W9-AQV-946

THE BURNING DARK

By Adam Christopher

Empire State
The Age Atomic

Seven Wonders

Hang Wire

The Burning Dark

THE BURNING DARK

ADAM CHRISTOPHER

A Tom Doherty Associates Book
New York

This is a work of fiction. All of the characters, organizations, and events portrayed in this novel are either products of the author's imagination or are used fictitiously.

THE BURNING DARK

A Tor Book
Published by Tom Doherty Associates, LLC
175 Fifth Avenue
New York, NY 10010

www.tor-forge.com

Tor® is a registered trademark of Tom Doherty Associates, LLC.

Library of Congress Cataloging-in-Publication Data

Christopher, Adam, 1978–
The Burning Dark / Adam Christopher.—First Edition.
p. cm.
"A Tom Doherty Associates Book."
ISBN 978-0-7653-3508-1 (hardcover)
ISBN 978-1-4668-2086-9 (e-book)
1. Science fiction. 2. Suspense fiction. I. Title.
PR6103.H76B87 2014
823'.92—dc23

2013025214

Tor books may be purchased for educational, business, or promotional use. For information on bulk purchases, please contact Macmillan Corporate and Premium Sales Department at 1-800-221-7945, extension 5442, or write specialmarkets@macmillan.com.

First Edition: March 2014

Printed in the United States of America

0 9 8 7 6 5 4 3 2 1

For Sandra, always

Acknowledgments

My thanks to everyone who made this book what it is, including my crack team of early readers: Kim Curran, Amanda Lynn, Mark Nelson, Andrew Reid, Sharon Ring, Amanda Rutter, Kate Sherrod, James Smythe, and Jennifer Williams. Thanks also to Danielle Stockley for her valuable insight (and for introducing me to the best hot chocolate in New York City).

I'm grateful to two people in particular, whose life-changing notes and edits helped shape this story from when it first appeared as something luminous and fragile called *Ludmila, My Love*: my agent, Stacia J. N. Decker, of the Donald Maass Literary Agency, and my editor at Tor, Paul Stevens. Stacia's eye for detail and deep understanding of the text were vital (we in Team Decker are a lucky bunch of writers, no doubt about it), and Paul's suggestions on what might *really* be going on aboard the U-Star *Coast City* were a revelation. You're holding this book in your hands because of them. Thanks also to Pablo Defendini for the Puerto Rican Spanish and the suggestion Serra probably knew a thing or two about Santeria. And to Will Staehle—my friend, you've done it *again*.

This book has a *long* history, so my apologies if I've left anybody out, but a big thanks to Lauren Beukes, Joelle Charbonneau, Mur Lafferty, Emma Newman, Kaaron Warren, and Chuck Wendig.

Finally, to my wife, Sandra, whose endless support, enthusiasm, understanding, and love make everything worthwhile. Thank you, and I love you.

THE BURNING DARK

YOMI

In the shadowland of the dead, she sat and cried for her husband, but the prison was sealed and she could not leave and nobody could hear her.

The shadows surrounded her, swarming like living, breathing creatures. The shadows caressed her skin, holding the rotting flesh onto her bones. Things crawled over her and ate the flesh, but the shadows kept her firm, kept her whole as the things ate, and ate, and ate.

It was too late.

She had eaten the food of the underworld, and she could not return. So she sat in the shadows, and cried for her husband, and things ate her flesh.

Abandoned, imprisoned in the dark, her fury burned like a black sun. Trapped in the basement of the world, she waited, and grew resentful. Her mind didn't break, not exactly, but it grew as black as the walls of the prison in which she sat. The walls that rippled and cracked and filled her head with the roar of the ocean when she touched them, but that did not yield or break. They were solid, inviolable.

He had left her here, left her trapped while he returned to the land of the living. He had tricked her and betrayed her. The one she loved had betrayed her.

They were *one;* they were *kindred*. Yet here she sat, in the dark, imprisoned beyond time, beyond space. In the dark, her despair turned to hate.

She knew now that she could not return, that she was changed and that the world had changed. She also knew that he would pay, one day. She would have vengeance. She would have revenge.

Her tears dried as the last scraps of flesh were eaten from her face. The endless night of her prison grew even blacker as her dead eyes were sucked from their sockets like rotting eggs by something crawling and screaming in the shadows. In their place a blue light shone, the cold blue light of the end of the world. Her eyes lit the prison. The things that crawled squirmed to escape her.

In the dark she burned.

She stood in her prison for the first time in eternity and screamed for revenge. She would return to the world outside, not to life, never again to life, but to find him, and punish him, from here to the end of time. This she vowed.

Then she sat in the black nothingness and waited. Her husband had sent her here; there was no way out. Someone would need to free her. But she knew someone would, in time. The living were curious, and the dead were patient.

And then it came: a knock and a voice, from somewhere else, somehow. An offering, a proposal. A way out. And it was so simple, all it needed was power, just enough to crack the walls of the prison. And if there was a crack, she could reach out and touch the world. She could reach out and drink her fill of life, a thousand souls a day, until she was whole again. And then, when she was whole, she would be able to break free. She would be able to escape, and her husband would not be able to flee her wrath.

In the dark she burned, and she pressed her skull to the wall, and she listened.

THE RELIEF OF TAU RETORE

This is how the shit went down. Lemme tell you about it, right now.

We came out of quickspace at oh-fifteen, which, even pushing warp as we were, was still too damn late. And when we popped back into the universe above Tau Retore, there was already a gap in the arrowhead. One ship hadn't made it—engine burn-out in quickspace, or some such. That can happen, and the loss—hell, any loss—was a shock. But we had a job to do first and my crew was fast, filling the gap without even needing an order, sliding the pack of cruisers together just *so*. It was pretty sweet, lemme tell you.

So, formation tight, one ship down. We spin down into planetary orbit, braking hard so the cone of warp exit didn't knock the goddamn planet off its axis. That's why you don't pop quickspace until you're far off out into the unknown. It's bad enough pushing just a spaceship through the gap between *now* and *now,* but, trust me, you don't want a planet dragging in your wake. The whole universe shakes when a single mote of dust leaves it to fly quickspace. Shove a spaceship through the hole, the universe shakes, gets mightily pissed off, and then gives you a smack at the other end. Universal punishment. God doesn't like you messing with his shit, that's for sure. That's what the quantum dampeners are for. A whole planet? *Forget about it.* They don't make dampeners big enough for *that*.

Anyway.

We came in hot and close, but we were too late. They were there already, on the other side of Tau Retore, and we couldn't see the main body, but we could see its claws stuck deep into the mantle of the planet, the liquid interior spilling out around the talons like hot blood. And the claws. *Jesus*. Shit, man, I've seen them do it before, the way they crack a planet open, then spin it—*spin it!*—like a spider. Don't know how they do it, how they find the sheer mass to build machines as big as moons. At the heart of a Mother Spider lies the guttering embers of a star, we know that much, and as the claws reach the core of their victim, the planet's magnetosphere gets all fucked up to shit, and they siphon the energy off that too. That's some crazy tech, way beyond what we got. And it's an amazing sight, the death of a planet—a planet physically pulled into pieces by the biggest fucking machine in the universe. You don't forget a sight like that, not in any kind of hurry.

You could hear it on the bridge. The viewscreens were green with the shitstorm of quickspace, then they flashed, then we're almost in fucking orbit around Tau Retore and that *thing* sucking the power and the life out of it. And everyone, everyone on the bridge of each of the twenty-three ships left in the arrowhead cries out in horror, and the captains give their pilots the command to decelerate and change course to deflect the nose of the warp cone past the planet, but they're already doing it and cursing blind as they do. Because in front of us there's a Mother Spider eating a planet, and the planet is bleeding. And on our ships, the comms channel is choked with one hundred people shouting in surprise and praying to whatever gods or goddesses they hold dear and precious.

I mean . . . *Jesus* . . .

Anyway.

We were too late to save it, really. We knew it, but that didn't mean we weren't going to try. So the arrowhead is in formation and we push the warp cone up just as it fizzes out over Tau Retore's north pole and we slam it toward the Mother Spider. If we can take that out, then the planet will at least stay in orbit, and if it stays in one piece, then when this whole crazy shit is over they can send out some terraformers to reconstitute the landscape and restabilize the core while whoever is left alive goes on vacation to Elesti or Alta or somewhere nice with beaches and sunsets.

Now things start to get interesting, because the Mother Spider has seen us. It's weird, it really is. I don't think the Spiders have actual spiders wherever they're from, but they sure as hell built their whole space tech around them. You know those little spider egg sacs, those balls of web on a leaf that you flick and then they break and about a million of the shits swarm out over everything? Just like that. The Mother Spider's still chowing down and we're flying toward it—and the U-Star *Boston Brand* is right in front, leading the charge, because I'm goddamn Fleet Admiral for the day and I want to get there first—when the main body *splits,* kinda like one of those paper folding games that girls make in school. You know, it's a kinda pyramid, you stick your fingers in, and it opens up, like a flower, and there's writing and jokes and suggestions about who loves who.

You know?

Anyway.

The Mother Spider opens and more Spiders come out—little small ones, half the size of our U-Stars, coming out of these shells that they shuck off like cocoons, and then they unfold their legs and head toward us. There's some more swearing but I order comms silence. Then—*Bang!* The ship that filled the gap in the arrowhead? Gone. These Spider babies are like their momma. They don't have weapons; they have *claws.* So they close in and latch on to your hull, and start chewing it up, and with so many of them swarming—hundreds, *thousands* maybe—they take just a second or two to reduce a U-Star to particulate matter. I don't know whether they ever developed projected energy, or even projectile weapons. Maybe they just think eating enemy ships is funny. So: *Bang!* U-Star *Gothamite* is history, nothing but metal and vapor. But we're in comms silence now, and that seems to keep everyone cool, I guess because they're now looking at me for instructions and trying not to think about how a U-Star can be taken out just like that. It takes the responsibility off them, let's them disengage, the conscious mind giving way to training and experience. Which is good for battle. You need your cool, and you don't need your emotions. Plenty of time for that later.

Of course, I'm standing there watching the other Spider babies getting too close and I'm as angry and scared as the rest of them, but nobody knows that. I signal my pilot and then hit the comms, ordering the arrowhead to break up. So long as everyone stays the hell out of one another's way and shoots at the right thing, hunting season is officially open. The Spiders are going straight to whatever hell their creepy insect intelligence believes in.

I can see the arrowhead split on the screens to the left and right. About a dozen ships on each flank peel upward and apart like an aerobatic display, and a few seconds later the same screens are filled with flashes and sparks and flames as the Spider babies are put into the grinder. I let myself smile, just a little, because I know that everyone on the bridge isn't watching the fireworks outside, they're watching my face, waiting for their orders. And if I smile—just a little—they'll smile too and they'll do their jobs just another one percent better than before. That's leadership, *yessir.* You gotta show and *project* it to everyone. They're depending on you, and this time it's not just the arrowhead; it's Tau Retore. That's a whole planet with a giant machine Spider trying to crack it open to make a galactic omelet. We're here to save the day again.

I'm smiling because, although we're still blasting toward the center of the big Mother Spider, right about where the main body splits to spit out the babies, I see the U-Star *Stripes* and its twin ship the *Stars* swing in ahead, rocketing in from underneath the *Boston Brand.* I smile because when the *Stars* and the *Stripes* are flying side by side, they're cool as shit. Those are the cruisers that everyone wants to be assigned to. They've got the kudos, the cachet, the shiniest damned paint jobs in the whole of Fleetspace. But, I mean, what a mouthful. The U-Star *Stars*? Huh.

Anyway.

So the *Stars* and the *Stripes* pull up ahead, and the screen goes pink automatically as the pair empty all their torpedo tubes at once at big momma's belly and the *Boston Brand*'s AI doesn't want its crew to go blind. Ammo spent, the two cruisers curve off out of the way. It's going to take a few seconds for the missiles to hit, and that's when I decide to give them a little push on their way.

Now, you gotta understand, I've got no rep in particular. I don't take risks. I do things by the book, and I know how to lead, and I get results. And that's what counts—boy, does the Fleet need results. And true, there have been those who have taken risks and acted with rash strokes of genius, but those guys are mostly assholes and mostly dead.

But look. When you see a Spider up close, it's one thing. When you see a Mother Spider with twelve legs, each ten thousand klicks long, *eating* a planet like it's a goddamn apple, it affects you. Something stirs in the back of your brain, like you're watching a movie or having a dream. So sometimes you get ideas, and then you know what it's like to be one of those assholes, and you start hoping to hell you're not about to find out what it's like to be one of those *dead* assholes.

I think somebody on my bridge says something but my head is buzzing and my ears are full of cotton wool, and not just because I've got a pink-tinted Fourth of July show outside. Do they still do that back on Earth? They must. I haven't been back in . . . Well, I'm not *that* old, but sometimes a five-year tour on the edge of the galaxy can feel a lot longer. Could be worse. There was this friend of mine, commander on one of the *really* big ships. "Wraiths" is what their crews call them, these ships that stay out for so long, hiding like an old-fashioned submarine just in case the Spiders pop up. After his last tour, he found me at Fleet Command and he said to me, Ida, he said . . .

Um. Anyway.

I'm sure somebody says something but I'm on the first pilot's back, pulling his position around and grabbing the sticks. Maybe it's the other pilot saying something, but then he sees what I'm doing, and looks at the screen ahead, following the green trail of the torpedoes through the pink wash—and that looks fucking freaky, I tell you—and he grabs his sticks and nods. That's it. He sits there, and nods, and looks ahead.

See? That's leadership, right there. He trusts me and is ready to follow me into hell if need be. Which actually isn't far from the truth, because I count to three and open quickspace right there, with the torpedoes in front of us and the Mother Spider in front of *them*. The warp cone pops ahead of our nose, and the screen goes from pink to blue.

Well, it's crazy and suicidal, and now people really are standing up and shouting at me, and the comms kicks into life with so many people all screaming at me that it sounds just like the wild roar of the universe.

But it works. The warp cone shunts the torpedoes forward at a speed way, way, *way* beyond their design tolerance, and when they hit the big fat Spider, they don't just explode, they go fucking *nova,* the energy spilling from our warp cone the same as throwing gasoline on a barbecue. You ever done that? Well, next time you're planet-side and can afford to take a trip out somewhere natural and you don't mind a little smoke. But this, it's like a new star has just sparked up, right over Tau Retore, right in our flight path. If there's anything left of the Mother Spider

(The star falling and burning as though it were a lamp and then they died one and all and)

we never found it. The only shit left was a few trillion tons of scrap metal and a high percentage of helium floating in high orbit around the planet.

But we're still heading right into this fucking mega-explosion and the warp cone is decaying quickly, so I give the order and we pop quickspace for just a second and fly *through* the explosion, and then the second pilot—promoted, needless to say—kills the engine and we slide back into space just a million klicks north. Of course we cooked the engines and the nav computer went offline to run a diagnostic, or maybe it was just really pissed off that we popped quickspace without telling it first and it went into a sulk. It was a rough ride too, and something burns out in the control console in front of the pilot and then there's a bang and something pings against my leg, but I don't notice, not yet. We've got enough juice in the tank to turn her around and coast back in. All the baby Spiders have been mopped up too, with only a few U-Stars damaged. One of which was the *Stripes,* and already someone has cracked a joke about scratching the paint job. Goddamn boys and their toys.

And you know what? We *were* in time. Tau Retore took a fucking pounding, but they'd been clever and got nearly everyone evacuated just as soon as the Spider appeared in the system. Just about the whole planet was saved, almost three hundred million of them. . . .

Now, that's a result. We actually won something, and won it big. I mean, I don't know if you heard, but things . . . well, things are not all rosy in this great and wonderful war. The Fleet is mighty and the Fleet is all, but, the Spiders? They might not think like us or act like us, but, goddammit, there are so many of them. I mean, it seems like we're taking one step forward and two steps back all the damn time and . . .

Anyway.

So guess what? I'm a hero. A genuine, bona fide heroic sonovabitch. So then I call up the commander of the U-Star *Castle Rock,* which I see up ahead, and I ask her about how many medals she'd like to have, and then someone says my leg is bleeding and . . .

"Abraham?"

"Hmm?" Ida paused, hand reaching for the cup. His head was a little light but his throat was dry . . . if someone would just be so kind as to pour another shot of the strawberry liqueur, that would do nicely, very nicely indeed. He rolled the thought around in his mind and glanced at Zia Hollywood, seeing nothing but his own reflection in her mining goggles.

"Shut the fuck up."

Zia's lips hadn't moved. The woman's voice was coming from the other side of the table. Ida frowned and turned his head too quickly. The room spun in surprising and interesting ways.

"Excuse me . . . Serra?"

She'd called him Abraham. He hated that.

Serra shook her head, looking at him with a mixture of disgust and pity. It wasn't a pretty expression, no matter how perfect her olive-skinned face was. She stood up and pushed her chair back, looking away.

"Come on, let's go." Serra's voice was almost a whisper. Disgust was now outright embarrassment. Carter, her inseparable lover, six and a quarter feet of military might wrapped in tight olive fatigues, nodded and muttered under his breath, but Serra was already stalking away from the table. Carter stood and threw Ida a look you might call dirty.

"Jackass."

And then they were gone, and Ida was left with the two VIPs. Fathead's permanent grin was as wide as ever, and oddly hypnotic to Ida's pickled brain. Zia's face was set, expressionless, and he noticed she hadn't had much of her drink.

Ida's head settled a little, and he glanced around the canteen. It was late now, but a couple other crewmen of the U-Star *Coast City* were still here, backs turned to Ida's table, apparently happy to keep out of the way of the space station's guests.

Zia Hollywood said nothing as she stood and tapped Fathead's shoulder. She walked off in silence, leaving her big-haired crewman to pull Ida's empty cup away from him before picking up the red bottle and the bag it came in from the floor and following his boss out.

Ida was alone at the table. His hands played at nothing in front of him. He wished the cup would rematerialize.

Well, fuck you very much.

Ida stood quickly, chin high, chest out, and he took a breath. He was better than this. He took a step toward the canteen's serving bar. Then his knee protested, and he relaxed his stiff-backed posture into his more regular, round-shouldered limp. The servos in his artificial joint didn't seem to like alcohol much.

Alcohol was forbidden on all U-Stars, and while the expensive liqueur had been brought in by the famous crew of the *Bloom*

County, Ida wondered if there was some of the marines' home-brewed engine juice around. Didn't hurt to ask.

"Hey, can I get a drink, my friend? Something . . . *special.* Anything you recommend?"

The canteen server had his back to him. Ida coughed, but the man didn't turn around.

"You've had enough. Any more trouble and I'll be talking to the marshal."

Ida blinked. "Huh," he said, tapping the counter. No progress then. Four weeks on board and he was still Captain No-Friends. The U-Star *Coast City* was turning out to be a real nice place.

Ida turned, regarded the silent backs of the other crewmen still seated at the other table, and limped out the door.

It was late in the cycle and the station's corridors were cast in an artificial purple night. Three turns and one elevator later, Ida was back in his cabin. He flicked the main light on, the autodimmer keeping it to a warm, low, white yellow. He tended to dim it during "daylight" as well, as the low light helped hide the nasty, functional nature of his quarters. What you couldn't see, your mind filled in for you. He liked to imagine the dark shadowed corners were crafted out of fine mahogany and teak paneling. Just like he had at home.

"Ida?"

Captain Abraham Idaho Cleveland was called Ida by his friends. Nearly everyone on the station called him Abraham, or worse. Mostly they called him nothing at all.

But not her.

He smiled, limped to his bed, and lay back. The damn knee . . . Ida raised his leg and flexed it, trying to get the psi-fi connection between the prosthetic and his brain to re-pair manually, but his leg was heavier than he remembered and lifting it made him feel dizzy. He dropped his leg and sighed, and closed his eyes.

"Hello, Ludmila," he said.

The woman's voice crackled with static as she laughed. It was high, beautiful. It made Ida smile.

"How was your night?" the voice asked.

Ida waved a hand—then, remembering he was alone in his cabin, switched the gesture for another dramatic sigh. "It was . . . bah. Who cares how my night was. How's yours going?"

The voice tutted. "You've been drinking, haven't you, Ida?"

Ida's smile returned. "Oh, maybe one or two."

The laugh again, each giggle cut with noise. She was so very, very far away. "Time for bed?"

Ida nodded and turned over. "Yeah, time for bed. Good night, Ludmila."

"Good night, Ida."

The room fell quiet, and the lights autodimmed again to match the purple dark of the rest of the station. Ida's breathing slowed and became heavy. Underneath the sound of his slumber the room pulsed with static, faint and distant.

Ida dreamed; he dreamed of the house on the farm. The red paint on the barn behind it shed like crimson dandruff in the sun and the same sun shone in the blond hair of the girl as she beckoned him to come with her, come into the house. But when he held out his hand to touch her, he was holding her father's Bible, the one that sour old man had pressed into his hands the very day he'd first met him, insisting Ida read the damn thing each and every night.

Ida felt afraid. He would not go into the house. He looked into the sky, at the sun, but saw that the sun was a violet disk, its edge streaming black lines. He frowned. An eclipse? There hadn't been an eclipse that day. He turned back to the girl, but she was gone and the door of the house was open, a rectangular black portal. Had her father sent her away already? Ida wasn't sure . . . it hadn't been then, had it? He and Astrid had another summer left, surely.

He took a step forward, and as he breathed the country air, the farmyard pulsed with static, faint and distant.

. . .

The static from the radio cracked sharply, and Ida jerked awake, dream forgotten.

"Mmm?"

"Ida?"

"Mmm?"

"Can you tell me the story again?"

Ida shifted. His bed was soft and the dark was pleasant on his eyes. He lay on his back and looked up into nothing. His knee seemed to have sorted itself out and didn't hurt anymore. He had a vague recollection of a red barn and a heavy book, but he shrugged the thought away.

"You mean Tau Retore?"

"Yes. Tell me again."

Ida chuckled and turned over. The still, blue light of the space radio was now the only light in the room. Ida stared into it, imagining Ludmila, wherever she was, watching her own light in the dark.

"Well," said Ida. "This is how the shit went down. Lemme tell you about it. . . ."

SOME KIND OF HERO

>> . . . please wait . . .

>> FLEET_WIKIA_REVISION_889

>> ~cleveland_AI_835401

>> . . . please wait . . .

>> last login: Sun Jan 12 06:18:53

>> WELCOME BACK, CAPTAIN

>> /rpos_intro_CC-SECURE.rtz

>> password: ********************

Union-Class, Fleet Starship; Research Platform and Observation Station (RPOS) configuration. Catalog reference: Psi Upsilon Psi. Nameplate: COAST CITY.

Summary:

The U-Star COAST CITY was one of only two RPOS-configured stationary orbital platforms put into service by the Fleet. Although twenty-four such space stations were ordered, production problems with kitset modules for both the COAST CITY and its sister COLLINSPORT resulted in curtailing of the RPOS program by then–Fleet Admiral LAUREN AVALON. After a lead-in time of seven years, the Fleet station program was retooled, resulting in the now ubiquitous Multipurpose Orbital Platforms (MOPs), the STAR CITY, the METROPOLIS, and the [REDACTED] being the first science platform and command center stations put into operation.

After the COAST CITY and COLLINSPORT were commissioned, a series of [REDACTED] structural failures and robotic system malfunctions during assembly at each site resulted in [REDACTED]. While both stations were completed and activated to schedule, their history made them unpopular tours for Fleet personnel and both facilities were plagued with morale problems and petty crime. Following an [REDACTED]

The COLLINSPORT was decommissioned after twelve years of service, its demise hastened by a failure of the main power pack and [REDACTED]. Originally designed as a monitoring station and launch point in the Oort cloud for Fleet craft entering and exiting the Home System, the unpowered U-Star was towed to Jovian orbit, where it was disassembled. Components of the station were recycled and reused as part of the helium-3 robotic mining systems in orbit around that planet. For more information, please see /JMC_27s_intro_CC-SECURE.rtz, "History of the Jovian Corporation."

The COAST CITY was assembled in a stationary orbit at a distance of 1.2 AU around SHADOW, an asymptotic giant branch technetium star in the constellation of Upsilon. The COAST CITY served a dual role as science base for the study of the star and the properties of its radiated energy and also as a forward warning post against SPIDER aggression in the SHADOW system, as it was believed at one point that the sentient machine race would attempt to harness the unusual properties of the star as part of an attack on Fleet space. This concern proved to be unwarranted and no SPIDER activity was ever recorded in the system. For more information, please see /antag_SPIDER_techspec_high_CC-SECURE.rtz, "Spider high-energy experimentation and special weapons development."

The COAST CITY was placed under the command of Commandant PRICE ELBRIDGE, seconded from the PSI-MARINE CORPS on the personal orders of [REDACTED]

Specifications:

Station hub

Diameter: 1,627 meters

Circumference: 5,112 meters; housing 23 levels of habitable space plus robotic service levels

Spire

Length: 2,063 meters (including communication antenna and sensor probe packs)

Diameter: 200 meters (widest point, housing bridge and command centers [habitable space] plus robotic service levels and computer bays) tapering to 13 meters

Power pack

Three Rolls-Royce Dreadnought cold fusion reactors, output 3.9 GW per unit

Crew complement

2,200; consisting of crew, executive and scientific personnel, one Marine battalion, and one Psi-Marine company

"Long way out, sir."

Ida looked up from the screen. Sitting in front of him in the shuttle, the pilot didn't turn around but nodded at the viewscreen that occupied the entire forward wall of the cockpit, wrapping around each side a little to simulate an actual window. Ida let the computer pad rest on his leg and adjusted himself in the narrow seat, the leather beneath him creaking.

"It sure is," said Ida. Background reading on his destination forgotten for the moment, he took in the spectacular view.

The U-Star *Coast City* was a giant doughnut floating on its side against a starry background bruised purple with the expanded gas cloud that enveloped the Shadow system. The pilot rotated the shuttle, and the *Coast City* flipped to the horizontal. At this angle, a more natural one that followed the station's design, Ida could make out the windows of the bridge and other structures familiar from a hundred other platforms. Everything in the Fleet was constructed from the same prefabricated sections, after all; everything from tiny one-man hotseats, used on extended EVAs, to cruisers to the largest star bases. The entire Fleet was modular, allowing for an infinite number of combinations and functions, limited only by the imagination of the Marine-Engineer Corps—which meant that, actually, the vehicles of the Fleet only came in about five different forms. Efficiency was a higher priority than imagination, so really there was no need to mess with tried and tested configurations. And every war machine produced by the Fleet was given the Union-Class Fleet Starship designation, which no doubt made the accountancy and logistics departments of the Earth government happy, but it meant you couldn't tell what a ship was from just the name. Including the U-Star *Coast City,* which, in this case, was a space station.

As familiar as Ida was with Fleet "vehicles," the *Coast City* was an older boat, and, as he'd just learned, one of only two of this type assembled, so while the shape was more or less what he expected, the torus was a little fatter, perhaps, and the spire that punched through the center of the hub had antenna extensions that were far longer than standard.

Ida hadn't quite seen one like this before, and he'd never seen one being taken apart either. As the curved outer ring of the station moved around in the viewscreen, the shiny solidity of the hub changed to a ragged, torn framework. The superstructure was all still there, leaving the torus and spire shape perfectly intact. But as the shuttle orbited the station, its skeletal innards were revealed. Lights flickered here and there, betraying the progress of construction drones carefully separating plates, girders, bolts, and rivets, making sure not a single stray particle was left floating in space as they repackaged the kitset form of the station back into a series of long, cuboid boxes that stuck like limpets at irregular intervals on the strongest parts of the exposed frame.

A minute later and the shuttle had returned to the intact half of *Coast City,* all solid metal and lights and Fleet insignia. Ida saw another shuttle, similar to the one he was currently in, heading away from the docking bay. Even during demolition, Fleet routine held sway; the Shadow system was clearly still being patrolled for Spider activity, the secondary function of any platform.

The *Coast City* had primarily been pushed into orbit around Shadow to research the peculiar properties of the star. Ida leaned in toward the shuttle's curved viewscreen; glancing to the left, he could just see the very edge of the star's violet corona. He let out a low, long whistle. The light from the star was described as "toxic" in his briefing and the Fleet wikia reported it as "unusual," but that was all he knew. Now, seeing it even via the viewscreen, which processed the light as much as possible, he thought he might agree. When he looked back toward the station, his vision flashed purple and he felt a little dizzy and sick, like he'd been standing on the top of something very tall and someone had come by and given him a shove in the small of his back. He blinked for a few seconds and the feeling dissipated.

"You here on leave, sir?" The pilot's hands moved over the controls, lining the shuttle up for docking.

The question surprised Ida. He was in uniform, so he supposed there was no reason why anyone wouldn't think he was still on active duty if they didn't know. But this pilot was positively chatty. Ida considered reprimanding him, telling him to focus on his job, which was 90 percent automated. One last little flex of power, perhaps. Then Ida laughed.

"Sir?" Now the pilot turned his huge fly-eye goggles to his passenger. Ida saw a dozen tiny reflections of himself, then turned back to the screen.

The *Coast City* now filled nearly the whole view. On a small display inset into the console that showed the rear, the U-Star *Athansor* was just a hulking silhouette with a few rows of lights that might have been nothing but far-distant stars. Only the ship's nameplate, lit in neon red, was any indication that the black mass was an artificial construct.

Ida clapped a hand on the back of the pilot's seat, and then quickly removed it, realizing that while the docking procedure was nearly automatic, the pilot probably needed to keep concentrating as they made the final approach. Ida slid the computer pad on top of the console beside him and adjusted his straps.

"I'm retired," Ida said. "But I've one last duty for the Fleet, signing the final decommission order for this old crate. That and getting some TLC for this thing." He knocked on his right knee, and the sound came back hard and dead. The pilot nodded, although he wasn't looking.

The window was now showing an expanse of metal, tinged purple by the evil light from Shadow. In the center of the metallic wall, an octagonal patch of light allowed them to see into the station's shuttle hangar.

"Early retirement," said the pilot. "Sounds nice." Then he activated the main comms and began swapping technical chatter with the hangar controller on board the station.

Ida sat back with his hands linked behind his head. He smiled and closed his eyes. The purple spots had gone, at least.

Yes, sounds nice.

"Groups four and five, embark."

Finally, things were moving again. Serra swallowed, her throat dry, as she glanced to her left. Half her row turned smartly, fell out, then grabbed their bags and kit and jogged over to the ramp leading up into the gaping loading bay of the transport.

"Taking them long enough. Jesus Christ."

Serra nodded. Beside her, Carter was chewing his lip as he watched the marines get herded into the back of the ship.

He was right. It was taking fucking forever. This was the last-but-one transport ship off the *Coast City,* and it was supposed to take nearly everyone that was left aboard, leaving just essential support crew. Having nearly a whole battalion of marines stuck at the ass-end of the galaxy was not much use to the Fleet, not when the Spiders were making moves all over the damn show. The sooner the station was disassembled and the sooner the combat troops and other Fleet personnel were off it and doing something useful somewhere else, the better.

They'd been standing around in the *Coast City*'s hangar for a couple of hours now. The operation was supposed to be efficient, the whole production running practically on automatic. But there was something up with the computer on board the U-Star *Sunken Treasure.* Something about the manifest system getting stuck, refusing to update the catalog of personnel sitting patiently on the transport. Apparently it had been rebooted several times already, but until it was working, they couldn't load any more. But, finally, things seemed to be happening.

The *Coast City* had four berths available in its hangar: two small bays for shuttles, two for larger ships, including troop carriers like the *Sunken Treasure.* The carrier itself belonged to a larger

U-Star, *Athansor,* which sat out in space a few hundred klicks away. As well as picking up the bulk of the remaining station crew, it was here to drop someone off. Why anyone new would come to the station at the end of its life, with half its structure nothing more than a delicate framework of girders and open space, Serra didn't know. She didn't care either. All she cared about was getting off the damn thing. She didn't like it here. She never had, not really, but over the last few weeks there was something else bothering her.

On the other side of the hangar, away from the huge featureless box that was the *Sunken Treasure,* the first small bay was empty, the station's own shuttle out on routine patrol. In the other bay sat another shuttle, the one from the *Athansor.* It looked newer than their own craft.

As the marines began to be loaded into the transport again, Carter and Serra stood, kit at their feet, waiting for their group to be called. As they idled, they both watched the new shuttle as a single passenger disembarked. He was middle-aged and uniformed—an officer, although it was impossible to see his rank from this distance.

Carter tilted his head as though that would give him a better look. "Any idea who that is?"

Serra shrugged, but from the row of marines behind her came a deep voice as DeJohn leaned forward, his breath hot on the back of her neck.

"Heard he was some kind of hero. Supposed to have saved a whole planet, or some shit. But fucked if I've heard of him."

Serra felt Carter stiffen as he stood next to her. He craned his neck around to DeJohn.

"What, there's no record of it? That means Black Ops."

Ah, shit. Serra glanced at Carter and saw his face blush red. DeJohn gave a *Hey, don't look at me* expression and stepped back.

"Charlie . . . ," Serra whispered. Carter looked at her, his eyes narrow.

Black Ops. DeJohn didn't know—nobody aboard the *Coast City* did outside of the officers, and of them only a small, select group—about a small but important slice of Carter's service history. Serra knew, of course; Carter had told her, even though it would mean court-martial and an unpleasant, violent end for the both of them if it ever got out.

Black Ops. It was not a topic to bring up, not around Carter. Serra mouthed "Charlie" to him, and he seemed to relax a little, his shoulders falling and the heat leaving his cheeks.

Serra turned and watched as the new arrival was met by the station's temporary commander, the provost marshal. The marshal was supposed to be in charge of security, but with the commandant suddenly absent, he'd stepped in as the last officer of sufficient rank on board, all the other senior officers having left on the previous transport. Serra frowned.

"And you know this how, exactly, Corporal?" Carter asked.

DeJohn sniffed. "Didn't you read the briefing?"

Carter grinned and turned around. "Wait, you can read?"

Serra laughed along with the other two. That was better. Good.

"Shame the commandant isn't here to meet him, then," she said.

Behind her, DeJohn sighed. "Not this again."

"Look," said Serra, turning. "It's fucked up. How come the commandant isn't here? Isn't he supposed to stay on the station until the very end?"

DeJohn laughed. He was standing with his hands behind his back, his own row of marines forming a scraggly, disorganized group as they waited for their orders.

"You expecting this boat to sink, marine?"

Serra spun around and snapped to attention. The warrant officer in front of her held a computer pad in one hand, his attention apparently fixed on it as he tapped at the screen with his finger. Carter stood to attention too, but snuck a sideways glance at Serra, his lip curled in a smirk.

"Well, Psi-Sergeant Serra?" The warrant officer's eyes didn't leave his pad.

"No, sir," said Serra. Damn, did she want to get off this boat.

Nobody said anything for a moment. The warrant officer

continued to tap on his pad. Serra and Carter stood rigid. Serra could hear DeJohn breathing behind her.

Finally the warrant officer dropped the pad to his side. He took a step back and raised his voice to address the several ranks of marines still waiting in the hangar.

"Okay, there is still a problem with the transport manifest, so we can't take everyone. Groups six to nine will embark on my order. Groups ten and up, you're staying put."

The sound of several dozen marines, all packed up and ready to go, sick to death of their current posting and sick to death of standing around in the hangar, murmuring their displeasure as they shuffled to collect their kits, filled the hangar. DeJohn sighed more dramatically than the rest.

"The fuck?" he said, and then added, "Sir."

The warrant officer glanced over Serra's shoulder at the marine. "Them is, as they say, marine, the breaks. Any problem, you're free to take it up with Commandant Elbridge."

"The commandant isn't even on board this U-Star," said DeJohn, *"Sir."*

"And life is hard and unfair, marine."

Serra tried very hard not to smile. From the corner of her eye, she could see Carter having even more difficulty.

Over on the other side of the hangar, the new arrival and the provost marshal were heading out.

The warrant officer stepped closer to Serra and raised his computer pad again.

"Fleet regulation specifies that at least one psi-marine is to remain on any U-Star at all times. Lafferty drew the card and is on the way out, which leaves you on duty, Psi-Sergeant."

At this, Carter and Serra exchanged a look. As much as she wanted to get off this godforsaken space station and out of this system with its fucking evil star and all the crap its fucked-up light was causing, she didn't want to be away from Carter. She could see it in his eyes too. One day they'd leave the Fleet altogether, the both of them, get married, move out to a quiet colony, have kids. Carter was getting an itch, and Serra would follow him wherever he needed to go.

The warrant officer sniffed. "Problem, marine?"

Serra stood to attention, eyes-front. "No, sir."

The warrant officer glanced at Carter, catching the tail end of his grin. He raised an eyebrow, then shook his head and began tapping on his pad again. Then he walked off without another word.

Serra relaxed. When she looked at Carter, she was grinning too.

A heavy hand clapped her on the shoulder, making her jump. DeJohn leaned between the two of them, his shaved scalp glistening in the hangar lights.

"Looks like time to have a party, girls and boys."

"If by 'party' you mean make sure the demolition drones don't take us apart when they go haywire," said Carter, "then sure, let's party." He grabbed his kit and motioned to Serra. She nodded and picked hers up.

"Hey," said DeJohn, stepping forward as his row of marines fell out. Carter turned but Serra made a point of keeping herself pointed toward the exit. If she was staying on board for the remainder of the station's life, she would unpack her kit in Carter's cabin. Being the sole occupant of the psi-marine berth was going to be a real drag, and there was no one left aboard who was likely to make a fuss about her and Carter breaking Fleet regulations by sharing quarters. DeJohn was right, in his own, stupid way. It was party time at the edge of Fleetspace.

"Hey," said DeJohn again. Serra turned with a much-exaggerated display of boredom, but DeJohn didn't notice. He waved them back over and dropped his voice.

"Look," he said, "it's just us. We got this whole damn boat to ourselves—"

"And two hundred other marines," said Carter, folding his arms. DeJohn screwed his face up like he'd just bitten something very sour.

"Naw, I mean us. We're a fireteam now, am I right? One marine, one marine-engineer, one psi-marine."

Serra folded her arms too. "Your point?"

"Think we need to say hello to our so-called hero. Show him a thing or two, you know?"

DeJohn rubbed his fist into the palm of the other hand with relish. Carter stood still, not doing anything except sucking in his cheeks. Then he turned quickly and patted Serra's shoulder for her to follow.

Out of DeJohn's earshot, Serra asked her lover if he was okay, but he didn't answer.

Ida shifted on the couch. Looking up, he was blinded by the light that hung in the steel globe directly overhead. He turned his head to look at medic, a young Japanese woman who had introduced herself as Izanami.

Ida wasn't sure this was entirely necessary—the only part of him that needed medical attention was his robot knee, and only as part of a routine check. He was on his way *out* of the Fleet, not a raw recruit whose psychopathic tendencies were to be identified and, if possible, developed. But psychotherapy was all part of standard Fleet procedure, and his training died hard.

Izanami sat perfectly still, hands clasped in her lap. She smiled, the white of her teeth matching the white of her medic's tunic and skirt, contrasting a little—but not that much—with her pale skin. She was practically monochromatic.

Ida had been on board not quite two cycles, and so far Izanami was the only person other than the provost marshal who had spoken more than a few words to him. She'd turned up at his cabin, knocking politely on the door before appearing around the frame with a big, friendly smile. She introduced herself as a neurotherapist, but like most of the station's crew, she was no longer on active duty, merely stuck on the *Coast City* until the final transport ship arrived. With a skeleton crew of just over two hundred—and a full complement of medical drones capable of dealing, at the extreme end of the spectrum, with ten thousand war-wounded—she was surplus to requirements.

Ida shifted on the fake leather couch. To hell with it. The couch was comfortable.

"So, tell me about yourself," said Izanami.

Ida laughed. "Please don't tell me they teach you that opening line at the academy?"

"Sorry," said Izanami. She gestured to the room. "Old habits! I haven't had much to do here. I'm clearly dying to psychoanalyze someone, and you seem to be a willing victim, Captain."

Ida waved a hand, dismissing her apology. "I'm joking. But, let's see. . . . I was born in Avebury, England, 2920, Anno Domini. But only by accident. My father worked for the Fleet, so we traveled around a lot and were only in the Britannic States for a couple of months when I decided to make an early appearance. He was from Idaho—well, what used to be Idaho, before the Fleet Confederacy reorganized the United States in . . . *whenever.* He still called it that, anyway."

Izanami smiled, but there was something off about the expression, and Ida didn't like it. It was years since he'd been on a Fleet shrink's couch, and he thought perhaps he was straying from the point. He frowned and tried to find a better place from which to continue his personal history. He turned back to face the ceiling, closing his eyes against the dazzling light globe directly above. He cleared his throat.

"Well . . ."

For a second Ida thought he felt Izanami's hand on his bare forearm. Her fingers were cold, almost painfully so, and he flinched, jerking his head up from the couch to look.

Izanami hadn't moved, her fingers woven together on her lap. Her smile was somehow warmer now. Ida felt himself relax. He was jumpy; that was for sure. Maybe the whispers he'd heard around the place were worrying him more than he thought.

"So," Izanami said, "who are you going home to, now you're retired?"

Ida looked at Izanami, annoyed at the question. But, of course, she didn't know. She sat still in her chair, clearly expecting an answer.

"Oh," he began, then paused. "Not much time for family life in a job like mine. But . . . there was someone, though. Once."

Ida stopped, and frowned. He hoped Izanami would move on.

"Tell me about her."

No such luck. Ida coughed. "Ah, well, her name was Astrid. She had blond hair, and she . . . she died." He raised himself up on one elbow. "Do we need to talk about this now?"

The room seemed colder. Izanami met Ida's gaze, her face now expressionless. Her eyes seemed to catch a reflection from the steel lamp and flashed blue for a second.

"I have a husband," she said.

Ida raised an eyebrow.

"He left me," she continued. "Sometimes I think that is harder than death."

Ida's jaw worked as his brain tried to catch up with the conversation.

"I'm . . . ah . . ." Ida lay back on the couch. He squinted into the lamp; when he looked away he saw purple spots and streaking shadows until he blinked them gone.

"It's okay," said Izanami.

Ida glanced sideways at her and she was smiling again, and for a moment he was lost in her eyes. Then he saw that they actually *were* blue, a rare color indeed for a Japanese woman.

"You're not serious?"

DeJohn's face split into a wide grin. Serra looked across the canteen table at Carter, daring to hope he at least saw some sense, but he was smiling too. Except . . . there was something else, something behind the smile, behind his eyes. He was bored—hell, they were all bored—and he seemed content to let DeJohn take the lead on practically everything now. Carter was better than that; she knew it. If only he'd snap the hell out of it. If only DeJohn would just let it go.

"Hey, hey," said DeJohn. He looked first over one shoulder, then the other, like he was worried someone else in the canteen would overhear them. That was bullshit too; DeJohn didn't give a flying fuck what anyone else heard. But he still leaned in to the table and lowered his voice. All part of his stupid game.

"He's an officer with a Fleet Medal, jackass," Serra hissed at DeJohn. Her eyes remained on Carter's face, though. His smile thinned a little.

"He ain't no such goddamn thing, marine," said DeJohn. "Some kind of hero, right? Bullshit. I checked. Bull*shit.* There's no record of him or anything. Saved a planet? There's no way we wouldn't know about that. No *way*! Hell, save a planet? That doesn't happen. That's called winning. Which is something we sure as hell ain't doing."

"But if he was Black Ops, he wouldn't have a record, would he," said Carter quietly.

"Bah!" said DeJohn, sitting back in his chair. "You telling me Black Ops are saving planets now? A little difficult to keep something like that quiet. And you're telling me they hand out Fleet Medals in Black Ops? Black Ops is called Black Ops for a reason. They do the nasty shit so we don't have to. They don't give out medals for that."

Serra tried to catch Carter's eye, but he was staring, unblinking, at DeJohn. She glanced down—she couldn't help it—at the silver bar sewn into his tunic.

FOR SERVICES RENDERED

"You're right," said Carter. Serra blinked. There was a light in Carter's eyes, a fire. His smile crept up at the corners. "He's a goddamn liar."

Serra slumped in her chair as DeJohn laughed. *Damn. It.* She'd try to talk him down, but later, not here.

"So," said Carter, leaning in across the table, "what do you think we should do about it?"

Serra folded her arms and gazed into the air somewhere above the table as DeJohn told Carter exactly what he had in mind.

Idiots, she thought.

. . .

This had to be it, surely. Ida checked the computer pad in his hand, rotating the screen to view the station map from a different angle.

Left, Corridor Eleven, Omega Deck. Then left again, and then straight on. Service elevator to the next level, keep on going. Ida traced the route on the pad, his finger leaving a red trail on the station schematic. He tapped the "home" button and stroked the station locator icon on the pad's main screen. The device bleated, then came back with an error. Ida looked around, but the plating had been taken off this section of corridor already, taking with it the level and corridor ident signs.

Somebody had screwed up. His duties weren't exactly onerous—he was officially retired and merely an observer on the station. But as such he'd been given a few minor chores, including demolition sign-offs for each section, as well as a list of station modules already packed away that he had to cross-check against the master manifest. It was stupid, really. They were the kind of checks that the demolition crews would be doing anyway, so all Ida was doing was duplicating the paperwork and, no doubt, pissing off the skeleton crew who were doing their best to get on with their difficult and dangerous work without him slowing them down. King too—the provost marshal hadn't been exactly thrilled to welcome him on board and had been a little frosty ever since. Perhaps he thought that by sending Ida here, Fleet Command were butting in, questioning whether the marshal was capable of running a tight operation.

So far, the one adjective Ida thought of when describing the marshal was exactly that: tight.

But this? Either his pad was bugged or they'd sent him on a wild goose chase to get him out of their hair. One of the greatest heroes of the Fleet, stuck down a maintenance access tunnel on the toilet deck of the station with a glitching computer pad.

Ida frowned at the notebook-sized screen and thumbed the station layout again. The two-dimensional map sprang into life, showing an area of the *Coast City* Ida was pretty sure was nowhere near where he was. He was right out on the far edge of the station torus, as far from the inhabited section as it was possible to get. This whole segment of the base was not only unused but in the process of being dismantled as well. The walls and flooring were bare metal grilling, revealing a mess of cables and pipes behind the façade. It was also cold, the life support automatically cycled down to minimum just to keep atmospheric integrity with the rest of the station.

Ida turned, but as with the life support, the lighting was also on auto-minimum. As he'd passed each section of corridor, the next section lit in front of him, and the one he'd just been through turned off. Which, when you're lost with a bugged map and no corridor markers, in a station you've been in only a few cycles, was a real pain in the ass. There weren't even any comms boxes—or at least Ida couldn't see any, being stuck in a bubble of light between two near-black envelopes ahead and behind. And they hadn't given him an internal comms badge and ident tag yet either.

Ida took a deep breath and coughed, his throat catching on the cold air. He took a few paces forward, and the next corridor section faded into view as the lighting powered up. Satisfied, he set off to try to retrace his steps.

Now that he thought about it, this was a rather interesting section of the *Coast City* hub to be in, away from where the rest of the crew were installed. He wondered if there were any empty berths nearby, or whether the cabins had all been stripped by the demolition drones. If not, it wouldn't be a bad place to haul his gear and set up camp.

Ida walked on for a few minutes, following the grilled but otherwise featureless corridor, then slowed as he noticed his breath steaming even more in front of his face. Perhaps he was taking it too fast for the atmospherics to power up and keep the corridor heated. Ida stopped and, holding the pad firmly in one hand, patted his arms around his body to try to warm up.

No, it was too far around the hub, and the section was in too fragile a state to be comfortable. He'd settle for the regular crew quarters, but he could at least shift right to the end of the berths, put a little distance between him and the rest of the crew, even if it was just a handful of empty cabins. Better than nothing. Out here, the cold made his knee hurt.

Then the lights went out, and Ida was in darkness punctuated only by the glowing screen of the station control pad in his right hand.

"Well, that's nice," said Ida. He flicked the pad back to the home screen and selected the notepad feature. The screen lit with a blank cream page so bright in the total dark of the corridor that Ida squinted before he turned the screen away from him to act as a flashlight. It was remarkably effective, throwing a whitish light several feet ahead. Enough to get back to the service elevator, for sure. Ida kept walking, surprised at the loud, metallic sound his footfalls were making on the bare grille decking. The dark was playing tricks.

Ida stopped when he realized his boots *weren't* making that sound at all, but the sound stopped at the same time he did. He turned, holding the control pad in front of him like a shield. The corridor was empty, but while the light from the pad was bright, it was diffuse, producing a glow that left the edges of the corridor in shadow. Ida watched his breath puff out in front of his face.

There. Again, the sound. He swore it sounded like footsteps, but whoever was walking around was a long, long way off, the sound echoing from some distant corridor. Ida took a step forward. Then he shook his head. He'd had enough of this game.

"Hello?" His voice didn't carry as far as he'd thought it would. The rough grilled surface of the walls, floor, ceiling dampened the sound.

When the footsteps sounded again, Ida felt his heartbeat quicken. The footsteps *were* echoing, no matter what the corridors were lined with. They continued for a few seconds, getting fainter as the mystery walker moved away.

"Huh," said Ida, feeling stupid but also wondering if this was all part of the joke. He turned and, pad lighting the way, headed for the elevator in the opposite direction of where he thought the footsteps had come from.

As he turned the corner, Ida pulled up quickly to prevent himself from walking straight into two huge men in regulation olive green T-shirts.

Ida shone the light up, into the faces of the two marines, but their heads were wrapped awkwardly in more olive cloth. The disguise was childish, but quite effective in hiding everything but their eyes.

Those eyes had a spark in them. Ida had seen that light before, in the heat of battle. It was the light in the eyes of a killer that the Fleet selectors looked for when choosing frontline troops. And now Ida appeared to be locked in a space station with them, all clearly with a touch of cabin fever.

"Abe, Abe, Abe," said one of the marines, stepping forward. "Fancy meeting you here."

Ida shook his head. Enough of this nonsense. "Stand aside, marines." He took a step forward, only to be stopped by a large hand pressing into his chest. The marine turned to his companion.

"You hear what he's been telling everyone?"

"You mean that bullshit about saving a planet?"

Ida knocked the hand away. "What the hell are you talking about?"

"Some jack-shit story, right?" said the first marine. "Nice little tale for the grunts out in deep space, eh? Because those fucking space apes will believe any shit, right?"

The second marine shook his head and turned back to Ida. "He's a goddamn liar."

Ida felt his heart rate spike. "Now, wait one minute—"

"Serving the Fleet is an honor, you sonovabitch," said the first marine. "Now, you tell me what kind of cowardly shit would make up a story like that, huh?"

Ida made to turn, but it was too late.

"Look, Captain . . ."

Ida closed his eyes, took a deep breath, and began to count. It was supposed to be relaxing, helping him clear his head and focus.

Now the deep breathing just hurt, as somewhere inside, a cracked rib creaked. He winced, skipped from three to ten in his head, and opened the one eye that could still open. The ready room flipped in his vision in a way that made Ida nauseated, just a little, and when it righted itself it was fuzzy at the edges and slightly out of focus. Not good.

"Sir, do you expect me to explain how I fell down some stairs last night? Take a look. A good, long look. It was two of your marines, Carter and DeJohn. I know it was."

King leaned back, pressing his body into his leather chair, and looked at Ida down the length of his not insubstantial nose. There was no chair on the other side of the desk. The commandant—who should have been occupying the ready room—probably didn't want to wear out his fancy rug. Importing it from Earth, along with the fancy wooden desk and the fancy leather chair, had cost the Fleet a fortune; of that Ida had no doubt, no doubt at all. So he just stood and ignored the shooting pains that tap-danced down his side from armpit to ankle, and tried to ignore the fact that Provost Marshal King was the most obtuse officer in the galaxy and that he really, *really* wished the commandant himself was still on board.

"Captain Cleveland," King said. He kept looking down that mother of a nose.

Ida supposed this was his idea of appearing all-important and commanding to his subordinates; considering the jackasses left on the empty hulk that was the U-Star *Coast City,* perhaps it worked. On Ida? Not so much. Not least of all because the space station's security chief was a couple years younger than he was. Didn't King know who he was talking to? Who he was trying—and failing—to make sweat on the fancy little rug? Ida had been busy saving a whole goddamn planet from the Spiders while the provost marshal here got the *Coast City*'s canteen roster nice and straight. And now, with the commandant gone, King was the ranking officer.

Maybe it was just lack of experience, the self-important paper-pusher suddenly finding himself elevated to commander of a powerful, if only partially active, piece of Fleet military hardware. He seemed a born bureaucrat, content to manage the affairs of the Fleet from a safe distance while field servicemen like Ida were actually out there, taking the fight to the Spiders. Except now he was supposed to be in charge of the station and in control of its personnel, and Ida had just told him that he was anything but. The marines knew something was wrong—Ida had sensed that already, the commandant's absence clearly a sore point among the station's crew. And, Ida thought, the marines also knew that the marshal wasn't capable of replacing their respected commandant, even temporarily. Ida started to feel sorry for King.

King coughed. "Something funny, Cleveland?"

The feeling quickly passed. Ida tried opening his black eye, but all he could see through that one before it filled with tears was the provost marshal framed in a dark, grainy slit. Ida let it close again, and noted that King had not only dropped Ida's title but gone from his first name to his last. King was slipping, beginning to think Ida was part of the shitty little crew of the *Coast City*. And Ida wasn't going to let that pass.

"It's Captain, sir, and there is a whole lot that I find amusing on board this U-Star. Not the least of which is the deliberate obfuscation of a criminal act, namely the attack on myself by two crewmen under your direct command."

King pretended to look busy behind the desk, turning his attention to a stack of papers in front of him that were in desperate need of alphabetizing. He seemed uncomfortable, nervous even. "Captain Cleveland, let me assure you I take such accusations with a certain level of seriousness."

Paper shuffling while you told someone who was clearly an annoyance to get the hell out of your office was standard procedure. Ida had used that old trick countless times himself. Back in the day, before saving a planet and getting a robot knee had brought him here, to the back end of a particularly nasty little nowhere.

"But . . ."

Here it came.

". . . right now we're in the middle of a complex mission, and we're against the clock. I need all of this station's personnel working to capacity. Taking apart a platform like this is a difficult and dangerous operation—I don't think I need to tell you that. While I'm in command I need this ship running as smoothly as possible. I'm happy to discuss your report, when we're back at Fleet Command, but until then we have a job to do. All of us." King looked up at Ida, papers suddenly still.

Ida felt his molars grind together. So, he was right. King was out of his depth. Pushing the matter would do little. At the moment, anyway.

"Sir." Ida shifted his weight from right foot to left but this only amplified the pain in his side so he shifted back. He kept his breathing controlled and tight, but he sure as hell needed to lie down right about now. At least the knee wasn't acting up again.

King put the papers down and tapped his fingernails on the top of the desk. "The Fleet, in its infinite wisdom, sent you here to oversee the final phase of the demolition. I'm not entirely sure your presence is strictly necessary, but if that's the way they want to do things, then I'm not going to complain. Orders are orders. But let's make it easier on ourselves. Carry out your assigned duties, such as they are, but if you can stay out of my way, then I'll stay out of yours, and then maybe we can get this job done quickly and get out of here."

"And your marines? Carter and DeJohn?"

The marshal gave a curt nod. "The marines, Carter and DeJohn, everyone."

Ida relaxed his jaw. To hell with it. "Sounds like a plan, Marshal."

"Look. It's just a few more months. I know time may hang heavy on your shoulders—you're supposed to be a guest here, and your assignments are hardly taxing."

"That's true, sir."

"So fill your time. Read something. Take up a hobby. The station's facilities—what's left of them—are at your disposal."

Ida considered the marshal's proposal. Maybe that wasn't such a bad idea. Distraction, something to pass the time, something he could do on his own that would keep him out of the way of space apes like Carter and DeJohn.

Ida had an idea.

"Well, when I first joined the Fleet, I built, ah . . . I built things."

King's eyebrow went up. "You built things?"

"Well, electronics. I dabbled, here and there. Just little projects. My father taught me back when—"

The provost marshal held up his hand. "Fine. Electrical stores are yours, help yourself."

"Thank you, sir."

"Is it on?"

The device was six inches square and two inches tall, just a low silver box sitting on Ida's table. There were four large screws at each corner, flush with the top, and across the front was a row of small embossed buttons that ended in a larger dark circle.

"It's on," said Ida.

Izanami reached forward and scratched at the LED with an immaculate fingernail. "Are you sure? I don't hear anything. Is this light supposed to be on?"

Ida's hand dwarfed Izanami's, and he gently brushed the medic's delicate, almost skeletally thin fingers away so he could fiddle with the controls.

"Huh," he said. He hit the box with his fist. The light flickered white briefly, then began to glow, dark purple at first, brightening to a near-white blue.

Izanami clapped excitedly. With Ida bent over the space radio, she laid a hand on his shoulder. She was cold; he could feel it through his shirt.

"Well done, Ida!"

Ida smiled and tightened the radio's housing with an old-fashioned screwdriver, then stood back to admire his handiwork. Izanami's hand fell away, and she stepped back politely. When he glanced over his shoulder, he saw her smile was as wide as his.

Ida scratched his chin with the blade of the screwdriver. He regarded the plain silver box with the glowing blue light; then he slid his finger over the surface, like he was wiping dust off the spotless device.

A space radio. It had taken just two cycles to assemble it, using components from the electrical stores and the plans Ida had committed to memory nearly thirty years before. The device was actually quite simple, certainly easy enough for the ten-year-old Abraham Cleveland to build with a little help from his father.

Izanami tilted her head, clearly intrigued by Ida's handiwork. "So, what can you listen to?"

Ida looked into the blue light of the device. This was going to be fun.

"Well, that's a good question," he said. "Let's see, shall we?"

PART ONE

THE SIGNAL

1

"You ever seen a chick from Polaris? I mean, holy schnikes. You need level-ten protective eyewear just to look at them. Naw, seriously, they radiate UV when they get turned on. Some kinda survival mechanism. So yeah, it's risky and you need to prebook yourself ten weeks in a class-three ICU afterwards to get your DNA rebuilt, but man, what a rush. What a *goddamn* rush. There was this one time—"

Ida flicked the volume of the radio set down by half. It was Clive's Friday night. Let him have it.

Clive was a pilot orbiting a lump of ice near Polaris. In a few hours he was due to break cover from behind his asteroid and spearhead a lightning strike on the hidden Omoto base on Polarii Inferior. Chances were this time tomorrow Clive would be a patch of brown radioactive dust drifting in the Polarii solar wind, the residue of his beloved Polarii women with him. Because no matter what the outcome of the attack—be it Fleet victory or a successful defense by the Omoto—there wasn't going to be any sentient life left on the planet afterwards.

So, let him command the air awhile. Ida felt bad and hoped Clive made it, but he wondered if perhaps he should stay off the radio in the next cycle or so, busy himself with those damn checklists he'd let slide. As boring as Clive was, he wasn't sure it would be the same without him, and he wasn't sure he wanted to hear about the outcome of the Omoto sortie, good or bad.

It was a waste, one that Ida objected to. Strategically important but ultimately futile. The universe was a big place and maybe the Omoto could keep their base. The Omoto weren't even the Spiders, and wasn't the Fleet supposed to be fighting those mechanical creeps instead of starting little wars over lumps of ice?

Given how the war was going, Ida wondered if maybe the Fleet wasn't focusing on the right thing sometimes.

A little interference on the line was obscuring select moments of Clive's monologue.

Ida flicked through a set of diagnostic routines on the space radio's three-dimensional interface. What was a hobby for, if not to present a series of tiny challenges that needed to be overcome, one by one? Talking to others out in space was only half of it.

The white noise of interference spiked. Ida leaned his chair back to the upright and cast an eye over one of the screens that hung on an arm over the desk. It wasn't part of the radio set, it was just a display from his cabin's computer, but he'd patched it into the solar observatory located at the very top of the station's spire. He found the data useful. It had been ten cycles since Ida first turned the radio on, and he'd quickly discovered that the physics of Shadow frequently threw a spanner in the works. And tonight it was no different.

But he had to admit it was really quite a fascinating academic study on the interaction between the star's strange light and the station's own artificial magnetosphere. As the amber glow of data flowed across the screen, he noted a few spikes of stellar activity that corresponded to the static on the set. He could try to retune, or perhaps, given an hour, come up with an algorithm to work the mess out of his signal. Ida poked at the screen, the amber of its data tables and the blue light of the radio the only illumination in the cabin.

Clive kept talking. Castle, a civilian mining engineer whose job supervising the construction of a drill head on one of the moons of Arbitri clearly left too much free time on his hands, butted in occasionally to express his satisfaction with the juicier aspects of Clive's adventures in Polarii love and to ask respectfully for more technical data on the difficulties of human–Polarii anatomical interaction. A newcomer too, calling himself Captain Midnight—Ida wasn't sure whether this was his rank and name or some kind of superhero identity—seemed to be enjoying the chat. Ida didn't quite believe he was calling from inside a black hole, but, hey, the radio hams of the galaxy were a bunch of sad, lonely losers with nothing better to do. If Captain Midnight wanted to be inside a black hole, then let him be inside a black hole. On the radio you could be anyone and anywhere you liked.

Ida wondered whether he should tell them about his adventures over the skies of Tau Retore, and whether he'd get a better reception here than among the jarheads that inhabited the *Coast City*.

DeJohn had been quite right about Fleet service being an honor. In the middle of a difficult, decades-long war against an alien machine intelligence, a citizen could do no greater service for humanity than enlist in the Fleet. And Ida knew full well how he would feel if he came across someone claiming a heroic action that they had no right to.

But was he really so far out on the edge of Fleetspace that the news about Tau Retore hadn't made it? He'd saved a planet and seen off a whole Spider cluster—including a *Mother* Spider. Why else did they think he'd been awarded with the Fleet Medal?

And, he thought, an artificial knee, an enforced honorable retirement, and a final posting to one of the most remote backwaters in Fleetspace. To oversee the decommissioning of an unremarkable space station well past its use-by date.

Ida absently flexed his robot knee, which had grown stiff as he sat at the desk.

He sat and thought.

Something was well and truly FUBAR, and not just on the *Coast City,* but at Fleet Command itself.

Something that, maybe, he should look into.

2

Space is black. Everyone said so—in verse, prose, even song. Except in the Shadow system, space wasn't black; it was *purple*.

Serra took a breath. She stared at the violet-tinged metal wall in front of her, her eyes flicking over the green HUD projected onto the inside of her helmet visor. Among other things—suit status and integrity, temperature, oxygen, constant (and pointless) system notifications from the *Coast City*'s main computer—the HUD's main features were two glowing brackets on either side and an upside-down T right in the center, showing which way was up and which was down. Although such things lost meaning in space, the Fleet liked to impose its own order on the universe. The slice of it occupied by humans wasn't called Fleetspace for nothing.

She wanted to turn around, but, clamped on to the outer hull of the space station, she could only manage to get her helmet around enough to look awkwardly over one shoulder. She wanted to turn, *needed* to look, but she was afraid.

"Carminita . . ."

The voice again.

"Date la vuelta, m'ija."

Turn around, my child.

It echoed inside her helmet, washed with static, and she swore whenever it spoke the comms indicator on the HUD flickered. But she knew the voice wasn't coming from the station. And it certainly wasn't coming from Carter, working just a few meters away on the hull.

"Carminita, está bien, nena. . . ."

It's okay, baby.

Serra closed her eyes and took another breath, pulling on the atmosphere a little harder than the suit expected. She heard a whirr as it compensated.

"That's it. Cycle the power again."

Serra opened her eyes and turned her head slowly. The front of her visor was an inch from the station's hull, and she watched the metal slide out of her vision until it was replaced by the black—by the *purple*—of space. Until there, just at the edge, she saw something brighter, a violet-tinted white.

Immediately her suit's HUD changed from regular green to a bright, angry red. A countdown appeared, superimposed over the inverted T in the center: *4'38"*, and a third column that spun too fast to read.

"Ahí estás, Carminita!"

There you are!

She closed her eyes.

"Serra?"

Serra blinked and gasped, but the suit ignored it and didn't broadcast her sharp intake of breath to Carter. She turned back to the hull, and the HUD turned green and the counter froze on four minutes thirty-one seconds and remained in view for a few more heartbeats, just to make sure the reader got the message.

Serra got it: The light of Shadow will fuck you up. It wasn't hard to understand. First it would eat through the shielding on your visor; then it would burn your mind out through your optic nerve. Shadow was an evil mother.

"Earth to Carmina Serra. Come in, please."

Carter's voice was loud, exasperated—not quiet, not female, like the . . . *other.* The comm caught the rasp as he scraped his chin against the padding inside his helmet.

Serra turned and her partner propelled himself toward her. As he approached, he reached past her helmet and yanked at the manual power override switch she was floating right in front of. Serra watched the fabric of his suit's sleeve press against her visor, but it made no sound.

Carter sighed and pushed off again, back to where he had a service panel open. "You awake in there?"

"*Carajo.* Sorry, sorry." Serra shook her head. Should she tell him?

No. A psi-marine hearing voices—*a* voice—wasn't usually taken well by the regular crew. The psi-marines were essential to the Fleet, now more than ever as the fight against the Spiders seemed to be getting harder and harder. While this earned her class respect, she knew some found specialists like her more than a little creepy. She didn't want to give them the excuse. Not that Carter would tell anyone, but sometimes he joined in with the ribbing with the rest of them.

"Don't blame you if you need a little shut-eye," Carter said as he worked, arms deep inside the skin of the space station. "Didn't get much sleep last night."

Serra shook her head and smiled as Carter's laugh snorted across the comm. She wondered whether anyone in the station's bridge was listening in. She wondered whether she cared. The ship's manifest would have shown the two of them spending most nights in each other's cabins anyway.

"You hear what our honored guest has going on?"

Serra turned back to Carter. "Cleveland?"

Carter snorted again. He pulled something out of the service panel, checked a connection, and pushed it back in. "Got himself hooked up with a space radio."

"Oh." Serra wasn't interested. She wished she had more to do out here. She didn't like being in Shadow's light, but EVAs always had to be done in pairs and Carter had assigned her a simple task. "I didn't know they still used those."

"They don't. Nobody does. Seems he's a bit of a geek, among other things."

"We need to talk about that, Charlie."

"Not now." Carter grunted and floated a few feet back. He had another part in his hands, a long black pipe with silver connectors at either end. He held one end up to his visor, then the other. "Damned if I can find anything wrong with this thing. It's not the coolant conduits. I think in engineering terms, this whole thing is fucked."

Serra laughed. Carter's helmet turned slightly in her direction, and she could see her own golden-mirrored visor reflected in his.

And . . . something else. A black shape, like there was someone else out there, stuck on the side of the hull like a clam, just behind her.

Serra gasped. The comms ignored it again.

"Bridge, come in, please." Carter spun the black pipe and let go. It continued to revolve in the vacuum between him and the *Coast City*.

Serra turned her head quickly, the joint between her helmet and the neck of her suit clacking loudly. There was no one else outside. Of course there wasn't.

"M'ija, no tengas miedo. . . ."

My child, do not be afraid.

Serra closed her eyes and turned back around to the hull. It was the light of Shadow—that fucking magical radiation from the technetium star—that was the root cause of all their problems. The voices in her head. The instability of the station's internal environment system. Shadows where there shouldn't be.

Her comms clicked again. It pulsed a little with static as Shadow's light played with the data stream.

"Sergeant Major, I have Marshal King here."

"Sir, no faults out here," reported Carter. He pushed off a little from the hull and looked up. Above them, a demolition drone was crouched on the hull, parked temporarily but with a green winking light on its back indicating it was just waiting to continue its job. "The drone didn't report anything, because there's nothing to report. Fault must be elsewhere."

There was a pause before the provost marshal responded. He must have been holding the comms link open with his thumb, because Serra could hear a rushing sound in the background for a second before he spoke.

"Okay, back in. We'll just have to keep monitoring."

"Roger that, sir."

The comms beeped and went dead. Carter grabbed his spinning part and grabbed on to the door of the service panel to pull himself back toward the hull.

"Cycle the power back off, lemme get this piece of shit back together."

Serra nodded, and then realized Carter couldn't see it behind her mirrored visor. She acknowledged over the comm and flipped the lever back to the off position. She gave a thumbs-up, and Carter got back to work.

Serra closed her eyes and said, "Do you think there's anything out there?"

Carter grunted as he worked, but after a few seconds she heard his considered reply. "There's always something out there."

When Serra opened her eyes, the metal wall in front of her still had the alien violet hue. She could *feel* the star behind her, and . . . something else. A presence, something real, something alive right at her shoulder. It was impossible, they were alone, but—

"But the Shadow system is uninhabited, if that's what you're talking about," said Carter, the sudden appearance of his voice in her ear making Serra jump. "No planets. Nothing but slow-rocks and dust. Not exactly the kind of light you can grow plant protein under, right?"

Serra laughed.

Carter reappeared from behind the service panel. "Tell you what, though, those slowrocks are probably worth a bit. I heard the marshal a couple of cycles back. High yield of lucanol. Said something about someone coming out to take a look soon."

"Uh-huh," said Serra with total disinterest. If someone wanted to come out this far to look at some asteroids, then they were welcome to them. But there was something else in the Shadow system, she *knew*. Something watching, waiting for . . . something.

Carmina Serra blinked behind her visor, then turned her head back around to the left. The hull slid away, the purple of space reappeared, the glow of Shadow at the edge, her HUD red.

4:31

4:30

4:29

3

Ida lay on his bed. The lights were off and the room was dark but too cold and not particularly conducive to sleep. Even here, just on the edge of the occupied deck of living quarters, the station's systems were struggling. But at least he was left alone—there was nothing much beyond his cabin that hadn't already been sliced by drones and packed away, and the only person who bothered coming along to his end of the deck was Izanami, which suited him just fine.

But the environment was dodgy all over the station, with wild temperature fluctuations and deviations in the standard air pressure. A side effect of the deconstruction process. Ida had heard a crew went on an EVA to try to rig a fix, but so far they didn't seem to be having much success.

Not that he really *could* sleep. Ida was furious, but he'd pushed the feeling away and gotten on with his work, even though the remaining crew were not shy about their annoyance at his interruptions. Now, in the small hours, on his own, that ball of anger had changed into something colder, bitter.

He sat up and quickly swept off the covers, then slipped the top blanket off the bed and wrapped it tightly around his shoulders as he stood. Damn, it was cold, the temperature dropping even since he'd left the warmth of his bed. His breath didn't quite steam as it left his mouth, but the metal floor was ice on his bare feet.

He turned and hopped to the environment controls near the door, set the heating on full power, and then kicked his boots from where they lay against the wall into the upright position and slid into them. He hobbled to his work desk, boot tongues flapping against his shins. Sitting and securing the blanket around himself, he pulled one of the computer screens toward him on its articulated arm. He checked the clock in the top center of the home screen. It was three in the morning.

The *Coast City,* like every other U-Star in the Fleet, no matter if they were ships or stations or something in between, and no matter how far from home they were, was synched to a daily cycle that matched the rotation of the Earth, specifically to a cycle that matched the day and time at Fleet Command in the former state of Utah. Three in the morning there was three in the morning in space, no matter where you were hiding or the light of which star was shining on you. It didn't matter. War was a round-the-clock operation anyway.

He started poking at the display. Proving his involvement in the action at Tau Retore would be easy enough. All he had to do was access Fleet records and call it all up. Even jarheads like DeJohn and Carter wouldn't be able to deny one of the greatest—not to say *rarest*—heroic actions in Fleet history.

"E.T., phone home," he said, tapping the communications browser. The screen filled with the spinning insignia of the Fleet—rendered as a particularly nasty and old-fashioned three-dimensional model in scratchy blue—before resolving into a black empty square. Ida saw himself in a smaller window in the top left, and laughed. What the hell did he look like?

"Name, rank, and serial number," asked a voice from behind the black window. Ida gave his details, and an icon at the bottom of the screen flicked to green as the video link switched suddenly on. Facing him was an operator at Fleet Command, his chin the only visible feature of the man's face underneath a large, almost comical communications headset. Every minute movement of the operator's head made the insectlike eyes of his headset wiggle and catch the light on its myriad surfaces. Crew who worked as operators—the definition included nearly everything that was vaguely technical or skilled, whether it be communications, logistics, or even pilots—had two nicknames. The official one was Ops. The unofficial one, but the one much more widely used, was Flyeye.

"Ah, hi there," said Ida, pulling the blanket tighter but sitting up a little straighter in his chair. He didn't want anyone to think that a Fleet Captain—even a former one—was a slouch. "Put me through to Archives, please."

"Connecting you now," said the Flyeye; the video flickered with white lines before going black again. Huh. The interference from Shadow was getting worse, crossing over into the supposedly impervious lightspeed link channel. Sunspot activity or some such, no doubt. Ida made a note to check on the readings from the solar observatory again.

Ida waited, and waited. He peered at the tiny view of himself in the top corner. He frowned, and rubbed his face, and tried to flatten his bed hair. With the room heating up, he was beginning to feel drowsy. He shuffled, trying to get comfortable, and then was distracted by one corner of the blanket that had gotten caught under his chair. The room was dark, lit only by the glare of the computer screen and the few small lights on equipment scattered around the room.

Ida sighed and tugged at the corner of the blanket. He leaned down and freed the thick fabric from under the wheel, then sat back up and looked into the screen as he readjusted the blanket around his shoulders. He blinked and peered into the dark, reflective window where he expected a Flyeye from Archives to appear any second. He blinked again and his breath caught in his throat.

There was someone standing behind him.

Another blink, and it was gone, although there was a blur of movement on the screen that might just have been his eyelashes sweeping up and down. Ida felt his heart kick for a beat or two, and spun the chair around on its swivel.

Nothing. He wasn't sure who had been assigned to the room originally—it was large, clearly designed for an officer, maybe one with a higher rank than Ida's own. The cabin's door was on his left. On his right was the bed, which reached to just over halfway into the circular chamber. There was a low bedside cupboard on the side of the bed closest, stacking high with personal belongings not yet tidied away. On the other side of cabin were a couple of tall lockers, still empty, waiting to be co-opted into use. There was nothing else in the room, no place for anyone to hide unless they were on the floor on the opposite side of the bed or had squeezed themselves into one of the lockers.

Ridiculous. But Ida got up and checked anyway. There was nobody beside the bed. The cupboards were empty, and, besides, the doors were stiff and impossible to open without a harsh metal-on-metal scraping amplified by the quiet of the night-cycle. The main door was closed, and on the bulkhead control panel beside it the indicator glowed a pale red, *locked,* next to the environment control sliders. Nobody had come in or out.

Ida stood and flapped toward the panel, then stopped after a few steps, unhappy about the sound his unlaced boots were making. He had the sudden urge to be very, very quiet, and with the room warmed up, he shucked them off. Barefoot, he crossed the rest of the floor to the room controls, double-checked the lock—as though the red LED could give a false reading of security—and tapped the environment down a couple degrees.

When he turned back to the table and chair and faced the rest of the room, he found himself doing it with some trepidation. He was a career military man, and he didn't like being spooked—mainly because he never was. But he was tired and worried, and he knew sleep deprivation, no matter how mild, could amplify anxiety about the smallest things. He felt a surge of anger. The fucking space apes who inhabited this godforsaken space station were getting to him.

The video link flared into life again. Ida scooted to the chair and sat down again, blanket now abandoned.

"Archives," said the Flyeye, this time female. "What is your request, please?"

The video link rolled, for just the blink of an eye, and when it restabilized, it took a second or two for the white lines of interference to vanish. Ida ignored it.

"Reference Fleet action 2961, May to September. Sortie of the First Fleet Arrowhead to Tau Retore. List of commendations and awards, please."

"Thank you," said his new Flyeye. "One moment, please."

Ida tapped the mute and pushed the screen back on its arm to give him some room as he leaned forward on the desk. Head in hands, he massaged his cheeks, trying to wake himself up. He wondered if he should go down to the canteen to get some coffee. He quickly decided against it.

The Flyeye's head tilted. "Tau Retore System, 2961, sir?"

"Yes, Operator," said Ida before realizing he was still muted. He tapped the screen and repeated for the Flyeye.

"No commendation list available. The last Fleet action for the Tau Retore system is . . . December 2960."

Ida felt an adrenalized pang in his chest, enough to snap him to full wakefulness.

"Can you confirm, Operator? Tau Retore, 2961."

The operator paused only a moment, her multifaceted goggles bobbing as she inclined her head again to read the data off a display out of sight of the camera. When she spoke again, she was shaking her head.

"Sorry, sir. Do you have the correct reference? 2960 is the last action. I have the authenticated order command on file."

"Okay," said Ida. He rubbed his chin again, and then pulled his hand away. It was shaking. He slapped it down on the desk and hoped the operator didn't notice.

"Can you pull sortie sheets for Fleet ships?"

"Yes, sir. Nameplate and date?"

"U-Star *Boston Brand*. May 2961. No, wait . . . make that September 2961. Should be a log of repairs out in one of the dockyards. She took quite a battering. Warpcore was burnt clean out."

Ida tapped his fingers on the desk while the operator a thousand light-years away searched the servers of Fleet Command. He smiled to himself. Yep, the warpcore burned clean out because he had a bright idea that ripped the solar heart right out of a Mother Spider.

(Burning as if it were a lamp and then they died one and all and)

Ida coughed.

The search took longer than it should have, long enough for Ida to find his socks and pull them on. He felt a dull ache creep up his chest with every passing moment.

Something was up.

"U-Star Kappa Alpha Omega Omega. *Boston Brand.* Listed as out of service, January through November 2961."

Ida felt dizzy. "The hell?"

"That's what it says here, sir."

"Reason?" Ida snapped, causing the operator on the video link to jerk back at her console. Another pause. Ida could just see the top of the op's hands as she typed.

"Q-Gen coil failure. Replacement of the whole coil assembly. Any further information requires engineering classification, sir."

Ida swore, just remembering to hit the mute as he did so. The Q-Gen coil was the part of a U-Star's engine—a tiny component compared with the rest of the thing, but a vital one—that tore a hole in the universe and let the ship push into quickspace. He knew exactly how it worked—all U-Star commanders had to know the mechanics of quickspace and the technology that allowed them to abuse it. He knew that the Q-Gen coil had nothing whatsoever to do with the warpcore, the central component of the main engines that did the actual business of moving the ship past lightspeed. He also knew that such repair work was exceptionally rare and, as indicated by the operator, took nearly a year to complete.

The mute came off again.

"Q-Gen coil failure? The Q-Gen coil was fine. The warpcore needed replacing because I was the one who burnt it out. We pushed quickspace without engine warming!"

The operator said nothing. Then she licked her lips. To Ida she looked less like a fly and more like a praying mantis considering its next meal.

"I don't have any more information, sir."

Ida felt like reprimanding the operator, but he knew she was just reading what the terminal showed her.

"What about the U-Star *Stars* and the U-Star *Stripes*? And the *Carcosa*." He clicked his fingers. "Yes, the *Carcosa*. Gotta be a big report on that one. Same system and flight time."

The Flyeye glanced down, and Ida heard some tapping as she pulled the data sheets up.

"The *Stars* and the *Stripes* are both out of service. No further engineering notes. No entry on the . . . *Carcosa*?" The Flyeye repeated the name, then spelled it out. Ida confirmed it was correct.

Ida felt that deep, sinking feeling in his stomach, a mix of nausea and adrenaline that left him hollow and dizzy.

Maybe he was dreaming. Maybe he could just slide back into bed, and Astrid would be waiting for him. He remembered the farmhouse and the red barn. He'd been seeing those a lot, lately.

The Flyeye moved her head to look at someone off-screen; exaggerated by the operator's headset, the motion was enough to snap Ida out of his reverie.

The Flyeye turned back to her camera. "Do you have another request, sir?"

Ida considered. He had a hundred requests, a thousand individual entries he wanted the operator to look up. The flight histories of every ship in the First Arrowhead for the last two years. Service records and notes on every crewman on board the *Boston Brand*. The same again for everyone in the whole Arrowhead, including the list of the dead from the U-Star *Carcosa*. Reports on Tau Retore for the same period. News items. Observations on Spider movement and activity in the Tau Retore system and the next dozen closest.

He wanted a detailed listing of his own service history, including retirement remarks, commendations, and awards, along with medical records.

"Sir?"

Ida sighed and reached forward, hand hovering over the "terminate call" button.

"No further requests," he said, tapping the screen. It went dark. "Thank you," he said, all too late.

4

The "food" was spicier than usual, but Serra didn't mind. Next to her at the table, Carter spooned in mouthful after mouthful of the stuff. He normally hated anything remotely approaching hot, but even just a few hours outside the station on another EVA to try to fix the environment controls seemed to have spurred his hunger.

Serra didn't mind at all. In fact, she rather enjoyed it, the pleasant glow in her mouth replacing that thing called "flavor" that she thought she could remember if she tried hard enough.

"Heard the Omoto got fucking hammered," said DeJohn. "Heard it over the link. That rock was fucking toasted."

"Damn!" Carter held his hand up, and DeJohn gave him a high-five.

Serra grinned. Nothing better than news of a victory, no matter how far away, no matter how small. Victories were few and far between, moments to be savored, celebrated.

DeJohn sucked a sporkful of protein slime over his teeth. The sound was revolting, but manners weren't high on the priority list for combat troops. Combat troops taking apart a stupid space station. She shook her head and took her next mouthful.

"What?"

Serra glanced up. DeJohn was looking right at her, but it was Carter who had spoken. He had half turned toward her and seemed to be staring at her plate.

"What?" she said.

"You shook your head."

"I guess that's the end of the Polarii," said Serra. She tapped her spork on her tray and winked sideways at Carter before looking at DeJohn. "Shame."

Carter collapsed in mirth. Serra and he both knew about DeJohn's predilection for Polarii women. DeJohn looked slightly worried as he processed the information, before Carter reached forward and slapped his shoulder across the table.

"Relax!" he said. "Man, you are *so* easy."

DeJohn laughed, but it was unconvincing. Carter rattled his tray on the table and stood.

"Gonna get some more," he said, glancing at Serra. "Coming?"

Serra's tray was half full. "Nah, I'm good."

Carter gestured to DeJohn, but DeJohn waved him off. Carter stood and joined the back of the queue of marines slowly shuffling past the serving counter.

Serra ate some more, but there was no conversation. When she looked up after a few mouthfuls, she saw DeJohn was looking at her. Fuck. She shouldn't have mentioned the Polarii. Now DeJohn was wired, and when he was wired he was a fucking pain in the ass.

Serra shifted in her chair. She was smaller than he was, but still muscular; any difference in strength between the two marines would have been compensated by Serra's increased agility. She shook her head again and returned to her food. DeJohn was fine, but he was also a creep sometimes, especially when he started thinking with his dick. It didn't particularly bother Serra—life in the Fleet, am I right?—but it was fucking boring. Then again, maybe she didn't blame him. Months and months out on this wreck and hardly a female left among the crew. She was pretty sure there was something about shore leave that Fleet Command had conveniently ignored.

They ate in silence for a while, Serra doing her best to ignore DeJohn's gaze. By the time Carter returned, she'd nearly finished her tray. Carter dropped into his seat, spork hanging from his mouth and fresh mountain of something grayish green on the table in front of him. He pulled the spork out with a wet sucking.

DeJohn tore his eyes off Serra. "Been around the hub lately?"

"Nope," said Carter, hunched over his new tray. "Why?"

"Heard that fuck Cleveland shifted his shit around to the end of the officer's row on Omega Deck. Fucking prick scared as shit." DeJohn laughed.

Serra and Carter exchanged a look. "King said to keep away, remember?" Carter said before popping another mouthful.

"Fuck King," said DeJohn. "And we can just take a look. I wanna know what that prick is doing here, anyway."

Serra frowned and turned back to her plate.

"Carminita?"

Serra looked up. "What?"

Carter and DeJohn slowed their chewing. Carter raised an eyebrow. "Huh?"

Serra bit the inside of her cheek. She felt cold, and . . . somehow she didn't feel alone. She was in a canteen full of crew, sharing a table like she always did with Carter and DeJohn, but she had this feeling that there was someone else, somebody sitting in the empty chair to her right.

And she looked, just to be sure. The chair was empty, of course.

"I think we should stay away from Omega Deck," said Serra, her voice almost a whisper. She blinked and turned back to her food.

Where did that come from? She didn't know. Then again, she didn't know where the voice was coming from either.

DeJohn sniffed loudly. "There's a good little marine. The marshal asks you to suck his dick, would you do that too?"

"It's not King," said Serra. "We should stay away because . . . just because," she said, feeling stupid. She stopped eating and pushed her tray away. She saw DeJohn scratch his ear, his eyes flicking between her and Carter.

"Not this shit again," said DeJohn. Carter frowned at him and leaned over the table toward her.

"What's up?"

Serra held his look a moment, then shook her head and returned her attention to her tray.

"Anyway," DeJohn said, "there're better things to do off shift, right?" He nudged Carter, but his friend ignored him.

DeJohn chuckled, low, deep, his eyes crawling over Serra again. She sighed, then stood and began to walk away, empty tray dangling from one hand.

"Hold on, I'm coming," said Carter. She could hear him quickening his pace as he fought to clear his second tray.

Serra nodded but didn't turn around. By the time she'd dumped her tray on the collection trolley by the canteen's doorway she was unsteady on her feet. But only when she reached a little farther down the corridor, where there were no people around, did she allow herself to lean on the wall. She bent over, hands on knees, fighting the dizziness.

Someone called out her name again, the name only her long-dead grandmother used, but she ignored it, took a deep breath, and then stood up straight and kept walking.

5

Ida found Izanami six hours later, as the *Coast City*'s artificial day cycled toward midmorning.

After he'd cut the connection to Fleet Command, Ida sat in his room in the dark for what felt like a thousand years. There was a hell of a lot to take in.

Stuck in a space station full of jarheads was, in a way, like being back in the academy. All it took was someone taking a dislike to someone for rumors and stories to spread. Ida had seen it happen before. But picking out Ida as a liar who hadn't earned his medals was a surprisingly specific storyline for DeJohn to take up. Ida wondered who had started it. Carter, no doubt. He was the leader of the engineering team DeJohn was in, and the most senior noncommissioned officer left aboard. Maybe that was part of it—Ida had seen the silver bar of the Fleet Medal on Carter's tunic too. The Fleet Medal offered certain privileges that Carter no doubt enjoyed, only now there was someone else aboard—someone with a higher rank, even though no longer on active duty—with those same rights. Carter probably felt threatened, in some way, no longer the special one. And so a whisper about Ida's award being fraudulent had started, with DeJohn just happening to be the loudest.

But it seemed it was more than a whisper campaign. The more Ida thought about his late-night call to Fleet HQ, the more surreal it felt, like it really had been a dream. Maybe he'd given the Flyeye the wrong date, and the Op had looked up the wrong records. Or the Flyeye was working on too much caffeine and had made the mistake herself. Perhaps a computer glitch had caused the wrong data to be displayed; someone had screwed up the entry accidentally or—worse—deliberately.

He needed to do more digging, get it sorted out.

Not that he needed to prove himself to Carter and DeJohn. But . . . but it *bugged* him. Being sent out to the Shadow system was the most obscure retirement duty he'd ever heard of. If he didn't know better, he would have said that someone at Fleet Command had it in for him.

Izanami was in the surgical unit. She jumped when Ida called her name.

"This a new hobby, sneaking around the station?" She glanced down. Ida followed her gaze, realizing he was still in his socks. He sighed. Bootless, in grubby shorts and T-shirt, he must look crazy. But the feeling of self-consciousness passed as he began to describe the conversation with the Flyeye at Fleet Command. As he explained, Izanami's expression changed from a puzzled smile to a frown, her forehead creasing deeply.

"How is that possible? A mistake with Fleet records?"

Ida scratched his unshaven cheek. "It's possible, but even if it was a mistake, it seems to match with what DeJohn and the others think. None of them have ever heard of Tau Retore. It was six months ago, but this wreck isn't *that* far around the edge of Fleetspace. There's no way the news could have passed by."

Izanami dropped into her chair silently, tapping a pen against her teeth.

"Well," she began with some hesitation, "the lightspeed link hasn't been that reliable."

Ida curled his lip. "Interference from the star? Yeah, I had that myself. But bad enough to cut the station off so they missed the reports? Were you guys cut off?"

Izanami just shrugged. Ida thought maybe she hadn't been on the station then.

"But . . . you believe me, right?" he asked.

Izanami's pen stopped and she looked at him, her eyes narrowing. "Of course."

"I think you're the only one who does."

Izanami sank deeper into her chair. "What are you going to do? Try Fleet records again? If you asked the marshal—"

Ida shook his head. "It runs higher than him—it has to. If the commandant was still here I could ask him—maybe that's why he left before I arrived. No, I need to talk to Stockley, Stevens. The other commanders of the First Arrowhead. See if they've landed in the same mess." Ida frowned and looked at the floor. "How, though? The lightspeed link to Fleet Command is just going to lead me around the same circle."

Izanami smiled and stood. She reached out and laid a hand on Ida's shoulder. Her touch was cold and so light, he could hardly feel it through his thin T-shirt. "Well, you have your own link now. There's nothing to stop you."

Ida looked at Izanami. "The radio set?" He felt the smile grow on his face. "That might work. If I can find out their current postings, I could try getting in touch directly, bypassing Fleet Command."

"You'll need to use Fleet Command to get their posting first, though?"

"Yeah," Ida said. He frowned again. "Maybe. I'm not sure I have clearance anymore. Maybe I can pull a favor or two. . . ."

Izanami withdrew her hand. "You'll get to the bottom of this. I know you will."

Ida smiled and nodded his thanks and headed back to his cabin. The station was cold again, and he picked up his pace, rubbing his upper arms and looking forward to putting a second pair of socks on his frozen feet.

Ida slumped on his bed and ordered the cabin lights to darken. He lay still and closed his eyes, collecting his thoughts. He was exhausted, physically and mentally.

His efforts had been fruitless. Talking to Fleet Command via lightspeed link had been a frustrating and time-consuming process, given the clearance required for the information and the endless delays that caused. He'd spent hours on hold, or being transferred between operators and departments, or repeating his original request over and over again to new operators and supervisors who had no clue who he was or what he wanted. His original plan to call in favors owed evaporated when it became clear nobody could locate the people he wanted to speak to.

But it was the interference from Shadow that was the most frustrating. It had grown progressively worse the longer Ida kept the lightspeed link open. Several times it had gotten so bad, the link automatically disconnected. Ida had never seen anything like it, but then he'd never been in orbit around a star like Shadow. When he patched into the *Coast City*'s solar observatory again, the graphs flew wildly over the screen as numbers that meant little to Ida hurtled past. Shadow was active; that was for sure. Flares and sunspots and a lot of stuff Ida had no clue about; the activity even seemed to be affecting his knee, the psi-fi field periodically glitching in time with the rhythms of the star as he sat motionless at the desk.

If Shadow continued to act up like this, the station would be cut off from the rest of Fleetspace. Which, thought Ida, might not be such a bad thing—the last transport wasn't due to swing by and pick up the station's last remaining crew, Ida included, for a couple of months. If the Fleet lost contact with the *Coast City,* they'd more than likely send the ship early. Which suited Ida just fine.

Except right now, when he needed to get answers from Fleet Command, the increased activity of Shadow was just what he *didn't* want.

Between the endless waiting and signal dropouts, what information Ida had managed to gather was next to useless. Even when he had persuaded someone to impart the data he wanted, or even just look the damn thing up in the first place, there were either no records or a single-line description. Commanders Stockley and Stevens, no record. Lieutenants Yung, Martin, and Hazlett—two listed as deployed, with no further information, and the third an empty record. It was the same with all the command crew of the First Arrowhead. Like the U-Stars they had captained just a few short months ago, the men and women who had been under Ida's command were mysteriously unavailable, their records vague, their status indeterminate. Swept under the carpet. Just as Ida had been.

No doubt with proper authorization he could probe further into the records and mission status of the crews, but that would mean convincing Provost Marshal King, as *Coast City* commanding officer in the absence of Commandant Elbridge, to put the request in. Ida once again reflected on the early and unexpected departure of the commandant. There was another situation Ida didn't feel entirely comfortable with.

Ida closed his eyes. His lack of progress was worrying. Something was going on at Fleet Command, something revolving around him, his former compatriots, and the action over Tau Retore. The interference from Shadow was the icing on the cake. He almost felt the star was doing it deliberately.

Ida opened his eyes.

The brightest light in the dark cabin was the blue dot on the front of the radio set. It was the first thing he saw every morning, the pale, sky-colored LED drawing his gaze toward it. It represented so much—not just the effort of building the thing in the first place, but the link it formed with the rest of the galaxy. With the radio, he could escape from the *Coast City* and the weird nightmare he now found himself in. With the radio, perhaps he could find the answers out there in the black. Maybe Izanami had been right.

Ida sat up on the bed, his eyes used to the dim of the cabin, lit in pale blue by the radio, the red and yellow LEDs scattered on the other equipment and the walls of the cabin itself nothing more than an abstract star field of pinprick lights. He pushed himself off the bed with his knuckles and slid into the swivel chair, rolling it back over to the desk.

He coughed and looked around the empty room. He had no idea where to start—if the Fleet didn't know where his former colleagues were, then what chance did he have of finding them?

He waved a finger over the uniformly silver top of the radio set. The blue LED flicked to a brighter setting, and the cabin filled with the background white noise of the universe as it breathed. The sound swam until Ida found his headset. As soon as he snapped it to the sides of his head, the main speaker cut.

Ida was alone with the universe.

He closed his eyes, listening to the rush of static until his brain began to impose order on the sound, introducing patterns and rhythms Ida knew were nothing but figments of his imagination.

As a child, back on the family farm, he used to lie in the dry grass of summer, staring at the brilliant sky until his vision went white. Then he'd roll over, dust tickling his lips and the smell of dry dirt and leaves in his nostrils, and watch the patterns play out in purple black behind his tightly closed eyelids. Sometimes, if you stared long and hard enough, the patterns didn't just form geometric shapes and figures that danced left and right. Sometimes whole narratives played out. How long he used to spend lost in this nonexistent world, he had no idea. Years later he taught Astrid the same trick, and together they would lie in the grass and describe what they were seeing to each other, Astrid weaving intricate fairy tales and scary ghost stories.

Ida blinked and pushed the memory away.

The noise rose and fell, waxed and waned. The echo of the Big Bang, reverberating on for all eternity.

"*Sonovabitch,* where you been?"

The voice that erupted in his ears practically threw Ida out of his chair. Heart thundering, the next thing he heard was howling laughter. Ida coughed as he drew breath.

"Clive! You're alive!"

The laughter cranked up again. "You're a poet, and you know it."

"How was the, ah, sortie?" Ida winced. He wasn't asking about Clive's holiday in the sun, after all.

There was a sloshing sound, followed by a hollow pop. Clive was on the sauce. Probably quite deserved.

"Oh man, we hammered the Omoto. It was a beautiful thing.

Also, I rescued some damsels and got me some prime Polarii pussy for the ride home. Listen to this—"

Ida bounced forward on his chair. "Tell you what, maybe later. Good to hear you're in the land of the living."

Clive didn't notice the snub. He supped from his bottle again and gave a friendly holler over the air. "Take it easy, bro!"

"I'll try my best," said Ida, pointing a finger and rotating it in the air. The channel shifted, and the warm static filled his ears. Good old Clive. Nice to hear someone made it.

Ida leaned back and rubbed his face, allowing the virtual dial to keep spinning up as he considered where to start looking.

After a moment, the white noise changed, lowering in pitch, taking on a harsher edge. Ida's eyes flicked open in surprise. He glanced at the display hovering in the air in front of him and sat upright very quickly.

The radio's tuner had cycled down through the regular frequencies but had kept going. All Fleet communications equipment had built-in fail-safes, preventing certain frequencies from being accessed. Ida's rig, constructed entirely from memory, was clearly flawed, as the set should have hit the bottom of the dial and then stopped.

The sound in his ears was different. He was in unknown territory. Dangerous territory.

The set was tuned to subspace.

Ida frowned, hesitant to continue but also hesitant to turn the radio off. The frequencies of subspace were illegal, but despite his misgivings at the alien sounds that now filled his ears, he had to admit he felt a little thrill. Not just because he was breaking Fleet regulations, but also because he was doing so on board the *Coast City*. King would probably burst a blood vessel if he found out what Ida was doing . . . but what the marshal didn't know wouldn't hurt him, right?

Ida closed his eyes, leaned back, and listened. The sound of subspace wasn't just white noise and it had nothing to do with the Big Bang. The sound of subspace was the angry roar of the nothing that resonated *between* space. It was weird, *alien.* Ida couldn't remember quite what the penalty for accessing subspace frequencies was. He didn't imagine the regulations had been enforced in years. In fact, he wasn't even sure why they'd been drawn up in the first place.

Ida knew what every U-Star crewman knew about the physics of space travel—and maybe a little more than most. That interest was probably the only reason he'd even known *how* to think of pushing a whole U-Star through a Mother Spider via quickspace, the "hidden" dimension of the universe, the one that allowed objects, such as U-Stars, to travel faster than light, and which the Fleet's entire communications net—the misnamed lightspeed link—depended upon.

But subspace . . . subspace was different. Scary, even.

Back in the day, when quickspace and other dimensions were first probed, everybody thought subspace was *it.* Mankind had hit the jackpot and discovered the legendary hyperspace, the key to interstellar travel and faster-than-light speed, the subject of hundreds of years of science fiction. But, as it turned out, you couldn't push anything through subspace except energy, which made it useless for travel but perfect for communication. Then quickspace technology was developed, and by the time U-Stars were powering toward distant stars, subspace had been long abandoned, the lightspeed link having become Fleet standard.

No, subspace hadn't just been abandoned—it had been *banned* by the Fleet. Ida scratched his cheek, trying to remember the reason, trying to remember if he ever knew it. It had been a long time ago, he knew that much, nothing more than a footnote in Fleet academy textbooks. Nobody thought anything of it.

The noise flared, and Ida opened his eyes again. He blinked in the dark, eyes drawn again to the blue light on the radio set, and he frowned.

Maybe he did remember, just a little.

There was a story—probably just nonsense, a bit of spice to explain why subspace was prohibited—that the sound of subspace, that exotic static, was *bad* for you. Listening to it would drive you mad or rot your brain or make you curse your mother and start drinking at an early age. Some said the sound of subspace was an echo from another dimension, something *deeper,* a place where monsters lurked. A name had even been coined for the imaginary lower level: hellspace.

Hellspace was just a story and the name itself was a joke, but sitting in his cabin in the dark, Ida felt unsettled. The roar in his ears was a little weird, but it sounded more or less like regular white noise . . . but he had to admit there was something else there, a rolling sound that was beginning to make him feel dizzy. Maybe there was a reason, a real one, stories and legends aside, why the Fleet didn't want anyone tuning in to the roar of subspace.

Ida reached forward and gestured above the radio set, turning it off. The empty noise clicked off sharply.

Ida sat in the silence of his cabin, suddenly feeling alone. The sound of subspace had almost been like a physical presence.

Despite himself, it took Ida a few minutes to get the courage to move to the cabin controls and turn the lights on full.

6

The desk in the commandant's ready room and the green-shaded lamp that sat upon it were not standard Fleet equipment, but by tradition the most senior officers were allowed to bring their most treasured personal effects with them on long tours. Across the U-Star fleet, many wonders were held—rare and valuable books, sculptures, antiques and heirlooms. The officers of the Fleet liked to think they were a cultured lot. And having such objets d'art on display didn't hurt when welcoming representatives of other cultures and planets aboard a Fleet ship. The Fleet had to impress sometimes, and not just with firepower.

Roberto King didn't like the desk, but then it wasn't his desk, and it wasn't his office. The contents of the ready room belonged to Commandant Elbridge; indeed, since taking command of the *Coast City,* the only change the provost marshal had brought to the ready room was an adjustment in the height of the chair, itself as old as the desk it was placed behind. King was less interested in aesthetics and design and more interested in functionality. Give him a psi-couch and an earpiece, and he'd happily sit in the ready room and control without distraction the final few spins of the *Coast City* as it orbited toward full demolition. The chair was less comfortable, the desk less functional, but despite this, King spent most of his time in the ready room anyway.

He reached forward, the ancient springs in the chair protesting as he did so, and flicked to the next page in the book on the desk in front of him. He regarded the image on the thousand-year-old paper with distaste, but when he sat back into his chair he didn't take his eyes off it.

The provost marshal didn't like the desk or the chair (or, for that matter, the rug or the lamp), but he did appreciate the art on the wall behind him. He also appreciated the fact that the art was hung on that wall in particular, because it meant that while sitting in the chair, he didn't have to look at it.

He liked the artwork, wondered at the artistry of it, found the palette interesting and the brushwork exquisite. Of the subject, he was less sure. It was a ship in a stormy sea, the prow of the vessel about to crest a titanic wave that was sure to overwhelm and drown the crew. It was Japanese, and rendered in classic blues and grays and greens that, despite the subject, made the scene bright, if highly stylized. Perhaps Elbridge had a fondness for the art of the Far East. Perhaps he liked it because it showed that, no matter what measures were taken, nature could not be tamed by mere mortals. Perhaps he felt that the picture represented the *Coast City,* its mission to study the technetium star around which it orbited akin to trying to sail in a stormy sea. Shadow was dangerous. King knew that now, and Elbridge certainly had.

Or perhaps there was another reason for having the picture on the wall. Because the picture went with the book, and the book went with the desk.

Elbridge had volunteered to command the *Coast City* from the very inception of the mission. He'd had the desk installed as soon as his office was ready. The desk was made from the timbers of a sailing ship, one with a famous name, although it was a name Elbridge had kept to himself. He'd written about it on the inside front cover of the book—a leather-bound first edition of something called *Spate's Catalog,* published in New York in 1903—which had been hidden in a secret drawer. When King took over the office, that drawer had been left open, and it hadn't taken much to figure out how the mechanism worked.

After only a little reading, King knew full well why the book was hidden. He knew why the desk was here. He knew what the picture on the wall behind the desk showed.

He also knew why Captain Abraham Idaho Cleveland, retired,

had been sent to oversee the last orbits of the U-Star *Coast City*. He knew why the station was due to host Zia Hollywood and the famous *Bloom County* in just a short while.

King reached forward and flipped another page, feeling his stomach flip in synch. And then he leaned back again, and this time he closed his eyes.

7

The *Coast City* rotated into Earth-dawn. Ida yawned, stretched. He'd managed a few hours' sleep, at least.

The cabin lights were still on.

He rubbed his eyes, wishing that when the purple shapes appeared he could tell a story about them to Astrid. That wasn't going to happen. Ida's fingers stopped moving, and he sat with them pressed against his eyeballs.

He had to keep it together. He had to get to the bottom of it all.

He sighed, loped out of the cabin and down the hall to the vast communal toilets and shower room. As far as Ida knew, he had the place for his own private use, right on the edge of the habitable deck as he was. The nearest occupied berth was a good three hundred meters back toward the elevator lobby. Not far enough for Ida's liking, but any farther away and the station got a lot less comfortable.

Ida left the door of the stall open as he relieved himself, and thought about whether he could be bothered trekking to the canteen for a proper coffee instead of the caffeine simulant he kept in his cabin.

He zipped up, and stood stock-still for just a moment. He glanced over his shoulder, into the empty men's bathroom, wondering whether it was time for another of Carter and DeJohn's hilarious pranks. The space apes hadn't bothered him for a while.

Ida moved, the rustling of his T-shirt suddenly loud. Then he stopped. He wasn't imagining it. From down the corridor came the unmistakable rise and fall, rise and fall of subspace static. Faint as it was, Ida felt the hairs on the back of his neck prickle.

He'd turned the radio off last night, and he hadn't touched it since as far as he could—

Ida drew in a sharp breath. There was something else in the noise—not a rhythmic pattern, but . . . a voice.

Someone was talking on the subspace channel. It was faint, unintelligible, but Ida could tell it was female. He jogged back to his room.

As he sat down at the desk the static swelled, obscuring the transmission. Ida adjusted the tuning and the roar popped a few times; tapping the panel displaying data from the solar observatory, Ida watched as the popping coincided with spikes of activity from Shadow. More interference, this time strong enough to penetrate even subspace. The purple star at the heart of the system certainly was a strange beast.

There! Faint and distorted, behind the wall of noise. As she spoke, her words punched the static, and it flared and danced around her voice, like Shadow was reacting to the signal, fighting the transmission. Ida brought up the tuning dial and carefully adjusting the channel.

"Hello? This is Captain Abraham Idaho Cleveland of the U-Star *Coast City*. Come in, please."

The static buzzed and popped, and he repeated his call twice, fine-tuning the channel as he did so. Nothing. He'd lost it.

"Pyat, cheteeree, tree, dva, raz . . . " The woman's voice crackled suddenly, filling the room. Whatever she was speaking, it wasn't English. Ida frowned. English was the Fleet's official language, used for all communication. It was hard to tell with all the noise, but it almost sounded Italian.

"Can you repeat? You are very faint." Ida turned up the volume, and then grabbed the headset in a hurry and jammed it on. The rush of static was like a slap to the face, and he quickly turned the volume down again.

"Raz, dva, tree, cheteeree, pyat . . . "

The woman's voice rose and fell in the unfamiliar accent, making it impossible to tell whether she had realized Ida was on the line and was talking to him or she was in the middle of a conversation with someone else. Ida kept talking, stopping quickly as the woman spoke again, but soon he realized she couldn't hear him. He was eavesdropping.

Words and phrases were being repeated; he could tell that much. There were pauses; then she would repeat a phrase, sometimes quite loudly, as though she was trying to make herself heard. Ida realized that he could hear only one side of the conversation, as the pauses and phrases sometimes sounded like answers to questions, the speaker's temper rising as though whoever she was talking to didn't understand or couldn't hear.

Ida didn't like it. There was something about her tone as she went on, her speech quickening and her voice becoming higher and higher. She sounded scared and angry.

But . . . he couldn't turn it off, not yet. Who was she? Where was she? Was she in trouble, in danger? He tried to tune out her voice and listen for anything in the background that might provide a clue, but the channel was uniformly awful. The static was punchy, sharp. Ida watched the graph of solar activity crawl over the nearby display. If anything, that scared Ida more than the mysterious and frightened voice broadcasting, impossibly, from the depths of subspace.

But there was nothing he could do. She couldn't hear him, and he couldn't hear who she was talking to. He removed the headset and there was a brief second of silence before the subspace radio's speaker clicked in, filling his cabin with the static and the voice. It echoed oddly around the hard walls of the cabin.

Ida knew he should turn if off, but a part of him wanted to keep listening. It made him feel uncomfortable, and sad, and very, very small. The universe was a big and terrible place, and she was very far away, and there was nothing he could do, even if he knew what the trouble was. He suddenly felt that his own situation—most likely the result of a clerical error—was ludicrously insignificant.

Before he lay on the bed, he checked that the message and

data stream was being recorded. If he was lucky, he might be able to analyze it later and get a position on the signal. Not that that would be of any use.

Then he closed his eyes and lay with his hands behind his head. Listening, watching the purple patterns behind his eyes, wondering who she was.

8

M'ija, no tengas miedo.

Serra woke with a start. She might even have called out, she wasn't sure, but what she was sure of was the cold dampness of the sheet and the way her heart was trying to break out of her rib cage. She sat up quickly and breathed shallow and fast in the dark. The voice again. The dreams.

She should have left the station, insisted that Lafferty—whom she outranked—stay instead. But as her pulse slowed she also knew that a psi-marine who regretted past decisions was one with a much abbreviated lifespan.

The cabin was dark, and when she glanced to her left she saw the other side of the bed was empty, the blanket drawn back and the mattress still sunken from the weight of her companion.

There was a click from the other side of the room. Serra jumped again and this time she did call out, something colorful and Spanish that made Carter chuckle as he sat at the table, his naked back to her.

"You scared the crap out of me, Charlie." Serra sat up against the wall and readjusted the blanket around her. Damn, it was cold. The station's faulty atmos controls were becoming a drag, fast. "What are you doing, sitting in the dark?"

The clicking sound came again. Carter sat with his forearms on the desk and he wasn't moving, but Serra saw something bright flash in his hands. A small metal something, narrow and silver. Charlie Carter's Fleet Medal. FOR SERVICES RENDERED.

"You okay, baby?" she said. The Fleet Medal was the highest honor available to them both, but Carter didn't like to wear his, preferring to leave it in its fancy box back in his quarters. He's said several times that he didn't need to wear it all the time, only for special occasions, and there weren't many of those on the *Coast City*. Besides which, there was a smaller bar, a placeholder for the medal itself, sewn onto the breast pocket of his tunic. It was less conspicuous, which Serra knew suited him just fine.

Serra had learned to stop asking, anyway. Whenever she brought it up, he changed, withdrawing into himself. She knew that if she had a Fleet Medal, she'd wear it all the time and damn well write poetry about it, but Carter's was a different kind of medal. He'd been part of the Fleet Marine Corps Black Ops division—that much Serra knew, but little else. He shouldn't even have told her that. The commendation on the medal was standard, deliberately and officially vague; covering their asses, Carter said whenever she asked him about it. Which was rarely.

Except he'd clearly been thinking about it again, with the arrival of Captain Cleveland. She didn't blame him, especially not with that idiot DeJohn stirring things up.

Serra had thought Carter's medal was locked away in the cupboard where it usually was, but he had it now, at the table, rolling it between his thick fingers. He must have started carrying it around with him.

Carter didn't speak or move, except for the slow motion of his fingers, turning the metal bar over and over and over, the light it caught like a star glittering in the dark.

She tried again. "Can't sleep?"

No answer. Serra drew her legs up to her chest. Her breath was now clouding in the air in front of her face.

"Wanna talk about it?"

The Fleet Medal clattered to the tabletop and Carter got up. He was wearing pants but Serra could see his torso glisten with sweat as he moved across the room toward the door. He must have been freezing.

Almost in tune with her thoughts, he flicked the environment control on the wall next to the door up a couple of notches. Above her head, Serra heard the air unit whirr into life as it began gently blowing in warm air.

She smiled, and then, unsure if he could see, patted the bed next to her.

"Come back to bed."

Carter stopped by the door. "You know what they give out the Fleet Medal for?"

Serra pulled her legs up tighter to her chest. "For services rendered," she said.

"'For services rendered.'" Carter smiled. "You know what that means when you're in Black Ops?"

"I—"

"Means you weren't afraid to follow orders, no matter what they were. Means you weren't afraid to get your hands dirty. Means you did things for the Fleet that nobody else could know about. Means you did things that sometimes keep you awake at night."

Serra nodded. "You think he was Black Ops too?"

Carter sighed and walked back to the bed. The tension in the room seemed to ease a little as he sat down heavily, rocking Serra on the mattress. She reached out to him. His skin was cold but she ignored it. She was warming up and he would too, soon enough. He rubbed his chin slowly, but said nothing.

"Think he's cooked up that story to, what, cover his involvement with something else?" she asked. "Turning his Black Ops medal into something heroic?"

"Something heroic," said Carter. He laughed and shook his head.

"I didn't mean it like that."

Carter nodded and slipped back into the bed, facing her. He didn't look her in the eye, so she took his face in her hands and softly pulled his chin up. His eyes shone in the dark and she kissed him, but his lips only twitched in response.

"You're not okay," she said.

He smiled, but it was a sad expression. He brushed the hair from her forehead and sighed.

"Forget it," he said. "It's just another bad dream."

He settled onto his pillow and pulled the blankets up to his neck and closed his eyes. Serra watched him for a while. He didn't fall asleep, but he seemed calm, more relaxed.

She understood, or maybe understood just a little more, anyway. Carter lived with the shadow of the Black Ops cast over him; whatever it was he had done, whatever it was he had been *ordered* to do, it had affected him—broken him, a little—and they'd given him a goddamn medal for it. He hated the medal; really, deep down, she knew he hated the Fleet too and was looking for a way out.

And now they had Cleveland, a man with no past, with a Fleet Medal of his own, won in an epic and heroic battle that nobody had ever heard of. Here was a moment, a chance for Carter to act on his anger, his self-loathing. Cleveland was everything Carter hated about his own past.

Serra sighed, and she slid down under the covers. Maybe Carter realized that too. Maybe he'd reached a turning point. She glanced at him and saw he was now asleep, his breathing soft.

The room was warming up and she felt a little more comfortable, but as she closed her eyes she thought perhaps the shadows in the room were moving, and as she drifted off into sleep, her face twisted into a grimace of fear and her eyes moved under their lids rapidly.

Ahí estás, Carminita!

And the cabin was still and quiet and dark, and the shadows moved.

9

"My *God*."

Ida raised an eyebrow at Izanami, but the medic was staring at the floor. The subspace recording from the radio looped and echoed around Ida's cabin as the pair sat and listened.

"What?"

Izanami looked up at him, her face drawn. If she'd had any complexion to start with, he would have said she looked quite pale. But it was hard to tell. Her opalescent skin rarely changed hue. "Can't you hear it?"

Fear. He'd heard it before, the first time, but the more he listened, again and again, the worse it sounded. "She is—*was*—in trouble," said Ida. "Some kind of accident?"

Izanami listened for a moment more, and then shrugged. "Have you pinpointed the origin?"

Ida rolled on his chair to the desk. He reached out and stopped the playback; then he pulled a computer screen toward him. His fingers spread over the display as a scrolling table of data transformed into a simple vector map he'd constructed. A solar system. *The* solar system. Proper noun. Home.

"Near Earth, as far as I can make out. There's a lot of data loss in the signal. Most of the information has been stripped out by the interference."

"Interference from Shadow, I presume?"

Ida nodded. He felt Izanami peering over his shoulder at the screen.

"And near Earth? That doesn't make sense."

Ida tapped his index finger against the plastic frame of the computer screen.

"Not much about this does," he said. "Subspace isn't used for communication—it's a banned channel, has been for, oh, years and years—"

"Banned?" Izanami's eyes went wide. "Is this going to get you in trouble?"

Ida waved away her concern. "No one will find out. U-Stars aren't fitted out to monitor subspace, so it's not like anyone can listen in. Anyway, my point is: what's the signal doing there in the first place?" He scratched his chin and regarded the silent silver box on the table. "A signal broadcast from somewhere near the Earth, using a disused, prohibited system, spoken in something other than the Fleet's official language."

He poked the computer display, rotating the map of the solar system, new vectors drawing themselves from several points near the schematic representation of the orbit of Earth, each line suggesting possible source coordinates.

"I wish I knew what she was saying," said Ida. "I don't think anyone on the station speaks Italian, and the signal sounds too poor to feed into the station computer for a translation. If King would let me near it, of course."

"Italian?"

Ida turned and looked at Izanami. She looked confused.

"Don't you hear the accent?" he asked.

"Oh," she said with a shake of the head. "That's not Italian. Russian."

Ida's eyes widened. "And you know that because?"

She shrugged and turned away from Ida. She walked to his bed and sat delicately on the edge. "I worked in Russia once. That's the beginning of the recording—she's counting down, then up, like she's testing something." She held a hand up before Ida could ask the obvious. "That's as much as I can manage, sorry."

Ida crinkled his nose. Then he spun his chair around to the computer, switching the map back to the data tables. He flicked a hand near the radio, and the playback began. On the computer screen, the table began scrolling as the audio ran, a smaller window beneath plotting another graph of the audio analysis.

"She's talking to someone else, that much is clear. I only patched on one side of the transmission."

"Why do you care?"

Ida stopped, hands frozen above the computer's touch screen. He turned slowly. Around them the Russian voice crackled on. "What do you mean?"

Izanami had lain down on Ida's bed. *Well, make yourself at home,* he thought.

"You don't know who the recording is of," she said, looking at the ceiling. "You don't even know where it is from. If she was in an accident, she's probably dead. And even if she is or she isn't, if it was near Earth, the Fleet would have picked her up, because if it was some kind of distress call, or if she was reporting on something, she wouldn't have been using subspace. She'd be on the lightspeed link. What you patched into was an echo. That would explain the quality of the signal."

Ida didn't know what to say. He played his tongue along his teeth, and he felt cold again. Another environmental glitch. But she was right. The signal couldn't have been broadcast in subspace at all. What'd he'd picked up, completely by chance, was some weird echo bouncing around the hidden dimensions of the universe.

"More to the point," she said, "weren't you supposed to be working on something else? Your old crewmates?"

Ida blew out his cheeks. Why *did* he care? Izanami's question was fair enough: the signal was a distraction, something to keep him from going slowly mad as he tried—fruitlessly, it seemed—to get answers to his own little mystery.

But the lightspeed link was a waste of time now, the interference from Shadow growing so strong as to make it almost unusable. Even if he could break through the static, all he could do was call Fleet Command again and get some Flyeye to read him the same abbreviated reports he'd already heard a dozen times now.

"Ida?"

Ida coughed and looked at Izanami. The recording had looped again. "I'm working on it."

"Okay."

"Yes, okay." Ida felt a tightening in his chest. He sucked cool air over his teeth and changed the subject. "An echo, you think?"

Izanami shrugged. "Could be?"

Ida frowned. He'd never heard of signal leakage from one dimension to another, but it sounded feasible, especially when there was a strange star just next door pulling all kind of tricks on the communications networks.

But Izanami's question scratched at something in his mind. He repeated it over and over to himself, looped like the recording.

Why do you care, Captain Cleveland?

"Hmm," he said at length. He turned his chair around a few degrees and looked at the radio set and computer screen on his desk. She was right, it was a pointless exercise. But . . .

"Distractions can be useful sometimes," he said, turning back to the medic.

She nodded, and her smile reappeared. "I'm sorry, I didn't mean to make you feel guilty."

Ida laughed, but maybe that's what the feeling was. He tried a smile, and found it worked a little. "And, you know, there's something about her voice . . . it makes me feel . . . sad. But in a good way, somehow. I don't know. That doesn't make much sense."

Izanami tilted her head, her frown a thoughtful expression. "Melancholy can be good for the soul."

Ida blinked. "So says the neurotherapist."

They looked at each other, then both laughed. Izanami closed her eyes and pointed at the ceiling as she lay on the bed.

"Play it again."

Ida pushed his screen away, waved at the radio, and sat back with his eyes closed as the Russian woman's voice faded into the cabin.

"Pyat, cheteeree, tree, dva, raz . . ."

10

After another replay or two, Izanami left Ida to it. It was very late, and Ida wanted to use the main comms deck on the bridge to start a translation running before he tracked down Carter and got the marine to sign off on the next demolition briefing. And boy, was he looking forward to that meeting; he'd delayed it as long as he could, but the paperwork had to be done eventually. Over the last few cycles, Ida had realized his official duties took up maybe an hour per cycle, which made it easy to let them slide altogether. The marines resented having him poking around, giving them small, annoying extra tasks in order to get the demolition signed off. And the provost marshal, despite his apparent love of procedure, hadn't asked to see any completed documentation yet anyway.

Ida shifted on the bed and lay awake for a few minutes, then absently turned the recording loop back on and listened to it as he lay in the dark.

He dozed and dreamed of the farm, Astrid leading him into the red barn. When they got to the door, red paint streaming off in it a breeze that was colder than it should have been in summer, he discovered it led to a corridor of the *Coast City*.

Standing by the door was her father, his eyes narrow as he and Astrid argued. Argued about Ida, probably. But every time the old man opened his mouth, nothing but white noise came out. Astrid screamed and ran off down the corridor.

Ida woke with a start, thinking there was someone standing over the bed, watching him. The cabin was silent, the playback having stopped apparently by itself. Ida sat up and watched the blue light of the radio set for a while, thinking he'd probably turned it off sometime during the night and didn't remember.

He got up, showered, and headed to the bridge, subspace recording in hand and the silver Fleet Medal insignia shining on his breast pocket. As he walked, it crossed his mind that his self-imposed isolation was bad for his health. The last thing he needed now was to have some kind of breakdown.

It was the recording; he knew it. The mystery woman was becoming an obsession. Something mysterious but trivial to ease the wait until the interference on the lightspeed link cleared and he could try again to get some real answers about his missing past.

Ida picked up his pace. He was nervous, and more than once he checked over his shoulder, and more than once he thought he saw someone disappear just out of sight. Someone with blond hair, wearing a blue survival suit, like the one he'd last seen Astrid in.

Ida took a deep breath and shook his head, trying to snap himself out it.

He felt better as he entered the busier part of the station. Here the lining of the corridors was intact, and the station's remaining crew went about their duties, none paying him much attention as they rushed around. As he got closer to the bridge, he kept an eye out for his special friends, DeJohn and Carter, but he didn't see them among the green- and blue-uniformed personnel.

Normally the bridge of a U-Star was out of bounds except for those with explicit permission to be there or those of a high enough rank to make such a formality meaningless. Ida wasn't sure he had either, not anymore, but the elevator didn't protest as he requested his destination, and as he stepped out of it he fingered the Fleet Medal on his tunic, making sure it was still in place. Its constant presence made him feel a little better, anyway.

Despite the customized design of the space station, the bridge of the *Coast City* was fairly standard: the regular semicircle layout common to all Union-Class Fleet Starships was here extended around to form a completely circular room, with the elevator rising in a column in the center. The column continued up through the ceiling, leading ultimately to the top of the station's main spire.

Ida stood quietly by the elevator, jiggling the recording disk in his hand, scanning the half of the bridge he could see. It looked like only the minimum regulation crew were manning their stations: two pilots, who on a station had damn-all to do; two other officers Ida didn't recognize, both of whom were several rungs down the ladder from him; and a marine-engineer, recognizable in his olive green T-shirt and combat pants, checking something at the science station.

Ida frowned. The marine was DeJohn. But his expansive back was turned, and if Ida went left around the central elevator column, he could reach the unmanned comms deck, placing the column between him and his rival. He wanted to talk to DeJohn at some point, but it could wait.

"Can I help you, Captain?"

Ida jumped. He turned, finding his nose not two inches from Provost Marshal King's face. Ida smiled, trying to ignore the man's garlic breath.

"Comms deck free?"

King's eyes flicked sideways toward the side of the bridge that housed the communications station and then back to Ida. "The comms deck?"

Keeping his smile fixed, Ida casually strolled over to the comms deck and rested his hands on the back of the vacant chair. "May I use the communications deck?"

King stood stock-still near the elevator column, following Ida with only his eyes. He looked nervous. Ida could see it in his face, no matter how hard the bullethead tried to assert his authority. It was like the whole thing was a façade, one the man was desperate not to let slip.

"It won't make any difference," said King finally.

"What won't?"

King clasped his hands behind his back and slowly walked over, a ghost of a smile playing lightly over his lips. "The light-speed link is down, ship-wide. Interference from our friendly neighborhood star."

Ida frowned. "Happen often?"

The provost marshal shrugged. "Sometimes. The star has unusual properties. It's what this station was built to study, after all." King's smile tightened. "That comms deck will be needed when the channels have cleared."

Ida nodded. "Oh, no doubt. But while the lightspeed link is out of action, maybe I could borrow it for a little while?" He jammed one hand in the back pocket of his fatigues and offered the small black rectangle of plastic that held the subspace recording toward King. "Won't take that long. I just need to run some data from my little radio shack through the mainframe. You know, crosscheck some of my programming. I'm not as good as I used to be."

"Oh yes," said King. "I heard you built a radio set."

Ida grinned and waggled the disk in front of the marshal's face. "You did say I needed a hobby."

King's lips twitched, the tic pulling at one side of his nose. Ida widened his eyes expectantly.

"Very well." King had barely snapped out the words before he turned and marched swiftly back to the elevator. He pressed the call button, but as the elevator indicator light above the door began counting the floors toward the bridge, he turned back to Ida.

"One more thing, Captain." King folded his arms and took a few steps closer.

"Marshal?"

"I know you have relocated from your assigned quarters without authorization." King unfolded a hand from his arms and held it up, stopping Ida's protest before it had started. "And while I would normally issue a reprimand and insist you go through the regular channels, I'm prepared to overlook it for the moment. So long as our mission runs its correct and proper course, I don't care where you sleep at night."

Ida huffed a laugh. King's expression tightened.

"However, the station will be receiving VIPs in the next few cycles. If you could add your new cabin to the list of occupied spaces, I will add that stretch of the hub to the security detail."

Ida nodded. Anything for a quiet life. "Fair enough. I'll do it now."

"Thank you, Captain," said King. "Also, for the duration of the visit, all personnel will be required to wear their station tags and have them turned on at all times."

Ah. There it was. Always a catch. "So you can track my movements?"

King nodded. "So I can track everyone's movements, Captain. This station may not be in active Fleet service, but it is now a construction site. A *dangerous* construction site. For the safety of both our crew and the visiting party, we will need to keep security tight and to restrict access to some parts of the station."

"Don't want any important people stepping through the floor and floating away?"

King ignored the comment, turning away to head back to the elevator. The door slid open with a pleasant tone.

Ida called out after him. "Who's coming anyway? Anyone I know?"

King turned back, arms still folded, and the tight smile returned to his face. Ida didn't like it. Whoever was coming must have been a big deal, the way the provost marshal walked slowly back toward him. It was just short of a swagger. "You've heard of Zia Hollywood?"

Ida frowned and then shrugged. "Can't say that I have. She must be a hell of a VIP, name like that."

King drew an index finger along the bottom edge of his mouth. "She's a starminer."

"Ah," said Ida. That explained the name, then.

"You've been out in the black too long, Captain," the marshal said. "She's the most famous woman in Fleetspace. Hollywood and her crew will be stopping here to refuel on the way to that field of slowrock debris on the other side of Shadow."

Ida nodded, but he didn't care. He had no interest in the so-called celebrities of the Stellar Gold Rush. To have reached the top, she would be young, pretty, and 90 percent silicone, and she would spend her whole stay aboard the *Coast City* peeling frustrated space apes off her. Good luck to her. He'd register his cabin, wear his ID tag—turned on—and stay in his cabin for the duration of this special visit.

Apparently satisfied, the marshal stabbed the elevator button again to open the door and disappeared inside. Ida watched the indicator above the door begin to move again, King heading up the station's main spire.

"Zia Hollywood," said Ida quietly, shaking his head. He dropped himself into the comms chair, slammed the recording disk into one of the free slots in the console, and set to work.

11

The control room of the *Coast City*'s solar observatory was circular, very similar to the main bridge far below but condensed, with only enough room for a half dozen personnel at most. The provost marshal was the only one in the room, but he knew he was not alone.

The screen in front of him showed a view of Shadow, the image filtered with software so only certain wavelengths were displayed at the operator's request. King cycled the view through each in turn, and much as he expected, the image did not much change. The star was violet, light at the center and dark purple at the circumference, and stubbornly remained so no matter which wavelength he selected. The only change was in the corona, a shifting, diffuse halo that streaked off into space from the star's surface. As the images changed, so the corona changed with it, shifting in shape and size.

It was a failing of the solar observatory systems. It had to be. Although the systems were fitted and customized as best as possible for this particular mission, observing Shadow was a difficult task. The light from the star degraded the sensors and cameras with surprising speed, resulting in a constant need for replacement and recalibration.

The light that will fuck you up. King allowed himself a smile. It was a common refrain around the station. Nobody liked being out here, not within touching distance of a star so foreign, so *alien,* that it felt like it was alive, like it was watching. Maybe the *Coast City* wasn't watching the star; maybe the star was watching the *Coast City.*

King reached the end of the available filters, and he paused. He knew the truth, thanks to the book hidden in the desk, but he had to check for himself. Commandant Elbridge's notes may have been written in some personal code, but the comms deck had translated it without any difficulty.

The final filter would show it. King held his breath. He wondered if Elbridge had known what he was doing. Then he turned the selector switch.

The view of Shadow changed, the colors reversing, the bruised black of space a brilliant violet white and the star itself now black.

And at the center of the star, the blackness swirled, spiraling inward, black moving on black moving on black, like darkness being pulled in on itself, tumbling into a whirlpool. Darkness falling into an abyss.

King stiffened. The lights in the solar observatory were on low, twilight normal. The observatory was mostly run on automatic, the systems gathering data and piping it back to Fleet Command via the lightspeed link, while researchers who had until recently been stationed on the *Coast City* did their work in more comfortable surroundings down in the hub.

In the reflection on the screen in front of him, in the depths of the black star, King saw her standing behind him. Her eyes were blue, and the hand on his shoulder was as cold as the hull on the dark side of the space station.

"I know what you want," said King. He didn't move, but his jaw clenched as the pain of the cold crept into his bones and made him ache from head to toe. He closed his eyes. "You cannot have him. *Will not* have him."

When he opened his eyes, he was alone, and the observatory control room wasn't as dark as he'd thought it was. On the screen before him was displayed the regular view of Shadow in the visible spectrum, the violet white star a featureless globe, a purple halo licking out around it.

King turned off the display. He walked backwards until he was up against the opposite wall. Then he sank to the floor and wept.

12

"Fuck, Sen, you're a stone cold killer. Remind me never to—"

DeJohn's words were lost as the marine gunner next to him opened fire again with her heavy automatic rifle. Aboard a U-Star, all arms were switched from plasma pellets to soft ceramic shells so the hull wouldn't get punctured should a firefight break out. The shells were safe to use but made a hell of a noise, which made the practice range a popular place during a tour. Marines liked to make a lot of noise, and today the range on the *Coast City* was nearly full, the marines left aboard the station taking advantage of their light duties to get some practice time in.

Serra watched Sen's back as the gunner emptied her weapon at the target a hundred meters down her lane, reducing the somewhat dramatically drawn two-dimensional representation of a Spider groundcrawler to so much shredded fiberboard. Beside her, DeJohn had his hands clapped over his ears, the protectors hanging uselessly around his neck. He was laughing as he watched Sen practice. Heavy weaponry was her specialty, and leering at female troops was his.

A buzzer sounded and green lights lit above each firing point as the range commander called a halt. As the *Coast City*'s complement of marines was lower than normal, a roster had been drawn up; today the range commander was Corporal Ahuriri, and aside from punching the buzzer, Corporal Ahuriri didn't really give a shit. Regulations were loose now there were so few marines left on board, which meant practice at the range was perhaps a little more fun than it should have been. DeJohn even had a plastic drink bottle filled with something that smelled far stronger than their standard electrolyte solution sitting on the shelf in his firing point. Serra wondered if she cared enough to report it, and wondered if sucking on engine juice while holding a live weapon made DeJohn more dangerous or less.

The light on the barrel of Sen's rifle flicked to blue as she raised it, smoking, to the ceiling, balancing the stock on her hip and glancing sideways at DeJohn's grinning face. Serra couldn't resist grinning herself as Sen turned and, weapon safe, gave her a nod. DeJohn, meanwhile, started getting his own weapon ready on the shelf in front of him. He whooped as he checked his magazines.

"Some things a man never gets sick of," he said. "Am I right or am I right?"

Serra took her position at Sen's vacated station. The range of weaponry available to her as a psi-marine wasn't as wide or as heavy as the gunner's, just the standard light rifle and pistol. It was the latter that she was working on today; it had been a while since she'd used it. She positioned her feet carefully and then looked up, but DeJohn hadn't been talking to her. On the other side of him, Carter stood at his own firing point, pistol in hand but barrel end resting on his shelf. He was staring at his target. He didn't seem to be listening.

Serra frowned. Carter was acting like nothing had happened during the night, but he seemed distracted. She knew not to bother him, not after she'd seen the Fleet Medal in his hands. She wondered again about what had happened in his Black Ops tour. Being out on this derelict station probably wasn't helping either, not with DeJohn hanging around, not with Cleveland aboard.

DeJohn didn't seem to notice his friend's snub. He whistled to himself and returned his attention to his weapon. He'd chosen the light rifle. When it was ready, he flicked the safety off and the barrel light went from blue to red. He glanced over his shoulder at Sen, who leaned back against the wall and did nothing except look him up and down with a smirk on her face before pointedly slipping her ear protectors on. DeJohn grinned.

"They say it's not what you've got, it's what you do with it, am I right?"

Serra rolled her eyes. "Oh please," she said, and readjusted her footing before punching the button on her left. A new target slid into her lane fifty meters ahead.

The buzzer buzzed. The indicator lights turned red.

She fired six shots. Then DeJohn opened up with his rifle in the neighboring lane. Further down, a handful of other marines began firing as well, the combined sound of exploding ceramic ammunition pressing on Serra's eardrums despite the protectors. She lowered her weapon, regarded her shots with some disdain, and stepped back.

Carter hadn't moved. He was breathing quietly, his chest rising and falling beneath the tight olive T-shirt. Serra removed the clip from her pistol and walked over to him. She waited for the buzzer to sound again before speaking.

"You okay?"

Carter jumped at her voice, then closed his eyes and sighed. But when he opened them again they came with a grin. She smiled in return, and she felt a little better.

"Yeah, no problem," he said. "Didn't get enough sleep last night."

Serra laughed. "No kidding."

From behind her came a low chuckle from DeJohn. Serra turned and lifted an eyebrow. "You have a one-track mind, marine."

"You'd better believe it," he said, slamming another magazine into his rifle. He winked at Sen, who just shook her head. She was smiling too.

"Never see Captain Asswipe down here," said DeJohn, punching his target button and raising his rifle sight to his eye. "Girl has probably never handled a gun in his life."

Sen smirked and pushed herself off the wall. "Girl, huh?"

DeJohn snickered. Sen trailed a fingertip over his back. "And you'd show him a thing or two, wouldn't you?"

DeJohn lowered his gun. "That I would, marine. That I would."

Sen placed the back of one hand on her forehead and buckled at the knees. "Oh, Captain! My Captain!"

Then she burst out laughing, DeJohn and Serra too.

"Marines, ten-hut!"

There was a clatter of weaponry as the range came to attention, Serra, Carter, and Sen all standing tall. DeJohn stood relaxed, rifle hanging loosely by his side. With his other hand he grabbed his drink bottle and sucked noisily on the straw.

Captain Ida Cleveland stepped toward the insubordinate marine, computer pad under one arm. As he walked forward, his eyes flicked here and there, taking in the others in the firing range. He was frowning, the typical disappointed officer, but Serra could sense a lack of control. He wasn't in charge here, and he knew it. DeJohn knew it too.

"Thirsty, marine?" asked Ida. DeJohn looked him in the eye and kept sucking on the straw for a good few seconds before setting the bottle back on his shelf.

"Thirsty work, being in the Fleet," he said. Then he sniffed and raised his rifle. Pointing the barrel at the ceiling, he thumbed the safety off and manually reloaded the chamber.

Ida didn't move, didn't take his eyes from DeJohn's. "That's thirsty work, being in the Fleet, *sir*."

"I don't see no officer in here." DeJohn nodded at Carter. "You see anyone, Charlie?"

Serra could almost feel Carter vibrating next to her. She glanced sideways and saw his lips flicker, his eyes staring straight ahead.

Nobody moved; nobody spoke. Ida took a step backwards, his footfall loud in the quiet firing range. Then he turned on his heel and offered the computer pad to Carter.

"You're the demo leader on lambda section, marine. I need you to check and authorize the last drone run."

DeJohn hissed and turned back around at his firing station. He began fiddling noisily with his weapon.

Serra turned her head, breaking her stance. Carter looked pale. He licked his lips.

Ida lifted the datapad higher, until it was practically under Carter's nose. "Problem, marine?"

Carter exhaled, blowing the air out with puffed cheeks. He

box with the blue light. "Get anything new this time? I think I've heard it enough myself, actually."

Izanami nodded, much to Ida's surprise. "I think so too. I just wanted to hear it a few more times, in case there was something we'd missed."

"Like what?"

She shrugged. "I don't know. But it's fascinating, isn't it?"

Ida frowned. "Yeah, but I'm thinking maybe it's best to leave it for a while. There's no information to be had, nothing that tallies with anything recorded in that time period. The station's computer put the recording in low Earth orbit, but that's probably wrong. Could be anything, from anywhere. The only thing we know is that the message was sent a millennium ago." He slapped both hands down on his thighs. "Not much to go on, really."

"So you managed to get some more time on the comms deck?"

"I did, yes." The corners of Ida's mouth turned up at the thought. King would throw a fit if he found out, but Ida had been clever, disguising his computer time under a stack of fake processes that would swamp any activity list an operator would bring up to check. King seemed to be using the deck to run some analysis of his own, but with the lightspeed link down, it seemed as good a time as any to use the spare capacity. "One last pass, trying to filter the noise out. I've left it running. Should have something tomorrow, I think."

Ida leaned back and closed his eyes, and was halfway into a yawn when a knock came from the cabin door. His jaw snapped shut with an audible clack. He didn't move, thinking King had hauled himself around the hub to berate him personally for using the computer without authorization. The knock came again, and this time Ida quickly got to his feet.

The cabin door had a small square window set at an average head-height. It was a rubbery, thick plastic, scratched and slightly cloudy. As Ida approached, he could see someone moving outside the door, but the corridor was mostly in darkness and the person was just a shadow. The head was large and round, a helmet of some kind, and the person seemed to be bouncing a little, as though he or she were agitated.

Not King. It was Carter, or Serra, or DeJohn, in a better disguise than a T-shirt mask this time. Time really was lying heavy on their hands.

Ida turned, motioning Izanami to get back against the far wall of the cabin. She nodded, expressionless.

Turning back to the door, Ida exhaled quickly, rolling his shoulders, loosening them up. If someone wanted a piece of him, they'd have a fight on their hands.

The cabin door slid sideways the instant Ida jammed his index finger on the control. He held his breath and hopped backwards a little, balancing on his toes, fists clenched.

There was nobody there. Ida darted out into the corridor, checking to the left and right in a half duck, expecting someone to swing out from shadows on either side of the door.

Nothing, nobody. Ida stood to his full height but kept his fists clenched. Turning to reenter the cabin, he glanced up at the security camera he now knew was in the corner of the next bulkhead. This time he'd seen someone at the door. This time there would be evidence and King wouldn't be able to brush him off so easily.

"Who was it?" Izanami was still pressed up against the far wall, peering out from around the edge of one of the floor-to-ceiling cabinets. With the lights at one-quarter power, the cabinet cast a near perfect shadow across the angle in which Izanami hid. The room was cold again, and Ida caught sight of Izanami's eyes reflecting the dim blue glow of the light on the radio set.

"Didn't see, but I have a fair idea," said Ida, pausing at the threshold. "I need to talk to King. The camera should have got the asshole this time." Ida shuffled on his feet. "You coming?"

Izanami shook her head. She must have gotten quite a fright.

"Okay, but stay here and don't let anyone in who isn't me. If someone has it in for me, they might have it in for you as well. You seem to be my only friend around here. Don't think that has gone unnoticed. Back soon."

The door closed behind Ida, cutting the light from the corridor down to a dirty square thrown onto the cabin floor through the small window. Eventually that light dimmed as Ida moved down the passage and out of the section.

Izanami stepped out of the shadow in total silence, her eyes glittering. She padded to the door and, with a smile, placed the flat of her hand against the cold metal.

A shape appeared at the window, a black shadow at first barely distinguishable from the orangey gloom until its face resolved, pressing up hard against the cloudy plastic. Pale skin, sickly and white; yellow eyes wide; mouth pulled into an unnatural grin as the flesh squeezed against the window, revealing teeth as yellow as the eyes.

DeJohn writhed against the door, his hands now appearing beside his face, pressed hard enough against the glass to bleach the color from them. His mouth was open and he rocked his head from side to side, pulling the skin and flab into hard geometric shapes. His grimacing face, shoved hard against the window, was a horrifying, insane mask in the dark corridor. If he was screaming, no sound penetrated the cabin. His eyes rolled, shot through with broken blood vessels.

Izanami watched, the smile growing across her face.

Finally DeJohn calmed, his convulsions becoming less and less. His huge eyes lolled in their sockets until they fixed on the face on the other side of the door.

Izanami drew her hand away from the door, put a finger to her lips, and shushed the engineer. DeJohn's twisted mouth flickered. Then he pulled himself away from the window, leaving a thick, slimy residue of saliva and sweat on the frosted plastic.

Smiling, Izanami opened the door. In the near blink of an eye, it slid to one side.

The corridor beyond was empty.

Izanami stepped into the passage, cast a look at the lens of the security camera high on the bulkhead, and then turned and walked deeper into the hub, into the dark skeleton of the station.

18

"The provost marshal is busy, Captain, I'm sorry," said the Flyeye.

Ida blew out his cheeks and almost jogged on the spot in annoyance. The door to the commandant's ready room was locked, and the Flyeye had been quick to leap from her chair nearby and stop Ida from punching the doorbell.

"What the hell does he do in there?" asked Ida, waving at the sealed bulkhead. "Polish his precious desk?"

The Flyeye didn't speak, but her hand was held out as though to prevent Ida from charging the door with his shoulder.

Ida sighed. If the marshal didn't want any visitors, fine—he could use the security console himself.

As soon as Ida turned on his heel, the lock on the ready room door chimed. Ida turned back to see the indicator change green and the door slide open. King stood on the threshold. Behind him, the ready room was dark, lit only by the old-fashioned green-shaded lamp on the antique desk. Ida could see an open book—a *real* book, made of bound paper.

"Captain?" King's voice was steady, his eyebrow raised in the marshal's favorite expression.

The Flyeye began to explain, but King waved her away. He drew a breath to speak but Ida held up his hand. King sighed and nodded, and began to rub his forehead.

"I saw him this time," said Ida.

King shook his head. "We're a little busy here, Captain. Do you wish to report another burglary?"

Ida realized he was standing on his toes, and he gently rocked back onto his heels.

"No, I don't," he said, ignoring the weary look on King's face.

"But I caught him snooping around. He was wearing a helmet, maybe a spacesuit."

King kept his eyes fixed firmly on Ida's.

Ida breathed slowly, trying to keep his cool. What was King waiting for? "Marshal, if one of your crew is wandering around playing practical jokes in a spacesuit, I don't think our incoming guests are going to think much of Fleet discipline."

King blinked, jaw muscles working as he ground his teeth.

"I'm all for a little fun and games," Ida said. This was not strictly true and both Ida and King knew it, so Ida picked up the pace before the marshal would notice. "But aren't you going to have to file a report on Ms. Hollywood's visit? A crewman taking a suit without authorization to fool around in isn't going to sit well with Fleet Command, is it?"

Ida widened his eyes a little, playing the innocent, and King finally clacked his tongue against the roof of his mouth and, arms folded, turned and strolled over to the security desk. Ida was at his heel, checking his step, trying not to overtake the marshal in his impatience.

King tapped the operator, who stopped his furious typing and turned his huge, multifaceted goggles up at his superior. King nodded his head toward Ida and stepped back. Ida exhaled loudly and leaned over the desk, eyes scanning the array of screens suspended above the console. The Flyeye glanced at King and then back at Ida before signaling his readiness.

"Okay, camera feed outside my cabin—there we go. Wind back about twenty minutes, and also bring up crew scan records for the same period." Ida stood and rubbed his top lip. "No, further—go back an hour, let's see what we have."

"I wouldn't rely too much on that."

Ida turned to King, standing behind him. "The crew scan?"

King nodded. "There's a bug in the manifest. Crew tracking is a little flaky at the moment. That's what Operator Jagger here was busy with, trying to locate and correct the error without having to reboot the entire ship-wide net."

Ida frowned and scratched at the back of his head. He'd never heard of a manifest bugging. Keeping track of everything on board a U-Star was one of the provost marshal's main responsibilities. Everything from pencils to protein sachets, from neutron missiles to the crew itself was traceable and trackable. Their current whereabouts could be called up instantly on the automated system, and any movement watched in real time from the security desk. Fleet personnel had subcutaneous ident tags that couldn't be removed without a lot of blood and trouble—Ida's had been removed when he retired, hence King's requirement he wear an old-fashioned tag card on his belt.

"Huh," said Ida, turning back to the console. The two largest rectangular computer screens were showing the results of his request, the left-hand panel an amber diagram of the section in which Ida had made his quarters, the right showing the camera feed from the passage outside his door.

Ida watched one, then the other, his eyes flicking between the two screens. He saw his green ID indicator on the schematic. It was mostly motionless—him listening to the recording in his cabin, he realized. But the manifest scanner only showed him in his cabin, not Izanami.

"I see what you mean about the manifest," said Ida, glancing sideways at King.

The marshal raised an eyebrow but merely grunted in response.

The camera feed showed the half-lit passageway from the same three-quarters top-down view as it had before. The picture was almost entirely still, and if not for a few red and blue LED studs embedded in various wall panels that periodically flashed or changed color, Ida could have sworn the picture was on a freeze-frame.

"Wind them on together."

The operator acknowledged, fingers moving over analog jog controls on the desk. The pulsing of the LEDs on the security feed increased, and Ida could see his own green indicator on the map wobbling a little as he shuffled around the cabin. But aside from that, nothing was happening.

"Fascinating, Captain."

Ida turned to King. "Watch and wait," he said. He turned back to the desk and saw his green indicator move quickly across the schematic diagram of his circular cabin.

"There!" Ida tapped the desk and the operator slowed the recordings to normal speed.

Ida's green dot stopped by the door, and then moved forward. On the camera feed, he darted out of the now-open cabin door, fell into a crouch, and looked left and right in quick succession. Finally he straightened up and, fists clenched, walked back through the door and out of view.

Looking at the manifest scanner, Ida saw his green dot move back into the cabin a little before turning and leaving in a curved trajectory. On the camera, Ida reappeared briefly as he strode out of his cabin and headed to the bridge, walking under the camera and out of sight.

King sighed, and Ida felt a heavy hand clap him on the shoulder.

"Okay, Captain," said King. He looked at the floor and then flicked his eyes up to meet Ida's. "Thanks for the show. I'll be sure to look out for the rerun. Now, next time you step onto this bridge, I'm going to have a demo droid dismantle you and pack you away in one of the kit boxes along with the section of the hub that your cabin is in. Do we have an understanding?"

Ida shook King's hand off.

King stiffened, his eyes narrow and nostrils flaring.

Ida pointed at the two security screens, both now paused by the Flyeye. "You think I'm making this up? There was someone at my cabin. What? You think I'm seeing ghosts now?"

King clicked his tongue, then sighed and tapped the back of the operator's chair.

"Run it back, just before Captain Cleveland left his cabin the first time. There. Pause. Now go slow."

It was the same as before. Ida's green indicator unmoving in his cabin, then jerking into life and moving to the wall beside the door before passing through it. On the other screen Ida watched himself jumping into the passage and looking left and right.

King pointed at the screen. "Take it back, just a little. Slow, slow."

The Flyeye rotated the jog control, reversing the playback in ultra slow motion.

Bingo. Ida knew it. He pointed at the screen and looked at King. "Told you."

King looked at Ida, eyebrows knitted together over his nose. He looked back at the screen. "Operator, full manifest for that timestamp, please."

Ida folded his arms and took a step back, admiring the view on the two security screens as the operator and King busied themselves at the console.

The more he looked, though, the less he liked it. Ida began to feel a chill, and an odd, tight sensation in his chest, as the feeling of triumph over King abated.

The camera feed on the corridor was paused, a millisecond before Ida was due to make his exit from the cabin. The corridor was empty, except for a faint black shape. Hardly more than an outline, it was the size and shape of a man in an old-fashioned bulky spacesuit, complete with spherical helmet.

But even though the image was still, the form seemed to melt back into the shadows. In fact, the more Ida looked at it, the less it looked like anything at all, certainly less like DeJohn—the marine was a muscle-bound six feet, and the figure in the corridor was shorter, thinner. Ida squinted at the screen. It was a shadow, nothing more, maybe a simulacrum formed by the poor light of the passageway. He began to feel less and less confident.

But it was something, right? He was right. He'd seen something. Even if it meant he was jumping at shadows, this was proof it wasn't all inside his head.

"No suits missing," said King. He turned back to Ida. "Captain?"

Ida shook his head. He blinked and took a step back toward the console, where King was pointing at a smaller display set into the desktop. "No crew either," said the marshal.

"I thought you said the manifest was bugged?"

King pressed his tongue into the side of his cheek. Then he nodded. "Better check it manually."

He flicked the comms panel on the security desk. Nothing happened, and he flicked it again. Static popped sharply, making King jump.

"Problem?" asked Ida.

King whistled between his teeth. "No," he said sharply. Then he swore. "Where the hell is DeJohn? Carter, report, please."

"DeJohn isn't showing on the manifest, and there might be a suit missing. That's it, isn't it? That guy's been itching for me since day one."

King squinted at Ida, then glanced down at the Ops seated beside him. "Get a security detail here. Now."

"That's more like it," said Ida.

King stepped forward. There was something about his expression that Ida didn't like.

"You're right, Captain. It's time we started doing this by the book." King smiled a smile without any pleasure. "We're entering lockdown for the arrival of our guest, and you are operating an unauthorized communications deck. You are to surrender it immediately."

Ida almost took a step backwards. "Excuse me?"

The marshal placed his hands behind his back, now clearly in his element. "When I told you to take up a hobby, I didn't say anything about breaking Fleet regulations. I am aware you have tuned your radio set to subspace, which is a prohibited frequency."

Shit. He knew. Ida's mind raced. How? Clearly someone had told him—probably the same people who had broken into his cabin earlier. Ida wondered if anyone had been listening in on his radio chatter too. He wondered if anyone else had heard the strange message.

"Look, marshal," Ida began. He was on thin ice here, and he knew it. He just hoped that with the operations on the station winding down, King would continue to be lenient. He opened his mouth to speak again when King held up a hand.

King nodded to someone just over Ida's left shoulder. Ida saw

King's hand twitch just before a heavy hand enveloped each shoulder.

"Security, escort Captain Cleveland to his quarters and supervise the deactivation of his space radio set. Bring the confiscated equipment to me when you are done."

The grip on Ida's shoulders tightened.

"Captain Cleveland is to remain in his cabin until our VIP has departed." King looked between the two marine escorts and seemed to choose one at random. "Ahuriri, remain outside the cabin. If the captain tries to leave, manacle him to something heavy."

King's eyes flicked back to Ida's. The marshal was in his element now. Ida knew, after months stuck on a barely functioning station, he must have been itching for a chance to reestablish order and control.

"I'm under arrest now?" Ida's voice was almost a whisper.

King regarded Ida and folded his arms. "You are a security risk, Captain. But believe me, I am doing you a favor. If you were on active duty, this would be much worse. Dismissed."

The marines, each fully kitted out in the security detail's helmet and body armor, pulled harder on Ida's shoulders, and he knew if he didn't comply, they'd lift him up and carry him by the armpits back to his cabin. He shrugged them off, holding both hands up in surrender, and turned and walked to the elevator column ahead of his escort.

The walk back to his cabin took nearly ten minutes from the bridge, but Ida barely noticed. Instead his mind was racing. He'd got off easy, for sure, and he should have known not to dabble in the forbidden subspace frequencies, even if he'd found them accidentally in the first place.

But without the radio, he wouldn't have the message, the recording. Which was exactly what needed to happen—provost marshal aside, Ida had to get the damn thing out of his head.

None of which made Ida feel any happier about losing the ghostly, crackling voice of the woman who had died long ago.

"You going to open this door or what?"

Ida's head snapped around, and he looked at himself in the reflection in the marine's helmet. They were standing outside his cabin.

Ida nodded and, glancing up at the security camera on the bulkhead, tapped the entry code into the door panel.

19

Carter swore and slid off Serra's body. She sighed and kicked at the tangle of damp sheets at her feet. He laughed.

"What?" she asked.

Carter helped push the bedding off onto the floor with his feet. They lay together, heat radiating off their slick bodies.

"You," he said. "Aren't girls supposed to sigh delicately and pull the sheets up to their chin when they're done?"

Serra laughed now and stretched her arms above her head. Carter's eyes were fixed on her breasts as they were pulled taut against her rib cage.

His lip curled and his hands moved over her body. Serra giggled and moved in to kiss him, then jolted under his grip, pushing herself up the narrow bed quickly. Carter snarled and poked his tongue between his teeth, but his grin quickly vanished when Serra said *"coño"* and then "fuck," and knocked his hands away.

"What is it?"

Serra looked past him, her eyes searching the cabin, but it was dark, twilight-normal, empty. Carter craned his neck around.

"There was someone looking in." Serra pointed at the door as Carter rolled over and swung his legs over the edge of the mattress. She sat up and leaned over, scrabbling for the bedsheets so recently discarded.

Carter sat on the edge of the bed, elbows locked as he pressed backwards on the mattress, ready to spring up. After a few seconds his shoulders relaxed and he turned back to Serra.

"There's no one there. You okay? You're pretty edgy, you know?"

Serra frowned and pulled the sheet tight against her chest. It was getting cold in the cabin. She could hear the environment control kick in, faintly roaring like a distant sea.

Carter was right; that was the thing. Serra wished that she'd gone with the other psi-marines instead of Lafferty and met up with her lover back on Earth, later. Life on the *Coast City* was fucking her up.

Carter sniffed and looked back toward the door, apparently oblivious of the dropping temperature. "You think we got a Peeping Tom?"

Serra nodded. She wanted to say more, to tell him about the voices, to tell him about the purple light in her dreams, to tell him that she felt an almost constant presence now, tailing their every move around the station.

But she just pressed the sheet against her chest with her left forearm crossed protectively over it. Carter stared at her, his own face expressionless. But there was something in his eyes. She knew he trusted her instincts. That was her job, after all. He was a frontline marine, one of the best. That was *his* job.

Carter sighed and he pushed himself off the bed, padding over to the door. Placing his hands on either side of the square window, he pressed his nose against the panel and looked left and right as best he could. Serra shuffled on the bed behind him.

"I must have imagined it," she said.

"Huh," said Carter, still trying to look down the passageway outside the cabin without opening the door. "Y'know, if we've got a peeping perv, I have a feeling there's only one person on this boat that it'll be."

"DeJohn?" Shit. It wasn't a surprise. They'd given up trying to find him after nearly two hours of chasing shadows around the hub, Carter finally calling it and reporting back to the marshal. If DeJohn was playing a game, it was a fucking tiresome one.

"Yep. Prick." Carter turned from the door. "You've seen how he's been lately. He's high on engine juice most of the time. This tour is seriously screwing him up." Carter gave one more glance out the window. "Anyway, looks like we're alone now. Maybe it wasn't him. Maybe it was your imagination. Now," he said, turning and advancing toward the bed, a wicked grin on his face. "Where were we, exactly?"

Serra relaxed, letting the sheet slacken as Carter leaned forward to grab it off her. They both laughed, and Serra braced herself for a tug-of-war. Jerking forward, Serra glanced over Carter's shoulder, toward the door.

They weren't alone. She screamed. She couldn't help it.

Carter cried out and tumbled back as Serra's grip on the sheet suddenly loosened. He regained his balance on his heels and slid off the bed, spinning around to face the door, stopping just short of slamming straight into it.

They had a Peeping Tom, all right, and Carter had been right. The face was pressed tightly against the Plexiglas, rolling from side to side, dragging the fleshy cheeks horribly, exposing yellow teeth and sickly pale gums.

"DeJohn!" yelled Carter. "What the fuck?"

Carter slammed a palm against the locking mechanism. The door whined but didn't open, and for a moment DeJohn's distorted face stopped squashing itself against the glass just long enough to look Serra in the eye.

"Fucking *fuck,*" said Carter, slapping the door control repeatedly.

There was something wrong with DeJohn, thought Serra. He'd never had the best teeth in the world, but through the slightly cloudy glass of the cabin door they looked yellower than ever, and ragged, almost chipped at the edges, pointed. But it was the eyes—the whites were almost a dark shade of yellow, shot through with a bright spiderweb of red. DeJohn was grinning, his eyes so wide as to be almost perfectly circular.

"Get fucking rid of him," Serra called from the bed. She'd brought her legs up to her chest now and pressed herself against the wall at the head of the bed. On a fucked-up space station like the *Coast City,* the last thing she needed was DeJohn being a fucking *carajo.*

Carter looked down at the door control. "The hell is wrong with this thing?" He slapped it again, his palm smacking with a wet sound against the silver-chrome surface. The door whined again, and this time, after just a second's pause, opened.

The passageway was empty. Carter muttered under his breath as he strode out into the corridor. As soon as he crossed the threshold into the passage Serra saw him tense, his skin suddenly crawling with gooseflesh, the cold outside the cabin enough for him to reflexively pull his head back as though avoiding a blow. His body shone metallically with sweat in the dim light.

As Carter paced outside the cabin, Serra screwed her eyes tight. She was a marine, a fucking marine, and a little cold air and someone being a dick was nothing, *nothing*. But she'd had a surprise, and she was annoyed at her own reaction. She'd been more on edge before than perhaps she realized, and this made her uneasy, uncomfortable. Right now she'd rather have been at the front line of a battle against the Spiders, using her ability to plug into the Spiders' own psi-net and fuck with their communications.

"What the *fuck* is up with the environment control?" Carter's voice drifted out of the passageway. He reappeared at the door, sweat steaming off him as he stepped back into the cabin.

Serra thought of the purple light of Shadow. "I'm not going back outside to try to fix it again," she said quickly.

Carter paused and gave her an odd look. Then he nodded.

"Freezing out there. This hulk is fucked, I tell you. Environment control is all screwed up again." Carter reached behind him and hit the door panel. As the door slid shut, he knocked the cabin's environment control to high and sighed as warm air gently blew in through the vents near the ceiling. Carter walked over to the bed and began separating his clothes from Serra's.

"This demo job is really beginning to piss me off," he said, pulling on his pants. He swore again as his foot got tangled in the leg.

"So what the hell was DeJohn doing out there? Did you tell him to fuck off?"

Carter huffed. "Where's my shirt?" Finding it, he yanked it over his head and unrolled the T-shirt down his chest and back while shaking his head. "There's nobody out there."

Serra stiffened under the thin sheet. "What do you mean? What did you tell him?"

"I said," Carter growled, hopping on one foot as he pulled his boots on, "there's no one fucking out there."

"But . . . he was there!" Serra pointed at the door, waving her finger around as though that emphasized her words.

Carter glanced up at her and shook his head again. "He must have run out of the section."

"Where are you going?"

Carter hooked a thumb over his shoulder, toward the door. "Gonna see if I can find him, then see King."

"King?"

"Yep. Something isn't right."

Serra buried her chin in the sheet. The Fleet-issue bedding was terribly thin, and despite the warm air filling the cabin, the sweat on her body refused to dry, making her feel wet and cold. But she didn't want to move. It was ridiculous. She was a marine, a trained solider, just like Carter. And yet . . . and yet she had to bite back the urge to ask Carter to check under the bed, just in case. *And then when he leaves,* she thought, *I'll lock the cabin door, turn off the lights, and hide in the corner, and wait for him to come back.* She didn't want to be in view of the window in the door. Or, more important, she didn't want to be able to see out of it herself. Because . . .

"You see his face?" she asked.

Carter blinked at Serra. He was standing over the bed now, dressed. The muscles on his chest were tight, stretching the fabric as he clenched his fists.

"His eyes . . . ," she said quietly.

Carter nodded.

Serra sat up a little. "Is he sick? He looked sick. Maybe that's why he didn't respond earlier?"

Carter nodded again. "Stay here," he said.

But he needn't have bothered. Serra just watched as her lover opened the cabin door, standing in the frame for a good few seconds as he checked left and right and left again. With a final look over his shoulder and a small frown, he disappeared down the passage. The door snicked shut behind him automatically, and the light dimmed as the passageway darkened as he walked away.

In the corner of the room, on the bed, under the thin green sheet, Serra sat, every muscle in her body tense, not wanting to move, not wanting to close her eyes. If she edged back, just a little, the angle of the door window was enough that nobody could see her easily. Perhaps that was enough, but she didn't dare move across the room, not even to get dressed.

Shivering with cold and shivering with fear, Serra lifted the sheet over her head, plunging herself into a world of cold, green dark.

This fucking spaceship.

Carter walked slowly at first, then picked up the pace once he realized the environment control had at last decided to play ball, switching section lights on around him as he moved, keeping the ambient temperature just so. Still, it played havoc with his sinuses. The inside of his nose was cold and dry and it hurt when he sniffed. His lips had a layer of cracked skin on them.

The second passageway, then the third. Each gently curving corridor was separated by a bulkhead and door, the edges of each premade section that, when assembled together in space by the robot drones, formed the kitset space station.

Carter reached the end of the third passage along from the cabin he now shared with Serra. The bulkhead door slid upward silently as he approached, the ship's sensors timing it so that he didn't have to pause to pass through no matter what his travel speed.

Serra. Now, *there* was a marine. Her gunnery scores were higher than those of anyone else Carter had met in service, specialists like Sen aside, helped by that goddamn freaky sixth sense she had going on. But that wasn't the half of it. For the first time, he'd met someone who really understood him, who knew what it was like not just to be a marine but also to be ex–Black Ops. She knew what this meant, more than anyone he'd met who hadn't actually *been* there. She helped him deal with his past—it was a slow process, but he was getting better, he knew it, and it was all down to her, too, not the army of shrinks the Fleet threw at him. Serra was special, in more ways than one. And if they could only escape from the Fleet one day, then he knew, he *knew* she was the one he wanted to grow old with. Time spent with her helped him forget, more and more, about the Fleet and its business.

Carter stopped on the other side of the door, peering ahead. He was heading toward the demolition zone proper, marked by a red line running at eye level on the walls on either side of him. The metallorubber floor tiles had already been lifted, leaving a shallow grid of black metal. The corridor was very long, and although it was nearly pitch dark ahead, the bright red LEDs on the next bulkhead door did a fine job of illuminating the end of the section in a dreamy, misty light.

Carter sighed, tapped his fingers against the doorframe behind him, and then turned to leave. He needed to see King.

Just as he turned, the red light at the end of the passage flared in his peripheral vision. He stopped and snapped his head back around. Something had moved across the red LEDs. A shape, indistinct and blurred.

"DeJohn?" Carter stepped back into the section, trying to see through the mist now filling the dark passage. Lit by the low LEDs on the walls, it created an eerie violet glow.

"DeJohn? Hey, Niels, you there?" He shook his head, muttering, and kicked his feet at the clouds forming near floor level. The environment control had gone loopy again. Mist? "What the—?"

Carter took two steps forward, each footfall ringing out on the metal floor grid. Then he stopped.

He was there.

Standing at the far bulkhead, the figure in the spacesuit was unfocused and rough at the edges, the mist curling around it, crawling up its legs like it was alive, aware. It was standing in front of the door panel, and the glowing air made it look like you could see through it, see the lights behind.

Carter blinked and took another step forward. The door behind him, sensing his progress, closed.

"DeJohn, you fuck. What do you think you're doing? King is going to eject you into space, man. But not before you've explained yourself to me. Hey! I'm talking to you!"

The figure in the spacesuit didn't move. It was DeJohn, wasn't it? They'd seen him at the cabin window, although he'd put his helmet back on now. Although . . . the figure was somehow shorter and thinner than DeJohn, even in the bulky suit.

Carter suddenly had a feeling he should have ducked into the armory and signed out a sidearm. His fingers curled at his belt, searching for a holster that wasn't there.

But he kept walking forward. The figure in the suit didn't move, not really, although he shimmered in Carter's vision.

Carter's skin was pricking with a cold sweat, chilling him even further in the fucked-up atmosphere of the semi-deconstructed passageway, each step illuminating the next ceiling light tile to half power, enough to make sure you didn't walk into anything but not enough to see properly. Ahead, the figure rippled again.

Carter frowned. The ceiling lights above the figure in the suit were still dark—another environment glitch—but the section where the guy was standing was lit better now by the lights above Carter as he approached. He could see now that the figure in the suit was standing almost hard up against the bulkhead door. The door was unlocked—Carter could see the indicator light through the spacesuit—but remained closed.

Through the spacesuit? Carter stopped and pinched the bridge of his nose between forefinger and thumb. He felt dizzy suddenly. He sighed and strode forward.

"DeJohn, quit fooling around. You shouldn't have that suit out of storage. King is already in a bad mood and you're going to drive him truly apeshit, man."

Carter stopped. He could feel the cold air move around him, the thin mist cloying on his bare arms.

He blinked and was alone in the passageway. The figure in

the suit had gone. The bulkhead door was still closed, and he'd never heard it open.

The corner of his mouth curled into an irritated snarl, Carter looked at the frame of the door panel, as though an explanation might be printed there alongside the standard Fleet insignia. He stepped forward, just to check, and at the appropriate proximity the bulkhead door slid open, left to right. Beyond was another corridor in an identical state of deconstruction. The ceiling light across the bulkhead faded on, and, caught in the yellow-white light, Carter watched fingers of the cold mist drift into the clear air of the next section.

Carter swore, then stood and breathed deeply for a while. The nausea had passed, but his chest hurt. It was an unfamiliar feeling, being in a situation in which he wasn't in control. You could never let that happen in space, nor on the battlefield. Calm, control. Think. He shook his head, like that would clear his mind. He focused on facts rather than on supposition, ignoring the uncomfortable way the image of the man in the spacesuit had been a blurring, shifting black shadow in the passage. He quickly came up with a theory, one that better satisfied him.

DeJohn had snapped at the same time the *Coast City* manifest had bugged. He'd dropped off the scan and was now running free around the station, high on engine juice. He must have fallen into a paranoid delusion, stealing the suit, convinced that the U-Star was going to fall apart around him at any moment. He was sick; he needed help. Carter had seen plenty of cases of space madness. The theatrical nature of the environment failures was just triggering the latent, primitive, superstitious parts of DeJohn's mind. Carter understood—lighting and door failures, temperature drops and problems with humidity and condensation, it was enough to flip anyone out. And maybe with the station not altogether there anymore, they weren't shielded from the light of Shadow. Shadow scared even Carter. The light of that star would fuck you up. That was something else to report to King. The *Coast City* may have been decommissioned and in the process of demolition, but it was probably important for the demolition crew itself to survive the process. Maybe they could move the station farther out from the star. There was no scientific crew left aboard to study the stupid thing anyway.

He turned around. The figure in the suit was a couple of meters away, now standing in the passage through which Carter had just come. Carter felt a lump in this throat and instinctively swore just as he took a huge intake of breath. The result was a strangled gasp that didn't quite fill Carter's lungs. He stood, back straight, and whooped for breath again. In an impossible second the figure was now standing right in front of him, close enough to touch. It reached forward.

Carter's last thought before the blackness descended was that it wasn't DeJohn in a spacesuit. It was a woman, her curves unmistakable even under the silver padding. And it wasn't a Fleet-issue spacesuit. It was old-fashioned, like something from an old movie. Silver quilting and white plastic, and across the front, four large, bold letters in red: CCCP.

Carter stared at the closed helmet visor, trying to work out who the reflected image was. A man with cropped hair and a mouth stretched wide and screaming.

20

"What the hell?"

Ida heard the scream, and so did the two armed marines. The one inside his cabin shifted, helmet turning toward the door. Through the semi-frosted square window, Ida saw the guard stationed outside turn his head, looking down the passage. Ida stood quickly from the bed, where he had been reading a book on his computer pad—with no space radio, no mystery recording, he actually felt a lot better, and had started to think about his edited personal history again and what he would do and whom he would see back at Fleet Command in a couple of months to get it sorted out.

He put the pad down beside him and looked at the marine. The marine said nothing but shifted on his feet, clearly itching to check out the sound.

Ida pointed at the door. "Aren't you going to see what that was?"

The marine looked between his prisoner and the cabin door.

"Come on, don't be a jackass," said Ida. "Someone's in trouble. It's your duty to check, marine."

Outside the cabin, the second marine had been joined by somebody else. It was impossible to see who, but they were shorter and weren't dressed in battle gear like the guards. The marine's helmet, nothing but a dark spherical shape, bobbed as he conversed with the newcomer.

"Oh, for crying out loud." Ida took a step forward, hesitating only a moment as his robotic knee panged with pain. *Too much lying idle,* Ida thought.

The marine snapped back to full attention and made a move to stop Ida, but then seemed to think better of it and nodded instead. Ida slapped the chrome control panel next to the door, which snicked open.

"I can't get through to the bridge." It was Serra. She was dressed in her off-duty fatigues, her green singlet damp with sweat; clearly she'd come straight from her cabin at the sound.

"What's going on?" Ida's gaze flicked between the marines.

Serra looked at him; her eyes were wide and wet, her lips parted and quivering slightly with rapid breaths.

"Marine?" Ida looked at his guard.

The guard raised a gauntlet to the side of his helmet, and Ida watched his index finger twitch as he manually cycled through the comms channels. Normally it was automatic, controlled by a combination of jaw movements inside the helmet and selective thoughts as part of the combat suit's low-level psi-fi field. The manual control was there as a backup only.

The marine shook his head. "Some kind of interference on all channels."

Serra's face dropped into a worried frown. "Me too." She tapped the silver comms tag slotted onto her belt.

"Interference?" Ida stepped back and, standing in the doorway to his cabin, reached around to the door control panel. The room's main comms channel control was embedded next to the lock.

Ida thumbed the call button. "Bridge?"

As soon as he released it, the cabin was filled with a harsh burst of static. First the lightspeed link, now the station's internal comms channel? It was impossible. Ida flicked the button a few times, each resulting in a burst of noise. He bent over and absently rubbed his artificial knee, which seemed to throb in time to the static.

There was something else in the noise. Ida depressed the button and held it, focusing on both the sound and the way his knee ached. There was something else buried underneath the random sound. A rhythm, a roar that waxed and waned with a sharp edge that made the edge of Ida's jaw tingle like he was sucking on a lemon.

He'd heard that sound before. He had been listening to it just recently.

The static of subspace.

He hit the button again and again. "Bridge! King, come in." Nothing, just the empty roar of the universe that lay underneath their own.

He pressed the button one more time, but then he saw Serra wobble on her feet, her hands on her forehead. She was a psi-marine, he knew that . . . Maybe the alien noise of subspace affected her like it affected the psi-fi link between his knee and his brain.

Serra closed her eyes and rubbed them. She muttered something in Spanish, just a whisper, and looked at the floor.

Ida turned to the marine next to her. "Go to the bridge. Inform the provost marshal that we have a ship-wide communication failure and that there may be crew in danger. Go."

The marine turned his visor from Ida to Serra and back again, before looking over Ida's shoulder at his companion now standing in the doorway. The marine who had been guarding Ida nodded, the movement exaggerated by his helmet.

Ida tapped the first marine on the shoulder.

"Go!" he said, gently pushing on the jarhead's armor. The marine finally seemed to make his decision and turned, jogging down the corridor. The marine in the cabin pushed past Ida and made to follow, but Ida grabbed him by the elbow.

"Come with us. You're the only one with a gun. Serra?"

Serra snapped out of her reverie and raised her eyes to Ida's. "Yes?"

"What happened? Who's in trouble?"

"Carter. It's Carter. He . . . We saw DeJohn. He was acting up, so Carter went to get him. He didn't come back."

That snagged it. DeJohn, the nastiest, stupidest marine on board had finally flipped and jumped Carter. That had to be it. They were all in this together now.

"Come on," he said, and he led the way down the corridor.

. . .

They found him by a bulkhead, clockwise around the hub and only a few hundred meters from his own cabin. He was out cold, and Ida was pleased to see Izanami had got there first. The medic was kneeling on the ground beside Carter, his head in her hands, her long white fingers pressed into his face.

Ida was at her side immediately. "Is he okay?"

Serra dropped to her knees and rolled Carter's head toward her, brushing off Izanami's hands. "How should I know? He needs a medic. DeJohn must have jumped him. *Fuck.*"

Ida eased back a bit, giving Serra a good clearance around Carter's supine form. He was breathing, and as Serra clutched at his head he groaned and his eyelids flickered.

Ida looked him over briefly, not really sure what to look for. He wasn't bleeding and he seemed to be in one piece, although his uniform—off-duty greens like Serra's—was crumpled and saturated with cold sweat. Carter coughed and tried to get himself up onto his elbows, hissing in pain as he did so.

"Easy, marine." Ida laid a hand on Carter's shoulder, and the marine gave him a hard look.

But Serra's hand rested on his other shoulder, and she pushed him back. He looked at her and blinked, and seeing her face, he seemed to relax a little.

"What happened?" Ida asked. "Are you hurt?"

Ida gently took Carter's forehead between the fingers of one hand and rolled the marine's head to expose the back of it. There was a grid pattern in his closely cropped hair that showed where he'd lain, and the scalp underneath looked red, but otherwise he was unharmed. If he'd been attacked by DeJohn, the other marine hadn't managed to land a blow to the head.

Carter gave Ida an unfocused look, like he was concentrating on a particularly difficult engineering problem. He blinked again.

Ida recognized the signs of a concussion.

"Ah . . . that's a very good question, sir," Carter said quietly.

Ida smirked. He'd called him *sir.* Perhaps a concussion was good for him.

Then Carter's hand grabbed at Ida's chest, pulling the front of his shirt into a bunch as he sat up from the floor. Ida looked down and could see the veins bulging in the marine's biceps. His jaw was tight, the muscles under his ears bunched and white. His eyes were wide.

"I . . . remember . . ."

"Charlie, what is it, babe?" Serra asked, trailing her fingers around his face.

He flinched at her touch, but then relaxed, the red flush on his face sinking back into his bones. He breathed quickly in a controlled way, trying to calm himself down.

"I saw someone. It . . . I don't know who it was. A woman. Never found DeJohn. But . . . nah . . ." Carter shook his head, his eyes now fixed on the floor between his legs. The armed marine shifted to give him more room. From farther down the passage came the sound of more booted feet, running to the rescue.

Ida turned back to Carter. "Who was it? What did you see?"

Carter laughed. The laugh was empty, spent of emotion, an expression of fear and resignation at impossible things.

"Whoever it was, I don't think she's part of the crew. I didn't recognize the suit either. It was strange. Not Fleet issue. It had letters on it, maybe some kind of insignia." He moved his hand in the air over his own chest, miming his description. *"C—C—C—P."* He shook his head.

Ida frowned, unsure whether he should recognize the initials or not. He pushed the thought to one side.

Serra looked at Ida and then up at the armed marine. "A stowaway?"

"Or an infiltrator," said Ida. "That would explain the suit."

Serra nodded. "Spacewalk between the hub and their ship?"

"Could be. The manifest bug can't be a coincidence. If they've tampered with the station systems so we can't detect their ship, they might also be able to knock out life scanners *inside* so we can't see them as they sneak around the station. Maybe that's what's caused the manifest to bug, DeJohn to drop off the system. Right?"

But Carter was shaking his head, his agitation returning. He rubbed his greasy temple.

"No, there was something else, like . . . like they weren't really there, they weren't part of . . . ah, I dunno."

Ida stood up and stroked his chin in thought. A trio of marines jogged around the corner, pulling up as they saw the group standing around the man on the floor. Ida's former guard stepped toward the newcomers and filled them in on what was happening.

Ida glanced over at Izanami, who was standing well back in the shadows at the edge of the passageway, giving everybody room. He nodded to her, and then looked back at Carter.

"Okay, we'll let the medic take care of you, and then we've got to take this to King. This facility is supposed to be on lockdown."

Serra looked up at him. "He's not going to like this."

"Well, he can like it or he can lump it, but this time he can't brush it off." Ida rolled his neck a little, conscious now that he was bringing the subject back to himself. He felt everyone's eyes on him and quickly moved back to business. "We have an intruder. That's about as serious as it gets."

Ida turned on his heel. The marine at the front of the new group brought himself to a quiet attention, but Ida wasn't looking at him. He was looking past him.

Ida looked at Izanami. In the half dark of the corridor her eyes flashed with pale blue light.

Ida looked over his shoulder, down at Carter. "Do you think you can walk, marine?"

Carter snorted and bent his knees. "I'm not a cripple."

Ida smiled. Carter's old attitude was coming back, which meant he was feeling better. Damn.

Carter stood, Serra and a marine on each side for support. Ida stuffed his hands in his pockets and stepped back, eyeing Carter up and down, making sure there wasn't an injury he'd missed.

Carter froze.

Serra's eyes searched his face. "What is it?" she mouthed.

But he wasn't looking at her. He was staring straight ahead, into the shadows. His face blanched to a deathly white, and when he opened his mouth, his scream was long and high.

Ida swore and turned, following Carter's eye line. But there was no one there except Izanami, standing apart from the group, keeping out of everyone's way. Smiling in the darkness. Her eyes moved from Carter to Ida. Then she turned and walked away toward the bulkhead door.

Ida frowned. Behind him, Carter collapsed into the arms of Serra and the other marine.

21

"This is exactly what I don't need."

Ida snorted and shifted the weight on his feet. The provost marshal paced back and forth in the ready room, apparently talking to himself. Ida wasn't sure whether King was more concerned about possible infiltrators attacking his marines or about this screwing up his carefully planned schedule.

King stopped pacing and glanced at Ida and Serra. Serra stood to attention, looking pale and ill as she stared at the wall behind King's commandeered desk. Ida followed her gaze to the painting there—a print, Japanese, of some nautical disaster. It must have been as expensive as the desk and the rug. The desk was clear, the book Ida had seen open there now absent.

"Where is Sergeant Major Carter now?" asked the marshal.

Serra's heels clicked together. "He's been admitted to the infirmary, sir, and is under sedation, sir."

King nodded. "Very well. I'm moving this station to alert status. Our guests are due in just two cycles. We are going to sweep this station from top to bottom and get rid of our rats. Captain Cleveland . . ."

Here it came. Confined to quarters to twiddle his thumbs. He wondered if Izanami would at least keep him company. Ida glanced to his left, where she was standing demurely, smiling but staring ahead, her eyes apparently focused on the same point as Serra's. Maybe she knew what the print was about. Ida wondered who was looking after Carter.

"You and Psi-Sergeant Serra will lead the search. Dismissed."

Ida blinked, then coughed politely into his fist. "I don't believe I heard you correctly, Marshal."

King ground his teeth. "This station is operating on a skeleton crew, if you hadn't noticed. Retired or not, you hold the second-highest rank on board. For the moment I'm going to forget about the radio—"

Ida drew breath to speak but the marshal held up a hand.

"I said *for the moment.* Until we get this situation under control, I'm officially reinstating you to service."

Ida opened his mouth again, but he wasn't sure what to say. King raised an eyebrow.

Reinstated to service? It was a surprise, but it made sense. Orders changed all the time in war, often suddenly; Ida had plenty of experience with that. And King was right. If the station was under threat, they needed everyone to pull together.

Ida felt a smile grow on his face. He saw King look at him, and quickly brought himself to attention. He snapped a salute.

"Captain Abraham Idaho Cleveland reporting for duty, *sir*!"

King nodded and moved back around behind his desk. With the marshal's back turned, Ida glanced sideways at Serra, but she was motionless, her glazed eyes fixed on the wall. On Ida's other side, Izanami had that damn smile on her face again.

"At ease, Captain," King said as he sat behind the desk. "We need to flush out our rats, and quick. This station needs to be secure for our VIPs. I'm giving you a chance here, Captain. You say you're a hero? Show us. You and Psi-Sergeant Serra will assemble your teams. Dismissed."

Serra's heels clicked as she came to life. "Understood, sir." The marine spun elegantly around, snapped her heels again, and left the office at a formal march.

Ida and King regarded each other for a few moments. Then King nodded, and this time the smile on his face seemed genuine. Ida saluted and glanced at Izanami, who at last tore her eyes off the wall and looked at him, her smile still firmly in place. Ida turned back to the marshal, said "sir," then waved at Izanami. "Come on," he said, and he turned to leave.

"I'll monitor from here, Captain," said King.

Ida turned back. "Ah . . . yes, sir." He frowned, nodded at Izanami, and left.

. . .

Each of the twenty-three decks of the vast torus structure that formed the bulk of the *Coast City* had a series of large atriums at the four compass points that housed both passenger and service elevators and other access points. Ida had picked the northern lobby on Deck 20 as the closest one to Carter's incident. Ida told Serra he'd meet her in twenty minutes at the assembly point nearest to her cabin.

Then he returned to his quarters to prepare for the bug hunt. While the *Coast City* had an ample supply of uniforms, fatigues, and combat suits, Ida preferred his own, custom suit, brought with him from his own U-Star. He'd clung to it like a safety blanket, a reminder that he wasn't crazy, that he had served the Fleet and retired with honor. As he stood in his cabin, holding the combat jacket in his hands, he rubbed a thumb over the rank insignia and the small silver bar sewn onto the left breast. *You don't get that,* he thought, *from being a liar.*

Ida was surprised to find himself needing the combat suit again, surprised to find himself suddenly wielding authority after his confinement to quarters. But damn, did it feel good. He'd given his life to the Fleet, only to end up in forced retirement. But now the provost marshal had stepped up, shown his faith, and Ida was a captain again, combat suit and all.

Unfortunately, he'd have to wear it incomplete—the helmet sat on a shelf in the cupboard, the psi-fi link between it and the rest of the suit somehow unable to pair, no matter how many times Ida cycled the system.

"Are you excited?"

He turned, looking up from the jacket. Izanami was standing in the cabin's open door, and he realized that he'd been rude, leaving her to trail behind him while he was lost in his own world.

"How's Carter?"

Izanami stepped in, her eyes glittering in the cabin's subdued lighting. "Oh, he'll be fine. He's well looked after."

"Good, good." Ida tossed the jacket onto the bed and went to drag the rest of his combat gear out of one of the lockers. He thought he heard her soft footfalls on the floor and then a rustle behind him as she sat on his bed. He was about to ask who, exactly, was looking after Carter, but then he found the rest of his combat suit. He yanked it from under a pile of other bits and turned around.

Ida paused, then looked over at his desk. The silver oblong of the space radio was there, plugged in, the blue LED shining bright. Which was odd, since he didn't remember seeing it as he'd come into his cabin, and the blue light really was bright in the half-lit cabin. He walked over to the desk, running a finger along the top of the radio. He couldn't believe it was there.

"What's this—?"

"I brought it back," said Izanami. "Thought you might like to listen to her again."

Ida whistled. "King is going to throw you out of an air lock when he finds out." He turned to the bed. Izanami's words bothered him more than he cared to admit as he picked up the last pieces of his kit—gloves, belt, shoulder utility harness covered in pouches and metal snap-rings for holding additional equipment. "Time to get this bug hunt under way. Will you stay here? If there are rats, they may run. I can get a marine on the door."

Izanami shook her head. "I'll be fine. I'll lock the door."

Ida nodded. "Keep it quiet and keep it dark," he said. He adjusted his gloves and then nodded a farewell.

"She's a mystery, isn't she?"

Ida froze at the cabin door. "Um . . ."

"She blasted off from Baikonur Cosmodrome in May 1961 and never returned."

When he turned around, Izanami was standing right behind him. She smiled and Ida felt cold, even under his intelligent combat suit.

"A space pioneer," she said, "lost on reentry." Her eyes flashed blue, reflecting the light of the subspace radio. "Dead for a thousand years."

Why Izanami found the whole thing so amusing, Ida wasn't

sure. But there wasn't time to discuss it now. She was right, the message *was* a mystery, and clearly she'd spent some more time unpicking the signal, getting a better fix on its origin. But now there was real work to be done, hunting down the infiltrators and securing the station. As King had said, he had a chance now to show who he really was. It was time to move on.

"Fine," he said, surprising himself with the hardness of his voice. He pointed at the subspace radio. "As soon as we've secured the station, that needs to go back to wherever King stowed it."

Izanami took a step backwards, never letting her gaze drop from Ida's. Ida shivered. He supposed the recording had become a little obsession for her too. After all, she had nothing to do around the station. But he knew now that he should never have built the damned thing. Getting rid of it would be the best decision, for Izanami and for him.

"But right now I need you to stay here." Ida turned and headed toward Serra's rendezvous, adjusting the buckle on his equipment harness as he did, trying to remember why Carter's description of the red letters *CCCP* on the infiltrator's space suit was familiar.

22

Serra was waiting for Ida, and suddenly Ida felt he was out of place, his earlier bravado evaporating. His combat suit was a dark blue and he was missing the helmet, while Serra and her team were clad in the *Coast City*'s olive green battlesuits.

Get it together, Captain.

As he approached, Serra turned and flipped the visor of her helmet up and looked him up and down. Ida smiled tightly but Serra didn't say anything, instead tossing him a small rifle identical to the one she and the others were carrying. Ida caught the weapon and checked the small ammunition indicator display on the butt. It was loaded with soft ceramic shells, lethal to flesh and blood but, in the event of a full-on shoot-out, unable to penetrate far into the interior skin of the space station. The last thing you wanted to do in a crisis was breach the hull and pop everyone inside the station like overripe grapes.

"Thanks," said Ida, clipping the weapon to the webbing across the front of his combat suit. He felt better. "What's the plan, marine?"

Serra glanced over the assembled troops—Ida counted the two security officers who had kept him confined to his cabin among the ten marines present. The task force was a small but impressive one. Fully armored up and with helmet visors closed, they looked like a cluster of particularly angry turtles standing on their hind legs.

"The central core of the *Coast City* is locked off with marines patrolling key thoroughfares and junctions," said Serra. "Observation drones are monitoring other access points. That leaves us with the hub itself, eighty percent of which is uninhabitable."

"Observation drones?"

Serra nodded. "We've borrowed some demolition robots and set them to cover the access wells leading to the bridge and spire. Those areas are open to space, but might make an ideal access point for our rats."

Ida smirked. "I'd hate to come up against a demolition drone programmed to be a security guard."

Serra's mouth twitched into a smile. "Exactly."

"With the lockdown active, how many levels do we need to cover?"

"Just eleven. We split into two teams, start at opposite ends, top and bottom, then spiral toward the center clockwise and anticlockwise. Even if the rats manage to keep ahead of us, we'll have them squeezed between the two groups." Serra pulled a narrow rectangular computer pad from the holster on her thigh and held it up to Ida. As he watched, her gauntleted finger traced a map of their route through the station.

It was a nice plan, and a simple one. Ida had wondered whether scouring an entire space station was beyond the capabilities of the skeleton crew, even with him freshly recruited, but with the patrol points and observation drones doing most of their work, all they had to accomplish was a coordinated sweep that would force any infiltrators out into the open. Serra had done a good job, and he said so.

"Thank you, Captain."

Ida smiled. *Captain*. Yep, it was a good feeling. He was back at work.

Serra seemed to notice and grinned; then she turned to the other marines. "Decker, Blackmoore, Ahuriri, Reitman, with me. Lawrence, Perrett, Leena, Newman, follow Captain Cleveland."

She turned back to Ida. "Top or bottom?"

He looked at the ceiling. "Up, please."

Serra nodded. "Let's roll."

For the first time in . . . oh, a *long* time, Ida felt less like a spare part and more like the old Captain Cleveland. Taking point of his party of five, stalking forward slowly, rifle raised and sighted all the way, he immersed himself in the mission, losing himself in years of training and combat experience. He was in control, and that felt good, but there was more to it. He was *needed* and *trusted*. King's vote of confidence seemed to have brought Serra around too, which was, Ida thought, a small first step on the long journey to winning back the respect he deserved aboard the *Coast City*.

Ida stepped forward slowly, bulkhead to bulkhead, door to door, sweeping his weapon in front of him. It was pretty quiet so far, just the gentle tapping of the marines' boots behind him and the occasional plastic creak of their armor.

The provost marshal wasn't so bad. Uptight, sure. A manager rather than a warrior, but the Fleet needed both. It was just a shame, Ida thought, that the commandant wasn't aboard. He'd liked to have met him.

They kept moving. The passageways were still on minimum power, with the automatics turned off so that their progress wouldn't be heralded by the ceiling tiles lighting up as they moved. Ida regretted his lack of helmet, as it meant he had to rely on the enhanced sight on his rifle to see his way ahead clearly in the low light well.

"Leena," said Ida, still walking forward in formation, rifle sight playing the empty space in front of him as the squad crawled forward.

"Sir," came the marine's reply, her voice echoing electronically from behind her visor.

"When did the commandant leave?"

"He left before the last transport, sir."

Ida clicked his tongue, and they passed a bulkhead and began following the curve of the outer wall.

"Wasn't the one before that months ago? I thought he'd left recently?"

There was a pause before Leena answered. Ida could hear her breathing get heavier behind her helmet microphone.

"He left just before you arrived . . . I think."

Ida pursed his lips. "So he somehow managed to get off the station *between* transports?"

"Sir, I don't understand?"

"Never mind."

They walked on in silence. What had *really* happened to the commandant? Maybe Leena had got mixed up and he had left in a transport. That was the most obvious explanation, but with the current situation aboard the *Coast City,* Ida found his thoughts stirring some nastier suspicions. Had there been a coup, or a mutiny, King overthrowing his commanding officer? No, King didn't want to be in charge; that much was clear. Perhaps the commandant had been kidnapped by the infiltrators. Maybe what was left of his body was in orbit around Shadow, a carbonized ember floating in that star's toxic light a million klicks from the station. Maybe . . .

"Sir, shall we continue?"

Ida blinked and raised his eye from the gun sight to look back at Leena, following immediately behind. He realized he'd stopped moving. A trickle of sweat, salty and cold, ran onto his upper lip. Dammit, he needed to focus. But his knee had started hurting, and—

"Marine, what ambient temperature does your suit read?"

"Eighteen point five, environment normal."

"*External* ambient."

Leena's helmet tilted just a little as she called up the display inside her visor and scanned the data.

"Fourteen point three. No, point oh . . . thirteen two . . . thirteen . . . twelve five . . . twelve . . . eleven . . . ten five . . ."

The temperature was dropping rapidly. Ida nodded, and Leena stopped reading out her display. The marines behind her looked at one another.

The sweat on Ida's face was now like an icy cloth stuck to his skin. Environment failure had become an increasingly common occurrence on board the *Coast City,* and Ida knew it meant just one thing: Something unusual was about to happen. Something else was giving him a warning too—the psi-fi link in his knee was acting up. Interference.

There was a sharp click in Ida's ear. He let go of his rifle with one hand and touched the comms link on his collar.

"Receiving."

"Captain?" It was Serra, calling from several decks below his feet.

"Reading you, marine. Found any vermin yet?"

"I don't know. We're on Level Fifteen, Gamma Eleven-Two. Do you have any environment problems up there?"

"Affirmative. Temperature just took a dive in the last thirty seconds."

No reply.

"Hello?"

Ida thumbed the comms link twice, and suddenly it sparked back into life with a burst of static, loud enough to make him cry out in surprise. The sound receded quickly, but remained in the background as Serra's voice broke through. He couldn't catch her words, and asked her to repeat.

"Same here," she said. "We've tried the manual controls, but even the lights won't come on. Looks like some kind of general power failure."

Ida looked back at his team of marines. Leena was standing, gun down, listening to the conversation. Perrett and Lawrence remained alert, covering the front, rifles up. Newman had her back to the group, covering the rear with her rifle.

It was deliberate sabotage; it had to be. Which meant they were closing in.

Serra's voice was edged with white noise over the comms. "Captain, we've got company. There's someone up ahead."

Leena lifted her rifle and aimed just a notch over Ida's shoulder. Then she nodded at him. "Sir."

Ida snapped his head around. At the end of the passage, against the next bulkhead, was a dark figure, humanoid but bulky. Someone wearing a spacesuit. Ida clicked the comms.

"Serra, confirmed, so do we."

White noise, static.

"Serra? Come in?"

Nothing. Nothing but the angry roar of subspace.

Ida kept his eye on the figure ahead, noting that the bulkhead door hadn't opened despite the proximity of the intruder. That was it—they were controlling the environment, turning the lights off when it suited them, overriding the doors somehow, disabling the manifest and life scanners so they could move through the wreck of the *Coast City* unnoticed. Reducing the ambient temperature because—

Ida's comm sprang into life with a roar of white noise, just as the passage lights above Ida and his team flickered on to full for a second before falling back to the system minimum. The flare hurt Ida's eyes, and he drew an arm up instinctively to shield his face.

Ahead, the figure in the suit was somehow hard to focus on. Ida squinted. The outline was furry at the edges, streaking out like it was a reflection from somewhere being bent in the air. The shadows seemed to move, clustering around it like iron filings to a magnet.

More noise from the comms. Ida thumbed the control again and again, but each time, the roar seemed to come back louder and louder.

"Serra? Serra, come in."

Click, *static,* click, *static.*

"Sir?" Leena raised her rifle.

Behind her, Newman had turned from covering the rear and brought her gun to bear on the intruder. Lawrence and Perrett did the same. Ida pulled his own gun back to his face and put his eye to the sight, but the intruder ahead melted into the background in the computer-enhanced view. Ida released his safety and took a step forward. His boot crunched something on the floor; glancing down, Ida felt the blood drain from his face. It was his imagination, it had to be. The flakes of paint on the floor were red on one side, pale on the other. They swam around his ankles like autumn leaves on a nonexistent breeze.

He took a sharp intake of breath and realigned the gun sight with his target.

"Halt and identify yourself!"

The intruder began to walk forward, very slowly. With each step, the temperature in the passageway plummeted, and within seconds Ida's breath plumed in a cloud of steam in front of his face. The ceiling lights, already on minimum, dipped as the intruder passed underneath, almost as though their power were being siphoned away.

Ida adjusted his grip on the gun. As he shifted his weight, his boots crunched again. Something inside him screamed out, but he ignored it. "If you do not halt, you will be shot. You are unauthorized personnel. Prepare to be detained. Halt and identify yourself."

The intruder didn't stop. Ida felt his rifle, pressed hard against his bare cheek, become a cold, slippery block of metal as a dusting of frost began to grow on its surface. He shifted his grip again, pushing the sight hard enough into his eye socket to hurt. With the lighting fading, the scope automatically adjusted, enhancing the view even more so Ida had a crystal clear, if green-tinged, view of the passage ahead. He could see ahead to the closed bulkhead, but the corridor was completely empty.

Ida swore and raised his head from the gun. The intruder was still there, shuffling forward slowly like a sleepwalker. He checked the scope again. Nothing. More tricks?

"Marines," he called over his shoulder. "Do not use your scopes. Our equipment may be compromised."

"Sir," came the chorus of quiet replies.

Ida's comms link chimed. "Cleveland . . ."

Ida's hand shot to his collar. "Marshal?" The channel was clear enough, although the white noise pulsed steadily in the background, like the universe breathing. Or like a giant heartbeat.

"This is Commandant Elbridge. They're . . . here . . . don't let them get the . . . book . . . the ready room . . . the ready room . . . the . . ."

The commandant sounded like he was shouting in a hurricane, the roar that Ida knew was the sound of subspace drowning him out.

"Commandant? Come in, please. Where are you?"

The comm clicked and the white noise was so loud, Ida flinched, his hand a moment away from pulling the piece out of his ear.

The intruder stepped forward again. As it got closer, the edges of the suit seemed to resolve, as though the figure was coming into focus. A metallic blue spacesuit and narrow, elliptical helmet. A U-Star survival suit.

Ida's hand dropped and frowned. He recalled Carter's description of the intruder, but something didn't match. Behind him, Leena gave the order for the squad to take up a firing position. Ida automatically fell into a firing stance himself. His boots crunched; he glanced down again, willing the thick, heavy flakes of red paint to vanish in the same way they had magically appeared. Perhaps he was dreaming again. Perhaps, if he turned around, the bulkhead door would be made of rough wood, paint peeling off in a summer breeze. He closed his eyes and opened them again, but the paint flakes were still on the floor. He jerked his gun up. "That's enough. Stop right there."

The suited figure stopped just a few yards ahead. It was a woman, Ida could see now, as solid and as real as anyone.

"Identify yourself."

"Ida, it's me."

The barrel of Ida's rifle dropped an inch.

"It's me," she said again. The figure raised her hands to the sides of the helmet, twisting the globe anticlockwise until it clicked, and then lifting it off.

The woman was in her early thirties, strands of blond hair streaked with bright red and pink visible around the edges of the skullcap she wore.

Ida took a step forward, lowering his gun.

Leena took a step forward, gun rock steady and level, ready to shoot. "Sir?"

Ida waved her off. He was staring at the woman in the suit,

his mouth hanging open, forehead creased. Was it hot, or was it cold?

"Astrid?"

She smiled, her teeth shining pale blue in the low light and her eyes burning with the same color.

"It's good to see you, Ida."

Ida walked forward, mimicking the glacial pace Astrid had taken when she appeared at the bulkhead. He smiled, but his eyes were still narrowed in confusion.

"Astrid? I . . ."

She shook her head. "It's okay, Ida, don't worry. I forgive you."

Ida stopped and raised his gun, pointing it directly at Astrid's forehead. He slowly curled his head down to the sight. It showed nothing but empty corridor in front of him. He raised his head again. There she was. The barrel of the gun was less than six inches from her head.

"Come with me," she said. Astrid glanced behind Ida at the tight pack of marines, each with a gun pointed in her direction. "All of you. Come."

"Astrid . . . I . . ."

Astrid smiled. "Come with me."

"Astrid, you're dead."

"All of you. Come."

"You died. You all died."

"Oh, Ida." She laughed.

The sound made Ida dizzy, but he pushed his cheek so hard into the side of the rifle that it hurt.

Astrid tilted her head. "You can't stop us," she said. "Come with me."

Ida touched the comms tag on his collar, and when he spoke, it was through clenched teeth.

"Serra? Come in! Serra, you there?"

When he released the call button, the static popped out again, rising and falling, like the winds of a storm pressing against the shuttered windows of Ida's old family farmstead, back on Earth.

"Serra, dammit, come in."

Astrid smiled and reached out a hand.

Ida froze, rooted to the spot. He tried to turn around, to direct his marines, but suddenly he was swimming through syrup, trapped in a slow-motion nightmare. With a huge effort, Ida pushed himself back and opened his mouth to shout an order to his troops.

The order never came. The comms flared into life again with the screams of Serra's team, decks below them. He recognized her voice at first, before it melted into the wails of the marines with her, impossibly loud for the tiny earpiece pumping the sound into Ida's skull.

Ida let go of his gun, letting it drop and then swing from the short line clipped to his chest. He yanked the earpiece out then pressed the heels of his hands into his ears, trying to shut out the terrible cacophony, the sound of pure primal terror that reverberated around and down the passageway.

The marines didn't seem to hear it, couldn't have heard it, because they just stood, ready for action, frozen. Ida's artificial knee sent a pain signal so pure, so intense that the whole side of his body felt like it was on fire. Then it disconnected from his psi-fi field. The knee buckled, and Ida fell. Even that seemed to be in slow motion as the force, a presence so thick, emanating from all around them, threatened to swamp his senses.

Then he saw them, the shapes, tall and thin and black. As the overhead lights flickered and dimmed, each new shadow moved of its own accord, peeling itself off the wall, forming a misshapen, unfinished figure. Long, flaring human silhouettes flickered like guttering candle flame. Within moments they surrounded Ida's team, and he found himself separated from the marines by an ever-decreasing circle of darkness.

It was only when the circle of figures finally closed in that the marines sprang to life. Beneath the screams of Serra's team, piped out of the earpiece dangling over Ida's shoulder, Ida heard his own unit cry out. Two of them fired their guns, lighting the passage in brilliant flashes of white-blue light, each flare showing a passageway entirely empty. Ida looked back over his shoulder and watched as Astrid's image flickered in time with the gunshot flashes. He winced at the sound of the shots, each loud enough to punch through the roaring static and the wailing screams, and within seconds he could feel hot gritty dust coating his bare face as the soft ceramic shells were pulverized against the walls of the passageway. The marines were shooting at nothing. Ida found his voice and called on the troops to cease fire.

More barrel flashes and he felt something tug at the fabric of his combat suit, then an odd, wet sensation. Ida's leg jerked, a blackened smear appearing on the side of his robot knee. Underneath the torn fabric of his suit, the silvery surface of artificial joint shone through a web of dark blood.

The static and the screaming suddenly increased in volume—so loud, Ida let himself slide against the wall as he pulled his hands to the side of his head. Ida cried out in surprise and pain, and looking up, watched as the black shadows drew to within touching distance of the marines. Watched as the marines—trained professionals, conditioned for space battle in the most deadly environments it was possible to exist in—turned to blind fear, throwing their arms in the air and wailing like cornered animals.

"Come with us. All of you. Come."

Astrid's voice was inside his head. Looking back at her, he could see her lips moving as she spoke, but her words echoed somewhere inside his own skull, her voice edged with metal and fire. She took a step forward, her outstretched hand now turned palm-up as she offered her help to Ida.

Ida looked back at the marines. They were writhing shapes, shadows cocooned in a deep black envelope, a frictionless absence of light that was impossible to focus on. Ida closed his eyes.

Astrid was dead. He remembered her scream and her plea for help as it echoed around the bridge of the *Boston Brand.* He remembered the faces of his crew as they listened to the dying cries of those on Tau Retore who hadn't escaped. The one part of his heroic victory tale that he never told: how he'd been responsible for saving an entire planet, but he'd also been the reason many on the planet's surface died, the ones who had stayed behind. Including Astrid, who had been taken away from him and sent to Tau Retore by her father, the Fleet Admiral. Astrid, the love of Ida's life. When he closed his eyes he could see the stellar core of the Mother Spider drop, released from the heart of the machine, and plunge down toward the planet.

the star falling as though it were a lamp burning shining bright annihilation holocaust extinction

He opened his eyes.

"You're dead, Astrid."

Astrid smiled widely. Her eyes were burning blue ovals, deep and impossible like the black shadows that swarmed the corridor around them. "Come with me."

Ida shook his head. He didn't know what she meant. Nothing made any sense. As he lay on the floor of a corridor on the U-Star *Coast City,* his hands dropped from his head, and his fingers curled on the flakes of red paint beneath him.

He said, "No."

Then Ida blinked, and he was alone in the passageway. The paint flakes were gone, and the floor had an icy sheen, cold against his cheek as his head flopped sideways. The ceiling lights stabilized and returned to the system minimum, spotlighting his prone form.

He lay on the floor, alone. The image of Astrid was gone, and the black shadows had evaporated, taking the marines with them.

23

"Help me, somebody!"

Maybe he'd been asleep. He felt stiff, tired, cold, and his right leg was wet. He moved, and a sharp pain shot up from his robot knee, all the way up to his shoulder. He'd been shot, he remembered now. He'd been talking to Astrid and someone said . . .

Ida jerked his head off the floor. One side of his face was numb, and the saliva in his mouth was cold. He swallowed, and coughed, and looked up and the down the passageway. He could hear the environment system purring, bringing the temperature back to ambient normal. The lights were on and tinged with purple. It was night on board the *Coast City*.

"Hello? Can anyone hear me?"

Ida pulled his right leg around to a better angle. He could move his toes, and his knee still seemed to work, luckily undamaged by the ceramic round. For the first time, Ida was thankful the joint was artificial—the shot would have completely destroyed it otherwise. Thank God the passage hadn't been stripped of the rubberized floor tiles yet, either; otherwise, he'd have a head injury as well.

"Come in, please, somebody."

He looked left and right and up and down. He was alone. They'd gotten the marines, taken them. And they'd sent Astrid to get him. A ghost from the past to tempt Ida away to . . . what? He shook his head. They? Who were "they," anyway?

"Help me, please, somebody."

It took Ida a few seconds to realize a woman was speaking. He closed his eyes and listened. Maybe he had a concussion. Yes, a concussion. Hit his head, not thinking straight. He'd been dreaming too, a woman's voice, far away, calling out. They'd sent Astrid to get him, and Astrid was dead. They'd . . .

"Can anybody hear me?"

Ida's eyes snapped open, and he swore. He had to get moving. Someone was calling, not over the comms but from somewhere on the same level, from behind the next bulkhead. Maybe Serra had escaped and made it to Ida's deck. Maybe she'd been hurt too.

Pulling himself awkwardly to his feet, using his good leg and the wall to support himself, he tested his knee. Each flex stung like all hell and his leg felt weak, but he could manage a limp. He'd get Izanami to patch him up. Gingerly testing his weight, Ida pushed off the wall and stood in the middle of the empty passage.

"Help me, please."

The voice was from the left, and it didn't sound like Serra. Maybe it was one of the other marines? Leena? Or Newman? No, the voice was different—it was hollow and had a strange accent.

Ida limped down the corridor, through the bulkhead door, and toward the next section. The voice kept calling out, getting louder all the time. Ida replied, shouting that he was coming, but his voice sounded quiet and weak. The woman's voice had a crackle behind it, some sound that was so familiar to Ida, but he couldn't put a finger on it.

Hobbling as fast as he could, hissing at the pain and his own too-slow progress, he cleared the next passage and bulkhead and kept going. The woman's voice was getting stronger, and now Ida realized he was in familiar territory. Level 12, Delta-12. Omega Deck. The very edge of the crew quarters. His own cabin was just ahead.

He stopped. What if the voice was a trick, like Astrid and the dark shadows that had taken the marines? It *had* been her, hadn't it? Or had he dreamed the whole thing?

Ida closed his eyes and felt dizzy. He was confused, trying to untangle a million illogical thoughts.

"Help me, please!"

Ida sucked in a breath. He had to keep moving. Concussion and confusion were clouding his thinking. Someone was injured and needed his help. Someone familiar, if only he could place the voice.

Ida reached his cabin and punched the door control. As he stepped inside, the lights swelled to twilight-normal. On the desk in front of him, the blue light of the space radio pulsed softly.

"Is there anybody there? Come in, please!"

The woman's voice was coming from the radio set, punctuated by static, echoing across one thousand light-years of space. Ida recognized the accent, and recognized the voice. Moving to the desk, he saw that the radio wasn't set to receive; it was set on playback. The recording—the last communiqué of the lost cosmonaut—was running. Ida recognized the static and white noise and the distinctive crackle burnt into the signal as it crisscrossed space and time, bouncing around in subspace, across channels that didn't even exist in the real universe.

The recording of the woman dying in space, one thousand years ago.

The recording was speaking to him.

Ida coughed and gripped the back of his chair. It was a dream; it had to be. Or a nightmare. He was lying on the floor of the corridor, bleeding to death. He'd been shot and the station was under attack from saboteurs and infiltrators and assassins. The hull had been ruptured and he was being barbecued by the fucked-up light from the purple star. This was not the real world; this was a violet-tinged nightmare.

"Who's there?"

Ida flinched, looking at the radio. He cleared his throat.

"Who's there, please? I can hear you. Can you boost your signal?"

Mouth dry and leg on fire, Ida found himself reaching forward, adjusting the radio's controls. It was ridiculous, farcical even, increasing the antenna gain when the radio wasn't even on. It was just playing back the dead recording. The dead recording that was speaking to him.

Ida cleared his throat again. "This is Captain Abraham Idaho Cleveland of the U-Star *Coast City*. Please identify yourself."

He idly wondered who would find him first. Maybe the shadows had taken the entire crew off the station, and he'd condemned himself to a slow, lingering death alone in the corridor in deep space by refusing to go with Astrid. Or maybe Serra and her squad had fought off the attackers on the lower levels and were right now running up the maintenance stairs to his position.

"My name is Ludmila. Help me! Help me, I am lost."

Ida slumped into his chair. He felt his breath leave him in a warm, shallow stream, and then white stars filled his vision and the room turned sideways and then upside down, and everything went black.

THE STARCHILD

The Private-Profiteer *Bloom County* cruised lazily through space, in the light of the star Shadow, toward the skeletal remains of a large, doughnut-shaped space station.

It was Zia's father, Milo Hollywood, who had built the ship. True enough, at the heart of the vessel was an ordinary cargo barge—the original ship, the P-Prof *Herculanium Lady,* which had given Milo years of good use before being used as the framework for the *County.* But after the Spider attack on Earth—the historic battle that killed three billion and destroyed a hemisphere—it was Milo who saw the opportunity. He watched from the asteroid belt as the Spiders were defeated; then he piloted his barge into the shattered remnants of the moon to salvage what mineral wealth there was.

Well, he said, scotch on the rocks in one hand and flight joystick in the other, the moon was gone, no point crying about it, and hell if there wasn't 7.3×10^{22} tons of lunar rock just floating around in space that wasn't no good to anyone, not to mention it being one heck of a hazard to the spaceways, or it *would* be once the spaceways were cleared of any last baby Spiders. Okay, so maybe a few people protested the blatant capitalism, and maybe a few people registered their disgust at the desecration of the moon, at his turning the disaster into profit, but come on, it was the Spiders that chewed it up and spit it out like they had something to prove.

You can't fathom the alien mind. That's what Milo said when he announced his trip, and that's what he kept saying as the *Herculanium Lady* blasted off toward the Earth, skirting the cordon of damned hippie protest boats whining about the horror of moon mining. That's what he said again and again as the *Lady* weaved through the brand-new asteroid field a quarter of a million klicks out from the Earth, a slow-moving morass of gray tombstone rock and bone-white dust, a vast lunar graveyard. And Milo kept talking, even though, inside, he found it hard himself as the *Lady*'s belly was filled with the valuable mineral ore. Even though two of his crew nigh-on had nervous breakdowns at the very thought of scooping up great chunks of the moon—the *moon,* for God's sake. Even though perhaps he realized it *was* an act of desecration, pissing on the grave of three billion dead.

In fact, Milo kept saying you can't fathom the alien mind even as he cashed in the ore—making more money than existed in theory on the entire planet and plunging the Earth into a huge debt to its myriad colonies—and took off in the *Lady* with his riches, never to return home again.

Well, he couldn't, not really. The richest man in Fleetspace was persona non grata like nobody else. Sometimes, in the moments before sleep took him, Milo agreed with all his heart and all his soul.

But it was worth it. Because Milo Hollywood and his crew had found something else floating among the debris.

There was Fleet wreckage, of course, and whatever was left of the lunar colonies, but Milo didn't really stop to check, because the herculanium that formed the walls of the lunar bases and the engine housings of the U-Star hulks could be recycled just as well as the mineral ore could be processed from the gray lunar rock. The Fleet didn't seem to take any notice, being too busy patching that great hole in the Earth. The moon? Milo could have it.

But the near-intact Spiderbaby, barely a scratch on it—now, *there* was a prize. It had taken up nearly an entire bay of the *Herculanium Lady*'s mineral skip, and it had cost nearly a whole cycle of mining time retrieving it, but the loss in profit was well worth it. Because Milo Hollywood was one to tinker—tinkering with the *Lady* was what had enabled him to turn the standard G-class cargo barge into something bigger and faster, reaching the asteroid fields before his rivals and carving out the Hollywood mining empire. And now he had a Spiderbaby, its gigantic articulated legs neatly folded around its spherical body in the instinctive protective formation as it slept.

Milo couldn't exactly fathom why it was inactive. Perhaps this one was immature and underdeveloped, never having left its mother's belly with its hundred thousand siblings, and had somehow survived as the Mother Spider was blown to bits by the Fleet's finest all around it. *Whatever.* There it was, and it was his. All that alien tech, that living, thinking, adapting machine, eight giant legs and the beginnings of a mouth that would, in time—as the Spiderbaby became a Spider and perhaps even a Mother Spider—be able to render the ruined fragments of whole planets into so much particulate matter to fuel its growth and organo-technological systems.

Milo saw the potential. Sitting in his hopper was the perfect technology to pull open an asteroid like a piece of overripe fruit and process the mineral ore there and then, negating the need for bulk cargo trailers or unmanned barges to fill with raw, unprocessed ore and push back to home base on microkinetic rockets. The current technology was cheap but some of the haulers could take years to find their way back home, and some of them never did, each loss reducing the paycheck by a painful margin. If he could crack the alien tech, if he could turn the Spiderbaby into a mining ship, he'd go from commercial king to economic legend.

And Milo Hollywood was good, and he did crack it. It took twenty years, and most of his crew had by then left his employ, convinced the old man's mind had cracked just like the Earth's crust. But that was fine; he didn't need them. The *Herculanium Lady* drifted through space with no set course, stopping here and there only to refuel and restock protein and carbohydrate packs for the two remaining crew, Milo and his wife, Honey. Even without a running mine operation, their bank balance was large enough for colonial governors to offer their own beds for the duration of each port call. It didn't matter, none of it mattered, until the Spiderbaby had been cracked.

When he'd finished, the P-Prof *Herculanium Lady* was unrecognizable, its classic—if functional—lines hidden deep at the center of a new structure, eight insectoid legs folded around a cuboidal body, ready to twitch and grab and grasp at anything Milo landed on. The Spiderbaby's primitive mind was left intact, and it still slept, but the legs could operate independently and automatically. The new chimeric ship wasn't sentient, but it was alive, certainly.

Honey demanded the vessel be rechristened. The original ship had been named for her, but there was something alien and horrid about the new version that kept her awake at night. Sometimes her dreams were filled with dark shadows and alien whispers and the roar of the ocean, and sometimes when she awoke in a cold sweat in the middle of the night-cycle she felt she wasn't alone. It was the Spiderbaby; it had to be. She knew it wasn't dead, merely inactive, held in check by Milo's ingenuity and quantum dampeners, but really only temporarily imprisoned.

Milo eventually agreed, although he could never figure out what the darned fuss was about. You cannot fathom a woman's mind; that's what he said as he dug out the registration certificate and scrubbed the ship's name off with a short, thick finger, leaving the slightest trace of black dust on the pad screen as he did so.

It wasn't until later that he found the new name. Once the original registration had been deleted, they were theoretically illegal and weren't able to make port until the new registration had been filed. One cycle out from Arb-Niner and the little lady was giving him the ear about the state of supplies, so he had to do something. They had enough credits in the bank to buy all the real estate on Arb-Niner twice over, and as she paced the living quarters on board the *Herculanium* . . . the *whatever-the-hell-it-was-called-now,* she said she might well do that and evict the entire planet's population if Milo didn't take some responsibility for a change and maybe invest a few precious credits in something a little better than the compressed protein and carbohydrate ration packs that had been their diet for the past twenty years.

And maybe at five years old, their only child, Zia, could have some real food, and maybe they could even stop over for a while and Zia could meet some other people planetside. Zia was a starchild, born in space, schooled in space. Zia knew nothing but her ma and her pa and the tiny metal world of the *Herculanium* . . . the *something-something.*

You can't fathom a woman's mind; that's what Milo said as he watched his wife read to Zia in bed, the light of the pad she held shining brightly on their faces in the dark. There wasn't much use for reading when you're out there in the inky black, sorting rocks by the teraton, he thought, but the kid liked it and the little lady liked it, and if they were happy, then Milo was happy. Maybe they should settle down for a while, and maybe Arb-Niner was a decent enough patch. He lay on the bed next to his wife and his child, squinting at the too-bright screen that showed something from one heck of a long time ago, all small and black and white and like something Zia might draw herself. He asked them what they were reading. *Bloom County* came the answer. His wife said Zia didn't understand it, but Zia jumped up on the bed and said she liked the penguin, which tickled old Milo something. Later that night, he was sitting in the cockpit of his mighty new ship, watching lights on the panel flicker as the Spiderbaby's legs convulsed reflexively underneath them, when his wife came by, gave him a kiss, and told him to fix the ship reg or he'd have to swim the rest of the way to Arb-Niner. She laughed and he laughed too, but there was a hardness in her eyes. Goddamn it if the woman wasn't speaking the truth.

Milo Hollywood picked up his pad, called up the ship reg, remembered the penguin and the happiness on Zia's face, and thought of a name.

And so the famous P-Prof *Herculanium Lady* vanished, and the legendary P-Prof *Bloom County* was born.

PART THREE

THE GHOSTS OF SUBSPACE

24

Whispers in the dark.

Zia Hollywood's head jerked against the back of her command chair. She'd dropped off. It had been a long journey. Her three crew members, seated in front of her in the flight deck, each turned their heads around at the sudden leathery creak of her movement. She met their eyes, one by one, then nodded slightly. The crew turned back around.

Beep.

"*Bloom County,* this is *Coast City.* Welcome to the neighborhood, friend. Please transmit your preassigned clearance codes and security authorization. Channels are open."

Across space, a pencil-thin beam punched the radiation-soaked vacuum, carrying vital data from the *Bloom County* to the shadowed hulk of the station. The light from Shadow, the technetium star a hundred million klicks away, sucked at the transmission, stripping energy and data from it, introducing a rhythmic pattern of interference that sounded like a heartbeat, if anyone had listened to the raw feed. The computer on the *Bloom County* noted the energy loss automatically and boosted the signal; Zia glanced at the comms display on the arm of her chair, noticing a data transfer failure of more than 80 percent.

Beep.

"*Bloom County,* you are cleared for approach. Set your docking computer to ready and we'll guide you in. Enjoy the ride."

The message ended, and the air pulsed with static for just a second.

Zia heard it, even if no one else did. The static was odd, tinged with something metallic, something . . . screeching. She knew about the star, of course. Maybe, without her realizing it, it had made her anxious, because she had heard the sound in her purple-tinged dream too.

She leaned back, and the chair creaked again, and a warning tone sounded as the docking computer went online.

Beep.

One of her crew, Dathan, ran a finger along a data readout and flicked the comms channel back on.

"*Coast City,* this is *Bloom County.* Systems report a second-class alert on board our destination. We've been trying to contact you on the lightspeed link for several cycles. Can you confirm the nature of your alert and advise if your port is open? Please acknowledge."

Static swarmed. Zia leaned forward again, and somebody swore under his breath. The hub of the space station was an empty black void on the viewscreen ahead, a nothingness framed by the flickering violet light of the evil star beyond.

Beep.

"P-Prof *Bloom County,* this is the U-Star *Coast City.* Alert status negative. We have a minor technical issue due to the ongoing demolition of this platform, and increased solar activity is affecting the lightspeed link. Proceed as normal, no special instructions required."

"*Bloom County* confirmed. See you on the other side."

25

The ready room felt huge without the desk.

They—whoever "they" were—had attacked the beating heart of the station, somehow making it to the ready room and turning it over, turning Commandant Elbridge's expensive desk into so much expensive matchwood, at the same time as Ida's and Serra's squads had been confronted. "They" had got past guards, crew, Flyeyes at their posts, the works. The first anyone knew something was wrong was when the comms were filled with the roar of the ocean and the sound of destruction came from behind the ready room's closed door. When that door was opened, the room was a mess, the desk shattered, the provost marshal insensible in a corner.

Ida knew something had happened, even before he stepped inside and saw the wreckage. The commandant himself had tried to warn him that something was happening, something to do with the ready room. Ida didn't mention that to anyone. Not yet.

Whatever force, whoever the enemy was, they'd escaped, vanishing from the station with the eight marines led by Serra and Ida—they were the only two who were left behind. Worse than that, the station's manifest now reported less than half the crew there had been before. Those left aboard the *Coast City* were in a state of shock, impotent, with nothing to do but put armed guards everywhere and pretend to their VIPs that nothing was wrong. Pretend that the security was normal and that shadows and the cold were just an artifact of the station's half-demolished condition and that everyone was just tense because the end of the road was in sight, is all. And Ida pretended that the voice of the commandant hadn't come through his comm, that the absent commander hadn't tried to contact him, give a warning, as all hell broke loose.

Ida wasn't even sure that had happened, not anymore. Just a cycle later and he and Serra were standing in the ready room, he with his arms folded and she staring at the picture on the wall, which had survived intact. Ida glanced at her: she looked empty, burnt out. He knew she was a psi-marine, the last left on board, and he wondered what she was feeling and seeing and hearing that nobody else was. Like him, perhaps. He thought about the commandant's voice and about Astrid and paint flakes on the floor. Neither of which made him happy, not at all.

The ruins of the wooden desk had been removed. Now King had only a computer pad and a chair, and it looked as though he was making do with just that. There was hardly any point in refitting the room for the last months before the final sections of the *Coast City* were packed into their crates and rocketed on the long drag homeward.

Provost Marshal King stood square in the center of the room, arms folded, chin held high. Behind him, Ida heard the armor of the guard at the door crackle as he shifted on his feet. Red alert. Battle stations.

"So, what happens next?" asked Ida. Serra finally turned her head from the painting to look at him, but when Ida met her eye, her expression was still blank, like she was somewhere else entirely.

King's nostrils flared, but he remained otherwise motionless. "Next, Captain?"

Ida tightened the loop of his folded arms. "Yes, next. We have personnel missing. We have firsthand proof of intrusion. We have to tackle this now."

King shook his head. Then he held up his hand as Ida made to protest.

"Captain, I agree, but our VIPs have docked. We've put the station on alert and have armed guards covering as much of the hub as possible, but we're spread thin. We need to hold out until our guests have left, and then maybe we can accelerate the demolition. We have barely enough personnel to maintain operations, let alone go chasing after ghosts."

Ida found King's choice of words interesting. He raised an eyebrow. "Ghosts?"

"Intruders, then," said the marshal. "And with the lightspeed link down we can't alert other stations or call for any help, either. We're alone out here. We need to focus on internal security right now. We have a very valuable guest to look after. Her safety, and that of her crew, is paramount."

Ida folded his arms. "Where's Elbridge?"

King flinched, the corners of his mouth twitching downward. "What?"

"The Commandant, Price Elbridge. Do you know where he is?"

King turned away and paced back to his chair. He reached down and ran his hand along the edge of the computer pad as though he were about to pick it up. Then he seemed to change his mind, and he straightened up.

Ida stepped forward. "I was expecting him to be here when I arrived, but apparently he left before the last transport, but somehow after the one before that."

King's shoulders sagged. When the marshal turned back to Ida, his face was gray and the skin around his eyes tight.

"The station has two shuttles," said Ida. "One has been packed away and the other is still in use to patrol the system."

"I—"

"So where is he? Where did he go?"

Ida and King regarded each other in silence in the ready room. King knew something. He was hiding something. Ida knew it. He had to tell him about the voice on the comms, about the absent commandant getting in touch, or at least trying to. And then—

"Marshal, our VIP has arrived."

The Flyeye's appearance at Ida's shoulder broke the spell. Ida turned, suddenly angry, forcing himself to relax and to breathe, breathe, breathe.

Ida turned back to King. "Marshal, please."

But it was too late. King nodded at the Flyeye and strode from the room, leaving Ida and Serra and the marine on the door.

Ida sighed, and tried to think of something to say to Serra when he noticed she was squinting, like she was in pain.

"You okay?"

Serra rubbed her temples, spat out "fine," and turned on her heel. As she left, Izanami stepped out of the shadows on the other side of the room. Ida blinked. He'd had no idea she was there with them. In the dim light her eyes seemed to shine blue. Then she laughed.

"Sorry!" she said. "I didn't mean to intrude." She looked at the marine stationed at the door.

"I'm hungry," she said. She walked toward the door. "Come on, let's eat."

26

The woman on the screen cast a lazy look around the bridge, eyes hidden behind large rectangular dark glasses, while her entourage laughed at something. Beside her, King smiled, but everyone else on the bridge was as stiff as a board, standing to attention during the official tour. Armed marines stood against practically every clear spot of wall, conspicuous in their green armor.

Ida took another bite of the protein stick and peered closer at the screen hanging above the table in his cabin. The official welcome was, despite the current situation, being done by the book, broadcast on the station-wide information channel like any other important bit of Fleet business.

"She's pretty."

Ida looked over his shoulder. Izanami had crept up behind him and was peering around his folded arms.

Zia Hollywood was not pretty. She was flat-out gorgeous. Deep auburn hair streaked with black, cut into a long, angled bob that framed a delicate face with a snub nose. She was wearing black overalls, the top half folded down at the waist and the arms tied around her middle in a big knot, revealing a black sleeveless singlet. There she was, clad in the practical work gear of a space miner and somehow she outshone the stars. Her left arm was heavily tattooed, geometric patterns and floral motifs slowly moving over her skin. Intelligent, mobile ink was expensive. Her moving tattoo had probably cost as much as the pile of antique kindling that had been the commandant's desk.

Ida watched her on the screen as she glanced here and there, her eyes hidden behind what he could see now were square mining goggles. At the center of her entourage, she was silent and otherwise still. Her crew consisted only of three men. They were grimier than their boss, their overalls patched and marked, the bare biceps of one of them—a tall, thin man with an alarming scarlet Mohawk—matted with scar tissue. Ida had caught him being referred to as Dathan. He looked like he'd been handsome once, but his nose was angled strangely and the rest of his face was flat as a plate. He scowled at the camera and sniffed, the movement pulling his broken nose to one side. The other two were Ivanhoe—a very short, muscular older man, bald with a long graying beard—and an average-looking thirty-something with a huge, spherical Afro haircut who seemed to go by the name Fathead.

Ida shivered. Pulling himself away from the screen, he walked over to the environment controls near the door and poked at them. He didn't expect much to happen. The lights were now stuck on twilight-normal around most of the hub, and—sudden failures aside—the whole station seemed to be getting steadily colder. He thought Izanami must have been terribly cold in her thin, short-sleeved white medical tunic, but the temperature didn't seem to bother her.

The controls responded and warm air began to blow into the cabin. Satisfied for the moment, Ida turned back around.

"Where were you, anyway?" he asked. "Did you see anything when it happened?" *It* being the security breach.

"I locked myself in the med unit. Didn't see anything." She turned back to the screen and then she asked, "Why don't you like her?"

"Who?"

"Zia Hollywood. You don't like her, or her crew."

"Says who?"

Izanami brushed her hair from her eyes. "You don't like anyone, Abraham."

Ida worked his mouth. She . . . Actually, she was right, and he knew it, but her tone was surprisingly hard. And she had called him Abraham.

Ida turned back to watch the Hollywood gang fidget as King lectured them on the wheres and why-fors of station procedure before they were taken on a tour of the facilities. They were too far away to be heard over King's monotone on the feed, but Ida saw the Mohawked man glance at the Fleet personnel around him and then rock on his heels in a suppressed laugh, although what he could possibly find funny about being surrounded by a squad of marines in full field battle kit was beyond Ida. Behind Dathan, Ivanhoe and Fathead had lost interest in the briefing and were playing some kind of hand-slapping game while their boss stood, arms folded, mouth set, and expression unreadable behind the protective eyewear. Fathead gave his bald companion's hand one last sharp slap and then, laughing, sidled over to Ms. Hollywood. He trailed his hand over her arm as he swung around behind her. Then with one fingernail he traced the moving tattoo on her arm, the ink swirling like liquid under his touch. Hollywood remained still, but Ida thought she turned her head a little to look into the security camera.

"Admit it, you don't like her."

He found himself rubbing his chest through his shirt, trying to ease the tight feeling he now felt around his heart. "I don't even know her."

"Exactly," said Izanami, and she walked toward the door, and then out of it.

Ida bit his thumbnail and watched the empty space where she had stood, then sighed.

"What's wrong?" said the voice, thin and edged with static like the rolling waves of the sea. The space radio popped and crackled and Ida felt his heart kick.

Ludmila. She was real, apparently—an electromagnetic ghost bouncing around subspace, her voice echoing out of nothing but only when the recording was on playback. She was impossible. She was real. When she spoke, Ida felt afraid, knowing that he couldn't, shouldn't be talking to her. But then the fear faded, melting away, leaving Ida dizzy. They'd been in contact for little more than a cycle, but already he felt that he'd known her for years, that they had some weird connection, two spacefarers trapped in situations they had no control over.

Ida closed his eyes. If he thought about it too hard, none of it made sense, but there at the back of his mind he recalled a story he'd read years and years ago, a tall tale if ever there was one, but one that now made him take pause for thought. The story was that Marconi, the guy who had invented radio in the first place, hadn't been trying to build a new form of communication; he'd been trying to find a way to talk to his dead brother. That scared Ida too, and he was perhaps a little grateful that the light-speed link was down, as he wasn't sure checking the veracity of an urban legend like that would do him any good.

"Nothing," he said, opening his eyes. "I'm glad you stuck around, though." This much was true. She was a welcome distraction.

Ludmila laughed. Ida liked it when she laughed; the sound was high and young, and very happy. The background static pulsed in time with it, and then she sighed, the sound cut like dry leaves in an autumn wind. Ida couldn't remember the last autumn he'd had on Earth. He got as far as thinking it was red and orange before the memory was too fuzzy. He'd spent too long in space, too much time in Fleet service. He preferred to remember the summers on the farm, anyway. Or . . . he had, until recently.

Ida moved back to the door and glanced through the semi-frosted window, but the corridor to the right was just a faint orange smudge.

Then Ida looked to his left, and saw Izanami standing in the passage. He recoiled from the window in surprise; then he hit the control panel with his palm. The door snicked open.

"Izanami?"

Izanami took his arm, her fingers like ice even through Ida's sleeve. For a moment her eyes seemed to catch the light in an odd way, like they were spun blue with stars. Then the space radio popped and went quiet and Ida blinked, and the light was gone.

"I just walked around the deck," she said, pursing her lips. "I'm sorry, I didn't mean what I said before."

Ida smiled weakly, and gestured for her to enter his cabin.

27

The P-Prof *Bloom County* crouched on the side of the U-Star *Coast City* like the Spiderbaby it really was, customized mining legs folded into a symmetrical array of scalene triangles. From a distance it looked like a complex communications pod, myriad antennae pointing out into the inky black. Closer, it looked like a parasitic insect, a strange locust–spider hybrid, clamped to the side of the station, sucking from the belly of its prey. They hadn't used the station's hangar. They didn't need to—thanks to its unique design, the *Bloom County* could just sucker onto the side of the station, air lock to air lock.

There were many theories about the origin of the Spiders, about how an organo-metallic life-form might have evolved—or been *created*. About why the planet-eating, intelligent but not quite self-aware machine race looked so much like spiders. About why they had any interest in human affairs anyway. But for the crew of the *Bloom County,* the Spiderbaby at the heart of the ship was merely a very, very effective tool that helped them do their jobs. Out on the ragged edge of space, there was no time for theories.

The short, bald member of the Hollywood gang, who went by the name Ivanhoe, flicked a switch, dimming the lights in the *Bloom County*'s control cabin, and leaned back in the navigator's seat. He'd been born in the stars—just like the rest of the crew, each handpicked by Zia Hollywood with starbirth the most important parameter—and far preferred their light to the artificial illumination on board the ship. And while Shadow, the technetium star, was hidden on the other side of the space station, its high-energy emissions floodlit a shell of dust that enclosed the whole system nearly a tenth of a light-year out, giving the normally infinite black canvas of space an eerie—and with the cabin lights off, quite bright enough to work by—purple glow. This far out on the galactic rim, the star field beyond the glow was not as dense as Ivanhoe knew, or liked, but the scattering of distant suns that were visible were large and bright. So Ivanhoe sat for a spell, eyes flicking from one tiny solar body to the next, watching their outlines curl and flicker behind the dust cloud. He was happy to have gotten out of the VIP tour of the space station and glad to be able to look at the stars, even if he had a lot of work to do. They'd been lying about the security alert; that much was obvious from the number of marines on guard at every doorway. Unlike his crewmates, Ivanhoe didn't like guns much. Especially guns on board a spaceship.

Someone knocked a tool off the bench behind him. Dathan, probably, either finally managing to pull himself away from their boss or finally being told by said boss to go and fix the motherfucking ship. Either option was good for Ivanhoe. Tracing the fault in the navigation pod would be much easier with two people, and besides, if someone had to go out onto the hull and open up the pod itself, he'd rather it wasn't him. It wasn't the light of Shadow that bothered him. The pod, a box shaped like half an egg three feet in length, was within reach of the mining claws. *That* was what bothered him.

One day, Ivanhoe knew, just *knew,* those claws would turn on them. Zia said she knew what she was doing, and Ivanhoe had no doubt about that. But nobody really *understood* Spider tech, not her, not her father. And, well, those claws were *alive,* my brother. They twitched, and sometimes they even grasped, as the Spiderbaby slept. There, they were doing it now. Ivanhoe's eyes moved to the blinking indicator on the control desk in front of him. Two legs out of the four on the portside array were moving. Just a bit, just a flex, like someone who has sat on their hand for too long rolling their fingers to get the circulation back. Damn, it was as creepy as hell. But creepy as hell was paying the bills. Good old Spiderbaby. Sleep tight.

"I'll tell you now," said Ivanhoe to the shadows behind him, "I ain't going out there. Let's see if we can't get the nav pod re-jacked from here, my brother."

Silence. Ivanhoe tore his eyes from the flickering indicator and slowly revolved the navigator's chair around. The control cabin was empty, and the door was closed. The fallen tool—just a regular screwdriver—was on the floor in the middle of the cabin.

Ivanhoe sighed, pushed himself to his feet, picked up the screwdriver, and dropped it back on the tray of tools on the bench, not really thinking about how far the screwdriver had fallen from one side of the room to the other, not really thinking about how hot the metal tool had felt in his hand. It didn't matter. Space was strange. Artificial gravity wasn't perfect. Ivanhoe didn't trust it—he'd been born in zero-G, my brother, and like the water babies of Earth, anything else just wasn't natural. Falling through starlight. That's how he liked to describe it. It impressed the ladies, anyway.

He turned back to the control deck and put his hands behind his head, scratching his bare scalp as he did so. The mining leg motion indicator had gone dark, but the data screen showing the nav pod output was still a wash of amber nonsense.

"Well, fuck you very much, you spiky-haired freak show." It was clear what had happened. Even if Zia had told Dathan to go and help him, he'd probably stopped by the nearest dark corner of the station for a quick jerk-off. That prick had the slimy dirty hots for their boss. He made no secret of it, but it seemed to suit Ms. Hollywood. He'd jump to anything she said. To Ivanhoe and Fathead, it was free entertainment.

Ivanhoe stood from the seat and, reaching one leg forward, dragged a wheeled tool tray out from below the console with the toe of his boot. He looked at the tray for a minute; then he selected two or three items before kicking it across the floor over to the pilot's console on the other side of the flight deck. So, there it was. Once again it was up to him. Hours on his back under the consoles wasn't Ivanhoe's favorite horizontal activity, but the nav pod had to be fixed if they were going to find their prize on the other side of Shadow. And if he could fix the pod from here and not have to crawl out over the outside of the ship and take a look at it in person, all the better.

"Dominos . . ."

Ivanhoe jumped, dropping his tools with a clatter across the pilot's station. An electric socket wrench with a heavy handle bounced on the edge of the console and hit the floor, rolling noisily across it.

"Hello?"

There was no one. He was alone in the cabin, but someone had very clearly called his name. His real name, one that he hadn't heard in fifteen years and that, of the crew, only Zia knew.

He swore and stormed to the cabin door. Dathan again, playing some kind of trick. Maybe Zia had let his real name slip. Ivanhoe never wanted to hear that name ever again, and if she'd told Dathan, even accidentally, he was now officially pissed.

"Day, you fuck."

The wheel on the door spun counterclockwise for a few seconds. Ivanhoe watched it impatiently, knocking his knuckles against the heavy metal frame of it. Dathan was a dead man.

The door beeped as it unlocked. Grabbing the wheel with one hand, Ivanhoe pushed it to his left. Beyond was a short corridor leading to a ladder that went up to the crew quarters and down to the hopper and the working end of the ship.

The corridor was empty, and the hatches in the floor and ceiling were closed.

The *Bloom County*'s navigator drummed his permanently blackened fingernails against the doorframe, the thin metal plating making a harsh, tinny rattle as he tapped. The hatches were closed. The latches on both shone with the orange glow of the engaged indicator. Besides, the hatches beeped in the control cabin when the latch was shunted to green for open.

Well, if someone was playing games, they'd have to play by his rules. Ivanhoe walked the short corridor, hopped up the first two rungs of the ladder, and flicked the ceiling hatch from engaged to locked. Jumping off, he locked the floor hatch. If anyone was coming, they'd have to damn well ring the doorbell.

"Dominos Tararaz . . . Where is he?"

Ivanhoe spun around just in time to see someone duck around the lip of the open control cabin hatch. The corridor was only twenty feet long and just wide enough for two people to pass. With the hatches locked and in full view in front of him, Ivanhoe was positive nobody had come in. He'd been in the cabin for a couple of hours and he knew the ship was empty, the rest of the crew accompanying Zia on the formal tour of the U-Star.

A stowaway was impossible—the crew made it their habit, each of them, to inspect personally near to every damn rivet in the ship before a flight. There was no room, no room at all. Which meant . . .

Intruder.

"Mother*fucker,*" said Ivanhoe, shaking his head in disbelief. Some bored grunt from the station taking a look around and messing with his head. Shit, did that piss him off. He had a lot of work to do, and nobody but nobody got into the *Bloom County* without his permission—even the famous and rich Zia Hollywood, who *owned* the ship, asked him before allowing any visitors aboard. As navigator, Ivanhoe was responsible for steering the ship true toward riches and glory and, more important, away from and out of trouble. The lives of the crew and the safe and secure transit of their valuable cargo were in his hands. If they went in the wrong direction, if the charts were off and they missed their mark and lost a paycheck, it was his fault.

"Hey, come out here so I can kick your green-covered ass!"

Something clanked from beyond the door. It sounded like one of the tools being picked up. Fucker was arming himself.

"The hell you do," Ivanhoe muttered, and he jogged down the corridor. "You picked the wrong ship to play hide-and-seek in, my brother."

The control cabin was dark, much darker than it had been. Ivanhoe squinted in the gloom. The main window shutters were wide open and the purple light of the dust cloud shone in, a smattering of large white stars still visible. But there was something else inside the cabin, obscuring the windows with a blackish haze. Ivanhoe absently waved a hand in front of his face, but the mist (was it mist?) didn't move, didn't react like it should. He stood still, unable to decide whether this was smoke and something was on fire. But the blackness had no odor or taste, and it didn't move in the air. It was more like shadow, like swirling patches of air that were somehow less inclined to let light pass through them.

"Hello?" People were constantly asking him whether he liked the dark, or the night, considering he was a starchild. He usually answered that while space might be black, it was really full of light, as bright as can be, in every color—total baloney, but not many people he met were familiar with Olbers' paradox. And it hid the fact that no, Ivanhoe did not like the dark. In fact, he hated the dark.

Now, in the control cabin of the *Bloom County,* the black shadows disturbed him more than he liked.

"Dominos . . ."

He ducked away from the sound, a harsh whisper with an odd accent right in his ear. He banged the tool bench with his thigh and gasped at the pain, one hand automatically brushing at the side of his head. For a second he imagined the tickling sensation of someone's breath in his ear as the voice spoke to him.

"Where are you?" He squinted again. Something silver flashed in front of him, then another, then a third. Glinting with light, the objects wobbled in the air.

The tools. Two crescent wrenches, brand-new and still nicely chromed, and the heavy electric socket driver. They hovered five feet from the floor, dipping a little around their balance points, like someone was dangling them from above on thin wire.

"The poisoned sky weeps for my husband. . . ."

The navigator jerked his head away again as the whispering voice came from the other side. The intruder would have had to be crouching right on the control desk, up against the right-hand window pane, to breathe into his ear like that. The voice, feminine but not human. Empty and black. Like the dark shadows themselves were speaking.

The floating tools ducked and dived, then stabilized. Ivanhoe couldn't tear his eyes from them. He kept his distance as he walked around the edge of the control cabin, toward the main consoles.

What the hell was going on? It was that star, had to be, something to do with its light. The data sheet fed to them by the Fleet said it was "toxic"—whatever the hell that meant—and earlier one of the jarheads on the station had even said "that light will fuck you up," like it was some kind of a joke, although he hadn't been laughing. But the way their nav pod had scrambled as soon as they'd hit the system's heliosphere made Ivanhone think again.

"Dominos Tararaz . . ."

The light. It had to be the light. The weird star and its weird starlight.

That light will fuck you up.

Behind him the malfunctioning nav pod output screen flickered with new data, and the ship's computer alerted the navigator to that fact with a loud chime. Were those shapes moving around there? Long, thin figures, pulling themselves together out of the mist? Ivanhoe risked a glance over his shoulder. He saw enough on the output screen to know the nav pod had apparently not only fixed itself but aligned itself with the system's star. The information streaming across the screen didn't make much sense, consisting of a list of coordinates that looked okay but, he saw at a glance, were inverted, *negative,* like the computer was looking *through* the star and into someplace else, which was fucking nuts but—

The mining legs. Ivanhoe was drawn to the indicator lights, all eight flashing as all eight legs flexed. The Spiderbaby was dreaming, and dreaming deep. Maybe he was as well.

Ivanhoe looked up at the window, hoping for a reassuring, familiar look at the stars. But the windows were almost completely black now, the view transformed into a dull mirror. He saw nothing but his own face, floating in the shadows, lit from underneath by the scrolling amber text of the nav pod output and the flashing indicators.

Then over his right shoulder, another face. Ghastly white, angular, with a sharp chin and oval eyes that burned with a bright baby blue light. The face was that of a woman, pale and Japanese. Her hair was long and black and straight and blew in a nonexistent wind across her face. She looked Ivanhoe in the eye and smiled a smile from hell.

"Where is he, Dominos? Where is he?"

Ivanhoe's scream was not as manly as he'd hoped. But what the hell. The conscious centers of his brain relinquished the last vestige of control to his brain stem, and as his bladder emptied, everything spun to blackness.

28

Maybe I'm getting old.

Ida ran the thought through his head. He was forty years old, and he was tired and sick of spooning the blue protein gloop from plate to mouth in the canteen. Too much time in space. He was alone on one side of the eating area, watching Carter's space apes and the Hollywood gang merge into one shouting, swearing mass. Carter had recovered from his ordeal and seemed to be back to his old self. Serra sat by his side and laughed at the right moments but said nothing herself, and over the top of his spoon Ida could see her eyes narrow again, like she was fighting against a migraine.

The visiting crew of the *Bloom County* laughed and joked and slapped sides with their hosts, but they also exchanged looks and smirks and eye rolls among themselves that Carter's friends didn't notice. Ida did. It cheered him up no end.

Ida realized he was staring at the group when he saw Zia Hollywood returning the look. Eyes still wrapped in the mining goggles, she sat at the head of the table, cradling a shallow beaker of engine juice, the toxic liquid DeJohn had distilled out of the space station's cooling system before he'd gone missing. Ida had seen her laugh too, smile at the right people, but she wasn't really part of the group. She could never be—the fame and fortune attached to her name kept her distant from everyone around her, even her own crew.

Ida smiled, but not at Ms. Hollywood. In the time she'd spent returning his stare, she'd probably earned more in pure interest than the annual wages of everyone on the *Coast City* combined. She had the kind of wealth that could buy planets.

Ida sucked the spoonful of protein past his teeth and returned his attention to his plate.

"Fancy pulling up a pew and joining the party?"

Ida looked up. It was the first time he'd heard her speak. Her voice was strong and melodic, deeper than he expected and bathed in a golden accent. Her voice had a breathless quality; it crossed Ida's mind that she might be a good singer.

Zia's call had halted all conversation at her table, and Ida felt his face grow hot. Carter frowned at him, but Serra kept her eyes on the table. Ida knew he'd have to talk to her, and soon.

"We brought some food from our ship. Condensed nutrient from Earth, farm fresh."

Carter muttered something, and Serra touched his elbow. A few of the others laughed and turned back to the table.

"Well, I'm honored, but—"

"It tastes like chicken."

Ida dropped his spoon and pushed the metal tray away from him. "Count me in."

He picked a spot two seats down from Zia, on the opposite side of the table to Carter. Ida made sure he smiled and made eye contact with everyone at the table. On his right, between him and Zia, Fathead worked his jaw, the wet sound of his chewing obscenely loud as he looked Ida up and down.

"Now, ain't you gonna introduce us?" asked Zia Hollywood, seemingly to the table at large. Her chest moved as she spoke, the black singlet featureless but tight. Ida found himself swallowing a trickle of hot saliva. Oh, she was good. Being a genuine A-lister meant being able to turn it on and play the game anytime, anywhere.

Carter coughed, and Ida stuck out his hand. Ms. Hollywood looked at it and didn't move. Izanami's earlier comment played at the back of his mind.

"Captain Abraham Idaho Cleveland, ma'am. Pleased to make your acquaintance."

Hollywood pulled her bottom lip—pierced with a small silver loop just to the left of center—into her mouth, and Ida watched as she chewed it with her top teeth. Up close her square goggles had a greenish hue but were completely opaque, showing nothing but a double reflection of Ida grinning back at himself.

"Ain't captains supposed to salute?"

Ida let his hand fall away. "I'm retired, ma'am." He frowned. "Or . . . I was, and then I wasn't. It's a little complicated."

Fathead chuckled through clenched teeth, eyes half-closed in amusement. "You don't sound too sure. If you were retired, why are you here?" he asked.

"Good question," said Carter.

Zia raised a hand to the opposite shoulder, and from the corner of his eye, Ida thought he saw her moving tattoo dive down from her shoulder to her wrist, a thin twisting veil of black shadow forming a strange, streaking figurelike shape. He jerked his head back in surprise and blinked.

"Can't rightly say," he said, clearing his head. "Although upon the retirement of a senior officer—that's me, by the way—Fleet command is at liberty to issue one final set of orders. Usually it's a friendly gesture, like reporting to the Fleet college library to present your final log file to the custodian of special collections. Happened to a friend of mine. Sounded nice. Or it might be something more formal, like christening a new U-Star."

"And you?" Zia asked.

Ida laughed. "And then there's me. Well, apparently I have to close this hunk of junk down." He looked Carter in the eye. "Can't happen soon enough."

Fathead snickered and jogged Ida's elbow, passing him a plastic container stacked with gelatinous beige cubes. "Dig in, bro. It's on us."

Ida took the container and loaded his plate, then paused before carefully placing it back to the center of the table. He counted around the table again.

"Am I in someone's seat?"

Zia shook her head, mouth in her beaker. "Ivanhoe is back on the *County,* taking care of some last-minute work." Ida could hear the wet pop as Hollywood's lips parted when she spoke.

When she finished speaking, she held her mouth just so, in a moody pout perfect for the camera lens. Perhaps she wasn't just good, thought Ida. Perhaps she was a natural. "Our nav pod is temperamental, always has been. The Spider tech interferes with it something fierce. It went offline completely when we entered this system."

Ida nodded and started to say something about the nature of the star in this particular system, but as he squashed a cube of nutrient between his tongue and the roof of his mouth he was hit by the note-perfect taste of hot roast chicken, fresh from a farm oven. His words tailed off and he sighed, just a little.

Fathead jostled his elbow again. "Good, no?" He looked over the table at Carter. "Eh?"

Carter grinned and raised his spork in a toast. "Sure is, my man. I haven't eaten like this in years."

There was a murmur of agreement from the other marines, most of whom Ida didn't know by name. Ida caught Dathan and Fathead exchanging another look. This was the night's entertainment for them.

"The radiation from Shadow has a strange effect on electronics," said Ida, picking up the thread of his thoughts. "It's taken out our lightspeed link already. I presume you've got the right shielding on the pod?"

"Yeah," said Zia. "We're all good. Just needs recalibrating."

Dathan leaned forward on the table, peering around Ida at his boss. "We're gonna need that pod working if we're going to hit our target, Zia."

"Cool your boots. We're good."

Ida took another mouthful. The gelatin cube crushed to mush in his mouth, and when he breathed in through his nose he could feel the moisture of the steam rising from the nonexistent chicken meal.

Ida turned to Zia. "And what are *you* doing out here? Or is that a secret known only to you and Fleet command?"

"No secret, Cap'n." Zia seemed to relax, putting aside her beaker of drink and tipping a few food cubes onto her plate. On the other side of the table, Carter and his marines began talking among themselves, clearly refusing to be part of a conversation started by Ida. Zia chewed slowly and spoke with her mouth full. He watched his own reflection in her goggles as she ate.

"There's a small field of asteroids on the other side of Shadow. Hardly rocks even, more like a debris field of some kind. Maybe a half dozen big chunks, and a lot of dust and sand. They read mighty strange. Slowrocks. Nearly pure lucanol, ninety-eight percent, according to the readouts from your very own station computer. Lucky we got word before your lightspeed went south. So we hightailed it across Fleetspace to take a look-see. Your station is a pit stop. A bit of free PR for the Fleet in exchange for the tip-off."

Ida whistled and then dabbed his mouth with a canteen paper napkin. "Didn't think that was possible, an entire asteroid made of lucanol. How does it hold together? Must be as soft as your chicken cubes."

The two greenish black windows shielding her eyes were still pointed in Ida's direction, so he assumed she was looking at him. Then she smiled.

It was a beautiful smile, the kind of smile the paparazzi would have paid a fortune to see and to broadcast around the Earth and all her outposts. Ida thought he was probably very privileged to see it firsthand, sitting not one foot from the famous lips. Zia had a blue gray gem embedded in one of her upper teeth—spoils of her profession, no doubt. Ida suspected the tiny sparkling stone was worth more than the rug, the painting, and the matchwood in King's ready room put together. Ida knew at once that hardly anybody had a smile like this. This was the smile of a person rich and famous for a very good reason.

"That's what we're gonna go and find out," she said.

"And the Fleet just fed you the readings from this station, just like that? Would have thought that kind of data would be classified." Ida smiled. "Or encrypted, at least."

"That's what *they* think," said Dathan, tapping his metal spoon against the side of his tray four times, each tap with more force than the last until he let go of the utensil, letting it clatter across the table. Carter and the marines halted their conversation and looked at the spoon and then Zia's crewman.

Zia's expression tightened. "Go and help Ivanhoe with the nav pod."

The spoonless Dathan began rocking the edge of his food tray against the tabletop, making an annoying metallic clacking that increased in volume. Ida suddenly didn't feel like sitting between him and his boss.

"What in the name of Satan's tits are we doing here, Zia? We've come a hell of a long way on some spotty numbers. What if it's the starlight fucking with our instruments?"

"You'll get your cut."

"Oh, really? And what if there's nothing there? What if there's nothing shiny and gold at the end of your spectrograph?"

"Go and help Ivanhoe."

"Are you even listening to me?"

Zia leaned forward quickly, her expression tight, and when she spoke her voice was low and quiet. "If there's nothing there, I'll damn well pay you anyway. How does that sound, peaches?"

Everyone at the table looked at Dathan. He'd stopped rocking the dinner tray but his fingers were pressed against the rim, holding it up at an angle of several degrees. Dathan hesitated, perhaps aware that he'd pushed too far and the personal argument had become public. He sighed and let the tray drop with a crash. In the next few seconds, the only sound was Fathead chewing wetly on his chicken cube.

Then Dathan pushed his chair back and left the canteen without a word. Fathead was the only one who moved, turning to watch his fellow crewman walk out the door. Then he turned back to the table, grinning like this was the best night out ever.

"He always like that?" Carter finally broke the game of statues, reaching for another container of food cubes.

Zia's enigmatic smile reappeared. Ida was sure she'd been staring at him again. If only she'd take off the goggles. Ida felt that he'd not really even met Zia Hollywood yet. He was spending all his time talking to his own reflection.

Zia nodded, then tipped her drained beaker toward Fathead. The crewman reached down to a shoulder bag sitting at his feet. From it he extracted a tall, thin red bottle. It was elegant, expensive, and quite, quite illegal. Alcohol. The real thing.

"Oh yes!" Carter clapped his hands, and there was a murmur of appreciation from the other marines.

Zia took the bottle from Fathead. "Line it up, boys." She glanced and looked toward the door. "Your marshal isn't likely to walk in, is he?"

"Nah," said Carter. "Spends all his time in the ready room, if he's not asleep already."

Zia nodded and offered the bottle to Ida. Ida took it, calculating as he did the proportion of his wages that just a single shot of this would cost him on the black market, and how many years on a labor planet possession of a bottle that size would earn him.

By the time Ida had poured himself a careful measure of the liquid—revealed to be as bright in color as the glass of the bottle—Fathead had downed three shots. His face got redder and his smile wider. He bounced on his chair as he licked the remnants of the drink from his teeth, looking for all the world like a self-aware ventriloquist's dummy, the old kind Ida had once seen as a child. Fathead's eyes moved in the same way, keeping a glassy look on Ida as his head wobbled from side to side.

"So you're a real space hero, my good captain?" asked Fathead, grinning like a loon.

Ida paused, focusing on the intense fireball that exploded on his tongue as soon as it touched the red liqueur. He closed his eyes and willed them not to water. He heard Carter hiss out a laugh between his teeth.

When Ida opened his eyes, everyone at the table was looking at him. Carter with his favorite frown, Fathead with his smile. And for the first time since the incident down on the hub, even Serra seemed to be paying attention.

"Heard you were a hero." Carter and Ida both turned to Hollywood. She was, apparently, looking straight at Ida as she spoke, but with her mining goggles it was hard to tell. "I also heard you were a coward and a liar."

Ida couldn't take his eyes off her face, which was now completely, totally unreadable. Whose side was she on? "That so?"

Carter downed another shot of the liqueur. "Yeah, you going to tell them about that, old man?" he asked, his voice raspy with the kiss of the hard alcohol.

Ida allowed himself a slow smile and drained the remainder of his shot. He exhaled hotly through his nose, and immediately Fathead reached forward and topped his glass up. He made a wet clicking sound behind his fixed grin, which Ida took to be a sign of approval. Ida raised his shot to him as a toast, and then to Zia, and then sank it back. His mouth and throat were stung but numbing nicely. His tongue flopped fatly against the back of his teeth. He looked at Carter.

"Marine, I'm flattered my reputation preceded me across all of Fleetspace, but it's the utmost shame that it was a load of BS that got here first rather than the truth. Because, frankly, I'm not sure you can fit more than one idea and a half in that brainbox of yours."

Carter gave Ida a steely look, his face reddening a little, but Ida just leaned back and laughed. Whatever the liqueur was, it was starting to work. Serra smiled. Ida liked that.

"I'd like to hear the truth."

Ida looked at Zia and was surprised that when his head stopped turning, his eyes kept going. For a second Ms. Hollywood's image doubled, then trebled, clicking sideways in rapid succession like an out-of-synch video feed, throwing multiple silhouettes like a whole bunch of people standing behind her chair. He focused and held his glass out to Fathead. Fathead made the clicking sound and topped him up. Ida raised the glass a second time.

"Much obliged, man with the hair. And to you too, ma'am."

He drained the shot in one gulp. The alcohol burn was hot,

hot, hot, but now he could taste the drink. His mouth filled with rich wild strawberry. Now he knew why Fathead was so damn happy all the time. He could get used to this. He idly wondered if the *Bloom County* was in need of a retired—formerly retired—Fleet captain with a robot knee.

Ida waved his arms as though to draw the people sitting at the table closer over his campfire. Nobody moved, but he didn't notice. He had the stage. It was time to tell the truth.

"This is how the shit went down. Lemme tell you about it, right now."

29

Ida jerked up onto his elbows, eyes playing around the dark room, lit only by the faint blue LED of the radio set. A few seconds later and his head pounded, *onetwothree-twotwothree,* then settled into a steady, slower beat. That strawberry liqueur had been mighty fine. Too fine.

As he turned his head side to side, the rush of white noise swam with his movement. He imagined Ludmila listening, watching him sleep from her magical nowhere.

"Did you hear that?" Ida whispered, cocking his head. He'd been woken by a scream, but dreams and nightmares were becoming increasingly common. Maybe Izanami would prescribe something. If he could find her. The station medic seemed to be keeping to herself more and more since Ludmila had made contact.

There came a rustling across the subspace waves, like someone brushing against a microphone. "Mmm . . . Ida?"

"I'm here. Did you hear anything?" He squinted as his head thumped.

A pause, another rustle. "Maybe . . . I don't know. I was dreaming, I think. There was a girl, with black hair. . . ."

Ludmila was cut off by a second scream. It was very real, and not so far away. Ida was on his feet and at the cabin door, ignoring his headache. He stood at the threshold in the dim nightlight of the hub corridor. From inside the cabin it was hard to figure out from which direction the cry had come.

Ida stepped into the corridor, and the door slid shut behind him. For now, all was quiet. Ida noticed that the floor-level nightlights had come on for the first time he could remember. Their light was a soft blue, simulating the natural ambience of nightfall on some planet or another, he vaguely recalled. The *Boston Brand* had had them. Usually it was nice. But at times like this, the up and down angles of the light cast odd shadows that made Ida feel uncomfortable. When he looked down toward the far bulkhead door heading away into the demolition zone, blinking made it look like there were people moving in the dark corners of the passageway that weren't directly illuminated. And in his peripheral vision, Ida kept seeing fast sideways movement, startling enough to make his heart race. All tricks of the light, because the passageway was clearly empty, and Ida was alone.

He kept telling himself this for the next minute or so as he stood, unmoving, working up the courage to pick a direction and take a look. He was a Fleet captain, for God's sake. Getting spooked by shadows? *Gimme a break.*

For once the station wasn't an icebox, but the crosshatch flooring was hard on his bare feet. Ida was considering getting dressed when the scream tore the night air into little bits a third time, followed quickly now by the sound of running feet.

"Get in your cabin, let us handle this!" Carter appeared, shod in unlaced boots and stripped down to a stained olive singlet, carrying a plasma rifle. Behind him were two marines, armed and armored, with Zia Hollywood and Fathead bringing up the rear. Fathead was carrying a weapon as long as he was tall with a barrel approximately as wide at the business end as his hair.

"Where's Serra?"

Carter snarled. "Staying put where she was told to stay put. You gonna be difficult with me now?"

Fathead looked between the two men and waggled his finger at the pair. "I sense tension. Do you two need a moment?" He snickered.

Ida ignored him and looked at Carter. "The intruders didn't leave, did they?"

The marine looked him in the eye, his stare diamond hard. Then he nodded almost imperceptibly.

"Intruders?" Fathead turned to his boss. "Nobody said nothing about no intruders. You said everything was okay."

Zia said nothing, but her expression was set, her eyes still hidden behind her goggles, despite the gloom. Ida glanced down and saw she had one hand resting on the handle of pistol hanging from her belt. He hadn't noticed her wearing it before, but even with it mostly hidden in a holster, Ida could see enough of its curved back and handle to recognize it: a Yuri-G, a small but incredibly powerful pistol. They said it had enough kick to send a man into orbit, hence the nickname. Illegal for civilians. Restricted even for Fleet use. A stray shot would punch a hole straight through the *Coast City*'s herculanium shell. How a celebrity starminer had one strapped to her hip was a mystery to Ida, one that was more than a little alarming. Zia Hollywood moved in unusual circles; the pistol plus the alcohol—perhaps people like her really could operate above the law.

The sentient tattoo on Zia's arm swirled, perhaps showing annoyance, impatience, neither of which were evident on Zia's forever-cool features. Ida tried not to think about the way the tattoo's curling motion matched the way the shadows in the corridor swam out of the corner of his eye. His mind went back to Astrid. Then the image dissolved, almost without conscious thought.

There is no such thing as ghosts. There is no such thing as ghosts.

"I can help," said Ida, watching his own reflection in Zia's goggles. He turned to Carter, who seemed ready to keep arguing, when the fourth scream came. It was male, close, and terrible.

Zia stepped around the group and jogged ahead, Fathead on her heels. Carter glanced at Ida.

"Come on," the marine said. As he turned and headed down the passage, he touched the commlink on his belt and started calling for more backup.

Ida let one of the armored marines go first, then followed, the second bringing up the rear.

Ida struggled to keep up, his bare feet aching on the decking, the marine following behind forced to check his step. Zia, still at the front, clearly knew which direction to head in.

The auxiliary air lock. Her own ship, the *Bloom County*.

Ida and the second marine finally caught the group as they stopped by the air lock door. It was open, and dark beyond, and Ida was surprised to see the group hesitate. Zia was staring into the void, into her own ship, one hand resting on the bulkhead frame, the other on the butt of the Yuri-G.

"Ivanhoe?" she called out into the air lock. "What's happened? Day?"

Ida brushed past Carter, who caught him by the arm. Ida shrugged his hand off. He reached forward and touched Zia's shoulder, but recoiled almost instantly as her tattoo responded to his touch, crawling back up her arm toward Ida's fingers. The idea of an intelligent swarm of dye particles having free rein of her epidermis made Ida's own skin crawl.

"What's wrong?" said Ida.

Zia turned around to face him, and he once more found himself staring at a stereo reflection of himself, bed hair and all. He couldn't see her eyes, but her mouth was open, finally betraying her uncertainty and fear.

Ida pointed to the air lock. "Whatever's going on in there, we need to check it out. People don't scream for no reason."

He moved forward to take the lead, but this time it was Zia's hand on his shoulder. He turned.

"It's . . . it's dark."

Ida frowned and turned back to the passage ahead. It was short and unlit, but at the far end, no more than a few meters away, the lights were on at a junction, a service ladder leading up out of sight and down to a recessed hatch. There seemed to be options to turn left and right as well.

"Which way is the bridge?"

Zia hesitated. Ida watched the pulse in her neck twitch.

"Zia, which way?"

She nodded ahead. "Up. It's up and forward."

"Fine," said Ida. Without waiting for the rest of them, he turned and jogged down the passage toward the junction. The dark around him seemed to crowd in, blurring the lights ahead of him, but he kept his gaze fixed ahead and three seconds later was at the ladder. The metal rungs were icy against his bare feet and hands, but he powered upward and through the open ceiling hatch. Behind him, he heard the others rattle down the passage in their mix of heavy boots. Zia had been right about the dark. It was like moving through smoke. It crossed Ida's mind that maybe someone with a gun should be the one going first, but they were being slow enough already.

Ida emerged into a junction similar to the one he'd entered. The ladder continued upward to another hatch, and behind him a second black passage leading to a room, dim yellow light spilling hardly any distance at all from the opening. The flight deck. The yellow light shifted like someone was crossing in front of it.

"Hello?"

Nothing. Underneath his feet he saw Zia's reddish hair approach. He stepped off the ladder, and the others appeared one by one. It was cold—no, *freezing*—up here, Ida's breath pluming in front of his face and drifting outward, melting into the thin black mist that hung in the air. It was like standing in a walk-in freezer in a ship's galley.

Ida slowly approached the bridge, his bare feet on fire on the cold floor.

"Ivanhoe? Dathan?" Zia called out.

The passage was well insulated with a soundproof wrapper to keep vibrations from the mining machinery beneath their feet from rattling the crew's brains to gray paste when they were at work. In the dark, the complete non-echo of her voice was disconcerting. The bridge doorway was just a few meters away, but Ida had the feeling that Zia's voice had not even traveled that far.

Ida looked back as Zia took a step forward, but Carter held his hand up and shook his head. He raised the sight of his gun to his eye and took aim at the empty doorway. Following his lead, the two marines behind him did the same.

"This is the Fleet Marine Corps. If there are any unauthorized personnel on board this vessel, you are required to approach and identify yourself. Now!"

Carter waited a beat, then raised his head and looked out around his gun with his naked eyes. The yellow light continued to flicker, like someone had set up a campfire in the middle of the flight deck.

Carter sighted the gun again.

"You are in a Fleet-restricted area. We are authorized to use deadly force. We are entering the flight deck in five seconds."

The two marines clicked the safeties off their guns, the light on their barrels flicking from blue to red. Fathead pointed his weapon at the ceiling and stood back against the wall, ready to let the marines charge in before him.

Ida stood firm next to Carter. He could feel Zia tense beside him; he supposed she wanted to get into the flight deck first in case Carter started shooting her crew. Ida didn't like what was going on. He was glad the *Bloom County* was so cold, his shivering disguising his fear.

There is no such thing as ghosts. There is no such thing as ghosts.

Zia unclipped the Yuri-G and slipped it from the holster. Ida watched as her thumb flicked the safety off. The barrel of the tiny pistol lit an angry red.

Carter began his countdown. Ida readied himself, knowing this time he really did need to let those armed go first.

"One!"

Carter sprang forward, the two marines at close quarters. Ida waited, but then Zia swore and sprinted forward, the Yuri-G swinging as she ran to overtake Carter. Carter saw the movement out of the corner of his eye and sidestepped to let her pass, swearing as he did so, never once breaking his perfect combat crouch.

"Ivanhoe!"

Ida was at the door as Zia ducked ahead, crouching at the side of her crewman on the floor. He was alive, lying on his back and convulsing.

Carter signaled the marines to fan out and begin a search of the flight deck room as Ida joined Zia on the floor. Fathead rapidly paced about, his huge gun pointed skyward, checking computer readouts and flicking switches.

"Come on, baby, come on . . . ," whispered Zia. She'd dropped the Yuri-G and was holding her crewmate's bald head, trying to stop him banging it against the hard decking. Her fingers came away bloody, and his eyes rolled as a white foam trickled from the corners of his mouth and into the edges of his beard.

Ida looked at Zia, then over at the discarded gun. He picked it up carefully.

"Does he have a condition? Medication?"

She shook her head. "No," she said. "Not that I know of."

Ida was aware of military boots dancing around the small bridge. He looked up to see the two marines slowing their frantic patrol, Carter stationary in the center of the room. Carter swept his rifle around one more time; then he lowered the gun and relaxed his posture.

"Clear," he said. He glanced down at Ivanhoe and his two attendants. "What's wrong with him?"

Ivanhoe's seizure had stopped, and he now lay flat on the deck, head lolling to one side, breathing heavily and out cold.

Ida stood, hands on hips. "Don't know. Nothing here?"

Carter shook his head. "Small bridge, only one door out. No one in here except him."

Ida sighed, and crouched back down next to Zia. "He was fixing the nav pod, right?"

Zia stroked Ivanhoe's forehead. "Yes. Dathan was supposed to be helping him."

Ida nodded. Then he froze, his eyes wide. "So where's Dathan?"

Zia's head snapped up, and Ida blinked at his reflection. Zia looked back down to Ivanhoe and gently stroked his cheek with the back of her hand.

"Ivanhoe? Ivanhoe, where's Dathan? Where did Day go? Can you tell me, honey?"

Ivanhoe twitched, and his eyes flickered open. He licked his lips and looked around the flight deck, but his eyes were dull and unfocused. Zia pointed somewhere across the room and clicked her fingers. She looked insistently at the nearest marine when nobody moved.

"Water, over there!"

The marine went to investigate, and after fumbling with a wall-mounted dispenser, returned with a small plastic bag of water. Zia took it, uncapped the tiny spout at the top, and offered it to Ivanhoe's lips. He sucked greedily for a few moments, but then pulled away.

Zia leaned over him again. "Ivanhoe, where's Day? What happened?"

Ivanhoe coughed and rolled his head around. His lips moved, mumbling something, but Zia just shook her head and continued to stroke his cheek, repeating her question.

Suddenly he jerked and grabbed her wrist. Zia cried out in surprise as Ivanhoe pulled himself up on an elbow, pushing his face to within an inch away of his employer's. His eyes were wide, wide, wide.

"They took him, Zia, they took Dathan. They took him."

Then he flopped back down, agitated, flexing his free hand while the other continued to grip Zia's wrist.

Then his expression changed, and he looked . . . sad. Ida folded his arms and watched, uncomfortable, as the man's face twisted into a grimace and he began to cry and shake his head.

Zia pulled his fingers off her wrist. "Who took him, Ivanhoe? What happened?"

Ivanhoe sniffed and wailed, his sobs choking any attempt to speak. Finally he took a deep breath and said it.

"They came. Zia, they came. All of them. All dead. They came and took him. They took him. They took Dathan." He twitched and grabbed at Zia's arms, eyes wide. "Where's Momma? Tell me, please, where's Momma? When can I see Momma?"

Behind him, Ida heard two guns being released from their safeties. Turning around, he saw the indicator on the side of

Fathead's absurd cannon light up as he began sweeping it back and forth into the dark corners of the bridge. Carter had raised his rifle again, but not to eye level. The marine stood, face bleached of all color. When he met Ida's gaze, his jaw was slack.

"The fuck is going on?" the marine asked.

Ida shook his head. That was a very good question.

30

They carried Ivanhoe to the infirmary and hooked him up to a monitor, one of the marines, Ashworth, volunteering to keep an eye on the otherwise automated systems as the others returned to their stations. Ida went back to his cabin to get dressed; while there, he tried to raise Izanami on the station's comms, thinking she should really go take a look at Zia's crewman. But there was no response, just more interference. When Ida returned to the infirmary he found Fathead and Zia by Ivanhoe's bedside, Ashworth still by the monitor. Fathead held his cannonlike weapon in both hands, the lights on the barrel an angry, dangerous red.

Zia watched her crewman sleep for a few minutes, then turned and left the infirmary at practically a run. Ida glanced at Fathead, but the man didn't seem to notice his boss's departure.

Ida quickly ducked out and found Zia farther along the corridor, marching with some determination. She looked back at him as he approached but said nothing. Ida didn't know what to say either, so he kept his mouth shut. She was going to see the marshal, that much was clear; standing in the elevator, Zia waited impatiently as Ida realized she needed him to punch the access code to the bridge.

Her meeting was brief. Provost Marshal King sat alone in the middle of the ready room, computer pad on his lap. Marines guarded the door on the outside, but not within. Ida thought maybe they should be.

The marshal looked at his computer pad but his eyes were unfocused. He looked ill to Ida. So did everybody else left on the *Coast City*.

Zia stood and shivered. The room was cold and her face was

white and shiny. The famous pout was gone, her once ruby red lips dull and dry.

King glanced up at her, flexed his fingers, then looked back to the computer pad.

"I'm sorry for the loss of your crew member, Ms. Hollywood." His voice was low, quiet, not a whisper but close enough. "All attempts will be made to locate him. For the moment, I'm assigning you a Fleet security detail—"

Then she spoke. She said: "We're leaving," and then turned on her heel and walked out.

King didn't reply, his gaze fixed somewhere beyond the computer pad. He flexed his fingers again. It was an odd, mechanical motion, beginning with the little finger and ending with the thumb. Ida hadn't noticed King do it before.

Dumbfounded, Ida turned and watched, through the still-open door of the ready room, Zia stride across the bridge, toward the elevator.

"What just—?"

"Thank you, Captain. Dismissed."

Ida stared at the marshal for a second. Then he went to follow Zia. But when he stepped out onto the bridge, she was already gone.

As the door to the ready room closed, the marshal twitched in his chair, eyes flicking to his left, toward a shadowed corner of the ready room. But it was a movement driven purely by his autonomic nervous system. If Ida had been able to look him in the eye before he walked out, he would have seen the marshal's pupils contracted to pinpricks, his eyes glazed, unfocused.

Out of the shadows stepped Izanami. As she moved, the shadows seemed to kick up around her like dust.

She laid a hand on King's shoulder, and the marshal twitched again, flexed the fingers of his empty hand, and stared at his knees.

Izanami smiled. In the dark her eyes burned blue as she bent down, her lips almost touching his ear.

"You can't keep him from me forever, my dear Roberto. Not now that I took your book away, your precious book of secrets and codes. Did your commandant really think that would be enough, that if he wrote it all down in cipher like a child, that someone like you would be able to understand it? Would be able to carry on, as if the secrets in the book were enough? Perhaps he did." She laughed. "The Fleet is indeed full of the weak and the foolish."

King's eyelids flickered, but he did not respond. Izanami straightened and watched the main door. She stroked King's head with her hand, her smile widening.

31

Serra had been sleeping when Carter returned. It was real, uninterrupted sleep; a rare thing, sleep to be treasured, free of shadows and purple light and the voice of her grandmother and from the *other* thing, the noise, the roaring of the ocean that filled her head—the sound of the Spiderbaby sleeping in Zia Hollywood's hybrid ship. It was a sound Serra was familiar with from dozens of sorties where she had to infiltrate and disrupt Spider networks with her mind. But out here it was different. Spiders were never alone, and they never slept. And this one . . . this one was *dreaming.* And this close, the Spiderbaby within touching distance, Serra could see into those machine dreams and hear the sound of—

She rocked on the bed as Carter jogged her shoulder. She tried to ignore it until Carter did it again.

And then he said, "I saw her," and Serra was bolt upright in a second, as alert and ready for action as when the gunnery sergeant blew the trumpet to announce incoming Spiders.

Carter paced the small cabin. Serra watched as the sweat glistened on his forearms as he walked under the fluorescent strips. He moved his hands as he paced, like he was sculpting the description out of thin air. But Serra already had a fair idea of what he was talking about.

"On their ship?"

Carter nodded vigorously but didn't stop walking. "It was there, on the bridge. Back in the corner, against the wall. The shadows hid it—" He moved his hands as though kneading dough. "—like smoke, or dust."

Serra swung her feet to the decking and pulled the sheets

over her lap. "Why the fuck didn't you challenge, or tell the others?"

Carter stopped and looked at her. He was pale and his eyes were wide, his brow creased as he struggled with what she'd just said. "What do you mean?"

"You found the intruders, why didn't you challenge them?"

Carter's mouth twisted into what might have been a smile. Serra didn't like it.

"No, no," he said quickly. "They weren't there. That's the whole fucking point. Nobody else could see them, only me, because they weren't there."

He stopped, and Serra saw that he was shaking. His bottom lip began to quiver; he looked like a lost child.

Serra stood and took his cheek in her hand. "What is it, baby? Tell me."

Carter took her hand in his, and she winced, just a little, as he squeezed too hard. He looked into her eyes, and she saw them wet with tears. "She said I could see them again."

Serra blinked. "She? The intruder spoke to you?"

Carter nodded. "It's a woman. She's from far away. She said I could see them again."

The final barrier came crashing down, and Carter sobbed into Serra's shoulder. She brushed his hair and pulled him backwards toward the bed. He was leaning on her, and he was very big and very heavy but he moved without resistance when she pushed him to one side to sit on the bed next to her. His sobbing died but the lost look on his face remained. Serra was frightened and her thoughts were being drowned out by the white noise of the Spiderbaby dreaming. She focused, trying to cut the sound out before it gave her another migraine.

"Who is she, and what did she say?"

Carter sniffed loudly and wiped his nose with his hand.

"She's from far away. But she can bring them back." Carter turned and looked at Serra. She winced again at his too-strong grip.

"For fuck's sake," she said. "Who?"

"My parents. I can see them again, speak to them. She'll bring them here."

Serra's heart rate went up by half in less than a second. She shook her head and ran her hands over Carter's regulation crew cut. "*Nene,* you've had a shock. Ever since the security breach. You shouldn't have gone back to duty so quickly."

Carter snarled and yanked his head away. Serra wasn't surprised at the reaction and let her hands fall into her lap.

"She can bring them back," he said. He stabbed a finger down toward the floor, like his parents could materialize right in their cabin, right now.

But they couldn't. They couldn't.

Serra shushed her lover but he flinched, so she got to the point. "They can't come back, baby. They're dead. You know that."

Carter nodded, the snarl replaced with a smile. He sniffed again. "Yes, yes, they're dead. They're all dead, all of them. But they can come back. She can bring them back."

Serra shook her head. Carter had snapped. Spooked by the shadows and the environment failures and the general what-the-fuckery that had gone on for the last two months.

Serra reached down to pick up her discarded clothing. As she moved, Carter hopped from the bed and grabbed her arm. He squeezed and pulled her to her feet, the bedding falling away. Serra snarled at him. "What the fuck are you talking about, Charlie? Your parents are dead. You know that. They're dead."

But Carter just nodded. "Yes, they're dead. They're all dead—DeJohn, the commandant, the marines. She can bring them all back here. The gift, you gotta use it, for me. You can help me."

Serra searched his face for any hint of sanity, but saw nothing but eyes wide and wet and a rictus grin. She didn't like the way he called her wild talent the "gift." It was the word her grandmother used for her precious Carminita, a description of the raw, hereditary ability the Fleet had enhanced to a finely tuned battle sense. Serra had never called it that, not to Carter. She didn't like the way the conversation was going.

She pulled her arm free and turned to reach for her clothing again, but Carter grabbed her a second time.

"Charlie, let go!"

He shook his head. "You can do it," he said. "You can help me. Please, you have to help me. You can use the gift." He tapped his own temple.

She moved to sit back on the bed, and he let her this time.

The gift? In the middle of all this, he wanted her to reach out and make contact? Even the thought of it made the static in her ears rush in, like a gate had been opened. She closed her eyes and pressed the heel of her hand against her forehead, and listened to the noise.

"Who is 'she'?" she asked eventually.

Carter sat next to her. "She's from far away. From the other side of space. She's dead too."

Serra gulped and felt faint. She opened her eyes and saw Carter looking at her.

"She's dead, and she can help us. She can help all of us. She can help *you*."

Their eyes remained locked.

Help . . . me? At this thought, the static swirled, like the machine was listening in on their conversation. Watching from the dark. Giving approval.

Then Serra nodded.

"Okay."

32

The corridor swam with static, which made Ida pause, half-in, half-out of the elevator. The space radio had been off when he left his cabin, he was certain of that, and the first thought that jumped out at him was that someone was messing in his private space—again. Ida clenched his fists and his jaw and headed down the passageway.

It took Ida a few moments to realize how cold the air was and that the pain in his knee that had started back at the elevator was ramping up. He stopped mid-stride, his breath catching in a white cloud before him.

Not again.

"Ida? Ida, where are you?"

Ludmila calling, her voice punching holes in the white noise that surged and rolled to fill the gap when she was silent.

"Ludmila?"

"Ida, I can't stop them, I tried—"

Ida broke into a run, his artificial joint screaming. Ludmila's voice was different: it sounded even farther away, and the hard edge of fear had returned.

Ida's cabin was empty and dark, lit only by the half light from the passageway as he stood across the open doorway. The blue light of the space radio was piercing.

"Ludmila? What's wrong?" Ida moved to his desk, pulled the chair in tight, and hunched over the radio set. He tried adjusting the signal, but the static just popped and crackled and settled back into its usual pattern.

"I tried to stop them, I tried to stop them, Ida, but I couldn't, I couldn't—"

Another noise now, a chirping or clicking. Ida frowned and closed his eyes. Then he realized what it was, distorted by the bad signal. Ludmila was crying.

"Stop who? Ludmila, tell me what happened."

Ludmila sniffed, the sound of dry paper being torn.

"They're coming. It's sooner than I thought. I've tried to hold them back, but it's not working. They're getting stronger."

"Who is?"

"Ida, you must stop them."

Ida sighed and rubbed his face. "Who?"

"Your friend, Carter. And the others. They're going to try to bring them in. It's too soon, too soon."

Ida sat up. Carter? Friend was not the first term that came to mind. But, more important, how did Ludmila know what the marine was doing? How did she know anything about what went on in the *Coast City* outside of Ida's cabin?

"What's Carter doing?"

The rush of white noise snapped like a gunshot, making Ida jerk back instinctively from the radio set. When Ludmila spoke again her voice was loud and crushed.

"Stop him! Stop them all!"

Ida hopped to his feet and looked around, searching. Then he saw it. The Yuri-G was sitting on the bed. In the confusion aboard the *Bloom County,* Zia hadn't seen him pick it up. He grabbed it and checked the charge, almost telling Ludmila to wait there. He stopped, and had the oddest feeling that she really was in the room.

"Go," she said. "He's on Level Twelve, Mess Deck."

"How did you—?"

"Go!" Ludmila screamed. Her voice, meshed with the interference across the radio, was like a banshee's cry. Ida felt the hairs on the back of his neck stand up.

Without saying a word, he sprinted out.

. . .

In the empty cabin, the static died down to a baseline level, punctuated by the occasional pop as Ludmila cried. Then it snapped again, as it had before.

"Contact has been established . . . contact has been established," Ludmila whispered to the empty room.

33

Knock-knock-knock-knock-knock-knock-knock.

Hands clenched.

"It's not working—"

"Marine, shush."

"Sir."

Knock-knock-knock-knock.

"You really know what you're doing?"

"It's fine. It always starts like this." Serra fidgeted on her chair. Carter's hand was like sandpaper in hers.

Knock-knock-knock-knock.

"This is fucked up."

Someone else moved, knocking a knee against the table, rocking it.

"Carter, shut the fuck up. You were the one who asked me to do this." And now, sitting in the dark, in the circle, she wondered why she'd agreed so easily.

Then the machine sound was there, creeping in at the edge of her mind, and she knew she'd made the right decision.

"Fine," Carter whispered.

Knuckles white. More knocks.

"Carter," said Sen, thrown out of bed by Carter to complete the circle, "you are so fucking full of shit."

"That so, gunner?"

"It sure is. Just wanted you to know."

"Duly noted."

Someone snickered. Serra's eyes flicked open but the canteen was lost in pitch black. It was amazing, breathtaking, how dark they had managed to get it. Not even the night-lights in the passageway outside sent a single sliver sliding under the canteen door.

She closed her eyes again and concentrated. She wasn't that familiar with the rituals of Santeria, and she hadn't done this for . . . well, forever, really. And only one time before that, when she'd been six. Her mother had been furious, but even she bit her tongue. Her mother had been scared of Grandmother, always, of the things she could do. But it was working. The white noise in her head was clearing, slowly.

"This better work."

Serra's eyes snapped open again. It was ridiculous. Just an hour ago Carter had been a wreck in her cabin, crying for his mother. Now he was acting like she was *making* him do this.

"Are we going to keep trying, or do you children want to go play somewhere else?"

Someone yawned, and someone coughed. The blackness was like a blanket, enveloping, soft.

Nobody said anything for a few seconds, but nobody let go of her hands either. Finally Carter hissed; Serra could just imagine his face, teeth clenched, lips drawn, ready for anything the enemy could throw at them.

"Do it," he said.

Serra screwed her eyes tighter and tried to remember what her grandmother had taught her, twenty years ago. That it had been in the old house in Puerto Rico and she was now on an old station a thousand light-years away shouldn't matter. Carter had made direct contact. That was much more than her grandmother ever had, and she'd made a living out of the "gift."

She was old by the time Serra hit recruitment age, but cane in hand she'd stood by her beloved Carminita as she took the oath, as tall and as proud as her bones would allow. Next to her, her mother was also proud, but there were tears in her eyes and her hands shook. She was scared for her daughter. Service with the Fleet was honorable, but with Spider aggression increasing daily, the survival rate was enough to make any mother weep.

A sigh in the dark, from her left. Someone jumped in his or her seat and someone snickered again. This wasn't going to work. They needed a focus. They needed a light. They needed gifts.

Ida's booted feet pounded the crosshatch decking. It made a racket, which was fine by him. If the marines were in trouble, he had no problem letting them know someone was coming.

He came out of the elevator and headed left. The canteen was a quarter-way around the hub, between him and the next elevator lobby. For a change the passage lights were operational, the night glow flaring to regular operational white as Ida raced around the curved corridor. The environment control was holding as well.

Neither of these facts entered Ida's mind until the lights failed. He careered to a halt, animal instinct stopping his run as the darkness of the next passageway section reared up at him like a physical object.

Ida swore and, arms swinging, carried on.

It was all they had, but it would do. The lighter—illegal on the U-Star, but smuggled on board by someone—provided a tiny flame but one that burned with a yellow so dazzling in the complete dark of the canteen that even with Serra's eyes closed, the shapes moved brown and red behind their lids. Next to the lighter stood a plastic cup of canteen coffee, the steam rising in mesmerizing waves in the flickering light. The only thing missing from the offering was a cigar, but Serra was amazed enough that someone in the circle had produced the lighter. The gifts were better than she could have hoped for.

Serra exhaled, shook her sweaty hands, and then completed the circle again. All at once, everyone around the table jolted, like a circuit had been completed and an electrical charge conducted.

"What the fuck—?"

"Quiet," whispered Serra. Behind her closed eyes she watched the flame dance.

Knock-knock-knock-knock.

"This still ain't working. I gotta be on shift soon."

KNOCK-KNOCK-KNOCK-KNOCK.

Everyone jumped as the rapping sounded on the table in front of them.

"What the fucking fuck?"

The knocking continued, fainter. Serra leaned down toward the table, concentrating.

"Please, we have a code. One for no, two for yes. Do you understand?"

Knock-knock-knock-knock-knock.

Serra felt Carter's grip relax. He moved his fingers, threatening to break the perfect circle. They were so close.

KNOCK.

"What?"

"Wait."

KNOCK-KNOCK.

"Do you understand us?"

KNOCK-KNOCK.

Someone on the opposite side of the table drew a breath in sharply. One of the marines, another woman. Serra didn't really know her. She seemed quiet and timid, but she had more Spider kills notched on her rifle butt than the rest of the squad put together. Always the quiet ones.

"Is someone there?"

KNOCK-KNOCK.

Backs straight. Knees together. A gasp in the dark.

"You asked us to come, didn't you?"

KNOCK-KNOCK.

Serra opened her eyes, just a crack. Lit by the steady flame of the lighter, Carter's face was a grimace, sweat dripping down his forehead. Serra licked her teeth and watched Carter's eyeballs moving rapidly behind his eyelids.

"Is there someone there?" she asked. "Is someone coming?"

Nothing. Serra repeated the question, and then closed her eyes. As soon as she did, the red and black shapes reappeared, dancing with the flickering flame.

She took a breath and held it; then she opened her eyes again. The flame was still, steady, strong.

Then she looked up. Standing behind the group, in the gap between Carter and the protesting Flyeye, stood DeJohn.

Except . . . maybe it was the light, the way he was illuminated in yellow from the front and from down low, maybe it was the way the light flickered even though the flame was steady and true. Maybe it was the way that the blackness behind him moved. Whatever it was, the figure looked less like DeJohn and more like a photograph, or some weird mannequin. She realized DeJohn had his eyes closed.

"Hey—," Carter whispered, eyes closed. Immediately the darkness seemed to bulge, partially obscuring DeJohn's head. Serra pulled on Carter's hand.

"Quiet, dammit."

Carter did as he was told.

Serra closed her eyes. "Who is there? Do you know us?"

KNOCK.

KNOCK.

The raps came slow and deliberate. Somebody whimpered and Serra felt Sen's grip slip in the fingers of her left hand. She turned her head instinctively toward the sound, but kept her eyes closed.

She sat and watched the shapes moving in the flame light behind closed eyes, hypnotized by their dance.

The door was open, but the canteen beyond was just an empty black void. Ida stopped again, and listened. He could hear something, a knocking sound, far away. The temperature in the passageway was approaching freezing. Standing motionless, he could feel his eyeballs drying out.

The darkness had gotten thicker somehow as he approached, filled with a substance as thin and insubstantial as gas but impenetrable to light. It had no substance, no taste, no smell, and Ida knew full well that it wasn't gas or mist or smoke. It was shadow.

Ida was scared. Scared of what the shadows hid, of what might come out of the shadow, of going into the shadow and not returning.

"Ida . . . Ida . . ."

Her voice was caught on a nonexistence breeze, painted light and thin onto a background of static. The echo of subspace.

Ida spun around. The shadow had surrounded him, but back the way he had come the passage lights, now returned to their baseline nocturnal setting, were faintly visible. The passage looked old and granular through the fog.

She was there. Standing where he had come from. He wondered how long she'd been following him, but then he realized that she hadn't at all. Beyond, the elevator door remained open. It was possible she'd come around from the other side of the hub, but he knew she hadn't really.

Ludmila.

Her suit was silvered, her closed visor golden. Across her chest were four bold red letters.

CCCP.

And when she spoke, it was across the eternity of subspace. Ida wasn't sure whether it was sound acting on his eardrums or whether she'd tuned in to his very thoughts. But she spoke, and he listened. If he was afraid, she was terrified.

"I can't stop them, Ida, I can't stop them. Go, please."

And then her voice dropped to a whisper, reduced to a sibilant hissing against the interference.

"They are coming. . . . They are coming. . . ."

Ida needed no further encouragement. He spun on his heel, yelled blue murder, and dived into the black portal of the canteen.

"Carter?"

Someone sobbed. One hand, rough, grabbed Serra's hard enough, it felt, to snap bone. Another hand, soft and wet, twisted and slipped away. The circle broke.

KNOCK.

KNOCK.

Slow and sure.

She dared not open her eyes.

Dared not.

"Who is there? Who are you?"

A sigh—long, high, not from someone who sat around the table.

She must not open her eyes.

Must not.

But . . .

KNOCK KNOCK.

But she must . . .

"I feel . . . ," said someone not at the table. "I feel the darkness *breathe.*"

The voice was female, accented. Far East. Asian. Japanese. The voice spoke the last word like it was a blessed relief.

She must not open her eyes.

KNOCK. KNOCK. KNOCK. KNOCK.

A breeze. Ice. The flame flickered.

The voice was as cold as space as it asked, "Where is he?"

She opened her eyes, and it began. One scream, then another.

The light danced and the shadows swirled and the flame on the table was still, steady, small.

Between each sitter, a face. DeJohn. An older man in round glasses. Men in Fleet marine helmets reflecting the light that guttered and flared from nowhere.

Serra tried to close her mouth, tried to stop the scream, but she could not. Wide-eyed and wide-jawed, she turned her head, left to right, left to right, like a fairground attraction from old-time Earth.

And then she turned again, to the left. The chair was empty. Sen had gone.

And to the right. Carter crying.

And to the left. The chair was no longer empty. A woman sat demurely, hands in her lap. Dressed in white, with hair long and black. Skin as white as her tunic. Her eyes, oval, Japanese, closed.

They opened, and the woman smiled. Her smile was the death of a thousand children under a hot desert sun. Her eyes were blue voids in which stars exploded.

Serra's jaw clicked as it opened beyond normal endurance. The scream she uttered came from the ancient part of her brain. It was old and green, the sound of the Earth being split in two.

And the flame burned, white, steady. But it could not fight the darkness, the shadows. The blackness spun around the table, around the sitters, around the uninvited guests.

The Japanese woman held up her hands. One was empty, the palm facing forward. The other clutched a handle, long with a woven cover. Pointing downward, something long and silver sparked in the night.

She whispered, and the whisper became a rush of sound, a wind from nowhere, the static white noise howl of subspace. The Japanese woman stood and raised her sword.

"Where is he?"

Serra stared into the light.

"Where is he?"

Serra stared into the light and screamed.

Ida looked around, sweeping the Yuri-G in front of him. It had a white light on the front of it that projected a bright cone in front of the barrel, mixing with the red safety-off warning indicator and illuminating the table and chairs and the canteen's serving bar at the back in a washed-out pink.

The room was empty.

Careful to keep his senses alert to anything that might be hiding in the corners, Ida played the light from the Yuri-G over the table. There was a plastic cup filled with something black that had frozen into a solid block, and something smaller, metallic, that glinted. He leaned forward and snatched it up—a cigarette lighter. He held it close and shook it. It was still nearly full of fuel, and the cap and striking wheel were hot to the touch but the metal of the body was icy. He closed the cap and squeezed the lighter in his fist. His knee banged one of the chairs; he winced at the sudden sound.

He didn't know why he wanted to be quiet, but he did. There was something about the canteen. Not just the darkness, now that he'd passed through the strange blackness that had hung like a mausoleum curtain over the entrance, but something else. He turned to look back at the door, but the shadows seemed normal again.

Mausoleum. He turned back to the canteen and pointed the gun around slowly, rolling the word in his mouth like a glucose tablet. The canteen was the canteen, and he knew it well. But somehow, whether it was the harsh light of the Yuri-G against the soft blue of the night-lights, whether it was the odd way the shadows flitted around his peripheral vision, he couldn't tell. But the empty tables and chairs were . . . spooky.

Especially the table in front of him. With the chairs arranged like a group had just been sitting there. With the frozen cup and the lighter, the closed cap still hot in his hand.

It was like walking into a tomb. He'd experienced the sensation before, on several planets. Action against the Spiders meant infiltration or outright conquest of people and places, on both sides. He'd walked through enough sacred places, forbidden temples or tombs of kings, where the very fabric of the place pushed at you, telling you to turn around, warning you to go no farther.

And he felt it here. The canteen had become an alien landscape, a sacred, secret place. Ida had the feeling he'd interrupted something, something important, something of which he wasn't supposed to be a part. Something that, he knew, was terrible and dark and old, the result of foolish meddling by people who had no clue at all.

Had no clue, or were led into a trap.

Ida kicked a chair and shouted and recoiled at the sound, so loud and sharp in the cathedral silence of the canteen.

It was empty. He'd been too late.

"You couldn't stop it."

Ida turned. When he saw Ludmila in the doorway, he lowered the gun. Its flashlight spotlighted his feet absurdly.

She was getting stronger. As he stood there, watching the slim figure in her silver spacesuit, Ida felt the hairs on his arms and neck prickle. Fear, yes, but cold as well. It seemed that to manifest like this, Ludmila was sucking the energy from the very air. Any kind, whatever was available. Light and heat. His robot knee ached like someone had hit it with a hammer.

"Where are they?" was all Ida could manage. His face was stiff with the cold, his words sending clouds of steam billowing into the air between him and her.

She moved a gloved hand by her side so that the palm faced him. Maybe moving was difficult. The room reverberated with the faint sound of the ocean.

"They've been taken."

"Taken where?"

"I thought they were coming," said Ludmila, "that this would hasten their arrival. But someone stopped them. Not you, someone else."

"I'm afraid."

"So am I."

Ida's throat was dry. "I'm afraid of you," he said.

The gloved hand dropped.

"So you should be," Ludmila said.

Ida stared at the apparition. She was real, solid, three-dimensional. And then he saw that her golden visor was not reflecting the room or him, standing right in front of her. It showed a starscape and the edge of a blue-green orb. The Earth.

Ida jumped as the scream punched through the fog in his mind. His intake of breath was sharp and the cold air stung. He knew that voice.

Zia.

He turned back to the woman in the spacesuit, but she was gone. The canteen was empty once more.

When Zia screamed a second time, Ida flicked the safety off the Yuri-G and left the room at a run.

34

He found her in the corridor outside, halfway between the canteen and elevator lobby. She was curled into a ball and pressed into a corner, arms wrapped around her knees. One arm was bare but the sentient tattoo on the other had stretched out, enveloping the limb in a black sleeve. It made Ida feel sick to look at it.

"Zia?"

She flinched at his voice, and as he knelt down she crawled backwards even farther, trying to telescope her body into the smallest bundle possible. Small, safe, out of reach.

He caught sight of his own face looming toward the reflection in her goggles. At least that meant she was real, and she was here. Then he blinked and looked away. The reflection showed only blackness behind him. He had the irrational, childish fear that something was going to swim out of the darkness and grab him from behind; a single white hand with claws, creeping out across the floor to grasp at an ankle and pull him away.

He shuddered and then took a breath. "Zia, what happened?"

He gently took one shoulder—above the arm without the tattoo—and squeezed. Her curled form seemed to relax, and the tension in her forehead eased. Her lips parted, and she tilted her face up to his. Then her lips began to move, mouthing words that, somehow, Ida didn't feel were hers.

"Where is he? Where . . . Where is he?"

Then she let out a cry and jerked forward, pushing Ida away. He rocked on his heels as she scrambled forward on her hands and knees before she seemed to relax again and sat on her haunches.

"What's wrong?" Ida realized he had a fair idea. "What did you see?"

Zia coughed and brought her knees up to her chest. Her goggles were pointing dead ahead, but Ida had no idea where she was looking. Then she spoke in a small voice.

"Nobody. I didn't see nobody."

She fumbled on the floor; Ida backed off to allow her to push herself to her feet.

"You all right? Because you sure screamed like you weren't. And where is who?"

Zia paused as though considering an answer while she brushed herself down. Her glasses were now pointed right at him.

"I don't know what you're talking about. I'm fine."

Ida frowned.

"We have to leave. Now," she said, and she headed toward the elevators.

"Wait," said Ida, but she ignored him. He jogged to join her and touched her shoulder as he pulled level, but she jerked away. As she moved her other arm to rub the shoulder where he had touched, Ida noticed the tattoo springing to life, curling and swirling like an agitated eel in a tank.

Zia Hollywood hit the control panel and stepped though the sliding doors, Ida close on her heels. Ignoring Ida, she touched the personal comm unit on her wrist.

"Fathead, we all set?"

The comm clicked and her crewman's voice came through, acknowledging. Zia nodded.

"I'll be at the *County* in five. Start the engine warming." She released the comm and dropped her arm.

"So that's it? You're off, just like that?"

Nothing.

"Zia—"

She tapped her foot three times and then spun on her heel. Her mouth was set.

"Yes, Cap'n, I'm leaving." The elevator dinged. She shifted the weight on her feet, and the corners of her mouth twitched. "And if you had any sense, you would too."

Ida took a step forward. "What does that mean?"

Zia shook her head. "I need to get the fuck off this ship. You do too. Everyone."

The elevator doors snicked open. Zia's level, one floor up from Ida's hidey-hole. She made a line for the doors, forcing Ida to sidestep. By the time he turned around, she was already halfway down the corridor. And then the light panel behind her faded off as the one ahead faded on, and Ida watched as she became a series of vignettes disappearing toward the guest quarters.

She was waiting for him in his cabin. She sat on the bed and was smiling, like there was nothing wrong at all aboard the U-Star *Coast City*.

"What's the matter?" Izanami asked. The smile didn't leave her face.

Ida paused at the threshold, one hand on the doorframe, one hand rubbing his forehead. He was getting a headache, a real thumper. It was cold and there was a sound in his head, the rushing noise of subspace like some kind of tinnitus, echoing in his ears.

"I saw her," he said. He gasped for air. His body felt like it was made of herculanium armor.

Izanami hopped off the bed and went to Ida, her hands behind her back. She peered at his eyes. Ida held the back of his hand over his mouth like he was going to retch, but nothing materialized.

Izanami's smile grew a little at the corners. "You look like you could use a rest, Captain."

Ida shook his head and tried to straighten up, but his vision was going black and red at the edges. The shadows, crowding in. He turned to Izanami and was surprised by the blue light in her eyes.

"She's here," he said, shaking his head again. "And Zia's gone . . . going . . . she saw . . . I . . ."

Ida screwed his eyes shut. It felt like hot metal was being pressed against his temples. He staggered to the table, where he sat heavily in the chair.

Izanami turned but stayed by the door. "Who's here?"

From Izanami's tone, Ida thought for a moment she was addressing a small child. He opened his eyes, but she was looking at him. The room flipped momentarily in front of his eyes, and nausea crawled up his chest from somewhere lower down. He grimaced and gripped the arms of his chair so hard, the edges bit into his hands.

He closed his eyes again. The last thing he saw before he did was Izanami's eyes. They were blue, as blue as the sky, as blue as the light on the space radio and just as bright.

Behind his closed eyelids he wished for the purple shapes of summer, the breeze on his face, and the grass in his nose, but all he got was black shapes on a black background. They shifted, squirmed, rolled.

The *sound* filled his head. He sucked a breath in that was colder than he thought it should be.

"Where have you been, anyway?" he asked. He kept his eyes closed. He didn't want to look at her. There was something about her eyes. . . . "One of Zia's crewmen needed attention." He opened his eyes. The cabin was still dark, and Izanami was hidden in shadows. Ida stood, waiting a beat to make sure he wasn't going to keel over. Then he hobbled to the bed and lay down.

She shrugged. "I'm not the station's official medic. You should get some rest."

Ida turned over, the effort titanic. He opened his eyes and looked up and saw two Japanese medics sitting on his bed, the black shadow of a translucent third orbiting above them. He blinked and rubbed his eyes, and the image refocused. Izanami was still smiling.

"Sleep, Ida. Sleep."

Sleep. Yes. He was tired, very tired, and cold. He thought about Zia and about the empty canteen, but the roar of subspace was a like a blanket, enclosing, enveloping, smothering his thoughts.

"Good night, Ida."

"Guuhnmm . . . ," he said into the pillow, and she was gone.

On the table, the blue light of the space radio shone, but there was no static, no interference, no noise.

After a while, Ida jerked awake, but the room was empty. When he looked up, the radio's blue light shone straight into his eye, and he let his head drop back to the pillow.

"Good night, Ludmila," he said.

There was no answer, but Ida was asleep. In his dream he saw himself holding a gun and looking around an empty room. Red paint flakes fell like snow, and Astrid called his name.

As he was lying on the bed, his left hand unclenched, finally releasing the small, silver object onto the olive green blanket. Ida sighed in his sleep and turned over, knocking the lighter to the floor. It banged dully as it hit the rubberized decking, but not enough to wake him.

35

Ida woke and the nausea hit him like a punch in the stomach. He got to the communal bathroom down the passage just in time. After he threw up he felt better, at least physically. He knelt in the stall for a few minutes, collecting himself. He had to see King straight away, insist he put the station on full alert, get everyone available to work on clearing the lightspeed link. The *Coast City* and everyone in it—everyone *left* in it—were in danger.

As he shuffled back to his cabin, he found himself checking over his shoulder more than once, more than twice. The environment control had settled into a low twilight, which wasn't helping his state of mind.

Ida rushed into his cabin, immediately shutting the door behind him and leaning back against it as he took deep breaths, waiting for the panic to abate. He closed his eyes but that seemed to make it worse, and he quickly turned around to check through the frosted window. The corridor beyond was empty and silent. Ida exhaled loudly and rolled his neck. He had to see King, yes, but right now he didn't really feel like venturing out in the corridor again, not just yet.

The cabin was cold, so very cold. Ida scrambled to the bed and grabbed the blanket to wrap around himself; then he saw something glinting on the floor in the low light, a bright white-blue sparkle like a tiny star. He reached down and picked it up.

The cigarette lighter: old-fashioned, either a replica or maybe an antique, forbidden on a U-Star as part of standard protocol (no naked flames). Ida flipped the cap, shook it—nearly full—then flicked the wheel. The flame was short and shone brightly in the twilight.

"Ludmila?"

Ida's eyes flicked toward the space radio. It was on, the blue light shining. But the speaker was dead. Suddenly Ida missed the hiss and pop and crackle.

"Ludmila, are you there?"

Nothing. Ida dropped into the chair in front of the table. He adjusted the set, altering the volume, the gain, the everything.

Silence.

Ida swore and quickly pulled the radio set toward him so he could access the back panel. Nothing. It was all the same, all the jumpers were in the right place, the tune controls aligned. He pushed the box back and ran a finger over the manual controls on the front. All fine.

Ludmila was gone.

Ida pushed away from the table with a shout, allowing the momentum to spin his chair around and around, his face in his hands.

Had she ever been there? Maybe she'd been a product of his imagination, a voice conjured from the dark shadows of his mind. Maybe she'd never answered back. Nobody else had heard her, after all. Ida wasn't even sure now that he'd told Izanami it.

Maybe he was cracking up. Maybe he already had. Maybe the same thing had happened to DeJohn before he vanished. Being alone in the dark could break a man.

But . . . no, he'd *seen* her. She'd been there, an apparition, a warning. And Carter had seen her too, earlier. He'd described the red CCCP insignia on her spacesuit.

Ida flicked the lighter closed and swore.

The blue light of the subspace radio. Ludmila. She *was* real, and she was connected to whatever was going on aboard the station. Ida knew that now—she'd died when her capsule burned up a thousand years ago; what was left was an echo in subspace, some part of her personality imprinted on the fabric of that bizarre dimension. Intelligent, self-aware survival after death. A ghost in the machine. And right now, the only person—alive or dead—who knew what was going on.

He waved his hand in the air above the space radio. The blue light flickered as the set recognized his commands and the three-dimensional holographic control panel materialized in the air. Ida began scrolling through frequencies; every few seconds the radio auto-locked onto something, but it was all garbage, the signal destroyed by the interference from Shadow.

He searched, lower and lower. Ludmila's signal had been at the very bottom of the set's range, where it shouldn't even have been able to pick anything up: subspace, where the frequencies were thin and the signals weak, meshing with the background noise of the dimension itself.

Finally he was there, and the voices died down to be replaced by the roaring ocean of white noise that was so familiar, the roil of metallic static tinged with danger. He sighed and sat back, letting the sound roll over him and bounce around the room.

He was close. Close to her, he knew it.

He opened his eyes and scrolled farther, the noise, the poisonous, hypnotic, *addictive* pulse of subspace ebbing and flowing like a tidal current.

There. He jerked his head up. The patterns in the static had changed. Another signal, buried deep in the roaring. His eyes narrowed in concentration as he tried to focus on the sounds.

More pops and crackles and . . . a voice. His back went straight.

Ludmila.

He pulled himself closer to the table and yanked the radio closer to him so it practically hugged his chest. He carefully scanned the region he was tuned to.

"Ludmila? Ludmila, can you hear me? Come in, please."

Something there, scrambled. A woman's voice.

Ida's heart raced. The answer was within reach.

"Ludmila? It's Ida. You're very faint. Can you hear me? Over?"

"Ma . . Y . . . this . . . ty . . ."

More fine-tuning. The voice started to pull itself together like a jigsaw. A woman, yes, but the accent . . . Ida frowned.

"Ludmila?"

"Mayday . . . mayday . . . mayday . . ."

Ida gasped, hands busy on the ethereal control panel. "This is the U-Star *Coast City,*" he said, his training kicking in. "Please state the nature of your emergency."

The static surged like a wave, and the voice was lost. Ida tuned some more, rotating an invisible dial between finger and thumb.

"Come in, please. Ludmila, is that you?"

He knew it wasn't. When the voice returned, it was loud and crystal clear. His heart raced and there was a cold, hard ball in his stomach.

"Mayday, mayday, this is the P-Prof *Bloom County* requesting urgent assistance. We are drifting and need rescue. Mayday, mayday."

Zia Hollywood, surely not more than a few million klicks away. Ida wasn't sure what the *Bloom County*'s speed was, or how long he'd been out, but the ship couldn't have left any more than a few hours ago, at the very most.

"*Bloom County,* this is Captain Cleveland aboard the U-Star *Coast City.* Zia, it's me, Ida. What's happened? Where are you?"

Static lapped at Ida's ears like waves rolling on a beach. There was something else buried under the aural junk, and Ida realized it was Zia crying.

"Ida? Ida, help us. Help us, please."

"We're coming, Zia. Hold tight."

Ida stood, the blanket falling away as he sprinted out of his cabin.

Zia said something else, but it was lost in the interference. It popped and crackled and fizzed in the empty room.

Izanami stepped from the shadows, her eyes blue spinning diamonds of night. With each slow step she took toward the table, the white noise pulsed.

"Who's there? Ida? Ida?" Zia's voice came thinly over the air.

Izanami stepped up to the table.

"They're all dead, Ida. All of them. They were taken. They're dead."

Izanami waved a skeletally thin arm over the radio set. The static roared as her hand approached the receiver, and the last sound that came over the speakers before the set overloaded and turned itself off was Zia Hollywood, alone in her spaceship, screaming.

36

Darkness. Darkness and sound; enveloping, surrounding, penetrating. Pink noise and square waves and saw waves. Nothing random, nothing natural. A pattern: information, data. A *code.*

The language of machines.

Frequency modulation. The machine was awake.

Ahí estás, Carminita.

The roar of the ocean. The roar of language, ancient, artificial. Alien.

The sound was all around her and it was inside her. Nobody could hear it except her. This was what she was born for, born to do. A gift, a wild talent honed by training, polished and sharpened until it became a tool, until the tool became a weapon.

And she was the best of the best.

Contact has been established. Contact has been established.

In the darkness, Carmina Serra smiled and turned over on the hard floor.

In the darkness, the machine clicked and whirred and lights flashed, once, twice, and then went out.

AOKIGAHARA AND THE GIRL WITH BLUE EYES

She was there the next day too, standing by the tall pines that marked the edge of Aokigahara, the Sea of Trees. Tsutomu stood by the well and watched her for a while. Behind the forest, Fuji's perfect cone pierced a sky that was blue and clear. It was still cold that day, unseasonably so; the water from the well was so cold, it should be frozen, Tsutomu thought as he filled the two buckets and lifted their yoke onto his shoulders. Some in the village said it was the falling star that had brought the cold, but at this, most laughed.

And then she was there, watching him. For five days she had watched in silence. He didn't hear or see her arrive, or see her leave, for that matter. She never spoke and never seemed to move. She was wearing white, and her eyes were blue and bright, but Tsutomu knew that was just the strange cold playing tricks. People didn't have blue eyes.

He bent down to adjust his load, and when he looked up, she was gone and the forest was once more empty and silent. A cold wind blew across the black rocky ground and Tsutomu turned to start the long trek back to the village. Maybe today he would tell the elders at the village and they could go and ask the daimyo. The daimyo would know what it meant.

The girl had appeared the morning after the star fell from the heavens. The star roared as it fell, as loud as the scream of a shisa, and everyone came out to look toward Fuji. Perhaps the mountain was angry, angry as it had been before, when the gods rained fire on the Earth and turned the sky thick and black with rage.

But the mountain was still and in the morning the air was cold, like the winter so recently passed had returned anew. Tsutomu was sent by his mother to the well, and there he had seen her for the first time. Except she hadn't been a girl then, not on the first day. She was a . . . thing, something white, a light and a shape that slid along the ground and then stopped by the edge of the trees.

He had been surprised and wondered if perhaps he should have been afraid. Aokigahara wasn't cursed, not really, but it was said there were caves lost within the trees, caves in which *things* lived, things that slept but which sometimes woke, and when they did, they fed on those foolish enough to venture beyond the pines, into the forest proper. He wondered if the shape was one of the cave-things, but it didn't move from the edge of the forest and then it was gone, so perhaps he hadn't seen anything at all.

On the second day he returned and so did the shape. This time it stood, and it had arms and legs but no face. It stood by the tree and even though it had no eyes, Tsutomu knew it was watching him. He watched it too, and then between the blink of an eye it was gone and he was alone with his task.

On the third day he returned and she was there, dressed in white, by the tree. Now it had become a girl, no older than he, with long black hair like his. But her eyes were different. They were blue, and in the shadow cast by the tree they shone like coals.

Tsutomu returned home with his water and felt afraid. His mother hit him when he didn't do his chores properly, but he was distracted by his thoughts of the girl in the forest. And then his mother was distracted by the news that quickly spread through the village.

Hideo and Aki had gone. The two brothers had not returned from the woods. Not Aokigahara, never Aokigahara, of course. The other woods, the ones on the other side of the hill where the soil was rich and brown and where birds still sang. Hideo and Aki went to cut wood and never returned. That night a search party set out: seven men, with torches and axes and swords.

They were the next to go. When morning broke, the village was less nine souls.

But his mother still needed water and Tsutomu still made the journey, even though it took him near to the Sea of Trees and its strange black ground. Near to where they said the star had fallen over Fuji.

That night, Tsutomu told his mother about the girl, and she hit him over the head and told him not to talk of such things. But there was something in her voice and in her face that Tsutomu hadn't seen before. Later, when the village was quiet, he lay awake, unable to get the image of the girl's burning blue eyes from his mind, and he heard his mother talking to someone. It was Kanbe, one of the elders. He sat in silence as his mother spoke, and he left without a word. In the dark his mother wept and Tsutomu went to bed.

The next day the girl was there. Tsutomu set his empty pails down beside the well, and across the rocky ground the two watched each other.

Then she smiled, and there was suddenly someone with her. A young man, standing behind her in the shadow of the fir tree.

Aki.

Tsutomu recognized him at once, and he called out, but Aki moved back into the trees, into the shadows. The girl with blue eyes was smiling, and Tsutomu knew something was wrong. That day he ran back to the village without his pails of water.

And he returned, and soon, leading the men of the village to the edge of Aokigahara. Kanbe said Tsutomu was a good boy and had done well, and patted him on the shoulder as he drew his own sword and ordered his men to follow him into the Sea of Trees.

Tsutomu waited, and eventually the day drew in and the sun set behind Fuji, making it look in the cold clear sky as though the mountain were alight. And as the stars came out, there was a sound in the air, a roaring, like a waterfall, like the sound of the ocean far away, like the scream of a shisa. More stars fell that night. Tsutomu counted four, and then he screamed and turned as the girl stepped out of the forest, her blue eyes burning in the dark and behind her a group of men, more than two, more than seven, more than twenty. Aki and Hideo and the men of the search party and Kanbe's warriors. But now they were clad in dark shadows spun from the night itself, and when they stepped from the trees they moved quickly, flashing in time with the blink of Tsutomu's eyes.

Tsutomu ran back to the village, the demons of Aokigahara and those that had fallen from the heavens close on his heels.

PART FOUR

AND YOU WILL KNOW US BY THE TRAIL OF DEAD

37

She was quiet after that.

Gone were the black coveralls, the tight singlet. Instead she sat in the canteen, clad in a spare pair of blue and green marine overalls. They were the right size and she carried them off like the supermodel she might have been had her father been in a different business. Ida was perhaps surprised the most by the fact that she had covered up her bare arms—the right, which was elegant and beautiful and tanned, and the left, which was covered by the ever-changing tattoo.

That was just as well. He didn't like the tattoo, the way it damn well knew what was going on around it, and the way it moved to suit the mood of its wearer and, perhaps, those around her.

But gone too were the big square mining goggles, and without them, Zia Hollywood's face looked small. Here was her real face, naked, unhidden. And she looked unhappy. People tended to avoid her, though that wasn't difficult, considering Ida had counted less than a hundred remaining crew members. On a U-Star the size of the *Coast City,* that figure gave a very low population density per square kilometer.

The station's shuttle, the U-Star *Magenta,* had picked her up. Ida had wanted to travel on board the small patrol boat himself, but when he finally got the comms Flyeye on the bridge to tune in on the *Bloom County*'s distress call, echoing weakly over the lightspeed link, interference crawling over the signal only just strong enough to be picked up by the station, the *Magenta* was already out on its regular, routine patrol. Ida was happy at the response speed, but he knew that if he hadn't been scanning the illegal subspace frequencies, Zia's signal would never have been picked up.

King didn't seem to care anymore. He dragged himself from the ready room, but he seemed tired, worn out, just the shell of the blustering bureaucrat he had been. It was understandable; everyone left on the *Coast City* was on edge, going through their routines, carrying out their duties on autopilot as the undercurrent of tension and fear steadily grew. They were stuck, isolated. There was nothing left to do but just survive until the final transport arrived.

As for Zia's signal, King blamed it on Shadow, and perhaps he was right. The *Bloom County* sure as hell wasn't equipped to transmit over subspace, so what Ida had picked up was a freak occurrence, a random reflection of Zia's call. The light of Shadow, said King. Does strange things. Bounces a signal around to God knows where.

That Ida wasn't going to argue with. He thought back to Ludmila and wondered if she had had any reality outside of his own head.

And now Zia Hollywood sat in the canteen. She sat still and in silence, although she ate standard protein rations. They were a far cry from the real food stowed on the *Bloom County,* but after the marines dragged her screaming from her ship—which had been towed back to the station and now sat in the spare shuttle bay—she had refused to return to it.

Ida had stayed by her side since she returned to the station. She was unhurt, according to the automated scan in the infirmary. She and King had a debriefing that lasted no time at all, Ida waiting in the bridge, watching the closed door of the ready room. He wondered what they had talked about, or if Zia had said anything at all. As she exited the ready room, King stood in the doorway and glanced at Ida. Ida frowned, and the marshal, pale, looking ill, turned around and closed the door behind him.

Ida watched Zia in the canteen. There were four others eating: a pair at a nearby table and two others spread out across the large communal space.

He needed to talk to her. She *knew;* he was sure of it. There was something out there, hiding in the purple space between the station and the star. She'd seen it. As Ida had. As Carter had. And maybe like Serra and Sen and the others, before they'd vanished.

Ida grimaced. Now Zia was also alone. Her message had been no exaggeration. Her remaining crew members were gone, just like the others. Just like *that.*

When the *Magenta* docked, according to Private Chan—Ida had eventually cornered the Ops on the bridge as he waited—the *Bloom County*'s distress call had stopped. Zia, the only person aboard, was busy at the control deck erasing things—erasing everything, as it turned out: navigation files, computer drives, and the ship's log, all of it. All illegal acts: treason, conspiracy with the enemy, an automatic death penalty. But so intent had Zia been on her task that she had actually asked the marines to wait a moment before they realized what she, celebrity or not, was doing.

She hadn't finished erasing the log, so when the marines picked her up by her arms and carried her off the bridge, the screaming had begun.

Aboard the *Coast City,* the screaming stopped and the silence began. As she sat in the canteen, her eyes moved, left to right, up and down, like she was sitting in the dark, waiting for the bogeyman to appear. She'd moved her chosen table closer to the far wall, with just enough of a gap to allow her to squeeze in, her back hard against the wall. Even so, she'd occasionally look over her shoulder at the featureless gray green expanse behind her, like there might have been someone—some*thing*—there.

Ida frowned. He had no idea what to do.

"Are you going to talk to her?"

He jumped and his plastic chair banged against the floor of the canteen. Izanami was right behind him, had practically whispered in his ear. Across the canteen Zia started at the sound, but then she returned to her curled posture and closed her eyes.

Ida lowered his voice to a whisper. "I'm not sure she wants to talk. Not to me, or to anyone. She's traumatized."

Izanami straightened up, and didn't make any attempt to

lower her voice. "With no medic on board, I doubt she's getting the proper care. She needs counseling."

Ida turned and looked up at Izanami. Clad in her medical whites, she had her arms folded and was regarding Zia like a specimen to be observed.

"Jesus Christ," Ida hissed through his teeth. "You're a medic. Can't you do something?"

Izanami smiled, still looking at Zia. "I'm not part of the crew, Ida."

Ida tapped the table impatiently. Keeping his voice down became an effort. "I'm pretty sure the marshal won't care if you volunteer your services."

Izanami turned to Ida. Ida didn't like her look or her smile. Something at the back of his head began to hurt. Her eyes, they were blue ovals, burning bright, drawing Ida in. As he looked, his vision unfocused and her eyes seemed to spin with stars.

"Who are you talking to?"

Ida blinked and jerked his head around. At the opposite table, Zia still sat, knees drawn to her chest, heels balanced on the lip of her chair. Her arms were wrapped around her shins in a way that didn't look comfortable.

"Zia Hollywood, welcome back," said Ida with a nervous smile that didn't convey the relief he felt inside. "I was just thinking that Izanami here could help out. She's not part of the crew, but she's the only medic we have until the last transport arrives." He laughed lightly but it sounded fake, so he stopped.

Zia smiled, a shadow of her former, knowing grin. "And you think *I* need help?"

Ida's smile flickered. "I'm sorry?"

Zia lowered her legs to the floor and leaned forward on the table. "Who's Izanami?"

Ida gestured to the Japanese woman standing at his shoulder. "You weren't introduced before? Zia Hollywood, Izanami, the best neuro-psycho-physio-therapist this side of Fleetspace."

Izanami bowed slightly.

Zia's smile turned to a frown, and she rubbed her forehead with the heel of one hand. "You hum it, I'll play it."

"Ah. Pardon?" Ida felt confused.

Zia shrugged an apology. Then just said, "Okay."

"Okay?"

Zia nodded. "Okay."

Ida frowned. He had an odd feeling that he was listening in to only half of a conversation he'd thought he was taking part in. He glanced up at Izanami beside him. "Ah . . . is there anything you can do for Ms. Hollywood at the moment?"

"Ida—"

"Yes, Ms. Hollywood?"

"Who are you talking to?"

"Ah . . . what?"

Ida watched as Zia's eyes moved to the space over his right shoulder, and then back to his face. "There's no one there."

Ida coughed. His headache was starting to return. He turned and looked up at Izanami. The Japanese woman began to laugh, and this time her eyes really did spin into pools of pale blue light, scattered with diamonds and stardust. As Ida watched, she melted away, becoming nothing more than a black-silhouetted afterimage on the insides of his eyelids.

"You feeling okay, Cap'n?"

Ida stared at where Izanami had stood. When he blinked, he could see her outline, but then even that faded. He closed his eyes and screwed them tight and wished the shadows away.

"Oh, just fine, thanks," he said. Then he took a breath as the world wobbled around him. "Zia, what happened?"

The miner sighed. Ida's eyes were still closed, and he never wanted to open them again.

"We were attacked. They—"

"No, no. Before. Here. What made you leave early?"

"Oh, that," said Zia lightly. "I saw my father. He's dead, you know. Ain't that just a fine thing."

Ida exhaled, long and slow.

"He was with someone." Zia's voice got higher, and the words got faster. Ida shook his head, refusing to look. "There was a woman, behind him."

Something clicked in the back of Ida's mind. "A woman in an old-fashioned spacesuit?"

"No. She was laughing. Dressed in white."

Ida's stomach did a flip-flop. He opened his eyes to stop a sudden wave of dizziness and felt hot bile in the back of his throat.

He turned to look at Zia. She was sitting calmly, but her eyes were wide and she was as white as a ghost.

"Describe her."

Zia's eyes unfocused; although they remained on Ida, he didn't think she was looking at him. "A white dress, short. She had black hair, long and straight. And blue eyes, pale baby blue, very bright, as bright as the stars. She was Asian . . . Japanese or Korean. I don't know."

Ida swore, and prayed to whatever gods were listening to stop the walls of the world crashing in on him.

"She knew my name," said Zia. "She called to me. My father asked me to come with them. And then . . . then they changed. Became . . . I don't know. . . . She's looking for someone too. She asked me if I knew where he is. . . ."

She was shaking now. Ida watched her lips move, although no more words came. Then she squinted and pressed the heel on one hand to her forehead. Ida knew exactly how she felt.

Ida's mind raced. "When I found you," he said quickly, "before you left, that's what you said. You said, 'Where is he, where is he.' Who?"

Zia shook her head. "I don't remember that," she said. She closed her eyes tight, and her shivering increased.

He stood, pushing his own chair away noisily. She jumped at the sound but didn't open her eyes. He walked over, ignoring the way the shadows moved like smoke in the corners of the canteen. The others in the canteen had gone; Ida just hoped they had walked out rather than been . . . *taken*.

Ida grabbed Zia's shoulders firmly, not sure what he could do other than to let her know that he was here, that *they* were here, together.

Zia screwed her eyes even tighter, and her hands shot up and grabbed Ida's forearms. She squeezed them hard, hard enough to hurt. Ida grimaced, but then she opened her eyes.

"They're watching," she said, her voice a whisper.

38

They locked themselves in Ida's cabin.

It had been hours, although it was hard to tell, as Ida's override meant the automatic night cycle never came. For all he knew, the station was back in twilight outside. There was no way in hell he was opening the door to check. The frosted window was just a vaguely orange opaque square.

The shadows were dangerous, and they weren't *just* shadows. This they both agreed on.

And Izanami. He'd seen her fade with his own eyes—the only pair of eyes, he now realized, that had *ever* seen her aboard the *Coast City*. Individual ideas and suspicions finally coalesced in his mind, forming a picture he didn't want to see. The malfunctioning life scan that never showed Izanami in his cabin. Interrupted conversations. Izanami's insistence that she wasn't a member of the crew. It turned out she was telling the truth.

"Not sure we can count on the marshal, either."

Zia looked up. "Do you think he's a part of it all?"

"Maybe," said Ida. "He knows something, I'm sure of that. He's been frosty since I arrived, but the last few cycles it's like he's not really here."

Zia shrugged. "Sure he isn't just buckling under the pressure?"

"No, seems more than that. Like he's . . . I don't know, fighting something."

"What about the others on the station?"

"Well, there aren't many left. At first it was just a bug in the manifest, but now we know that crew members are disappearing. Carter and Serra were taken in the last group I know of. Six in total."

"Like Dathan and my crew."

Ida grimaced. "Like them."

"What happened to your commandant?"

"When I arrived, he'd already gone. But he'd managed to get off the station *between* transports."

"And we know what that means. . . ." Zia sucked in a breath.

"Maybe he was the first," said Ida. "I heard his voice later—calling over the comms, during the first security breach. The ready room was attacked at the same time."

Zia shifted forward on the bed. "But if you heard him, doesn't that mean that he's . . . well, that he's out there, somewhere? And the others too?"

"Maybe," said Ida. He rubbed his face and spoke into his hands. "They were taken to somewhere. Maybe they're still alive." He dropped his hands and watched the dark space under the bed, thinking back again to Zia's account of what happened on board the *Bloom County*.

Zia's crew were not only highly trained but highly paid as well, and when their employer told them to jump, they asked for the height, distance, and details of the bonus remuneration offered for the task. At Zia's call, Fathead had dragged Ivanhoe from the infirmary and readied the *Bloom County* without pause or hesitation. When Zia joined them, they didn't speak unless spoken to, and the trio blasted off to their destination ahead of the official schedule. Neither Ivanhoe nor Fathead asked about Dathan, and Zia didn't mention him. The only thing her two remaining crew members knew was that they had to get away from the *Coast City* quickly. As well as miners and pilots, they were bodyguards and minders. Zia Hollywood was one of the most valuable private assets in all of Fleetspace, and protecting her was a deep-drilled instinct. They were a three-person self-preservation society. Saving their asses was the prime directive.

The slowrock field lay on the other side of Shadow, forming a cone-shaped spearhead of rubble powering cometlike toward the star. Perhaps it *had* been a comet, one that had broken up into its constituent rocky parts. Over time, if it wasn't engulfed by Shadow or vaporized by its strange light, the field might separate until its density became almost undetectable in deep space. This was the bounty Zia had come to hunt. The readings were off the chart, making it a prize worth crossing half of Fleetspace for. Each bite-sized chunk, according to the data leaked to them by the Fleet, was composed nearly entirely of lucanol, a metalloid that, when combined with herculanium, made an alloy strong enough to construct the core filaments of quickspace drivers. Half a standard mining hopper of rough lucanol ore could buy you a small asteroid of your own to call home. A *Bloom County* skipful of the pure metalloid meant Zia could buy the Fleet itself. Maybe that was her plan.

Or had been. The new plan was to get the hell out of the system, and fast. The question of the slowrocks hadn't even entered Zia's mind until they came up close, quite by accident as the ship curled away from the *Coast City* and into a trajectory that would take them away from Shadow. The ship's mining computer got a lock immediately and started pumping out data without anyone even asking.

The readings were impossible. Lucanol was soft, reactive; that's what made it so rare. So either the readings were subject to the same kind of weird interference from Shadow's radiation . . . or they were being altered somehow. Deliberately.

Two hours later and they'd swung by the leading asteroid's perihelion, the debris looming large on portside as they raced along. It was black, solid, a single triangular wedge, something too perfect, too regular.

Then the Spiderbaby under their feet had begun to twitch. It was unusual, but within bounds, and probably due to the light of Shadow as they skimmed its corona. They were close to the star, far closer than they'd intended.

The first sign of trouble had been when the movement of the mining legs had stopped. A minute later and the *Bloom County*'s engines cut out. As Fathead scrambled over the controls, they went dark. The control cabin cooled a little as the environment systems shut off, giving Zia's crew just a few hours of life support before they'd freeze in space.

Ivanhoe worked on the engines while Zia and Fathead got the backup systems online. Minimal life support and emergency communications, and that was it. The flight deck was dark, lit by the weak orange of the emergency communications screen and the dull purple glow of open space coming in from the large window. Zia thanked the stars for their light, and the fact that their ship had real windows and wasn't reliant on viewscreens.

She'd seen it first. The starlight itself began to dim. The debris field was suddenly looming over them, much closer than it should have been as they'd drifted unpowered toward it. It was impossible. Unless the great black nothing had steered toward them itself.

As Zia watched, the window went dark, leaving them with nothing but a sick orange from the comms channel as it sprang to life, filling the cabin with a hard-edged roar of white noise. Then the light from even that dimmed, as the darkness came through the window and filled the cabin like a heavy, black gas being poured into a tank.

Fumbling in total blackness, Zia called for Ivanhoe and Fathead. At first her crew replied and Zia walked and stumbled, arms outstretched, the small flight deck impossibly large in the dark. Then the voices stopped. Zia realized then that there had been three responses: Ivanhoe and Fathead . . . and Dathan.

As her eyes adjusted, Zia could make out the comms deck ahead of her. The shadows seemed to move at her peripheral vision, black-on-black shapes darting out of sight as she turned her head.

And then a new voice.

Ida scratched his chin and looked at Zia. "The voice," he said, waiting a moment as Zia tilted her head quizzically "You sure it was him?"

"On the ship?" she asked. "I know my own father's voice."

Ida nodded.

"Y'know," she continued, "the very worst thing is that part of me wanted to go."

Ida glanced at her. She sat cross-legged on the bed, her hands twisting at the sheets beneath her. Ida thought back to his own temptation on board the *Coast City,* in the lifetime ago before Zia had even arrived.

Zia sighed. "D'ya think it was really him?"

Ida didn't answer for a long time. "It's either him, or something pretending to be him. Whatever it—they—are, they can get into our heads, into our minds."

"You've seen 'em too?"

Ida nodded. "I saw someone who was once very close to me."

"Dead?"

"Yes, she's dead."

They sat in silence for a while. The shadows under the bed didn't move.

"I couldn't go," said Zia eventually.

"No," said Ida. "Me neither."

"He said he'd forgive me if I came."

Ida looked up. "Forgive you for what?"

But Zia wouldn't meet his eye.

39

Quicker than Ida expected, Zia changed the subject. "What makes us so damned special?"

"What do you mean?"

Zia shifted on the bed. She let go of the bunched-up sheets and began gesturing with her hands as she spoke. It was good, Ida thought. She was focusing on solutions, not problems. First step: gather data.

"They . . . she . . . *it*—whatever 'it' is—is taking people. The marines, the commandant, everyone on this fucked-up space station. Fathead, Ivanhoe, Dathan. And who knows who else. How far does this go? How many people have vanished in Fleet-space?"

Ida frowned. "And this station—or rather, this system—is at the center of it. Must be. Shadow is an unusual star, unique. Can't be a coincidence. But more important, what are people being taken for? There must be a reason."

They fell into silence. For once, Ida didn't miss the static roar from the space radio.

Zia unfolded her legs and lay down. She looked at the ceiling, and then crossed her arms behind her head.

"So did all those fancy heroics really happen?" Zia asked.

Ida coughed, his train of thought broken. "Tau Retore? Yes," he said, looking at her. "It really happened."

"So if you saved an entire planet from the Spiders, how does something like that get erased from Fleet records? What I heard, the war isn't exactly going as planned. Win like that would be shouted to the heavens."

Ida felt the panic rise in his chest. Just a twitch, just enough to remind him that, weirdness aboard the good ship *Coast City* aside, there was plenty else wrong with the universe.

Unless, of course, they were connected. Another unlikely coincidence.

Zia sat up and leaned forward. "No, I'm serious. Damn thing never happened. I ain't never heard of it, and none of my crew have either. It's just smoke in the wind."

"What do you mean? How do you know?"

Zia raised an eyebrow. "I checked. We were given a crew list of the station when our stop was approved. It was a long flight. I looked you up."

"What did you find, exactly?"

Zia shook her head. "Nothing, is what. There ain't nothing recorded. No name, no rank. No record. Nothing at all. You, my fine Cap'n, don't even exist."

Ida laughed, but the laugh died and he stared at the floor. Zia shook her head again. "But . . ."

"But?"

"Well, here you are." said Zia.

"Here I am," said Ida, throwing his hands open. "Stuck out in the back end of nowhere, surrounded by shadows and ghosts. Tau Retore happened, and then I was sent here."

Zia blew out a lungful of air between pursed lips. "And so was I. . . ."

Ida straightened in his chair. "You were sent here? I thought you came of your own free will?"

"Well, yeah, but only because we were fed the readings on the slowrock field. If those readings didn't show a whole damn gold mine floating out in this fucked-up system, I wouldn't be here."

"So you and me—"

Zia nodded. "Yep."

"We were both sent here."

"Yep."

"For a reason."

"Yep."

Ida stretched his arms in front of him, turning his palms inside out and cracking his interlocked fingers. Then a thought occurred. A connection made, perhaps.

"I'm not the only one who seems to have dropped out of the history books," he said.

"What do you mean?"

Ida spun the chair around slowly until he was facing the table. There sat the space radio, narrow and silver, the blue light now a dead black dot on the front of its shiny casing.

"I made contact with someone with this thing, just before you arrived. Caught a signal and then found a voice."

"And?"

"And she didn't exist. The transmission was from a thousand years ago and had been bouncing around subspace ever since. The sender was a cosmonaut, mid-twentieth century. Except not one that ever existed."

"Subspace?" There was something in Zia's voice that made Ida want to sit very still, very still indeed.

"Ah . . . yes. Some malfunction, the set could pick up—"

"God*damn* it, Ida, you've been listening to a voice from fucking *subspace*?"

Ida turned the chair, surprised at Zia's outburst. But there was something else too, that cold fear again, somewhere in his middle. He could feel his heart kick up a gear and he watched Zia. She was sitting up on the bed again, her eyes wide.

Zia swore. "Jesus, Ida, don't you *know* about subspace? Didn't the Fleet send you a fucking memo?"

"I know subspace frequencies are illegal, but—"

"Holy crap. You know why they're illegal?"

"Um." Ida's breathing was fast and shallow. The quiet, creeping fear grew and grew and grew. His mind tripped over memories, trying desperately to claw back what he'd learned at the academy, searching for answers, facts that he felt he should know but that he now realized hadn't been taught by the Fleet, not to him, not to anyone.

The stories. The half-remembered whispers about subspace, about how it was dangerous. About what lurked below. Hellspace.

"Um," he said again. His throat was dry.

Zia sighed and slouched back on the bed, shaking her head. "Things," she said, like that explained everything.

Ida let out a breath and blinked. "Things?"

"Damn *it*." Zia rubbed her forehead. "There are things in subspace. Bad things. You could say they lived there, but they're not alive, not really. They live in subspace and deeper too. Hellspace. *Fuck*."

Ida swallowed. His throat felt tight, the sound so terribly loud in his ears.

Hellspace.

He rolled the word around in his head, trying to convince himself that this conversation wasn't happening.

"You've been hanging out in too many colonial bars, Ms. Hollywood," he said quietly, but he knew he was out of his depth.

She turned her head to look at him. "Don't you get it?"

"Get what?"

"Subspace is illegal because the *things* that live in it got out once. Followed a signal. Back in the early days of the Fleet, before the Spiders. Took everything we had to push them back, and then subspace was closed off. No one went near."

Ida stared at her, his mind racing. Then he shook his head and laughed—a nervous reaction, the laugh of a man afraid, one that quickly died in his throat. He closed his eyes and held up a hand.

"And how do you know this, exactly? I'm an officer of the Fleet and even I don't know—"

"Look," said Zia, and Ida opened his eyes. She was leaning forward, toward him. "Someone like me, I get to see a lot of things. *Hear* a lot of things. There's a whole lot of people, all of them want a piece—of me, of my money, everything. They want my ship, they want to be friends, business partners, lovers. When you're rich and you're famous, then doors get opened, you get to go places most people don't, not even officers of the Fleet. And you're told things, shown things."

Ida shook his head. "Told things?"

"You'd be amazed at how willing people are to talk when they think they can impress someone like me, thinking it can get them *in,* get them close. Trust me when I say that those stories about subspace and what lives there are all true."

Ida sighed. He believed her. And if what Zia said was true, then the stories, the rumors, about subspace and hellspace, they didn't even cover the half of it. There was something out there. Something the Fleet didn't want anybody to know about. Something that, Ida thought, was now stirring.

"What if they're coming back?" he asked. "What if someone made contact again and what if they're following the signal back out?"

"Then we're all dead," said Zia.

40

With only a fraction of operational personnel on board, the *Coast City*'s hangar was a rare hive of activity, the crew busying themselves with familiar routines and protocols, trying to keep order, control. It was the Fleet's way. In the middle of a difficult and protracted war, this is what you did. You carried on, and maybe you told yourself that the final transport was already on the way, having headed out early, as soon as the lightspeed link had gone down.

Maybe. But until it arrived, the crew went about their duties, running the hangar bay and readying the station's shuttle for its routine patrol of the system.

The *Magenta* was illuminated from underneath by landing lights, and from their position behind a row of empty loading pallets, Ida and Zia could see two crew members sitting at the flight controls.

Ida and Zia had a plan.

In his cabin, they'd patched into the comm channel between the bridge and the hangar and listened to the chatter between the two for nearly half a cycle before heading down to the hangar. Most of the talk had been the usual system updates and routine checks, although they learned that two crew members who were due on duty were not responding to calls and couldn't be found on the hub. More taken.

They waited, listening, until the *Coast City* cycled into night. The dark was dangerous, the domain of Izanami—the thing from subspace, Ida now knew. But they needed to risk it, because they had to get to the *Magenta*. Their objective was clear.

The debris field.

They'd pored over data from Zia's wrist computer. The field

density readings originally supplied by the Fleet said the slow-rocks were pure lucanol—a gold mine, as Zia had said, but one that was impossible. As Zia had seen firsthand, whatever was floating out on the other side of Shadow wasn't a cluster of asteroids at all, but something regular, artificial: a single solid object, one that had moved toward the *Bloom County* like it was being piloted.

Piloted . . . like a ship. Another coincidence too far. The answers lay aboard it. Ida knew it and Zia knew it and they also knew they had to get back there. They were clean out of options on the station.

They couldn't take the *Bloom County,* not without people noticing. And Zia had refused to get back on board it. But the *Magenta* was due to make its regular, routine flight. If they could get on board and bide their time as it went about its patrol, they could take the ship over and be at the target before anyone knew about it. Before Izanami knew what they were doing.

Space Piracy 101: Secrete yourselves on board, wait for the ship to blast off, count to a thousand, and, bingo, hijack. It was so simple, it might just work.

Zia was restless, and Ida didn't blame her. They'd been crouched behind the loading trays for more than an hour now. Ida flexed his fingers around the Yuri-G's molded grip; he looked back at the shuttle.

"Here we go," he whispered.

Two hangar crewmen walked down the *Magenta*'s rear ramp and headed toward the stairs leading to the control room, a large cuboid box that hung on one side of the bay. They looked tense, anxious, and as they walked in silence they both glanced around, into the shadows that draped the far corners of the hangar. The *Coast City*'s crew was holding on, but only just. The Fleet's training was good.

"Preflight routine complete," said Ida into Zia's ear. "The shuttle will be empty for less than an hour."

Zia nodded. Ida watched the hangar crew move up the stairs and into the control room. After disappearing around a door, they appeared briefly at the main window as they completed their check, then turned and walked out of view. Just to be sure, Ida counted to twenty, but nobody reappeared on the stairs.

"Go!"

Zia led the way, crawling around the side of the loader and then ducking under the superficial railing that separated the cargo pads from the shuttle landing pad. She dropped the three-foot step silently, and ran at a crouch to hide behind the *Magenta*'s front landing gear. She waited a count of three, just like Ida had told her, and then scrambled to the rear of the craft and up the exit ramp.

Ida counted to three himself, and then followed her pattern—railing, check; landing gear, check; exit ramp, and on.

Time to fly.

She fell asleep in the power conduit. Pressed against her, Ida watched as her gentle breathing bounced a strand of her hair against her lips. He hoped she wasn't dreaming.

They'd been in the conduit hatch for only another twenty minutes before Ida heard the *Magenta*'s crew climb the ramp and fire up the craft. Ida had tried to count the footfalls on the floor above their heads, but he hadn't been expecting so many and had lost count. It sounded like a whole squad of marines. Ida knew that this was standard, in case the *Magenta* was required to board any other craft in the vicinity, but with the *Coast City* at such reduced manpower and the Shadow system devoid of other activity, Ida was surprised they kept to the book. With King still locked away in the ready room, and without orders to the contrary, Ida imagined the marine commander on duty was just trying to do his job as usual.

The *Magenta*'s orbit would be short. It was pure routine. A single perfunctory sweep of the station's immediate vicinity, maybe out to a quarter of a million klicks. It crossed Ida's mind that the shuttle might not even be fully fueled, without enough energy to get them to the debris field on the other side of Shadow. But if everything was being run to routine, then there was no reason to suspect the shuttle didn't have a full complement of power cells loaded. More than enough to get them halfway to Earth, let alone a few million klicks around to the far side of the sun.

Ida pressed an ear against the metal panel beside him. The shuttle was small with disproportionately large engines, and every part of the ship was a perfect sounding board. He listened, and with a lifetime's expertise judged the engine throttle. It was slowing, imperceptibly at first, the drone of the drive system lowering in pitch as the shuttle approached the far side of its orbit. There the *Magenta* would pause, like a ball at the top of a throw, and then curve a graceful arc back around to the other side of the *Coast City*. The edge of the orbit was their target. It was nearly time.

He nudged Zia, and she jerked awake. He shushed her and raised the Yuri-G as much as he could in the cramped compartment.

"Did you dream?" he asked, hooking fingers into the webbed underside of the floor panel that was their temporary ceiling.

"No," she said, but she said it too quickly and Ida guessed it was a lie.

The short corridor that connected the shuttle's hold to the bridge was empty. The flight was running as normal: marines strapped into their flight harnesses in the troop compartment next to the hold, the four crew members (pilot and copilot, navigator and commander) in the cockpit flying the shuttle around the preset course, mostly on automatic, mostly in silence.

Ida crept down the corridor. The cockpit door was open, and he could see the back of the pilot and copilot's Flyeye helmets. The commander's chair was just out of sight, as was the navigator's.

Zia moved silently back along the corridor, toward the troop compartment. Ida glanced over his shoulder and nodded, and then watched as she gingerly pressed the hatch lock. The troop compartment would now open only from the outside, but they probably had only a minute before one of the marines on the other side noticed the lock status light change color. Zia returned to her position behind Ida and tapped his shoulder.

Eyes front, Ida held up a hand, three fingers extended. At an even pace, he dropped them one by one; when his fist was closed, he darted forward, Zia on his tail.

He burst into the cockpit so quickly that at first only the commander and navigator registered his entrance. Both reacted in the same way, moving quickly to leave their posts and confront the intruder, but Ida held the Yuri-G in front of him and they both gently sank back into their seats, hands raised in surrender. Zia saw the pilot twist his head around and jumped forward, pulling the commander's pistol from his belt as she passed him and moving around to stand directly in front of the freestanding control console, in the gap between it and the forward viewscreen.

"Everybody stand for the man with the gun in his hand!" she said, waving her own weapon at the pilot and copilot.

With Zia covering the cabin, Ida lowered the Yuri-G to a more comfortable position to cover the commander and navigator, now standing as Zia had instructed.

"This is treason," the commander said, looking Ida up and down. Ida recognized him from the groups that used to congregate back in the canteen. A noncommissioned officer—he couldn't remember the name—but one who had taken pleasure in sending sour looks over to Ida when they were in the same room. Ida squeezed the grip of the Yuri-G just that little bit harder.

"Technically, you're right. But you might just thank me later." Ida moved around the chairs at a sidestep so he was standing in front of the navigator. He wiggled the end of his gun, gesturing to the pair to return to their seats. He heard the Flyeyes move behind him, Zia having followed his lead.

"Navigator, you've got some new coordinates."

The copilot saw it first. They'd reached the approximate location recorded on Zia's wrist computer; dead ahead the violet disk of Shadow burned in the center of the viewscreen. As Ida watched tendrils of blackness curl from the pale star's horizon, he was grateful the *Magenta* had no actual windows.

And there it was: in the middle of the sun's disk, impossibly close, a black mark that could have been a sunspot if Shadow had had any blemishes at all on its perfect purple skin. Ida followed the copilot's pointed finger and watched with growing dread as the black shape steadily grew in size. Like it was coming out of the star itself.

The pilot had his eyes glued to the forward sensor reading, Zia standing at his shoulder. There, at least, the object was as large as life. Dead ahead.

"Is that another ship?" asked the *Magenta*'s commander. Ida glanced at the man and scratched his own temple with the barrel of the Yuri-G, safety on, before turning back to the screen.

The safety had been on the gun for a while now. Ida was pleased that the crew had offered only a token resistance. You didn't argue with a man holding a Yuri-G. The marines locked in their troop compartment had been somewhat more vocal, at least until Zia had told the commander in no uncertain terms to kill the comm link with them. The manifest scanner on the control desk showed the life signs of ten marines sitting in their harnesses along each wall, one standing by the door, and one pacing up and down.

"Now what?" The shuttle commander drummed his fingers on the arm of his chair behind Ida.

"We get close, we find out what that thing is," said Zia.

The commander snorted. "That's some plan, lady."

Ida turned back to the screen. "The best defense is a good offense. Didn't they teach you anything at the Fleet academy?"

The pilot slowed the *Magenta*. The black wedge ahead of them got larger, nothing but a deep silhouette against the star behind.

Then he leaned forward over the control desk and flicked a couple of switches. "Manifest failure, sir."

The commander creaked forward in his chair, but Ida waved at him to sit back. Ida stood over the pilot's shoulder and glanced over the screens.

"Report, pilot."

"Sir . . . ah, I mean . . ."

The commander began drumming his fingers on his chair again. "Go ahead, pilot," he said.

"Tracing the fault now, sir. Manifest scanner is misreporting crew complement."

Zia stepped forward to look at the pilot's display, upside down, from the other side of the console. She and Ida exchanged a look.

Ida looked at the small square display panel set into the desk that provided the standard shuttle system report. Energy reserve, engine throttle, and core temperature, a dozen other mysterious technical parameters that Ida once understood but had long since lost interest in. As on the *Coast City,* the ship's crew were counted among its equipment and assets.

The troop compartment was showing as empty. Where twelve life signs had showed as bright orange dots just a few moments before, the diagrammatic representation of the harnesses showed them all to be empty. Gone also were the two others who had been moving around.

An alarm chimed, and the pilot flicked another switch. The status screen refreshed, but the manifest report stayed the same.

"Can't trace any computer fault, sir. Trying again."

Ida's felt his skin grow cold. "Don't bother," he said. "That's not a fault. That's the manifest report."

Zia swore. The commander leapt out of his chair and pulled on Ida's shoulder, ignoring his own gun held in Zia's rising arm.

"Do you know what's going on, Captain Cleveland?"

Ida licked his dry lips and glanced at the viewscreen. Shadow was nearly all gone, obscured by the black nothing.

Another alarm pierced the silence, loud enough for everyone on the bridge to jump. The commander grabbed Ida's arm instinctively, but Ida threw him off and pushed him back into his chair. The commander made to stand again, but found the hot end of the Yuri-G in his face, the red light in the barrel indicating that the safety was now off.

The high, bell-like alert sounded again. Ida looked at the ceiling.

"U-Star *Magenta,* stand down and prepare for boarding. Do not deviate from your present heading or we will open fire."

The voice that came over the ship-to-ship was female, the accent American. Ida spun around and leaned on the control desk to stare at the viewscreen. There was nothing but an empty black void, lit violet white at the edges of the screen.

The alarm sounded a third time.

"Proximity alert, Commander," said the pilot, and the commander, navigator, Ida, and Zia all crowded the pilot's position. The sensory display showed the object ahead, close enough now to get a better reading: an oblong outline, with a set of three narrow trapezoids at one of the short ends. The shape was distinctive, recognizable to any Fleet personnel.

"What is it?" Zia looked at Ida.

Ida stood and pointed at the forward viewscreen. As the object blotted out the light of Shadow behind it, it came into sharp relief. It was metallic, silver, and very close, filling the entire forward view. "It's a U-Star. A Destroyer."

The ship-to-ship sprang into life again.

"U-Star *Magenta,* boarding in two minutes. Present yourselves at the loading bay air lock immediately, seated with hands on heads. Failure to comply will result in the use of lethal force."

The *Magenta*'s commander swung back into his chair and snapped on the personal comm panel in the arm.

"This is Commander Van Buren of the U-Star *Magenta*. You will identify yourselves."

There was a pause, but the comm channel stayed open. Very faintly, at the edge of hearing, there was a rustle, something like dry paper being crushed or someone walking on small pebbles. Or static, white noise, the sound of nothing. The sound of subspace.

"U-Star *Magenta,* this is Commodore Manutius of the U-Star *Carcosa*. You will stand down and prepare for boarding in one minute."

"Jesus Christ have mercy on our souls," Ida whispered.

Zia's eyes were wide. "Ida, what is it?"

Ida looked at Zia, and then the others on the bridge.

"That's not Manutius, and that's not the *Carcosa*. It can't be."

The commander and navigator exchanged an uncertain look. Zia stepped up and stared into Ida's eyes.

"How do you know?" she asked.

"Because," Ida said, "the *Carcosa* was lost with all hands."

"What? When?"

"At Tau Retore. The *Carcosa* was my ship."

41

They were kept in darkness for a long time. There was no need for hoods or blindfolds. As soon as the *Carcosa* had docked and its marines stormed the *Magenta,* the lights were killed. Standard Fleet procedure—the marines could all see in their helmets, but the prisoners were blind. In a way it was worse than being hooded, because with eyes wide in the total dark, the blackness became almost a physical object. It loomed right into your face, giving you the feeling you were about to walk into something very hard and very painful.

That was the idea. At the end of a march through darkness, prisoners would be in a state of near-panic. Considering most of the Fleet's human prisoners were civilians, it worked too. Captured Fleet troops were unusual, and for Ida and the crew of the *Magenta,* it was unpleasant but quite bearable if you knew what to do. Except as far as Ida and Zia were concerned, the darkness itself was dangerous, and both of them kept their eyes screwed tight.

Ida had got only a glimpse of the boarding marines. They were what he expected, helmeted and armored, although he wasn't sure if it was his imagination or whether there was something else there, something dark, misty, smokelike; shadows that moved with the men.

When the lights came on, Ida needed a few moments to adjust to the glare. Sitting cross-legged on a hard ceramic floor, Ida guessed before he opened his eyes that the flare of lights meant that they were now in the holding cages. He lowered his hands from behind his head and looked around.

Zia was sitting immediately on his left, the commander, navigator, and two pilots behind them. They were sitting in the middle of a cube made of a fine wire mesh, big enough to stand in and walk around comfortably with a dozen people in it. But if you strayed too close to the mesh, you could hear an unsettling buzzing coming from the wire. The walls of a standard Fleet holding cube were not something you would want to touch.

Their cube sat in a large, hangarlike room, and was just one of fifty identical cages set in a regular grid, filling the space. The holding cells of a large U-Star. Ida knew the design well. It looked like half the cages were occupied, a sea of blue and olive figures, some standing, most sitting, blinking as they adjusted to the lights. All Fleet personnel.

"So they got you in the end, huh?"

Ida turned at the voice. The next cube along the grid was three meters away, and was occupied by a full dozen. Hands on hips, Carter stood as close to the wire wall as he could. He shook his head, like a teacher disappointed with a problem student yet again.

Ida unfolded himself and stood quickly. "Carter, you're alive?" He ran his eyes over the other occupants of the cage. "Serra! Your whole squad?"

Carter nodded, and behind him, Serra's face broke into a grin. Carter looked back over his squad, and when he turned back to Ida, his smile curled up at the corners. He really seemed pleased to see Ida. Or, Ida thought, pleased to see his nemesis stuck in the same position he was.

"All but DeJohn," said the marine. He nodded, indicating the other cages. "They're keeping about half of us here."

Zia paced their cage, looking out at the other cubes. Ida knew what she was looking for.

"No sign?"

Zia's pace increased. She swore impatiently. "Nothing."

"They were here," said Carter.

Zia stepped up close to the wire next to Ida. "Were? You've seen them?"

"Your crew? You betcha. They were taken out a while ago. Look."

He pointed.

Between the holding cubes and the far wall of the room was a gap of twenty meters, an assembly ground where prisoners were brought in and sorted—in the dark—into their cube groups. The far wall had a large double door, the very one Ida's group had been marched through. This had now opened again, and a group of people walked in. Ida's jaw loosened as he watched.

They didn't really walk. They *glided,* their movements somehow in time with the blinking of Ida's eyelids. One moment they were ten meters away, the next five, and yet they didn't seem to be moving at all. Their edges were blurry and seemed to streak away to the left, like a faint smoke trail being pulled in a nonexistent wind, like the shadow figures he'd seen on the station—like the marines who had boarded the *Magenta.* Except these were no shadows; they were people.

In single file, ten figures—eight men and two women—traveled across the assembly space

Carter folded his arms as he watched. "Looks like they're coming to get some more."

As the people approached, their forms shimmered like the guttering flame of the lighter in Ida's pocket. Ida found himself stepping back from the wall of the cage. Were they still people at all?

They were all Fleet marines. None of Zia's missing crew were among them.

Ida looked at Carter, but the marine just shook his head. Serra caught Ida's eye, and she nodded, just slightly before quickly looking away. Ida frowned, unsure what she was trying to tell him.

The figures separated, each heading toward a different cube, including Ida's. As the shadow-man approached, Ida could read the name tag stitched onto the marine's fatigues.

"Garfield? Garfield, it's me, Cleveland? Remember?"

The marine that had been Garfield made no indication he knew Ida was there. Close up, he looked as real as anyone, except for an odd halo of darkness that seemed to outline him, a shadow clinging to his figure.

Zia joined Ida at the wire, peering closely at the marine. "What the hell's happened to them?"

Ida stood. "Carter?"

Carter was sitting on the floor again, next to Serra. A shadow-man had gone to their cage too, and was now standing, waiting for something.

"Every now and then they take people out," he said. "Sometimes they come back, and when they do, they're like this. Sometimes we don't see them again."

"What about the crew of this U-Star?"

"What crew? We haven't seen nobody."

"The commodore spoke to us, on board the shuttle."

"You came here by shuttle?"

Behind Ida, Commander Van Buren laughed. "Not by choice."

Ida sighed, but Van Buren told Carter about the hijacking.

Carter laughed. "The resourceful Captain Cleveland. Maybe you really are a hero."

Ida ignored him "What did you see on the station, marine?" he asked.

Carter stopped laughing, and the smile dropped from his face. "What?"

"Back on the station," said Ida, "I saw someone . . . someone I knew. Someone I know is dead. She spoke to me, even."

Carter's eyes widened.

Zia stepped forward. "So did I."

Ida smiled at Carter. "So, who did you see? What sent you to the infirmary for a whole cycle?"

"I don't think that's your business, *sir.*"

"Come on!" Ida slapped his arms against the sides of his legs in frustration. "You may not have noticed, but we're kinda in trouble here."

Carter sat back down. Ida looked around and realized the shadow-men had vanished. He turned, looking around his cage.

The two pilots from the *Magenta* had gone, leaving him and Zia with Van Buren and the navigator. In Carter's cage, half of the dozen prisoners had vanished. Ida was pleased to see Serra was still there. She sat cross-legged on the floor, her eyes closed, a smile playing over her lips. She was a psi-marine. Maybe she'd gone too, inside her head.

Ida whistled. "Hey, listen to me. You know where we are? We're on a ghost ship, marine. The U-Star *Carcosa*. That's a ship I happen to know very well. It was my ship, the one that didn't make it through quickspace when we hit Tau Retore."

Carter shuffled on the hard floor. "Didn't you say the *Boston Brand* was your ship?"

Ida shook his head. "I was on the *Boston Brand,* but I was assigned to the *Carcosa*. Commodore Manutius and I swapped commands for our attack. The *Boston Brand* had a few tricks the *Carcosa* didn't, and I wanted the *Boston Brand* out in front."

Zia's eyes widened. "So if you'd stayed on your own ship—"

"Yes," said Ida. He cast his eye over the interior of the hangar they were now in. "If I had stayed on the *Carcosa,* I'd be dead. Or not, as the case may be."

He raised his hand to the cage wall and felt the tingle of the charge play across his palm.

"Only delaying the inevitable," said Carter quietly. Ida pulled his hand away from the wall of the cage and turned to the marine. Sitting on the floor behind him, Serra laughed and opened her eyes.

"You okay, marine?" asked Ida.

Serra nodded. Carter uncurled himself to turn around, and peered into her face. Serra smiled again.

"It's okay," she said. "She won't get it."

Carter jerked back in surprise. "What?"

"The shadow demon. She thinks she has her prize within her grasp, but she doesn't."

Carter leaned forward and snapped his fingers in front of Serra's face. "Hey! Snap out of it. You've been funny since we got here."

Serra blinked, and her smile dropped away. She scooted back on her hands, shaking her head.

"She's here," she said, and then she screamed, and then the lights went out.

42

The dark was absolute, abyssal. Around him, Ida heard the other prisoners murmur and move in their cages.

"What's going on?" Zia at his shoulder.

"No clue." Carter in the other cage. From the same direction, Serra's breathing, quick, fearful.

Ida held his breath as he heard something else. Footfalls. He stood as still as he could, trying to locate the sound in the dark. Someone was walking between their cage and the one holding Carter and Serra's group.

"Hello?" His voice sounded uncomfortably loud. The footsteps continued, coming around to the front of his cage.

"Who is it?" Zia had her hand on the small of his back. Ida shook his head, then realized nobody could see him.

"Serra? You with us?"

"Yes." Her voice came softly from the other cage.

"Who's here? Izanami?" Perhaps Serra knew about her. Perhaps Izanami had made contact with her, a psi-marine. Perhaps Izanami had followed the signal Serra's mind had sent out into the dark.

Ida's thoughts turned to another kind of signal. Was . . . was he responsible?

"Who's Izanami?" asked Carter, breaking Ida's train of thought. Ida heard the squeak of Carter's boots and the rustle of his uniform as he stood up.

The footsteps were soft, rubbery, accompanied by a sliding sound, like someone wearing something bulky.

Ida turned over his shoulder. "Van Buren?"

"I'm here. Koch?"

The *Magenta*'s navigator confirmed he was still with them.

The footsteps stopped, right in front of them. Ida balled his hands into fists, not sure where to plant them and not sure there would be anything physical to hit. He closed his eyes to blot out the disorienting depth of the dark around them and concentrated on the sounds instead.

The buzzing of the cage's energized mesh walls increased gradually, like someone turning the gain of an antenna up. As the pitch increased, it began to break up into rough noise. White noise, like static, the rolling of an ocean. Ida felt his heart leap at the familiar sound.

The sound of—

There was a click, and then, "Ida."

A voice, far away but right in front of him. Tinny, thin, coming through an old-fashioned speaker. A female voice, accented. A voice brushed with interference.

Ida let out his held breath and choked in the process. He swallowed the ball of spit quickly.

"Ludmila?"

A ghost ship filled with . . . ghosts.

"Come," said Ludmila.

Ida opened his eyes. There was a light, yellowish orange, in front of him. He blinked and watched as the light moved, lighting up the cage. The light blinked, and then a brighter, white beam snapped on. A lantern, fixed to the left breast of the spacesuit.

Ludmila stood outside the cage, her golden visor catching enough light from her flashlight that Ida could see himself and Zia reflected in the mirrored surface, superimposed over other shapes that moved and swirled. It looked like the reflection of stars and a planet spinning beneath. The curve of the Earth.

Ida sighed. She was real, solid, a person in a spacesuit. The suit was some kind of metallic silver cloth, quilted in fat bands, with the red letters CCCP boldly printed across the chest. In one hand she held Ida's space radio, the light on the silver box a bright baby blue. With her other hand she reached forward to touch the cage. Ida watched, spellbound, as the silver fabric of her suit creased at the elbow as her arm moved, as her hand raised to show Ida the black fabric that covered the palm and underside of each finger—

Zia called out just as Ludmila's gauntlet touched the cage. There was a pop, and the entire framework of the cage flashed blue for a second. Zia flinched, but Ida stood rock still, watching himself in Ludmila's helmet.

Was there anyone there, behind the curve of the visor? Did Ludmila exist?

She withdrew her hand and turned, heading back to the holding bay entrance. "Come," she said, her voice crackling through the space radio.

Her pool of light was small but the floor was reflective enough for it to light a wide stretch of the hangar. Ida glanced over at Carter and saw the marine was watching Ludmila too. He could see her. They all could.

Ida pushed at the front of the cage. The mesh was warm and rough. He pushed again, and the door flicked open silently.

"Hey!"

Ida turned. Carter gesticulated at the cage around his group. Serra stood at his shoulder.

Zia pulled on Ida's sleeve. "We're going to need all the help we can get."

She was right.

"Ludmila!" he called. The flashlight's beam turned slowly until it was directed at them. Ida pointed at the other cage as the prisoners shielded their eyes.

"Can you release them?"

The light bobbed forward slowly. It was like she was walking against a high wind, or in low gravity. Maybe that was exactly what it was like, moving through a world you were not supposed to be in.

When she got to the cage, Ida watched as she touched the mesh. There was a flash, and Ludmila stepped back. Carter wasted no time in shoving the door open and releasing his squad.

"Come," said Ludmila. "There is not much time. The harvest has begun."

"What about the rest?" Carter gestured to the other cages that filled the holding zone. The shallow light of Ludmila's lantern caught the glittering eyes of those prisoners closest.

"We have no time," said the voice from the crackling speaker.

Carter began to protest but Ida raised his hands. "We'll come back for them. Let's just do as she says and see if we can't figure this mess out first."

He turned back to Ludmila, who was walking away at her infuriatingly slow pace. Ida, Zia, and the others followed, forming a single file as they quietly left the cells. Behind them, shouts erupted, the other prisoners protesting at being abandoned. Ida ignored them. He had no choice. None of them did.

They walked in the dark, Ludmila's lantern lighting the way, illuminating metal corridors in an eerie white yellow glow that bobbed up and down and left and right as she walked in her bulky suit. It felt like walking into a tomb, ancient and cold, except for the occasional wall panel with bright LED lights. Their footfalls were soft but they echoed oddly. It was as though the whole of the *Carcosa* had powered down to system minimum, the ghost hulk drifting toward its destination.

But it was real, all of it. It might have been dark, but it was solid. The metal floor, the walls. The same as any other Fleet U-Star. Ida touched the walls, trailing his fingers along the metal and plastic panels. Cool to the touch, as they would be on any ship. The metal was hard and shiny, with the finest of grains running horizontal to the floor. The rivets were perfect, almost seamless at the panel edges.

It was real. The *Carcosa* was part of the First Fleet Arrowhead. They'd all entered quickspace near Atoomi, and they'd all exited near Tau Retore—all, that is, except for the *Carcosa*. There was no engine failure. The ship had been taken, wholesale, as it sailed close to Izanami's domain. Ida's escape on the *Boston Brand* had been coincidental and, as he now realized, only temporary.

And Ludmila? She was right in front of him. He could reach out and touch her. He raised his arm to try but then changed his mind. She was real, as real as the passageway along which they now crept. A real person, taken a thousand years ago.

Zia's question resonated in Ida's mind: How many had been taken, and for how long? And the ultimate question—for what?

Ludmila's lantern beam diffused suddenly, and she stopped. They'd come to a larger space, a wide, low room. Ahead were a set of heavy doors. An air lock. Ludmila turned around, and Ida stared at himself and Zia and the rest of them in her golden visor. Her chest radio popped.

"This ship is now attached to the auxiliary docks of the space station. This will lead you back to it."

Zia stepped forward. "What? We can't just leave. We gotta spring the others, and find the ones they've taken away."

Ludmila said nothing. Zia's reflected face loomed as she leaned toward the cosmonaut, and then turned to Ida. Ida studied the reflection, lost in thought.

"It's not that easy, is it?" he said at last, eyes still on Ludmila's visor.

"The harvest has begun," said Ludmila. "She has enough power now to make her last moves before she returns. Time is short. We must act soon."

Carter gestured over his shoulder with a thumb. "We've got enough personnel locked away down there, and enough weapons on the station, to take this ship over from any hostile alien force, easily."

Ida watched it all in the helmet reflection.

"Ludmila?" he asked quietly. "They're not aliens, are they?"

"They are not anything," she said, the radio spitting the words out in a trebly squawk. "The Funayurei are neither alive nor dead. They are the souls of those lost at sea. They are her army. They wait, trapped like her, eager for release. And soon she will be free. She will, in turn, release her army, and her army will march."

Carter frowned. "This is no time for riddles, ma'am."

Zia exhaled softly. "Hellspace. She's talking about hellspace. That's where her army—these *Funayurei*—are."

A hundred thoughts entered Ida's head, all of them bad, all of them leading to the same conclusion.

"So that's where she takes them." He stared into the visor. "She's built an army, pulling people down from our world into hellspace. The souls of those lost at sea."

Zia caught his eye in the reflection. She looked very pale.

"I told you they were real."

Carter looked between Ida, Ludmila, and Zia. "What the hell are you talking about? Who is building an army? And what for?"

"*She* is," said Ludmila. Carter blinked and the crackling voice over the radio continued. "Izanami-no-Mikoto. She is almost here."

Ida shook his head. "But Izanami was my medic. She was on the station, looking after me."

"Shadow is *Ame-no-ukihashi,* the bridge between subspace and this universe. Here she could wait—still imprisoned, but able to move among you as her power grew."

Ida's heart raced. "How?" he asked. "How does her power grow?"

The radio clicked. "Before, she was nothing. A thing from subspace. Centuries ago she fell to the Earth and became Izanami-no-Mikoto. Others of her kind followed. Then she died, leaving only an echo in subspace where her husband, Izanagi, found her. She begged him to take her back into the world. She grew angry and tried to follow Izanagi out, but he sealed the gateway, trapping her forever."

"This is some fairy tale," said Carter. He huffed and folded his arms.

"Izanami vowed revenge. To rebuild herself and escape, she needs to eat a thousand souls a day. They nourish her, provide her with the energy to cross the bridge, to return."

Silence. The space radio crackled and Ida realized the truth. He turned to the others.

"The Fleet. They're in on it—they sent me here. You were tricked into coming," he said, looking at Zia before gesturing to Carter, Serra, Van Buren, Koch. "They were sent here too, as part of their tour." He turned back to Ludmila and looked at his own reflection. "We were *all* sent by the Fleet. The Fleet, who placed this station around a very particular and unusual star." Ida rubbed his chin. "And the war isn't going so well. . . ."

The space radio hissed and Ludmila spoke. "Izanami wields the power of subspace, if only she could be released."

"Are you out of your minds?" Carter stepped forward. "Are you saying that the Fleet sold us out to whatever it is trapped behind the star, in exchange for victory against the Spiders?"

Ida nodded. "The Psi-Marine Corps. Commandant Elbridge is from the Psi-Marine Corps. So are all the Fleet Admirals. The . . . whatever they are, the things that live in subspace, they escaped into the world once before, right?" He glanced at Zia. "And then the Fleet banned all subspace technology. But it was too late. They knew about what lived in subspace. They knew about Izanami."

Carter frowned. "So the Fleet cut a deal? This is insane."

"The souls she consumes become her army," said Ida. He looked up at the ceiling. "They even gave her a ship."

Zia swore, but Ida was already nodding. "And," he said, "the only Spider tech in human hands. The *Bloom County*."

Carter glanced at Ludmila. "And where does she fit in?"

Ida frowned. "The original incursion from subspace?"

Ludmila bowed her helmeted head.

"But there was no Fleet when she was taken," said Zia. "The Fleet wouldn't have been around for another, what, hundred years?"

"January the first, 2050," said Ida. "But there would have been records of the incursion—classified, but records all the same. And then the Fleet runs into trouble with the Spiders and the old project is opened up. The Psi-Marine Corps."

Ida turned to Serra. The psi-marine stood at the back of the group, her eyes downcast. She hadn't said a word since they left the cells. He remembered the odd look she gave him earlier, like she knew something.

She was smiling.

"They evacuated all of the psi-marines off the station," said Ida, taking a step toward her. "All except one."

The crackle of the space radio. "The commandant knew the plan," said Ludmila. "But he also knew that Izanami would not stop with the Spiders. She would destroy everything. All life is energy to be consumed."

Ida nodded. "So he was taken, but he made sure someone was left behind to fight. Someone with the right skills."

Serra looked up, her eyes bright in Ludmila's lantern light, but she didn't speak. Ludmila's voice crackled from behind Ida. "He ordered a psi-marine be left on board," she said. "The best psi-marine." Her helmet clicked as she turned toward Serra. "Is it ready?"

Serra nodded. "Almost."

"Good," said Ludmila.

Serra walked to the front of the group. "Come on," she said. "We need to get to the *Bloom County* before it's too late."

"The *Bloom County*?" asked Ida. Then he smiled. The only Spider tech in human hands, of course. "Right, let's go," he said, but when he turned around, there was no sign of Van Buren or Koch.

Carter cracked his knuckles. "Come on," he said, "before we disappear too."

43

"Sections Five and Six to embarkation point. Embarkation at oh-seven-oh-seven."

It was the third time the announcement had been broadcast to the crew of the *Coast City* since Ida's group had returned to the station, and it was just one of many instructions echoing over the internal comms. Ida was shocked to find the station's passageways glaringly bright, the hub alive with people—marines, Flyeyes, technicians, support staff. Everyone walking briskly in one direction. Ida knew the leftover crew of the *Coast City*—those who hadn't already been snatched by the Funayurei—must number only between fifty and one hundred, yet there appeared to be many more on the move. Such was the pace of the traffic that Ida feared they would be called out purely because they were walking slowly and uncertainly.

Ida, Zia, and Serra crouched at the corner of a side passageway as it curved away from the main thoroughfare. There was just enough cover provided by the curving wall that they could observe the main corridor without being seen. Ludmila had vanished as soon as they returned to the *Coast City*—Serra, in contact with her thanks to her remarkable abilities, telling the others that Ludmila hadn't wanted to slow them down. If the plan worked, she would meet them later. Ida asked what the plan was, exactly, but Serra just smiled. But he trusted her. He didn't have a choice.

"Here he is," said Zia. A moment later Carter was striding briskly toward them. He kept his eyes ahead and didn't slow as he approached, only turning and dropping into a crouch to scoot down the side passage when he had passed the group. They gathered around him.

"Everyone is being assembled for evacuation. They think the *Carcosa* is the last transport."

"But who are all these crew?" asked Zia. "There weren't this many when I arrived."

"They're from the *Carcosa,*" said Ida. "I recognize them."

"Well, that means you're a liability," said Carter. "They'll recognize you too."

Serra shook her head. "They're not really people anymore."

"The Funayurei," said Ida, and Serra nodded.

Zia frowned. "But what are they doing? There's hundreds of them."

"Remember what Ludmila said." Ida rested his artificial knee on the floor and leaned around the curve of the passage; the knee now ached constantly, a low, dull pain. In the main corridor there was no letup in the foot traffic. Fleet personnel passed by in a near-continuous stream.

"The harvest," said Zia. "They're swarming."

Serra shuddered. "Like locusts, coming in to eat."

"Something tells me the Fleet's plan isn't going so well," said Carter.

"We have to make sure ours does, then," said Zia. She turned to Serra. "You can talk to my ship?"

Serra nodded; Carter's eyebrow went up.

"I really wish you'd tell us what was going on," he said.

"Can't risk it," she said. "I'm talking to the ship, but others may be listening."

"Well, that's just dandy. So what do you want us to do?"

Serra scanned the corridor ahead of them. "Nothing at all," she said. "Just follow my lead. Help is nearby."

"Help?" Carter asked. Serra met his eye and nodded.

"You were wrong, before," she said.

Ida pursed his lips. "Wrong?"

"There are two members of the Psi-Marine Corps left aboard."

"Two?"

Serra nodded. "Two: me and the commandant, Elbridge. And this is our battle now."

Exhibit 1.1. Pro Forma Mail-Out Survey Budget, Cont'd.

V.	*Third Mailing* (480 nonrespondents receive additional mailing)		
	Prepare letter		
	Professional time		
	1 hour at $100/hour	$ 100	
	Typeset and print	100	
	Mailing service (processing mail-out—see first mailing for details)	75	
	Postage and return mail (100 returned)	260	
	Maintain inventory of respondents		
	1 hour at $20/hour	20	$555
VI.	*Data Reduction and Processing*		
	Clean returned questionnaires and postcode open-ended questions		
	5 hours at $100/hour	$ 500	
	15 hours at $20/hour	300	
	Computer input—approximately 100 keystrokes per questionnaire = 4,200 keystrokes; processed at 400 strokes/hour = 10.5 hours at $25/hour plus purchase of tapes	300	
	Computer input verification (should achieve 98% accuracy)	200	
	Computer processing and selection of appropriate statistical output (including 1 hour at $100/hour)	500[b]	$1,800
VII.	*Data Analysis and Report Preparation*		
	40 hours at $100/hour	$4,000	
	Typing, photocopying, binding	350	$4,350
VIII.	*Contingency for Unforeseen Occurrences*		$1,000
IX.	*Overhead Charges on Nonlabor-Related Expenditures*[c]		
	10% × $4,795		$ 480
	Total Cost		$16,415
	Mean Cost per Respondent		$ 41

[a] May be higher for specialized population list not generally available. Additional administrative research may be required.

[b] May vary depending upon access to mainframe/university affiliation.

[c] Labor expenses include overhead.

Exhibit 1.2. Pro Forma Telephone Survey Budget.

I.	*Initial Costs*		
	Same as for Exhibit 1.1		$5,100
II.	*General Costs*		
	Determine sample size and select sample in accordance with various sample selection techniques		
	5 hours at $100/hour	$ 500	
	Prepare initial sample lists for interviewers		
	2 hours at $20/hour	40	
	Type questionnaire		
	4 hours at $20/hour	80	
	Photocopy and staple questionnaire—6 pages[a] (500 questionnaires to compensate for incomplete interviews)	180	
	Miscellaneous supplies	100	$900
III.	*Recruitment, Selection, and Training of Interviewers*		
	Place recruitment advertisements		
	2 hours at $20/hour	$ 40	
	Cost (including printing of bulletins and classified advertisement fees)	150	
	Selection		
	Résumé review		
	2 hours at $100/hour	200	
	Schedule initial review of applicants		
	2 hours at $20/hour	40	
	Interview Applicants		
	5 hours at $100/hour	500	
	Train selected interviewers		
	4 hours at $100/hour	400	
	28 hours[b] at $12/hour (includes payroll tax)	336	$1,666
IV.	*Telephone Interview Process*		
	Interviews		
	200 hours at $12/hour	$2,400	
	Follow-up interviews: 10% recalled (4 calls per hour)		
	10 hours at $20/hour	200	
	Replacement sample selection/supervision		
	10 hours at $100/hour	1,000	
	2 hours at $20/hour	40	
	Telephone charges	200[c]	
V.	*Data Reduction and Processing*		
	Same as for Exhibit 1.1	$1,800	
VI.	*Data Analysis and Report Preparation*		
	Same as for Exhibit 1.1	$4,350	

Exhibit 1.2. Pro Forma Telephone Survey Budget, Cont'd.

VII.	*Contingency for Unforeseen Occurrences*		
	Same as for Exhibit 1.1	$1,000	
VIII.	*Overhead Charges—Nonlabor-Related Expenditures*[d]		
	10% × $2,380		$ 240
	Total Cost		$18,894
	Mean Cost per Respondent		$ 47

[a] Note difference from mail-out—no cover or return address is necessary.

[b] Assumption: Seven interviewers selected to complete 400 surveys within seven days. A work week of thirty hours per interviewer with two completed questionnaires per hour. Each interviewer to receive four hours training at one session.

[c] Can vary considerably based upon geographic range of interviews.

[d] Labor expenses include overhead factor.

Exhibit 1.3. Pro Forma In-Person Survey Budget.

I.	*Initial Costs*		
	Same as for Exhibits 1.1 and 1.2		$5,100
II.	*General Costs*		
	Same as for Exhibit 1.2		$ 900
III.	*Recruitment, Selection, and Training of Interviewers*		
	Place recruitment advertisements		
	Same as for Exhibit 1.2		$ 190
	Selection of interviewers		
	Same as for Exhbit 1.2	740	
	Training of interviewers		
	8 hours at $100/hour	800	
	56 hours[a] at $15/hour (includes payroll tax)	840	$2,570
IV.	*Preliminary Contact with Potential Respondents*		
	Prepare letter of introduction		
	2 hours at $100/hour	$200	
	1 hour at $20/hour	20	
	Photocopying	40	
	Professional mailing service—mailing list, labels	120	
	Mailing of letter (Mailing service—envelope inserts, folding, labeling, metering, sorting, bundling—$75/thousand)	75	
	2 hours at $20/hour	40	
	Postage—first class	100	$ 555

Exhibit 1.3. Pro Forma In-Person Survey Budget, Cont'd.

V.	*Telephone Contact with Potential Respondents*		
	100 hours[b] at $15/hour (4 contacts/hour)	$1,500	
	Telephone charges	100	$1,600
VI.	*Repeat Mail and Telephone Preliminary Contacts* (three additional iterations until 400 respondents are secured)		
	Sample selection (10 hours at $100/hour)	$1,000	
	Photocopying of letters	120	
	Mailing labels	360	
	Mailing of letters (mailing service)	225	
	Postage	300	
	Telephone contact		
	300 hours at $15/hour	4,500	
	Telephone charges	300	$6,805
VII.	*In-Person Interviews* (assume that 85% of scheduled appointments are maintained = 340 interviews)		
	680 hours[c] at $15/hour	$10,200	
	Mileage charges[d]	1,700	$11,900
VIII.	*Secure Additional Interviews for Unmet Appointments*		
	Sample selection (2 hours at $100/hour	$ 200	
	⅓ × $4,500 (see Section VI of Exhibit 1.2)	1,500	
	In-person interviews		
	120 hours at $15/hour	1,800	
	Mileage	300	$3,800
IX.	*Data Reduction and Processing*		
	Same as for Exhibits 1.1 and 1.2		$1,800
X.	*Data Analysis and Report Preparation*		
	Same as for Exhibits 1.1 and 1.2		$4,350
XI.	*Contingency for Unforeseen Occurrences*		$2,000
XII.	*Overhead on Nonlabor-Related Charges*[e]		
	10% × $7,355		$ 740
	Total Cost		$42,150
	Mean Cost per Respondent		$ 105

[a] Assumption: Seven interviewers selected to complete 400 surveys in thirty working days at the rate of two completed questionnaires per day—each interviewer to receive eight hours of training at one session. These thirty working days take place over an extended period in view of scheduling and sample replacement needs.

[b] Can vary considerably based upon geographic range of interviews.

[c] Assume two hours per interview, including travel time.

[d] Twenty miles round trip per interview at $.25/mile.

[e] Labor expenses include overhead factor.

expensive and should be used only when the other methods are found to be inadequate.

The researcher should also be aware that, generally speaking, smaller surveys will have a higher cost per respondent than larger surveys because of economies of scale that may accrue to larger studies. These economies of scale will be realized, for the most part, in terms of expenditures for professional time spent preparing the questionnaire, analyzing the data derived from its implementation, and preparing the final report. It would not be uncommon, for example, for very large sample surveys to realize cost reductions per respondent of up to 400 percent. In other words, the $41 per respondent mail-out cost in Exhibit 1.1 can conceivably be reduced to approximately $10 when the sample size is very large (for instance, several thousand) and highly concentrated.

Scheduling

Figures 1.1, 1.2, and 1.3 translate the pro forma budgets into feasible time schedules for the completion of the model projects, as described above.

Mail-out surveys will generally require three to four months for completion, much of which is due to the time allocated to the respondents for sending the completed questionnaires back to the researcher and to the printing of the questionnaires, which must be presented in a sophisticated and attractive manner.

The reader should note that the telephone survey represented in Exhibit 1.2 and Figure 1.2 is an extensive, original research study that requires substantial research in order to prepare the questionnaire. These figures also assume that a formal written report will be prepared based on the data obtained in the survey. By contrast, many telephone surveys, especially political opinion polls, require little or no advance planning or research and are reported to the client in the form of raw tabulated data. The time frame for the completion of such a survey is substantially shorter than that portrayed in

Figure 1.1. Time Schedule—Mail-Out Survey.

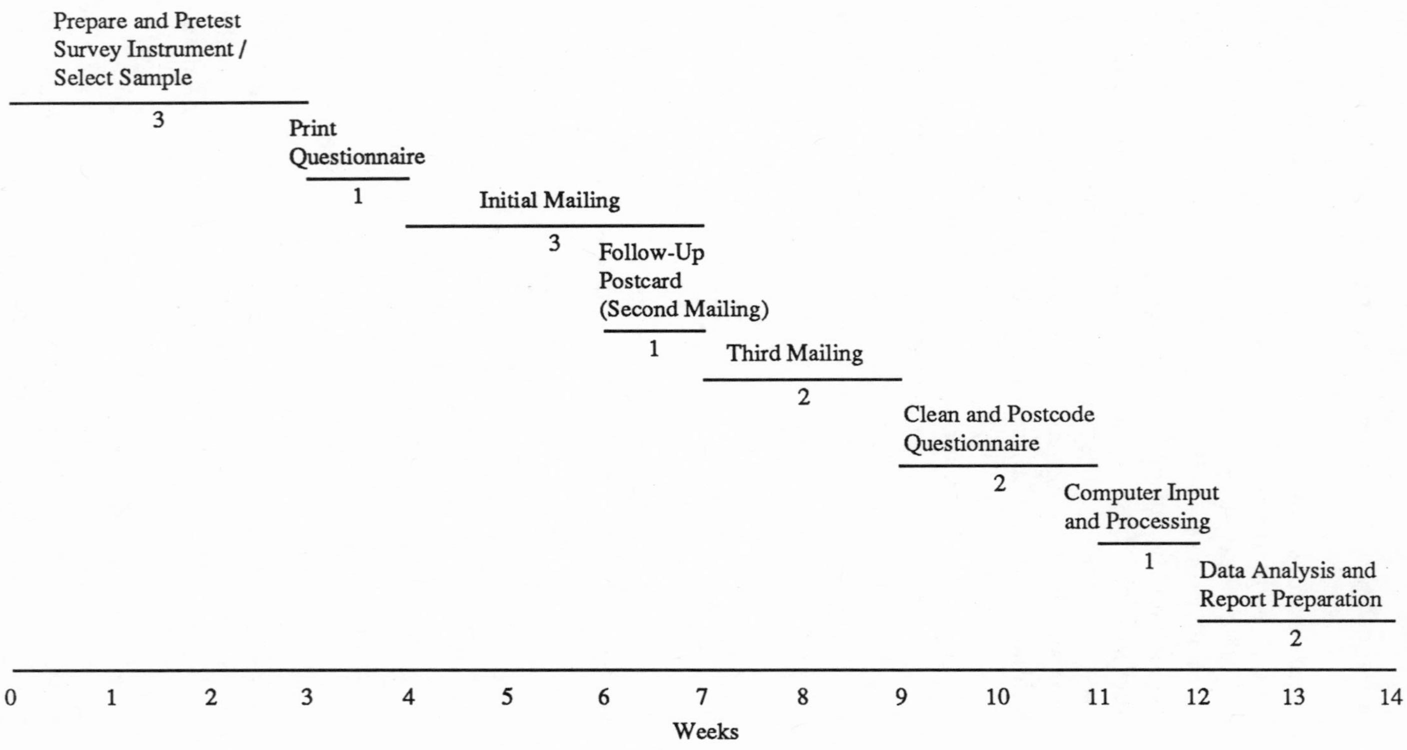

Figure 1.2. Time Schedule — Telephone Survey.

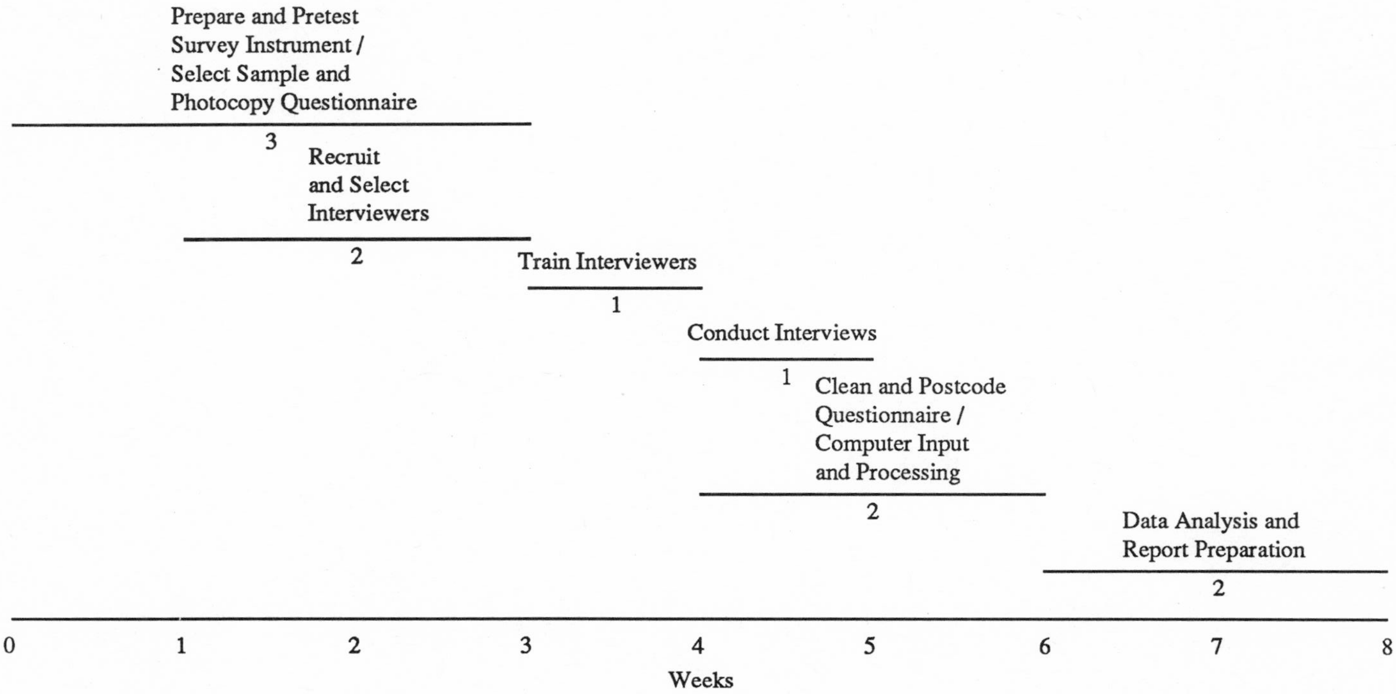

Prepare and Pretest Survey Instrument / Select Sample and Photocopy Questionnaire

3

Recruit and Select Interviewers

2

Train Interviewers

1

Conduct Interviews

1

Clean and Postcode Questionnaire / Computer Input and Processing

2

Data Analysis and Report Preparation

2

0 1 2 3 4 5 6 7 8

Weeks

Figure 1.3. Time Schedule—In-Person Survey.

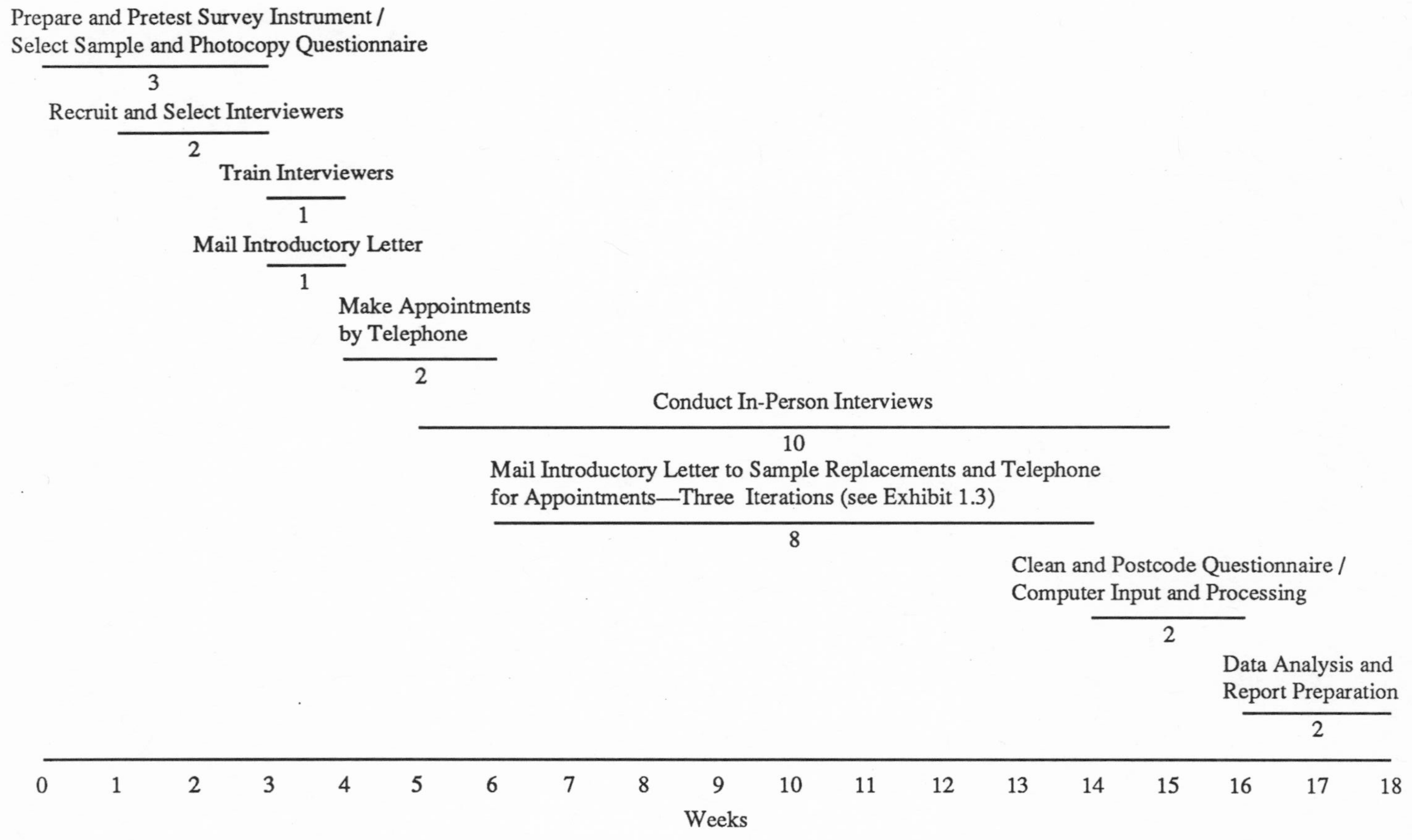

Prepare and Pretest Survey Instrument /
Select Sample and Photocopy Questionnaire
3
Recruit and Select Interviewers
2
Train Interviewers
1
Mail Introductory Letter
1
Make Appointments
by Telephone
2
Conduct In-Person Interviews
10
Mail Introductory Letter to Sample Replacements and Telephone
for Appointments—Three Iterations (see Exhibit 1.3)
8
Clean and Postcode Questionnaire /
Computer Input and Processing
2
Data Analysis and
Report Preparation
2

0 1 2 3 4 5 6 7 8 9 10 11 12 13 14 15 16 17 18

Weeks

Figure 1.2 and can, under such circumstances, be completed in less than two weeks.

The in-person survey process is the longest of the three interviewing techniques. This length occurs as a result of the time required to schedule the interviews and to conduct them on a face-to-face basis at a place and time convenient to both the respondent and the interviewer.

Conclusion

The primary purpose of this chapter has been to introduce sample survey research as a useful technique for gathering information. Its fundamental advantage is the capability of generalizing about an entire population by inference from a smaller portion of that population. Sample survey research can be applied to any facet of descriptive data, behavioral patterns, and attitudinal information about societal preferences and opinions.

PART ONE

Developing and Administering Questionnaires

Chapter 2

Designing Effective Questionnaires: Basic Guidelines

At the heart of survey research is the questionnaire development process. The key considerations in this process, including the placement of questions within the survey instrument and their format in terms of the method of implementation (telephone, mail-out, or in-person interviews), form the basis of this chapter. The discussion of these issues will take place within the context of sample questions and examples derived from actual questionnaires and survey instruments that have been implemented by the authors during the past several years.

The reader should be made aware that no questionnaire can be regarded as being ideal for soliciting all the information deemed necessary for a study. Most questionnaires have inherent advantages as well as inherent flaws. The researcher must use experience and professional judgment in constructing a series of questions that maximizes the advantages and minimizes the potential drawbacks. The guidelines detailed in this chapter recognize that there are a large number of considerations that the researcher must address in the process of questionnaire development. Sound questionnaire construction, therefore, is a highly developed art form within the structure of scientific inquiry.

In the initial stages of the survey research process, it is important to determine the relevant issues that bear upon the purpose of the research. Because social science research spans so many disciplines, it is impossible for any researcher to be fully knowledgeable in all the fields of study that might call upon survey research services and skills. In addressing the complex multidisciplinary nature of survey research in the social sciences, the researcher can respond in two ways.

First, the principal investigator often seeks to construct a team of experts who jointly plan and implement the research study. This team represents both technical expertise and substantive knowledge of the political, socioeconomic, and cultural environment associated with the project. Second, with or without such a research team in place, and as a prelude to the development of survey questions, the investigators must gather preliminary information about issues of importance from interested parties and key individuals. These issues will derive in whole or in part from the three types of information and requirements elaborated upon in Chapter One: description, behavior, and preference. This preliminary information is best generated in a group setting where issues and problems of relevance to the study can be debated, discussed, and refined openly and constructively. Foremost among these preliminary information-gathering techniques is the *focus group*. The focus group is a structured set of meetings in which individuals who are deemed to have some knowledge of the issues associated with the research study are brought together in roundtable discussions run by a group leader. The discussion that ensues should contribute significantly to an understanding of the key substantive issues necessary for the development of the questionnaire.

For instance, consumer research focus groups should consist of consumers, advertisers, and manufacturers of the particular goods and services involved. Focus groups on low-income housing might include low-income residents, representatives of local welfare agencies, redevelopment experts, and officials of the appropriate housing and planning agencies. A study of Native Americans who reside on reservations would require an even greater amount of preliminary information because of the unique character and specialized circumstances of reservation life. In this case, the focus group might consist of reservation residents, tribal leaders who understand Indian law and tribal customs and can relate them to outside researchers, Native American legal representatives, Bureau of Indian Affairs officials, and other parties who have some influence and involvement in reservation life.

At the conclusion of this preliminary information-gathering stage, the key issues that have emerged must be outlined and specified. This list of issues should be submitted to members of the discussion groups for clarification, confirmation, and, perhaps, further explanation. After this review, the researchers can prepare a draft questionnaire or survey instrument. If the research study has been commissioned by public agencies or private clients, as is frequently the case, the draft questionnaire should be reviewed by these parties for content and to ensure that questions are consistent with the objectives of the study.

Once the researcher is satisfied with the draft questionnaire, the next step is to conduct a *pretest*. A pretest is a small-scale implementation of the draft questionnaire that assesses such critical factors as:

- *Questionnaire clarity:* Are the questions understood by the respondents? The researchers may find that certain ambiguities exist that serve to confuse the respondent. Are the response choices sufficiently clear to elicit the desired information?
- *Questionnaire comprehensiveness:* Are the questions and response choices sufficiently comprehensive to cover a reasonably complete range of alternatives? The researchers may find that certain questions are irrelevant, incomplete, or

redundant and that the stated questions do not generate all the important information required for the study.

- *Questionnaire acceptability:* Such potential problems as excessive questionnaire length or questions that are perceived to invade the privacy of the respondents, as well as those that may abridge ethical or moral standards, must be identified and addressed by the researchers.

The sample size for the pretest is generally in the range of forty to fifty respondents. The researcher is not really interested in statistical accuracy; rather, interest centers upon feedback concerning the overall quality of the questionnaire's construction. Accordingly, the researcher will select respondents from among the working population but need not be concerned about selecting them through a random sampling procedure (Chapter Seven) or in accordance with sample size requirements as specified in Chapter Six. Because statistical inferences are not the primary intent of the pretest, the researcher can be particularly sensitive to cost and time considerations—hence, the relatively small number of respondents. For example, a study that attempts to obtain information about teenagers might conduct a pretest using one or two high school classes. The members of the classes are highly likely to be individuals in the appropriate age category, and the classes can be surveyed quickly, conveniently, and efficiently. Clearly, not all teenagers are high school students; therefore, the high school classes do not necessarily represent the exact characteristics of the respondents in the final study. However, this degree of precision in the selection of pretest respondents is not required. It is only required that the pretest respondents bear a reasonable resemblance to the study's actual working population.

Following the pretest, the researchers must revise the questions as needed. They may want to perform a further pretest if these revisions are extensive. Otherwise, the final questionnaire can be drafted and prepared for implementation in an actual study.

Introducing the Study

It is important to inform potential respondents about the purpose of the study in order to convey its importance and to alleviate any trepidations that potential respondents are likely to have. From the researcher's point of view, there is a need to convince potential respondents that their participation is useful both to the survey's sponsor or client and to the respondents themselves. Any fears that respondents may have regarding time and inconvenience, confidentiality, and safety should be allayed. The respondent must be assured that all answers are valuable—that there are no correct or incorrect responses.

An introductory statement should contain certain components. First, the *organization or agency* conducting the study should be mentioned, stating the relationship between the sponsoring institution and the potential respondent. A great deal of *credibility* can be gained for the study if the sponsor is a governmental body that in some way represents the respondent. An introduction that contains the following reference, for example, can be quite successful in establishing that credibility: "The City of Chicago is conducting a survey of residents in order to assess community opinions about services provided by your local police department."

A general statement establishing the *objectives and goals* of the study and the significance of the results to the respondents themselves should follow the client reference. Potential respondents are more likely to participate when they perceive that the study's findings will have direct impact upon their well-being. For example: "It is the purpose of this study to identify those needs that the citizens of the city feel should be addressed in order to maintain a peaceful and secure community."

The *basis of sample selection* should be made clear in order to make the respondent understand that there are no hidden agendas or undisclosed motivations behind the questionnaire. It should be mentioned whether the respondent was selected at random, or as a part of a census, or as a member of a purposive sample, and so forth, as appropriate. The *characteristics the respondent possesses* that led to inclusion in the sample should be clearly delineated. For example: "Chicago is particularly interested in the opinions of minority residents, and as such, you have been selected at random from a list of minority residents of the city."

The respondent must be assured that *participation is valued*, and that *answers are neither correct nor incorrect*. He or she must be assured that participation is strictly protected in terms of *confidentiality*. For example: "You should know that there are no right or wrong answers and that your responses will be treated confidentially. They will in no way be traceable to individual respondents."

Because of the more personal nature of telephone and in-person interviews, the interviewer should, as a matter of courtesy, identify himself or herself by name and obtain *permission* to proceed with the survey questions.

A telephone or in-person interview preamble might also include some *estimate of the time required* in order to complete the questionnaire. In the case of a mail-out questionnaire, the respondent should be able to judge this by direct observation of the instrument received in the mail.

A mail-out questionnaire should also include brief *return mail instructions*, such as, "Please drop your postage-paid, pre-addressed response in the mail by June 15."

Exhibit 2.1 is an example of a mail-out introduction that addresses the issues discussed above. The reader should verify that the preamble contains the essential information. Exhibit 2.2 is an example of a telephone interview introduction. Once again, the reader should cross-check the highlighted issues against the example.

Because of the personal, physical presence of the researcher in face-to-face interviewing, Exhibit 2.2 can be revised into a somewhat less formal, more conversational format in this type of questionnaire administration. Exhibit 2.3 reflects these changes.

Question Format

Open-Ended and Closed-Ended Questions

Most questions in a questionnaire have closed-ended response categories. Such questions provide a fixed list of alternative

Exhibit 2.1. Mail-Out Introduction.

Dear Baytown Resident [*applicable respondent characteristic*]:

We need your help [*participative value*]! The City of Baytown [*organization identification/credibility*] is conducting a survey of all households in the city [*basis of sample selection*]. The information you provide will be useful in helping your City Council provide services and programs to meet the needs and wishes of the residents [*goals/objectives of study*].

Please take the time to complete the enclosed questionnaire. There are no correct or incorrect responses, only your much-needed opinions [*neither right nor wrong*]. This form contains an identification number that will be used for follow-up purposes only. All responses will be treated confidentially and will in no way be traceable to individual respondents [*confidentiality*] once the survey process has been concluded. Please drop your postage-paid, preaddressed envelope in the mail by June 24 [*return mail instructions*].

Thank you for your assistance. We care what you think [*participative value*].

Sincerely,

Jean M. Wilson
Mayor [*credibility*]

---

responses and ask the respondent to select one or more of the alternatives as indicative of the best possible answer. In contrast, open-ended questions have no preexisting response categories and permit the respondent a great deal of latitude in verbalizing responses.

Advantages of Closed-Ended Questions. There are several advantages of closed-ended questions. One is that the set of alternative answers is uniform and therefore facilitates comparisons among the respondents. For purposes of data entry, this uniformity permits direct transferral of data from the questionnaire to the computer without intermediate stages. Another advantage is that the fixed list of response possibilities tends to make the question clearer to the respondent. A respondent who may otherwise be uncertain about the question can be enlightened as to its intent by the answer categories. Furthermore, such categories may, in fact, remind the respondent of alternatives that otherwise would not have been considered or would have been forgotten.

Exhibit 2.2. Telephone Introduction.

Good Evening (Afternoon/Morning). My name is Thomas Smith [*interviewer's name*]. The City of Flint [*organization identification/credibility*] is currently conducting a survey of Flint residents [*applicable respondent characteristic*] concerning the future development of library facilities for the City [*goals/objectives of study*].

Your household was selected at random [*basis of study selection*] to provide information and opinions regarding library facilities in the City of Flint.

We would greatly appreciate a small amount of your time [*time*] and your input on this important issue [*participative value*]. There are no correct or incorrect responses, so please feel free to express your opinions [*neither right nor wrong*]. Your responses will be treated confidentially and will in no way be traceable to you [*confidentiality*].

May I ask you a few short questions [*time/permission*]?

Exhibit 2.3. Introduction to In-Person Interviews.

Hello, my name is Janet Johnson [*interviewer name*]. The City of Flint [*organization identification/credibility*] is conducting a survey of its residents [*applicable respondent characteristic*] concerning the City's future development of library facilities [*goals/objectives of study*].

Your household was randomly selected [*basis of sample selection*] to provide information and opinions about library facilities.

Would you be willing to answer a few short questions [*time/permission*] on this important issue [*participative value*]? Please feel free to express your opinions because there are no correct or incorrect responses [*neither right nor wrong*].

The questionnaire form we complete today will not be marked in any way that would identify you [*confidentiality*].

The respondent's answers can be somewhat constrained by a fixed list of alternatives, which in turn limits extraneous and irrelevant responses. An example of a closed-ended question would be:

How much education do you have?

______Some high school or less

______High school graduate

______Some college

______Four-year-college graduate
______Postgraduate degree

If, instead, the question were open-ended, as shown below, the responses might not be quite so specific.

How much education do you have?

____

____

Sensitive issues frequently are better addressed by asking questions with a preestablished, implicitly "acceptable" category range rather than by asking someone to respond with specificity to an issue that might be considered to be particularly personal. For example, for medical purposes, an abortion clinic might require information about a client's history in terms of previous abortions. The question, "Have you ever had an abortion? If so, how many?" will tend to intimidate certain respondents who have had prior abortions and who perceive that abortion carries with it a strong social stigma. Their responses, therefore, might be biased toward minimizing the actual number. Recognizing that this tendency exists and always will in regard to socially sensitive issues, the researcher would improve response accuracy by constructing the question as follows:

How many abortions have you had?
______None
______One
______Two
______Three
______Four
______Five or more

Phrasing sensitive questions in this way, with alternative responses that extend significantly beyond normally expected behavior, implies that an accurate response to this question is not outside the realm of social acceptability, that many other young women may have similar histories, and that having had an abortion is not necessarily aberrant behavior.

Other types of sensitive questions may involve issues more closely associated with privacy than with social acceptability. This situation is encountered when the subject of a question is income. A respondent may very well feel that privacy is violated when she or he is asked "What is your annual household income?"

Giving alternative choices in the form of income ranges will tend to mitigate such feelings and will therefore generate a much higher level of response. The question about income is much better constructed to read:

> Please indicate the range that best describes your annual household income:
> ______Less than $15,000
> ______$15,000–$29,999
> ______$30,000–$44,999
> ______$45,000–$59,999
> ______$60,000 and above

Fixed responses are less onerous to the respondent, who will find it easier simply to choose an appropriate response than to construct one. Thus, use of fixed-alternative questions increases the likelihood that the response rate for the questions, in particular, and for the questionnaire, in general, will be higher.

Disadvantages of Closed-Ended Questions. There are, however, certain disadvantages of closed-ended questions that researchers should consider when developing a questionnaire. For example, there is always the possibility that the respondent is unsure of the best answer and may select one of the fixed responses randomly rather than in a thoughtful fashion. The advantage of ease of response, therefore, carries with it some negativity. In a similar vein, a respondent who misunderstands the question itself may also randomly select a response or may select an erroneous response. Open-ended responses, in which the respondent is asked to explain and/or discuss an answer in personally selected words, can mitigate these drawbacks. However, as will be discussed below, open-ended questions also have certain shortcomings.

Closed-ended questions, in a sense, compel respondents to choose a "closest representation" of their actual response in the form of a specific fixed answer. Subtle distinctions among respondents cannot be detected within the preestablished categories. This particular drawback is frequently addressed by inserting another alternative in the fixed-response format: "Other, please specify ______." This alternative represents an excellent compromise between closed- and open-ended response formats in that it is an open-ended question within a closed-ended format, as shown in the following example:

> Please indicate the activity you participate in most frequently at the community recreation center.
>
> ______Basketball
> ______Volleyball
> ______Swimming
> ______Table games
> ______Aerobic exercise
> ______Other
> please specify ______

For simplicity and ease of response, however, the use of this option must be carefully controlled. The decision to include an "Other" response category must be based on evidence obtained during the pretest of the survey instrument. If the evidence shows that a relatively large number of responses to the question do not conform to the preliminary set of fixed alternatives, then the researcher should formulate additional fixed categories for the responses that appear frequently and retain an "Other, please specify ______" category for the responses that appear less frequently. If there is no indication that an "Other" category is needed, it should not be included.

There is an increased possibility that the simplicity of the fixed-response format may lead to a greater probability of inadvertent errors in answering the question. For instance, an interviewer or a respondent may carelessly check a response category adjacent to the one that was actually intended. Open-ended questions eliminate the possibility of such unintended responses. In addition, closed-ended questions tend to constrain the breadth of subject matter addressed within the questionnaire and prevent respondents from expressing their opinions to the fullest extent possible. To obviate this shortcoming, the researcher may choose to use one or more general open-ended questions during the course of the survey.

Open-Ended Questions. Open-ended questions are used by researchers in situations where the constraints of the closed-ended question outweigh the inconveniences of the open-ended question for both the researcher and the respondent. It is recommended that open-ended questions be used sparingly and only when needed. To the extent that they are used, the researcher must be aware of certain inherent problems.

First, open-ended questions will inevitably elicit a certain amount of irrelevant and repetitious information. In addition, the satisfactory completion of an open-ended question requires a greater degree of communicative skills than is true for a closed-ended question. Accordingly, the researcher may find that these questions elicit responses that are difficult to understand and sometimes incoherent.

A third factor is that statistical analysis requires some degree of data standardization. This process entails the interpretative, subjective, and time-consuming categorization of open-ended responses by the researchers. And finally, open-ended questions will take more of the respondent's time. This inconvenience may engender a higher rate of refusal to complete the questionnaire.

Sequence of Questions

The order in which questions are presented can affect the overall study quite significantly. A poorly organized questionnaire can confuse respondents, bias their responses, and jeopardize the quality of the entire research effort. The following series of guidelines for sequencing questions has been created to enable the researcher to develop a well-ordered survey instrument.

Introductory Questions

The first questions should be related to the subject matter stated in the preamble but should be relatively easy to answer. Introductory questions should elicit a straightforward and uncomplicated opinion and/or derive basic factual—but not overly sensitive—information. The main purpose of the early questions is to stimulate interest in continuing with the questionnaire without offending, threatening, confusing, or boring the respondent.

For a study involving quality of life among Native Americans who reside on reservations, the authors developed a questionnaire that began with the following questions:

1. To what tribe of Indians do you belong?
   Pala________ La Jolla________
   Pauma______ San Pasqual______
   Rincon______
2. How long have you and your family lived on the reservation? ______
3. Please indicate your general level of satisfaction with life on the reservation using the following scale:
   Highly satisfied ______
   Satisfied ______
   Neither satisfied nor dissatisfied ______
   Dissatisfied ______
   Highly dissatisfied ______

It can be noted that the first two questions are of a basic, factual nature. The third question, although eliciting an opinion, is uncomplicated; however, it is germane to the key focus and sufficiently stimulating to evolve continued interest.

Sensitive Questions

Certain questions deal with sensitive issues, such as religious affiliation, ethnicity, sexual practices, income, and opinions regarding highly controversial ethical and moral dilemmas. It is highly recommended that these questions be placed late in the questionnaire for two primary reasons.

First, if respondents react negatively to such questions and decide to terminate the questionnaire, the information obtained on all previous questions may be usable in the overall survey results, because enough information may have been obtained to warrant acceptance of the interview as a completed case with only a few questions remaining unanswered. Second, if rapport has been established between the interviewer and the respondent during the course of the survey process, there is an increased likelihood that the respondent will answer sensitive questions that come late in the questionnaire.

Related Questions

Questionnaires generally have a certain frame of reference, as indicated by their goals and objectives. Within this overall context, there are several categories of questions. For instance, the questionnaire soliciting opinions from Native Americans contained questions relating to housing characteristics, schools, public services, crime and police issues, economic development, employment issues, transportation, tribal decision making, recreation, shopping patterns, and socioeconomic data.

Proper questionnaire design dictates that related questions be placed together within the questionnaire so that the respondent can focus and concentrate on specific issues without distraction. In order to facilitate this, it is sometimes appropriate to separate categories of questions by providing a distinct heading that characterizes each section. For example, in terms of police and crime-related issues, the following sequence can be considered to be an acceptable one:

1. How would you describe the current relationship between the police and your community?
   ______good ______fair ______poor
   ______no opinion
2. During the past five years, do you feel that this relationship between the police and your community has:
   ______improved ______remained about the same
   ______worsened ______no opinion
3. In what ways could police officers improve their performance? ____________________________

On the other hand, if these same questions were to be commingled with questions from other categories, the resulting questionnaire would be much less likely to produce clear, well-formulated responses. The reader should be able to verify this by examining the less acceptable question order below.

1. Do you or other members of your family participate in the tribal council decision-making process?
   yes______ no______
2. Would you be interested in participating in a job training program?
   yes______ no______
3. In what ways could police officers improve their performance? ____________________________

While it is generally desirable to arrange questions pertaining to a particular subject in the same section of the questionnaire, it is also important to be cognizant of creating a patterned series of responses. Consecutive questions that tend to evoke reflexive responses by the respondent, given without adequate thought, should be minimized.

The reader should note that the sequence of questions in Exhibit 2.4, which is part of a commercial business survey, could well produce an automatic, unidirectional set of responses unless the respondent is sensitized to the subtle, but important, differences among the questions. This process of sensitizing will tend to minimize the risk of reflexive responses and is accomplished in this example by underlining *and* italicizing the essential distinctions.

Alternative approaches to minimizing this risk of patterned responses may include the use of open-ended questions (without fixed alternative responses), questions that change the order of the fixed responses from question to question, or questions that vary substantially in terms of wording or length. The potential disadvantages of such tactics are that the respondent's thought focus may be disrupted or that the respondent might become confused, thereby defeating the purpose of grouping these questions in the first place. Because several considerations must be balanced in the grouping of questions, the pretest becomes of paramount importance to identify the potential for inadvertently eliciting response patterns and to minimize any such impact on the study.

Logical Sequence

There is frequently a clear, logical order to a particular series of questions contained within the survey instrument. For instance, an appropriate time sequence should be followed. If questions are to be posed concerning an individual's employment or residence history, they should be structured in such a way that the respondent is asked to answer them in a sequential or temporal order—for instance, from the most recent to the least recent over a specified period of time:

> Please indicate your places of residence during the past five years:
>
> 1. Current: ______________________________
>   ______________________________
> 2. First prior residence: ____________________
>   ____________________
> 3. Second prior residence: __________________
>   __________________

Exhibit 2.4. Series of Questions Demonstrating Sensitizing of Respondents.

1. What types of additional businesses, if any, do you feel are needed in the City of Poway to help serve *your business needs*? (Please check no more than *three* types of businesses.)
   Types of Businesses
   _______Food/market
   _______Food/specialty store (bakery, deli, etc.)
   _______Restaurant/dinnerhouse
   _______Restaurant/other (specify) ____________________
   _______Retail/department store
   _______Retail/specialty store
   _______Professional
   _______Services/supplies/equipment
   _______Light industry
   _______Other (specify) ____________________
   _______Other (specify ____________________
   _______Other (specify) ____________________
2. What types of additional businesses, if any, do you feel are needed in the City of Poway to help serve the needs of *your employees*? (Please check no more than *three* types of businesses.)
   _______Food/market
   _______Food/specialty store (bakery, deli, etc.)
   _______Restaurant/dinnerhouse
   _______Restaurant/other (specify) ____________________
   _______Retail/department store
   _______Retail/specialty store
   _______Professional
   _______Services/supplies/equipment
   _______Other (specify) ____________________
   _______Other (specify ____________________
   _______Other (specify) ____________________
3. What types of additional businesses, if any, do you feel are needed in the City of Poway to help serve the needs of *your customers*? (Please check no more than *three* types of businesses.
   Types of businesses
   _______Food/market
   _______Food/specialty store (bakery, deli, etc.)
   _______Restaurant/dinnerhouse
   _______Restaurant/other (specify) ____________________
   _______Retail/department store
   _______Retail/specialty store
   _______Professional
   _______Services/supplies/equipment
   _______Other (specify) ____________________
   _______Other (specify ____________________
   _______Other (specify) ____________________

Filter or Screening Questions

Other portions of the questionnaire might involve establishing the respondent's qualifications to answer subsequent questions. Through what are called "filter" or "screening" questions, as shown in Exhibit 2.5, the researcher can determine whether succeeding questions apply to the particular respondent. The first question requires that some respondents be screened out of certain subsequent questions. Only those who have participated in the city's recreational program are asked how they learned about the program. Both existing participants and nonparticipants, however, are asked about intended use of a community pool and preferred payment programs, with a further screening out of questions pertaining to pool use for those respondents who have no intention of using the pool at all.

Exhibit 2.5. Filter or Screening Questions.

---

1. Have you or other household members participated in the recreation program offered by the City of Poway Community Services Department during the past 12 months?
   ________Yes (Please continue with Question 2)
   ________No (Please skip to Question 3)
2. If yes, how did you find out about the City of Poway Recreation Program? (Please check only one)
   ________*Poway Today*
   ________*Poway News Chieftain*
   ________Community Services Department recreation brochure
   ________Poway Unified School District flyers
   ________From a friend/family member
   ________Other (Specify) ________________________________
3. A community swimming pool is being planned for Community Park at Bowron Road. If you and/or your family members plan to use this pool, which of the following payment methods would you most prefer? (Check one) If you and/or your family members do not plan to use the pool, please go on to Question 4.
   ________Unlimited-use membership (Annual fee)
   ________Purchase in advance a specified number of visits for a discounted price
   ________Pay each time you or your family members use the swimming pool
4. Do not intend to use the swimming pool (If you have checked this response, please skip to Question 6)

Exhibit 2.6. Screening Used to Disqualify Respondents.

1. Are you registered to vote in the City of San Diego?
   Yes .... ______(CONTINUE)
   No .... ______(DISQUALIFY)
   Not sure .... ______(DISQUALIFY)
   Refused .... ______(DISQUALIFY)
2. Did you vote in the 1986 elections for mayor or U.S. senator?
   Yes .... ______(ASK QUESTION C)
   No .... ______(DISQUALIFY)
   Not sure .... ______(DISQUALIFY)

Under some circumstances, filtering questions may be used to disqualify certain respondents from participating in the survey process at all. Exhibit 2.6 draws from a telephone questionnaire that was used in a survey of registered voters. It was the intent of the survey to query not all registered voters, but only those who were likely to vote. For purposes of the survey, those who were most likely to vote were considered to be those who had voted for the mayor and/or U.S. senator in the previous year's election. The survey screened out entirely those who did not satisfy the appropriate preconditions by providing explicit instructions for the interviewer concerning disqualification.

Reliability Checks

On occasion, when a question is important or is particularly sensitive or controversial, the degree of truthfulness or thoughtfulness of the response may be in doubt. In such situations, it may be appropriate to include in the questionnaire a check of the respondent's consistency of response by asking virtually the same question in a somewhat different manner and at a different place within the survey instrument.

In a survey research project seeking to identify the demand for market rate housing in downtown San Diego, the following question was asked of respondents:

> Please indicate the likelihood of your choosing to live in downtown San Diego?
> ______Very possible
> ______Somewhat possible

______Not very likely
______Highly unlikely

The researchers suspected that there might be a casual or less careful response pattern to this question in which respondents might indicate their willingness to live downtown without giving the matter adequate thought. Therefore, later in the questionnaire, another question was posed as follows:

When you consider the possibility of living in downtown San Diego, do you feel
______Excited
______Interested
______Indifferent
______Uncomfortable
______Frightened
______Other
Please specify ______________________________

In this study, in order for a respondent to be considered a "possible downtown resident," he or she had to choose the first or second response to *both* questions. Because any other combination might indicate a tentative or inconsistent willingness to consider downtown as a possible place to live, respondents with such answers were not considered strong candidates for downtown living. Without the benefit of this reliability check, respondents who were less likely to live downtown might well have been wrongly included with those who were more inclined to do so.

Follow-Up Open-Ended Questions

As mentioned above, it is desirable to have relatively simple, fixed-answer questions wherever possible. However, most surveys find it necessary to seek information that cannot be fully answered within the fixed-answer format. In such cases, follow-up open-ended questions are asked in a manner that connects them to the fixed-answer question. For instance, during the studies of Native American tribes, the following questions were asked:

1. Are you generally in agreement with the policies and decisions made through tribal decision making?
   yes ______ no ______
2. If no, how do you generally differ? ____________________
   ____

Efforts should be undertaken to place such open-ended questions as late in the questionnaire (or appropriate section of the questionnaire) as possible, while remaining cognizant of the need to have a logical and temporal order of questions.

Open-Ended Venting Questions

At the very end of the entire questionnaire, it is often beneficial to use one or more open-ended "venting" questions—ones in which the respondent is asked to add any information, comments, or opinions that pertain to the subject matter of the questionnaire but have not been addressed in it. For example, a citizen opinion survey in a midsized San Diego County bedroom community posed the following final question in its questionnaire:

> Thinking of your neighborhood as well as the City of Poway, in general, what do *you* personally feel are the most important issues or problems facing residents of this city?

Questionnaire Length

The questionnaire should be as concise as possible while still covering the necessary range of subject matter required in the study. The researcher must be careful to resist the temptation of developing questions that, although interesting, are peripheral or extraneous to the primary focus of the research project.

The purpose of being sensitive to questionnaire length is

to make certain that the questionnaire is not so long and cumbersome to the respondent that it engenders reluctance to complete the survey instrument, thereby jeopardizing the response rate.

As questions increase in complexity and difficulty of content, the questionnaire may be perceived as being tedious and longer than it actually is. Hence, the researcher must factor in such considerations as the number of questions and the time and effort required of the respondent to complete them.

As general guidelines, telephone interviews should occupy no more than twenty minutes of the respondent's time, mailed questionnaires should take thirty minutes or less including open-ended responses, and in-person interviews should be limited to forty-five minutes to one hour. These are maximum time frames. Ideally, telephone surveys should take ten to fifteen minutes, mail surveys should need approximately fifteen minutes, and in-person surveys should take less than thirty minutes.

Exercises

1. Choose a topic for a survey research study. Develop a list of at least five major interested institutions, organizations, and/or individuals whom you feel should be consulted for background information prior to the development of the questionnaire.
    a. What information would you seek from each of them?
    b. Whom would you select to pretest the draft questionnaire?
2. What are the primary components to include in a preamble or introduction to a survey questionnaire? Write a preamble to a survey questionnaire that focuses on the demand and use of automobiles and mass transit in a major metropolitan area.
3. Discuss the relative advantages and disadvantages of open-ended and closed-ended questions.

4. Write six questions for the hypothetical automobile and mass transit questionnaire in Question 2 above. Include both open-ended and closed-ended questions and place them in a sequence consistent with the principles outlined in the chapter. Identify the specific principles applied.

Chapter 3

Developing Survey Questions

The previous chapter has addressed overall questionnaire development and question sequencing within the survey instrument. No consideration of questionnaire development would be complete without a thorough analysis of the principles and potential problems involved in the actual phrasing and formatting of the questions themselves.

Questionnaire construction is a skill that is refined over time by experience. Each research project has its own set of conditions and circumstances; this renders the imposition of fixed and rigid rules impossible. This chapter is particularly sensitive to the need for flexibility, offering, instead of rules, a series of objectives and guidelines in the pursuit of clear questions. Two fundamental considerations are involved:

- Question phrasing
- Question formatting

The researcher must use considerable discretion in the application of the guidelines outlined in this chapter because there is a very fine line between appropriately and inappropriately constructed questions. Such appropriateness, or lack thereof, can prove to be critical to the success of the research project.

Guidelines for Phrasing Questions

Level of Wording

The researcher must be cognizant of the population to be surveyed in terms of the choice of words, colloquialisms, and jargon to be used in the questions. As a general guideline, wording should be simple, straightforward, and to the point. Specifically, the researcher should attempt to avoid highly technical words or phrases, words that require or are associated with higher levels of experience and/or education, and words or phrases that may be insensitive to ethnic or gender-related issues.

For example, in a questionnaire seeking to obtain information related to the use of illegal drugs, the following alternative questions may be asked:

1a. Have you or any member of your family been engaged in substance abuse during the past year?

or

1b. Have you or any members of your family used illegal drugs during the past year?

Question 1a uses the term *substance abuse*, which is not necessarily universally understood by the general population. Therefore, the responses to this question may not be consistent with its intent. Question 1b, however, uses the simpler and clearer phrase *illegal drugs*, and the responses should consequently be more accurate.

Obviously, the researcher is interested in making certain that respondents understand the questions well enough to provide accurate representations of their opinions, behavior, and characteristics for purposes of the study. If questions are not understandable, any one of three problems may arise:

- Information provided may be inaccurate.
- There may be a large number of "do not know" or "no opinion" responses.
- The rate of refusal to complete the questionnaire may be inordinately high.

Once again, the pretest looms large in importance in the detection of language-related problems.

On occasion, the general guideline of simplicity should be modified to accommodate special population groups. In a survey among attorneys concerning attitudes about courtroom procedures, it is appropriate to include words that are recognizable to those who have been formally trained in the law. If the survey were instead administered to the general public, the level of wording would, of necessity, be different.

Ambiguous Questions

Efforts must be devoted to avoiding ambiguity within the questions. Ambiguity can occur from the use of certain words or by the manner in which questions are worded. For example, if one is seeking the number of people residing together in one household, the question might be inappropriately worded, "How many people live in your household?"

Respondents faced with this question may not know whether or not they should include themselves in the response. The confusion can be avoided by rewording the question to say, "Including yourself, how many people live in your household?"

Similarly, in an attempt to determine household income, the question, "What is your income?" will produce a variety of unsatisfactory responses such as the respondent's annual income, the respondent's take-home pay, the respondent's hourly wage, or the total household income. What is generally sought in most surveys is total gross annual household income, before taxes. Generally, the question, "Please indicate the category that best represents your total annual household income, before taxes," will produce the desired responses.

Words such as *affiliate*, *identify*, and *belong*, when used in sociological terms, will often produce ambiguous results. For instance, asking an individual with what ethnic group he or she most closely identifies can be interpreted to mean, "With which group do I best get along?" rather than, "Of which ethnic group am I a member?" In the first interpretation, a respondent may provide more than one response in order to communicate a favorable inclination toward certain ethnic groups. However, the researcher is typically interested in ascertaining the respondent's own ethnic background and would find such a response uninformative. An appropriate phrasing for obtaining such information is, "Please indicate your race/ethnicity."

Multipurpose Questions

Multipurpose questions are those that might inadvertently confuse the respondent by introducing two or more issues with the expectation of a single response. A questionnaire was published in a small-town newspaper in order to determine public opinion about future land development in the community ("What Does Your Family's Future. . .?," 1989). The first question in that survey was worded as in Example 3.1.

Example 3.1:

> Do you believe the *VISIBLE* development at Alpine's freeway entrances will affect the image and property values of our whole community?
> Yes______ No______

The only way to answer either "yes" or "no" to such a question is to feel the same about both image and property values and about all entrances to Alpine. In other words, if a respondent considers such development satisfactory at one entrance and not at another or believes that image will be affected but not property values, there is no way to truly answer the question. Hence, responses to such questions are impossible to interpret accurately. Any question that contains the conjunctions "and" or "or" should be reviewed very carefully for the possibility that it may in actuality be composed of more than one question.

Inappropriate Emphasis

The use of boldface, italicized, capitalized, or underlined words or phrases within the context of a question may serve to place inappropriate emphasis on these words or phrases. However, emphasis can serve a constructive purpose when the researcher needs to clarify potentially confusing nuances that may exist within the questionnaire (see Exhibit 2.4).

Devices for indicating emphasis are inappropriately used when they are designed to evoke an emotional response or to impose the researcher's concept of significance rather than leaving the determination of what is and is not important to the respondent. Such tactics will tend to bias the survey results. Example 3.1 can also serve to illustrate inappropriate emphasis. Its focus on the word *visible* seems to be an effort to disturb the community's rural residents by ascribing some form of visual obtrusiveness to the planned development.

Biasing Words or Phrases

Although they may be clear, simple, and otherwise acceptable, certain words and phrases carry with them the power to elicit emotions. Survey questions must be as neutral as possible to obtain accurate results and to fulfill their obligation to solicit and welcome all points of view. Questions must invite true responses from the entire population and neither anger the respondent into an answer other than the one he or she would normally give nor shame the respondent into a similar distortion.

The following example, adapted from a public opinion survey prior to a major local election, clearly seeks to use emotionally charged words, thereby attempting to lead the respondent to answer the question in a particular way in reaction to a particular stimulus.

> There are some in the community who feel that the effort to change the name of Martin Luther King Way back to Market Street is racist. Others feel that the effort to change the name back to Market Street represents cold, economic motives. What do you think?
> ______Economically motivated
> ______Racially motivated
> ______Both
> ______Not sure

Words such as "racist" and "cold" are clear efforts to anger certain respondents and to shame, or intimidate, others. In general, slanderous and prejudicial language must be avoided, as must language that conjures up specifically positive or negative images. The question, "Do you prefer mountain village–like commercial zoning instead of open car storage, industrial zoning at the entrances to Alpine?" heavily slants the respondent toward the commercial zoning choice through the use of the phrases "mountain village" and "open car storage" to modify the competing land use choices. Such a tactic is inappropriate in that zoning itself does not necessarily dictate design or ultimate use, and it is very possible to have an unattractive commercial development and an attractive industrial one. The responses to the question were, as expected, 376 to 7 in favor of the commercial zone.

Manipulative Information

Certain questions may require some form of explanation to be presented to the respondent in order to provide necessary background and perspective. For instance, the following questions were contained within a citizen opinion survey of a city in San Diego County:

In July 1988, Caltrans will open a carpool/bus lane on I-15 ("High Occupancy Vehicle" or "HOV" lane). This will be a separate lane, from the Carmel Mountain Road interchange to the I-15/163 split, carrying traffic southbound in the morning and northbound in the afternoon. Use of the HOV lane requires that at least two persons be riding in the vehicle.

Will you use the HOV lane to commute to work or in the course of your work?

Yes______

No______

If a "park & ride" lot were available near the on-ramp, would you be more likely to use the HOV lane?

Yes______

No______

The researcher must be very careful that explanatory statements such as the one contained at the beginning of this example do not unduly influence the response by providing biasing or manipulative information. The objective researcher should not skew responses in one direction or another, but rather should solicit genuine opinions, behaviors, and facts from the respondents. An example of such manipulation is as follows: "One of the Ten Commandments says, 'Thou shalt not kill.' Do you believe that the state has the right to exercise capital punishment?" More often, manipulative information is less obvious. The following question derives from a survey of artists, whose input was sought as part of the development of a countywide arts plan.

In your opinion, what are the *three* top priorities that you feel should be addressed in arts funding for the Greater Cleveland metropolitan area (for example, direct funding for artists, new facilities, educational programs, and so on)?

1. ______________________________

2. ______________________________

3. ______________________________

The examples provided in parentheses served to strongly influence the responses in both substance and priority. In this situation, the examples should not have been provided at all.

Unfortunately, manipulative information is occasionally incorporated deliberately into a questionnaire. Some surveys are performed for specific clients and causes. It is not uncommon for these clients to want to use the surveys for publicity purposes or to influence voter opinion. The small-town newspaper survey referred to previously contains the following question, which can be considered manipulative:

> Do you agree with the current Alpine Planning Group's recommendation to build public trails on public right-of-ways and, if needed for safety, to enlarge the public right-of-ways?
>
> (This would enable our residents, as well as the outside public, to use Alpine-area public trails to access nearby Cleveland National Forest without crossing Alpiners' private property. *This would also minimize the liability, insurance, privacy, and safety problems posed to property owners by allowing public access to private property.*)

The manipulative information is in the lengthy explanation, which can serve to bias the respondent toward the affirmative response. The information contained in that explanation may or may not be correct. It is clearly subject to some interpretation. Furthermore, there may be a problem in invoking the endorsement of what might be perceived to be an organization or institution with particular expertise, as in the earlier reference to the Ten Commandments. Referring to the Alpine Planning Group does not present such a significant biasing problem, but the researcher must be cognizant of the biasing potential involved in citing authorities such as religious organizations or highly respected public figures.

Formatting of Questions

Whereas open-ended questions are relatively easy to present within the questionnaire, requiring simply an ample number of lines for the respondent to write an answer in full, closed-ended questions entail a greater range of considerations. The major issues related to the layout of closed-ended questions make up the balance of this chapter.

Levels of Measurement

Survey data are organized in terms of variables. A variable is a specific characteristic of the population, such as age, sex, or political party preference. Each variable is generally associated with a set of categories that describe the nature and type of variation associated with the characteristic. The variable, sex, is described by two categories: male and female. Certain opinions are solicited in terms of three categories of response—yes, no, no opinion; annual income, on the other hand, depending on the researcher's purpose and focus, can have numerous categories of response.

The variables used in a survey project have distinct measurement properties, referred to as levels of measurement or measurement scales. Some variables can only be classified into labeled categories (nominal scale); other variables are intrinsically capable of being ranked or ordered (ordinal scale); and still other variables not only imply a ranking, but also are associated with certain standard units of value that determine exactly by how much the categories of the variable differ (interval scale).

Nominal Scale

The nominal level of measurement simply involves the process of identifying or labeling the observations that constitute the survey data. In the nominal scale, data can be placed into categories and counted only with regard to frequency of occurrence. No ordering or valuation is implied. For example, a variable such as political party preference might be categorized into three possible responses: Republican, Democrat, and Independent. These response categories only serve the function of enumerating the number of survey respondents who indicate their respective affiliations. No ranking or ordering of the parties is specified or implied. Similarly, no valuation unit is available to permit the determination of the extent of each respondent's affiliation.

Ordinal Scale

The ordinal level of measurement goes a step beyond the nominal scale; it seeks to rank categories of the variable in terms of the extent to which they possess the characteristic of the variable. The ordinal level of measurement provides information about the ordering of categories but does not indicate the magnitude of differences among these categories. An example of the ordinal scale can be found in terms of education—specifically with regard to highest degree received. Potential responses for this variable might include Ph.D., master's, bachelor's, and other formal education less than the attainment of a bachelor's degree. It is clear that these categories possess an ordinality or ranking but do not reveal any specific measure of the amount of difference in educational attainment.

The Interval Scale

The interval level of measurement yields the greatest amount of information about the variable. It labels, orders, and uses constant units of measurement to indicate the exact value of each category of response. Variables such as income, height, age, distance, and temperature are associated with established determinants of measure that provide precise indications of the value of each category and the differences among them. Whereas with regard to age, ordinal levels of measurement might include categories such as infant, child, adolescent, and adult, interval levels of measurement will entail precise indications of age in terms of an established measure such as years, months, or days.

Basic Response Category Format

In formatting response category alternatives, the primary guideline to which the researcher must adhere is clarity of presentation. The choices must be clearly delineated so as to provide no confusion to the respondent or to the researcher when she or he examines the responses. The researcher must be able to recognize precisely what response has been indicated. Of particular importance is that each response should be unambiguously associated with one and only one response category, with no overlapping of responses. Generally, either a box (☐) or a line (______) is provided next to the responses, and the responses are, preferably, vertically organized with sufficient space between categories.

There may be occasions when the researcher wishes to conserve space in order to keep entire questions together on one page, for instance, or to save paper and printing costs. Questions that involve a relatively small number of response alternatives can be horizontally organized as long as adequate space is provided between the possible responses so that the respondent can easily identify the appropriate place to indicate the response and not inadvertently mark the line on the wrong side of the answer. Example 3.2 demonstrates the space conservation consideration as applied to Question 2, rather than the more space-consuming format taken by Question 1.

Example 3.2:

1. In your opinion, does San Diego need a rail transit system?
   ______Yes
   ______No
   ______No opinion
2. In your opinion, does San Diego need a rail transit system?
   ______Yes ______No ______No opinion

Some questions ask the respondent to circle the appropriate response. This device is not recommended in this book because circled responses tend to be less easy to read during the process of computer input, as will be discussed in Chapter Four.

Determining the Number of Alternative Responses

As discussed in Chapter Two, it is important to have as comprehensive a list of alternative responses as possible within each closed-ended question. However, the researcher must be careful that the number of fixed alternatives does not become so unwieldy that it confuses or intimidates the respondent. Ideally, in a mail-out survey, there should be fewer than ten response alternatives (this also has certain computer coding advantages—see Chapter Four). In some circumstances it may be necessary to increase that number of responses to an approximate maximum of fifteen. If it is suspected (either through professional judgment, previous knowledge, or the formal pretest) that there will be a large number of very distinct responses to a question that will be somewhat difficult to combine, and that those responses will each be represented by a respectable percentage (for instance, 3 to 5 percent) of the total responses, then the researcher is justified in expanding the number of alternative response categories to the maximum of fifteen. The balance of choices can be handled through the use of an "Other, please specify ______" category. When the number of alternative responses grows large and the survey is being performed in the in-person interview format, the interviewer can take advantage of the format by showing the respondent a card with the choices elaborated on it and can even extend the maximum beyond fifteen—up to twenty. On the other hand, the length of the response list takes on particular sensitivity in the telephone survey format, where fifteen to twenty response categories are far too many and the number of categories must be held to a maximum of six to eight, in order for the respondent to be able to remember and choose among them as they are being read aloud by the interviewer.

Structuring Categories for Interval Scale Variables

Interval scale variables pose special problems for structuring the alternative response categories. By the nature of their scale, nominal and ordinal variables have clearly identifiable categories in which there is, generally, little latitude with regard to assigning cases. For instance, a survey, planned for implementation at the local zoo, contained a question that was prepared to determine exhibit preferences among zoo visitors. It could be anticipated that such a question would elicit responses such as petting corrals, reptile exhibits, or a tiger pavilion. All responses could be placed in a few possible categories that would be both reasonable and informative. On the other hand, a question concerning the age of a respondent has an infinite number of possible ranges and interval sizes into which responses can be categorized. If, for example, the respondent is forty-three years of age, category alternatives for this one answer alone might include "35–44," "40–49," "40–44," "38–50," "over 40," and "under 50." Hence, deciding on the structure of categories for interval scale variables involves a greater degree of judgment and discretion on the part of the researcher.

There are several guidelines and rules of thumb that must be considered in this decision:

- Ideally, interval scale categories should be as equal as possible in terms of their interval sizes. In the case of age, fixed intervals such as "0–9," "10–19," and "20–29" should be considered an appropriate starting point.
- Each category should contain a reasonable number of responses. As discussed, a manageable number of categories should be provided, and categories with very few respondents should be avoided. On the other hand, categories with a very large number of respondents might tend to obscure details that are important to the focus of the study.
- The boundaries of the categories should conform to traditional breaking points wherever possible. It is more desirable, therefore, to use income categories such as "$10,000–$20,000" rather than "$11,100–$21,100."
- Each category should consist of responses that are anticipated to be evenly distributed throughout the category. This assumption is necessary in order to avoid a skewed distribution of responses and to facilitate statistical analysis. For example, suppose that a researcher is conducting a survey in

which respondents must be graduates of a four-year college in order to participate. For the variable of age, the category of "20 and less than 25" should be avoided, because most college graduates are at least twenty-two years old. Hence, the anticipated distribution within the category would be skewed toward the upper age groups rather than being evenly distributed. The pretest of the survey instrument is of particular importance in helping to predict whether or not these preestablished categories will yield a relatively even distribution.

It may not be possible to satisfy all of the above guidelines in any given situation. A potential difficulty in the application of these guidelines occurs when traditional category boundaries conflict with the principle of nonoverlapping categories. In the case of income, for instance, categories with traditional boundaries such as $30,000–40,000" and "$40,000–$50,000" are not acceptable within the same question because an individual who earns an annual income of $40,000 applies to more than one category. An acceptable alternative would be "$30,000–$39,999" and $40,000–$49,999," which assumes that all responses are rounded to the nearest dollar, or "$30,000–$39,999.99" and "40,000–49,999.99" without that assumption. Observations that in theory can assume the value of any number in a continuous interval require class boundaries that are inclusive of all such possible values. The use of the terms "under" and "over" can obviate any problems in the assignment of observations to the appropriate categories in such continuous variables. In point of fact, it is recommended that this format for class boundary determination be used for all variables except those for which whole number values are the only possible responses (for instance, number of children in a household). Hence, an even more appropriate format for these income categories would be "$30,000 and under $40,000" and "$40,000 and under $50,000," because of its clarity and simplicity and its conformity with traditional class boundaries.

Another deviation from these guidelines might arise with regard to interval sizes. Although it is desirable to maintain equal interval sizes for an income distribution, this objective may not satisfy the guideline that each category of the variable have a reasonable number of responses. Typically, the frequency of response declines at higher income levels. Therefore, researchers often expand the size of category intervals at the higher income ranges in order to ensure that a reasonable number of responses per category is maintained rather than burdening the audience with unnecessary detail of minor consequence to the study. There is an element of proportion that is also important in category construction. That is, the difference between annual incomes of $10,000 and $20,000 is effectively much more significant than the difference between incomes of $150,000 and $160,000. Furthermore, there will always be some individuals who earn enormous annual incomes. Intervals cannot reasonably be provided in anticipation of these relatively few responses. Therefore, income questions should provide an unbounded upper-income category to account for this likelihood. Age distributions and certain other socioeconomic variables also demonstrate these patterns of response and should be treated similarly. Example 3.3 shows a reasonable breakdown of income categories.

Another situation that may require an adjustment of category boundaries—in this case because of low frequency of response—is provided in Table 3.1, which indicates monthly rental obligations of respondents in low-income households. The frequencies stipulated were obtained in a pretest of the

Example 3.3:

Please indicate the category that best represents your total annual household income.

______Under $10,000
______$10,000 and under $20,000
______$20,000 and under $30,000
______$30,000 and under $40,000
______$40,000 and under $50,000
______$50,000 and under $75,000
______$75,000 and over

Table 3.1. Pretest: Low-Income Household Rents.

Rents	*f*	%
$150 and under $200	10	20.0
$200 and under $250	10	20.0
$250 and under $300	2	4.0
$300 and under $350	10	20.0
$350 and under $400	12	24.0
$400 and over	6	12.0
Total	50	100.0

survey instrument. In this case, the final questionnaire should be adjusted to account for the apparent absence of expected observations in the "$250 and under $300" category. This adjustment would require the elimination of the category by absorbing it into the immediately adjacent categories above and below it.

The revised categories might be as displayed in Table 3.2. This adjustment satisfies the guideline specifying that categories have a reasonable number of responses. It maintains traditional category boundaries, and it does not significantly deviate from the guideline specifying intervals of equal sizes.

Table 3.2. Pretest: Low-Income Household Rents (Revised).

Rents	*f*	%
$150 and under $200	10	20.0
$200 and under $275	11	22.0
$275 and under $350	11	22.0
$350 and under $400	12	24.0
$400 and over	6	12.0
Total	50	100.0

Ordering of Response Alternatives

The list of alternative responses may possess an inherent logical order. This order must be replicated in the elaboration of these categories within the question. Ordinal or interval data are obvious examples, as indicated in the following example:

1. How would you rate your day at Sengme Oaks Water Park?
   ______very good
   ______good
   ______fair
   ______poor
   ______very poor

It clearly would not make sense to reorder the responses in Example 3.3. Nominal data categories, on the other hand, should be randomly listed in order to deliberately eliminate any potential biasing effects of a particular ordering. Therefore, when conducting telephone or in-person interviews, the order in which these responses are read to the respondent should be periodically shuffled. For budgetary reasons and computer coding purposes, this shuffling is frequently not feasible for mail-out surveys.

Multiple Responses

On occasion, a question may require more than one response, as demonstrated in Examples 3.4 and 3.5. These two examples represent the two basic types of multiple-response questions: one in which the respondent is asked to rank preferences and the other in which choices are indicated without regard to their order. In constructing the questionnaire, it should be made very clear to the respondent if more than one response is acceptable or if a ranking is requested. In questions where the researcher requests only one response but where there may be an inclination on the part of the respondent to supply more than one, instructions to "check only one" must be very clear, as in the following example:

> For which of the following pool activities would you most prefer to have "adult only" time periods designated? (Check only one.) If you do not want designated "adult only" time periods, check the last choice.
> ______Lap swimming (exercise)
> ______Water aerobic exercise classes

______General recreational swimming
______Organized competitive swimming
______Instructional swimming/swimming lessons
______Do not want "adult only" time periods

Example 3.4:

What kinds of entertainment would you most like to have scheduled at the new Performing Arts Center? (Indicate your highest priority with a *1*, your second priority with a *2*, and your third priority with a *3*.)

______Plays
______Musicals
______Lectures
______Classical music
______Rock music
______Country & Western music
______"Popular" music
______Dance
______Other (please specify) ____________________

Example 3.5:

In what ways could police officers improve their performance? (Interviewer: If respondent indicates that no improvement is needed, check the first box.) Check the two most important.

______No improvement needed
______Concentrate on important duties such as serious crime
______Be more prompt, responsive, alert
______Be more courteous and improve their attitude toward community
______Be more qualified in terms of training
______Need more Native American policemen on the reservations
______Other (specify) __________________________
______Do not know

Scaled Responses

Some questions require the use of a scaled response mechanism in which a continuum of response alternatives is provided for the respondent to consider. The following example demonstrates a Likert scale used in a survey of a small city's business community. A Likert scale entails a five-, seven- or nine-point rating scale in which the attitude of the respondent is measured on a continuum from highly favorable to highly unfavorable, or vice versa, with an equal number of positive and negative response possibilities and one middle or neutral category.

What is your general impression of how the Susanville city government affects your business?

Highly positive				Highly negative
1	2	3	4	5
______	______	______	______	______

The extremes of such scales must be labeled in order to orient the respondent. It is also acceptable to label each numerical category on the scale. Generally, scaled responses work best horizontally to allow respondents to perceive the continuum. Caution should be exercised to provide adequate spacing between alternatives in the layout of the question.

The Likert scale works particularly well in the context of a series of questions that seek to elicit attitudinal information about one specific subject matter. Exhibit 3.1 is an example of such a series of questions that seek to elicit the attitudes of professional urban planners about their jobs and their degrees of satisfaction.

When a series of questions such as the one presented in Exhibit 3.1 has the same set of response categories, it would be prohibitively wasteful of space and monotonous to list question after question for several pages. In such circumstances, these questions can be efficiently grouped together in a matrix or gridlike format.

It should be emphasized that although the Likert scale is

Exhibit 3.1. Questions Designed to Elicit Attitudes.

Please indicate your opinion concerning the following characteristics of your present job.

Characteristic of Present Job	*(1) Strongly Agree*	*(2) Agree*	*(3) Neutral*	*(4) Disagree*	*(5) Strongly Disagree*	*Mean*
Opportunity to gain increased responsibility						
Opportunity to influence internal agency policies						
Opportunity to grow professionally (enhance skills and abilities)						
Opportunity to serve a useful public service						
Recognition of my contribution to the agency						
Sufficient remuneration for my efforts						
Opportunity to develop congenial relationships among colleagues						
Adequate resources to perform any assigned tasks						
Adequate evaluation of the quality of my work						
Reason to take pride in my work						

Exhibit 3.2. Scaled Questions Not in Likert Form.

Please indicate if you feel that the following services and facilities are *adequate* or *inadequate* in Columbus. Please indicate if you feel that these services have *improved, gotten worse*, or *remained about the same* since you have lived in Columbus.

	Check one		*Check one*		
	Adequate 1	*Inadequate* 2	*Improved* 3	*Gotten Worse* 4	*Remained the Same* 5
Street and sidewalk repair	______	______	______	______	______
Police protection	______	______	______	______	______
Fire protection	______	______	______	______	______
Paramedic services	______	______	______	______	______
Library facilities	______	______	______	______	______
Recreational programs	______	______	______	______	______
Park and parkway maintenance	______	______	______	______	______
Street cleaning	______	______	______	______	______
Activities for youths	______	______	______	______	______
Traffic movement	______	______	______	______	______
Animal control	______	______	______	______	______

quite common in survey research, it is only one of several types of scales available to the researcher. For instance, Exhibit 3.2 shows a series of scaled questions that are not in Likert form in that they do not solicit opinions ranked on one continuum from low to high or from high to low.

All scaled response series should adhere to certain principles:

- The number of questions comprising the series should generally consist of two to ten items, depending on the complexity of the subject matter and the anticipated tolerance of the potential respondents.
- The questions chosen for the series should cover as many relevant aspects of the subject matter under consideration as possible.

- The questions should be unidimensional; that is, they should be consistent and concerned substantially with one basic issue.
- The scale itself must be logical and consistent with a continuum.
- For each question in the series, the scale must measure the dimensions of response in the same order. For example, in Exhibit 3.1, the high end of the scale always measures dissatisfaction, while the low end always measures satisfaction.

Interviewer Instructions

Clear instructions are of great importance to both the mail-out respondent and the telephone or in-person interviewer. The mail-out survey respondent, in particular, must have explicit instructions concerning how to properly complete the questionnaire. The instructions that are incorporated as part of the question itself must be clear in terms of content and readily noticed. Although this is less important in telephone and in-person surveys because of the involvement of a trained interviewer, the instructions should still adhere to the principles of clarity and noticeability so that the interviewer does not occasionally forget the proper implementation of the survey instrument, which may happen no matter how facile he or she may have become in its administration.

In addition to filtering questions, instructions are needed to inform the respondent of the number of responses to be specified. Various examples throughout this chapter (such as Examples 3.4 and 3.5) illustrate this situation. Furthermore, in telephone and in-person interviews, it is possible that certain information should not be read aloud to the respondent and should only be tallied if it is volunteered, such as the "not sure" response in the following example:

2. [ASK IF "YES" IN Q. 1.] How would you rate your chances of voting in this year's upcoming elections for City Council and this year's ballot propositions?

   Excellent . . . ______ [ASK Q. 3]
   Good . . . . . . ______ [ASK Q. 3]

Fair ....______ [ASK Q. 3]
Poor ....______ [DISQUALIFY]
(DO NOT READ)—Not sure ....______ [ASK Q. 3]

Other information, such as the sex of the respondent, often does not need to be asked, especially in telephone or in-person interviews. In such cases, this information can be gathered directly by observation, and instructions should be provided to the interviewer to make certain that the information is noted, but not asked:

[DO NOT READ] Sex of the respondent
______Male
______Female

Exercises

1. Referring to the types of information that sample surveys solicit, as presented in Chapter One (description, behavior, and preference), write two sample questions for each of these three informational categories. Verify that none of the questions violate any of the principles of question wording.
2. Comment upon the sequence, wording, and layout of the following excerpt from a hypothetical sample survey. Do you feel that open-ended questions have been used appropriately? Explain.
   a. Do you see your business being in Carlsbad five (5) years from now?
      ______Yes (If yes, skip to question c)
      ______No (If no, continue with question b)
   b. Why do you not see your business being in Carlsbad five (5) years from now?
      ______Business expansion
      ______Business contraction
      ______Relocation because of nonbusiness factors
   c. How would you like to see the Carlsbad business community develop into the 1990s and beyond?
      ____
      ____

d. Where is your residence located?
______Carlsbad
______Oceanside
______Vista
______Encinitas
______Other North County city
______Other (please specify) ____________________

e. How long has your business been located at its present location?
______Less than 1 year
______1 and under 3 years
______3 and under 5 years
______5 and under 8 years
______8 or more years

3. [For students] Draft a survey instrument of approximately ten questions to be administered to other students in your program concerning their satisfaction levels regarding the curriculum and quality of instruction.
4. [For working professionals] Draft a survey instrument of approximately ten questions to be administered to personnel in your department concerning their overall job satisfaction.

Chapter 4

Administering the Questionnaire

The process of converting the survey instrument into survey data is accomplished through a series of stages. This chapter will begin with an explanation of how to precode the survey instrument for computerization and data reduction. It will then proceed with discussions of the interviewing process, including interviewer selection and training, the implementation and monitoring of the three primary types of surveys (mail-out, telephone, and in-person), and ethical considerations associated with interviewing respondents. This chapter will also address the issue of data editing or "cleaning," especially as it applies to postcoding responses to open-ended questions. The chapter will conclude with a presentation of various considerations associated with computer entry of the data.

Precoding the Survey Instrument

The nature of survey research is such that most survey projects will be too large for noncomputerized data processing. Computers, however, require the responses that are elicited to be translated into numerical codes. The most efficient coding process will be one whereby the computer operator can enter the responses directly from the survey instrument without the need for any intermediate step.

In order to facilitate data entry, numerical codes should be provided for each category of response at the time the questionnaire is prepared in final form. Example 4.1 represents the incorporation of numerical codes into the questionnaire. These codes can be entered directly for computer analysis. The placement of codes on the survey instrument itself prior to administration is known as *precoding*.

Example 4.1:

1. In your opinion, has County government been responsive to your needs? [12]
   a. ______ Yes
   b. ______ No
   c. ______ No opinion

There are several guidelines for precoding a questionnaire. First of all, codes should be unobtrusive in appearance and placement and should follow a consistent pattern throughout the questionnaire. However, they should still be clearly visible for ease of computer input. Second, only close-ended categories can be coded in advance. Clearly, precoding of open-ended questions is not possible because responses are not predictable.

Variables with nine or fewer categories should be coded with a single digit (1–9); variables with more than nine categories should be coded with two digits (01–99). In a few instances, it may become necessary to establish codes with more than two digits, for example, with ZIP Codes, telephone exchanges, and business standard industrial classification (SIC) codes. In such cases, an adequate number of digits must be used (001–999; 0001–9999).

The researcher frequently finds it necessary to include an "Other, please specify ______" response category, as discussed in Chapter Three. In such cases, when the number of fixed-

Example 4.2:

1. Which of these department stores do you visit most often? (Check only one) [44–45]

01. ____Nordstrom's		05. ____The Broadway	
02. ____May Company		06. ____Robinsons	
03. ____Montgomery Ward		07. ____J. C. Penney	
04. ____Bullock's		99. ____Other please specify ________	

response categories is close to the maximum allowable for the assigned number of digits (for example, seven to nine categories), the researcher should anticipate the possibility of having to provide additional response categories based on the information obtained from the "Other" category (see the section on postcoding below). The researcher can accommodate these anticipated additional responses by increasing the number of digits assigned to each response, as illustrated by Example 4.2, whereby codes of 01–07 are used instead of 1–7.

Codes of 9, 99, 999, and so forth should be reserved for the "Other" response category, thereby providing coding space for newly created postcoded categories adjacent to the other fixed alternatives. The codes of 0, 00, 000, and so forth are reserved in many computer programs for nonresponses. Therefore, numerical codes should begin with 1 for single-digit categories, 01 for double-digit categories, and 001 for triple-digit categories.

The far right-hand side of the questionnaire is frequently reserved for informing the computer technician how the code is to be read. Each response is assigned a series of spaces in the computer memory. In order for the numerical codes to be appropriately located within these computer spaces, the computer must allocate enough space to accommodate the number of digits that have been assigned to the categories of each variable. Example 4.1, for example, contains three categories, coded from 1 to 3. The computer must be instructed to reserve one space in its memory for this question, and the technician is so informed by the numerical notation of "[12]" on the far right. Similarly, Example 4.2, which contains two-digit codes, reserves two computer spaces with the notation of "[44–45]."

It is important to note that the numerical notations on the right are called *fields* and that each field corresponds to one variable. In general, questions that elicit two or more separate responses, as in Example 3.5, are considered to be made up of two or more variables. That is to say, each response must be regarded as a separate variable with its own distinct field. Example 3.5 must be precoded with separate field notations for each of the two responses. Thus, on the far right, two field notations would appear, arranged vertically in separate brackets.

The researcher may wish to reserve numerical codes for various other purposes—for example, to anonymously provide each respondent with a number in order to identify and correct computer input errors (see the section on computerized data entry later in this chapter), or to provide interviewer codes for purposes of quality control. In the case of respondent codes, an adequate number of digits must be provided and reserved in the computer's memory to allow each respondent to be individually coded. A survey of 1,000 respondents, for example, must reserve a field of four spaces. Generally, this field is reserved as the first few spaces of each respondent's entered data. In this case, a field [1–4] would be allocated and assigned digits of 0001–1000. The first variable, therefore, would start at field position 5.

Administering the Questionnaire

Once the questionnaire has been precoded and drafted in its final form, the researcher is ready to administer the survey instrument. The method of administration has been chosen prior to questionnaire construction, as discussed in Chapter One, and the researcher now must take the steps necessary to solicit the required data in accordance with the requirements associated with the selected method. This section presents detailed procedures for conducting these various types of surveys.

Mail-Out Surveys

Certain guidelines should be followed in administering a mail-out questionnaire. First, the questionnaire should be designed in the form of a booklet in order to ensure its professional appearance and to make it more usable by the respondent. Any resemblance to an advertising brochure should be strictly avoided. The aesthetic appearance of the questionnaire is important in terms of generating satisfactory response rates. There should be adequate spacing between questions, and questions should not be divided between two pages. Instructions to the respondent should be clear and easily distinguished from the survey questions themselves. Graphics, such as maps and illustrative photographs, should be carefully integrated into the design of the questionnaire.

The cover letter should be prepared in accordance with the principles of Chapter Two and should, of course, become the first page of the booklet. The last page of the booklet should be reserved for two purposes only: (1) to express appreciation to the respondents for their participation and (2) to provide a return mailing address and prepaid postage through a business reply permit. The last page should also contain instructions for returning the completed questionnaire. Alternatively, it is possible to provide postage-paid, preaddressed return envelopes, but the cost of this approach is somewhat higher.

Questionnaires should be stamped with an identification number for purposes of monitoring the follow-up process. This number must be explained to the respondent in the cover letter, accompanied by assurances of privacy and confidentiality (see Chapter Two).

The questionnaire booklet is mailed by first-class postage to the respondent in an envelope. The envelope is addressed either with the name and address of the respondent individually imprinted (in the case of small, more personalized surveys) or with a mailing label (most commonly used in large-scale, high-volume surveys). As will be discussed in Chapter Seven, mailing labels can be obtained from private mail services.

Follow-Up Mailings. As indicated in Chapter Two, a target date should be designated for the return of the questionnaire; this target date is generally recommended to be approximately three weeks from the initial mailing date. Two weeks after the initial mailing, a follow-up postcard reminder should be sent to those potential respondents who have not yet replied, as determined by their prestamped identification number. The reminder should be friendly in tone and contain language indicating that if the completed questionnaire and the reminder postcard have crossed in the mail, the respondent should disregard the reminder; appreciation for the respondent's cooperation is again mentioned.

Four weeks from the initial mailing, a second follow-up should be mailed to all survey recipients who have not yet responded. This follow-up should include a new cover letter that does not specify a target due date but instead stresses the importance of responding. Another copy of the questionnaire should accompany the letter in case the original questionnaire has been misplaced or discarded.

It can be reasonably expected that this procedure will yield a response rate of 50 to 60 percent for the general public and a somewhat higher rate for specialized populations. The researcher should wait two weeks after the second follow-up before closing the mailing process. A response rate of 50 to 60 percent can be considered satisfactory for purposes of analysis and reporting findings. If the researcher wishes to increase the response rate and has adequate resources and time to do so, the following additional procedures are suggested:

- In lieu of mailing labels, envelopes and the cover letter can be individually imprinted with the potential respondent's name and address.
- The cover letters should be individually signed in blue ink to avoid the impression that they were impersonally mass-produced.
- The follow-up mailings should include eye-catching, but tasteful, illustrations and graphics.

- Six weeks after the initial mailing, nonrespondents should be given a reminder telephone call.
- A third follow-up mailing, again with a new cover letter and copy of the questionnaire, should be sent to all nonrespondents eight weeks after the first mailing. This third follow-up should be delivered by certified mail.

These additional procedures are designed to achieve a response rate in excess of 70 percent for the general population and as high as 90 percent for certain specialized groups.

Special Considerations for Sample Selection in a Mail-Out Survey. Because the researcher has no control over which of the potential respondents will ultimately return the completed questionnaires in a mail-out survey, special sampling procedures must be adopted. It is expected that the process explained above will yield a minimum 50 percent response rate; therefore, the researcher should send the questionnaire to twice as many potential respondents as the number required for the overall sample. (See Chapter Six for a discussion of sample size requirements.) If, for example, 600 respondents are required, the researcher should randomly select 1,200 potential respondents to receive the questionaire by mail. It is possible to achieve a response rate greater than 50 percent. In this case, there may be more than 600 respondents to the questionnaire. The researcher should feel free to use these additional responses as part of the overall sample, thereby achieving a still higher degree of accuracy than was initially planned. The cost involved in mailing, receiving, and processing these additional responses is justified on the basis of making certain that at least the required 600 responses will be received under the 50 percent response rate assumption. If fewer than 600 responses are received, the survey will fall short of its established requirements.

Another factor that might require an even larger number of questionnaires to be mailed initially is *stratification*, which will be discussed in Chapter Seven. Some research objectives require that certain population groups be assured of adequate representation within the overall sample (generally, at least 100

Table 4.1. Total Population and Anticipated Questionnaire Responses from a Random Sample of Hypothetical Geographic Subareas.

Area	*Population*	*%*	*Anticipated Questionaire Responses*	*%*
A	10,000	10.0	60	10.0
B	20,000	20.0	120	20.0
C	30,000	30.0	180	30.0
D	20,000	20.0	120	20.0
E	20,000	20.0	120	20.0
Total	100,000	100.0	600	100.0

respondents for each such stratum or group). The researcher must, therefore, mail at least 200 questionnaires to identified strata, and perhaps more if it is suspected that these groups might be somewhat unresponsive.

By way of example, if the research focus requires analysis by geographic area, then stratification on the basis of geography is appropriate. Table 4.1 presents the population data for five areas within the city under study and also depicts the anticipated number of responses from each area based on a 50 percent response rate to 1,200 randomly mailed questionnaires and a proportionate response by each area.

Two choices are available to the researcher at this juncture:

1. Mail an additional 80 questionnaires to area A in order to achieve 40 more responses yielding the requisite total of 100. The initial mailing will, then, total 1,280 (1,200 to achieve 600 responses plus an additional 80 for the 40 more that are needed from area A).
2. Reallocate initial mailings from areas B, C, D, and E (all with sufficient anticipated responses) to area A, maintaining an initial mailing sample of 1,200.

Inasmuch as the mail-out is the least costly of the three formats, it is recommended that, budget permitting, the first option be selected based on its convenience in avoiding the need to reallocate the initial sample. In either option, the weighting procedure, which is explained fully in Chapter Seven, must be undertaken prior to data analysis.

Telephone Surveys

The telephone survey is less complex to implement than the mail-out. The most important aspect of this survey technique is the use of personal interviewers; the proper selection and training of these interviewers is critical to the success of the research project.

Selection of Telephone Interviewers. The researcher should be aware of the fact that there are a variety of sources through which individuals may be recruited to serve as telephone interviewers. The single best source of interviewers, when available, is a local university. Students, especially upper-division undergraduate students and graduate students, are motivated to become involved in the interviewing process for two basic reasons. First, there is frequently some substantive interest in the research project and its potential findings. Second, students often seek ways to augment their income in order to help fund their education and therefore may be willing to work for wages that are relatively modest in relation to their skill level. If the researcher does not already have an affiliation with a university, professors in appropriate disciplines should be contacted and arrangements made to recruit potential interviewers. University bulletin boards and newsletters can also be used.

When universities are not readily accessible or when additional assistance is required, newspaper "help wanted" ads are the second most effective recruitment tool. Newspapers that can be considered for placement of such ads include not only the major metropolitan dailies, but also neighborhood weekly newspapers. Another source of recruitment is contact with local organizations, such as social service delivery groups, civic organizations, and church groups, which are frequently able to publicize recruitment needs among their memberships.

The content of the recruiting advertisement should enable potential applicants to determine if they are interested in the job and if they meet its requirements. Thus, the job notice should include such information as work hours, pay rate, location of the work site (home or central telephone facility), and whether or not fluency in a language other than English is necessary. The job notice should also indicate times and dates for group meetings, which are designed to dispense additional information, answer questions, and receive interviewer job applications; these applications should contain questions about work history, education, professional references, and availability to perform the required tasks. Group sessions are an efficient way to avoid unscheduled and frequent individual recruitment sessions, which can be very time consuming for the researcher.

Having reviewed the job applications, the researcher should narrow the list of applicants by screening out those who clearly do not meet the basic requirements. After a brief personal interview, the remaining applicants are asked to administer a practice questionnaire as a final screening device. This process will enable the researcher to determine the applicants' ability to read at the appropriate level, follow directions, and relate to other people. Final selection should be based on the written application, the personal interview, the practice questionnaire, and any potential biasing characteristics that the interviewer feels the applicant may possess. A poor performance during the practice questionnaire should not necessarily eliminate the applicant from consideration; interviewer training after selection may help to mitigate some of the problems that are seen during the practice session.

Training of Telephone Interviewers. Interviewer training consists of a two-pronged process. First, the reseacher should provide the interviewer with general training regarding the fundamental techniques of the interviewing process, and second, the researcher should instruct the interviewer in proper administration of the specific survey questionnaire. Several procedures can be used to assist in the training process. To begin with, an overview of the questionnaire should be provided that is specific to the study, with the various types of questions identified, and all interviewer instructions pointed out, especially those pertaining to filtering and screening. It is advisable to pay particular attention to questions that permit more than one response, and to make certain that "other" categories and open-ended questions are recorded with precision. The researcher should also discuss the answer code format and explain the purpose of the variable fields.

Interviewers should be provided with a general understanding of the scope and substantive purpose of the research project. The organization sponsoring the survey should also be indicated. It is also important to make interviewers aware of the role they play within the survey process as a whole; that is, the interviewers should become aware of the sample size, the sample selection process employed, and how their role relates to the entire survey process, including data entry, data analysis, and the preparation of the final report.

The interviewer should be given the opportunity to practice administering the questionnaire. The first step in this procedure generally involves home study, in which the interviewer is sent home with a package of material, including the questionnaire and a small information sheet containing interviewer instructions. Home study should include rehearsal of the questionnaire with someone who is not associated with the study. Its main purpose is to allow the interviewer to gain facility with the survey instrument. After home study, and before actual interviews begin, interviewers should be contacted by the researcher for a final rehearsal of the questionnaire. All interviewers should be present, and they should alternate the roles of interviewer and respondent.

All telephone interviewers should be aware of some general ethical issues. The interview must be held in confidentiality and any information obtained through the interviewing process must be treated anonymously. The interviewer achieves the proper degree of confidentiality and anonymity by making no notations on the survey forms that would permit identification of the respondent. As stated in Chapter One, the telephone survey process permits the researcher to immediately note the disposition of the interview in terms of who has responded and who has not. The researcher will provide to the interviewer a sample list of telephone numbers upon which the interviewer should make the appropriate notations. In particular, when an interview has been completed, the corresponding telephone number should be crossed off the list. In contrast, in mail-out follow-up surveys, the researcher must identify each returned questionnaire. Although ethics demand anonymity and confidentiality in both formats, the proper application of the telephone interview provides a built-in safeguard that the mail-out survey does not.

The interviewer must be careful to minimize the amount of bias introduced into the interviewing process. The introductory greeting, as discussed in Chapter Two, should be delivered with sincerity. Questions should be read verbatim with appropriate pacing and in a pleasant conversational tone. The interviewer should be satisfied that the respondent understands the question and must be careful to record responses accurately, making certain that the respondent's answer is fully understood.

The interviewer should not express any opinions or make extraneous comments in reaction to statements made by the respondent. Despite these efforts to minimize bias, there is always the potential for the respondent's answers to be affected to some extent by her or his reaction to one or more characteristics of the interviewer, such as ethnic or regional accents, sex, or age. The researcher should be cognizant of these potential problems and plan the conduct of the research study accordingly. Interviewers should mark all responses directly on the questionnaire form. Direct use of the form itself makes it considerably easier for the interviewer to follow all intstructions and ask all appropriate questions, especially when filtering or screening questions are involved. If the respondent offers extraneous or supplementary information, the interviewer should be instructed to record it as accurately as possible on the blank side of the questionnaire form. Such voluntary statements may contain valuable information that may shed light on the issue at hand.

Interviewing should be conducted in the early evening (6:00 P.M. to 9:00 P.M. local time) and on the weekends (noon to

9:00 P.M.). Evenings provide the researcher greater opportunity to reach working adult household members, whereas daytime calling during the week would reach only those adults who are not working outside the home. After 9:00 P.M., the interviewer should stop placing calls to avoid disturbing those who may have retired for the night. Similarly, on weekends, calls prior to noon may interfere with needed extra hours of sleep or time spent at religious services. The overriding principle is to reach as many adult household members as possible at a convenient time.

If the interviewer encounters a busy signal, the call should be tried again in thirty minutes; if the line is still busy, the call is placed the next day. If the first call on the next day is once again met with a busy signal, the interviewer should wait 30 minutes and try one more time. When there are repeated busy signals, the interviewer is required to contact the telephone company to ascertain the working status of the number. If the telephone company indicates that the line is operating, the interviewer may try calling on another day at a time totally different from the previous attempts. If the line is still busy, the interviewer should classify the number as a "nonresponse" to avoid spending an inordinate amount of time in pursuit of one potential respondent. When, instead of a busy signal, the first call elicits no answer, the call should be repeated the next day. If, after three such attempts, there is still no answer, the telephone number can be treated as a "nonresponse."

When the sampling frame is composed of households, rather than individuals, the interviewer must speak to an adult member of the selected household unless the survey is specifically geared to minors. The interviewer should try to speak to a representative mix of men and women and sometimes may have to specifically request to speak to an "adult male" or "adult female" in order to maintain representativeness by gender.

When the interviewer has exhausted the sample list of telephone numbers, the researcher should be told by the interviewer how many nonresponses have been encountered. The researcher will provide the interviewer with a list of replacement telephone numbers selected in accordance with the appropriate sample selection method (see Chapter Seven). The interviewer then proceeds to make these calls as described above, returning to the researcher, once again, all nonresponses from the list. This process continues until the interviewer has completed the number of interviews assigned.

At the completion of each interview, interviewers should examine the completed questionnaire for missed questions, unclear open-ended responses, and general legibility. If necessary, a follow-up telephone call to the respondent should be conducted immediately.

There are a number of additional rules of interviewing that the researcher should insist upon having followed. These rules include:

- An interviewer should never interview more than one adult in the same household.
- A friend or relative should not be interviewed. If a friend or relative is part of the sample list, the researcher should be notified so that the person in question can be reassigned to another interviewer.
- The interviews should be conducted in as much privacy as possible to avoid distraction.
- The interviewer should not delegate assigned interviews to anyone else.
- Interviews should never be falsified.

In-Person Interviews

In-person, or face-to-face, interviews were at one time the dominant method of collecting survey data but have declined in popularity in recent years for three primary reasons:

1. There have been significant technological advances in telephone interviewing, especially the advent of random-digit dialing.
2. In the past, survey interviewers were homemakers who wished to work on a part-time basis. As economic conditions resulted in more members of this group being em-

ployed full-time, the supply of potential interviewers began to decline.

3. The rising number of incidents of crime has made it extremely difficult to find in-person interviewers.

However, as detailed in Chapter One, in-person interviews continue to play a role in survey research. As with the telephone interview, the selection and training of interviewers is critical to the successful solicitation of data.

Selection of In-Person Interviewers. The process of selecting interviewers should be precisely the same as that used for selecting telephone interviewers, with a certain emphasis on physical characteristics that is not as important in the telephone survey process. Because in-person interviewing involves face-to-face interaction between the respondent and the interviewer, the respondent's willingness to participate is highly dependent on the comfort level the respondent perceives to exist between them. Physical characteristics such as attire, cleanliness, neatness, manners, and overall grooming loom considerably larger in the in-person format than in the telephone survey, and they set the tone for the seriousness of the research study. Consequently, these characteristics must be emphasized in the selection process.

There is a secondary component of the interviewer's physical characteristics that can bear strongly on the in-person interview. A series of studies throughout the years has established that people have been socialized to react differently to another person depending on his or her sex, age, ethnicity, and social status (Bailey, 1982, pp. 184–192). These studies indicate that an interviewer with roughly the same characteristics as the respondent will tend to obtain more reliable information, especially if this information pertains to issues that are perceived by the respondent to be sensitive in nature. In the interest of obtaining as much reliable information as possible, the researcher must incorporate these considerations into the interviewer selection process.

Training of In-Person Interviewers. The principles of interviewer training that have been stated above with regard to the training of telephone interviewers apply also to in-person interviewers. A few additional considerations exist, which result from the differences in format between the two methods. These considerations are generally minor, however, and are relatively obvious.

Prearranging the In-Person Interview. It is important to remember that in-person interviews must be prearranged in order to protect the privacy and safety of both the respondent and the interviewer, in contrast to telephone calling, which is performed spontaneously. In addition to refraining from verbal reactions to the respondent, the interviewer should avoid any facial expressions or other gestures that may bias or otherwise disturb the respondent. It is recommended that all potential sample respondents be sent a letter not dissimilar from the one that introduces a mail-out questionnaire, including a description of the nature of the study and a statement concerning the importance of the recipient's participation. The letter should further state that a telephone call will soon follow in which the interviewer will seek to arrange an appointment for a personal interview at a place convenient to the respondent—often at the respondent's home or place of work. Approximately one week after delivery of the letter, interviewers should begin placing the telephone calls. The guidelines for conducting these calls should follow the same format in terms of time of day and follow-up calling procedures as telephone interview calls.

Monitoring and Supervision of the Interview Process

Telephone interviewing and the scheduling of personal interviews are best conducted from a centralized facility. This tends to produce higher response rates compared with interviews conducted privately from interviewers' homes or offices. It also affords the supervisor ample opportunities to directly monitor telephone conversations by listening to them. When such direct monitoring takes place, the respondent must be informed.

When telephone interviews and scheduling are conducted from private locations, the supervisor should randomly select at least 10 percent of the proposed sample and call these households to verify that contact has, in fact, taken place and to ascertain the respondents' degree of satisfaction with the conversation.

The supervisor should review the interviewer's work, be available for questions, and have frequent contact with the interviewers in the form of regular telephone or personal conferences. The supervisor should be prepared to reassign cases among interviewers if this is necessitated by such factors as language difficulties or varying completion rates. Production objectives should be established in terms of number of interviews to be completed in a given amount of time. It is the supervisor's responsibility to constantly monitor interviewer performance in terms of these objectives.

For larger projects, the supervisor should be hired by the researcher and should be expected to work at least twenty hours per week, especially in the early stages of the interview process. With smaller projects, the researcher may also be able to serve as a supervisor, thereby eliminating the need to employ additional staff.

Editing the Completed Questionnaire

As discussed above, a part of the interviewer's task is to examine the finished questionnaires for accuracy, legibility, and completeness. Despite this preliminary examination, the researcher must review each questionnaire for quality control purposes, especially in terms of filtering, multiple answers, and open-ended questions. Furthermore, since mail-out questionnaires have no intermediate interviewer examination, the researcher must be particularly careful in reviewing them.

In the review, the interviewer must be sure that questions that were designed to be skipped (through a filtering process) have indeed been skipped. If the interviewer has mistakenly asked an inapplicable question or has inadvertently marked a response to that question, the response should be deleted. In the case of questions that permit multiple responses and request a ranking, the first choice should be ranked by a code of 1 and the second choice by a code of 2. Such a question should be examined for accuracy in the following way:

- If only one response was made, it should receive a code of 1.
- Two responses should be coded with a 1 and a 2. If two responses are provided but are not ranked (they are indicated with a checkmark, for instance), telephone or in-person interviewers should recontact the respondent immediately. This is an important reason for interviewers to examine the accuracy of their completed interviews at the time they are given. In the mail-out format, if there are only a few such responses, follow-up telephone calls, using the cross-referenced identification code, are in order. If there are many such inaccurately coded responses, the researcher can establish a new category for response categories that have been indicated but not ranked (see the discussion of postcoding below for the procedure for introducing new variable categories).
- More than two responses are not permitted. The telephone and in-person formats enable immediate recontact. The mail-out can also involve respondent contact in the event of a few such errors; if there are many inaccurately coded responses, the category of "Indicated but not ranked" can be used, and the final report should caution the reader that some respondents provided more than two responses.

After the review of the questionnaire has been completed, the researcher can begin the postcoding process. In postcoding, responses are coded to questions that have not been precoded. To facilitate this process, the researcher should ask the interviewers to list all open-ended or "Other, please specify" responses to each applicable question on separate sheets of paper.

With regard to the "Other, please specify" response category, the researcher should first review the list of responses, identify those that reasonably belong to a precoded category, and code them in accordance with that category by boldly writing the code number directly on the questionnaire next to the response. This should be done in a different-colored ink from the one used to typeset the form and the one used by the respondent or interviewer to mark the questionnaire. This will permit the data entry technician to easily identify the postcoded response. The original "Other" response code of 9 or 99, for instance, should be crossed out for further clarity. The responses that cannot be categorized into the precoded response categories can be treated in one of two ways, requiring a certain degree of judgment by the researcher.

1. When there is a sufficiently large number of the same or similar responses, the researcher should consider creating a separate category with a new numerical code, starting with the first available number following the precodes, but before the code for "Other." If the frequency of any of these similar responses approaches the frequency of one of the precoded categories, it is probable that a new code is warranted. This code should be marked on the questionnaire boldly and in a different color. Recoding is a frequent necessity in survey research in order to accommodate unexpected responses.
2. All responses that have a relatively low frequency of response can be aggregated into a "Miscellaneous" or "Other" category, remaining in the 9 or 99 codes.

Example 4.3 can be used to demonstrate this process; a completed questionnaire contains a response that has been proven to occur with great frequency on other completed questionnaires and therefore merits a code of its own.

Example 4.3:

What kind of new business in Compton do you feel would give you the best opportunity for employment?
1. ____ Retail
2. ____ Light industry
3. ____ Heavy industry

4. ____ Office/professional
5. _x_ Other, please specify ____restaurant____

Open-ended questions require a similar postcoding process. That is, based on a verbatim listing of all responses to an open-ended question, the researcher again uses her or his judgment to develop categories into which these responses can be placed. The number of categories should be as close to ten as possible, with a maximum of fifteen to twenty, while adhering to the guideline discussed in Chapter Three that each should contain a respectable percentage (3–5 percent) of the total responses.

Table 4.2 was derived from the categorization of responses to an open-ended question: "How can the city government better serve your community?" By way of elaborating upon the process or categorizing open-ended responses, the category of "Improve zoning/planning process" in Table 4.2 contains such verbatim responses as "fewer apartments," "more open space," "make developers pay fair share," and "protect property values."

Computerized Data Entry

When they have been completed, edited, and coded, the questionnaires are ready for the data entry process, the specifics of which depend on the computer facilities and software that are available to the researcher.

Table 4.2. Ways in Which City Government Can Serve Community Needs.

	f	%
Provide improved local police protection	90	22.5
Ease traffic congestion	83	20.8
Enhance public education	74	18.5
Improve zoning/planning process	70	17.5
Provide more community funds	35	8.7
Improve communication	21	5.3
Other	27	6.7
Total	400	100.0

Universities, government agencies, and other large institutions and corporations frequently maintain mainframe computer systems. These systems process data that are entered on magnetic tape or disk, as well as directly (on-line) through the internal system of the computer itself. A researcher may wish to take advantage of the service offered by independent data processing companies, which will enter the data from the questionnaires onto tape or disks in preparation for statistical analysis by the mainframe program. These independent data processing companies may offer cost and time savings to the researcher because of their specialization and particular expertise in the computerized input of data. The data processing company must be informed as to the specific computer system involved, its format requirements, and the statistical programs to be used. Among the major mainframe systems are IBM, CYBER, and VAX. Two of the primary statistical programs for mainframes are the Statistical Package for the Social Sciences (SPSS) and the Statistical Analysis System (SAS). Both of these programs are sophisticated and comprehensive; they are capable of processing large amounts of data and generating both the very basic and the most highly advanced descriptive and analytical statistics and graphics. Chapters Eight and Nine explore some of this capability, but this discussion describes only a small portion of the potential utility of these programs.

Rapid technological advances in personal computers (PCs) have resulted in researchers finding that many of their data processing and analytical needs can be met by using these smaller computers. In many cases, the cost, convenience and accessibility of the PC is preferable to working with mainframe systems. The statistical packages that dominate the personal computer market are:

- SPSS/PC+ (Statistical Package for the Social Sciences)
- SAS-PC (Statistical Analysis System)
- SYStat (System for Statistics)
- Minitabs Statistical Software

The reader should be aware, however, that this list of statistical packages is by no means exhaustive. Several other excellent packages are available that the researcher may find useful for a particular project.

Although all of the programs listed above have the necessary features to accomplish almost any task required in a survey research project, they each have their own individual characteristics and relative advantages and disadvantages, which must be considered prior to selecting the most appropriate one for a given project. The size and scope of the project, the sophistication of statistical analysis envisioned, the importance of the integration of graphics into the final report, ease of operation, and program cost are all factors that bear upon the selection of the appropriate statistical package. The following section provides a brief description of each of the four major PC statistical software packages along with recommendations regarding their relative merits and utility. Because the researcher must have a working knowledge of statistical applications in order to select the best program for the project and must plan how statistics and graphic displays will be incorporated into the final report, the following information can be best understood only after the remainder of this book has been read.

SPSS/PC+

This program is an adaptation of the very popular mainframe program SPSS, which is primarily geared to quantitative analysis for the social sciences. SPSS/PC+ is a sophisticated and multifaceted program with a thorough tutorial on using the package as well as on understanding certain basic statistical procedures. The documentation is excellent. The system is menu driven, featuring context-sensitive help screens. Crosstabulations are produced efficiently and quickly. Graphics of presentation quality are available in several add-on optional packages. Overall, SPSS/PC+ is a comprehensive system, capable of performing for both the professional statistician and the less experienced researcher. Its only drawbacks are its relatively high price and its requirement for a large amount of storage capacity (12 MB). SPSS/PC+ has been available for DOS-based systems and recently became available for Macintosh computers.

SAS-PC

This program is a comprehensive statistical analysis package, usable through a new system or an expert command language. It is a difficult program to master, with sizable amounts of documentation and instruction for the basic system, for advanced statistics, and for its graphics procedures, which are excellent. SAS-PC's cross-tabulation capability is considered to be very good and its statistical functionality is wide ranging and of great depth. The cost of the SAS-PC package, which has only been usable on DOS-based systems, is significantly lower than that of SPSS/PC + .

SYStat

SYStat is a statistical package for both the DOS and Macintosh systems. It is a program that is capable of generating a full range of descriptive and analytical statistics and very attractive graphics. It has been found to be particularly user friendly, with logical and easy-to-follow commands. The manuals have numerous examples and are well written and highly readable. Unlike other manuals, SYStat does not attempt to instruct users in statistical analysis, but rather refers them to available statistical literature. Its cross-tabulations are produced in two or more parts, as opposed to others that produce consolidated contingency tables. The cost of the SYStat package is closer to that of SPSS/PC + than it is to the more affordable SAS-PC.

Minitabs Statistical Software

Among the programs discussed here, Minitabs is the one that can be characterized as possessing the most simplicity. It is particularly oriented for the nonprofessional statistician. It is entirely command driven, with no mouse and no "pull-down" menus. Its graphics do not measure up to the other programs discussed above, and Minitabs can tend to have memory-related shortcomings. The documentation, however, is excellent and the cost, although greater than that of SAS-PC, is less than the cost of

SPSS/PC+ or SYStat. Overall, as a general-purpose statistical program, Minitabs is well respected.

Exercises

1. Precode the following survey question:
   What type of business do you operate? (Check only one)
   _____ Automotive/automotive-related
   _____ Professional
   _____ Services
   _____ Restaurant
   _____ Retail
   _____ Entertainment
   _____ Other, please specify _____
   Hint: You should suspect that the list of business types is not exhaustive.

2. For the survey question in Exercise 1, postcode the following survey responses, which were answered as "Other, please specify."
   a. Dry cleaning
   b. Hotel
   c. Pediatrician
   d. Gas station
   e. Jewelry store
   f. Bar

3. Your staff has recorded and compiled open-ended responses to the following question into preliminary categories as designated in Table 4.3:

   > Thinking of your neighborhood as well as your city in general, what do you personally feel are the most important issues or problems facing the residents of this city? You may designate as many responses as you desire.

Table 4.3. Important Issues Facing Residents of the City of San Antonio.

	f	%
Road congestion	1,200	21.5
Too much growth and development	900	16.2
Need more open space	200	3.6
Preserve rural environment	100	1.8
Crime and drug abuse	350	6.3
School overcrowding	400	7.2
Poor-quality education	250	4.5
Parking problems	900	16.2
High taxes	175	3.2
Poor street maintenance	125	2.3
Need city beautification program	50	0.9
Inadequate library facilities	25	0.5
Inefficient government	150	2.7
Not enough jails	225	4.1
Need more jobs	300	5.4
Parks and recreation	200	3.6
Total	5,550	100.0

Using the principles and guidelines of Chapter Four, establish the final categories for data entry and recalculate the corresponding frequencies and percentages.

4. Prepare a short summary of the principles associated with the selection, training, and supervision of interviewers.

PART TWO

Ensuring Scientific Accuracy

Chapter 5

Understanding Sampling Theory

Statistical analysis is an integral part of the sample research process, especially with regard to understanding the theoretical basis of using a sample to represent the entire population. This chapter provides an introductory treatment of the statistical concepts necessary to truly understand the scientific basis of survey research.

The purpose of sampling is to be able to make generalizations about a population based on a scientifically selected subset of that population. Sampling is necessary because it is generally not practical or feasible to seek information from every member of a population. A sample, therefore, is intended to become a microcosm of a larger universe. However, the question posed in Chapter One asked how a relatively small subset of cases can be used to represent the much larger population from which the subset has been selected. In order to address and fully understand the implications of this question, it is important to establish the theoretical basis of sampling and its associated assumptions.

Describing Distributions of Data

Two primary types of statistics are used to describe distributions of data. They are measures of central tendency and measures of dispersion.

Measures of central tendency provide summarizing numbers that characterize what is "typical" or "average" for particular data. The mean (arithmetic mean), mode, and median are the three measures of central tendency. While the mean is the most important measure of central tendency for explaining the basis of sampling theory, it should initially be presented in the context of its two counterpart measures. The three measures of central tendency are defined as follows:

Mode: the category or value of the data that is characterized by possessing the greatest frequency of response. It conveys that category which is most typical of the population surveyed.

Median: the value of the variable that represents the midpoint of the data. One-half of the data will have values below the median and one-half will have values above it.

Mean: the mathematical center of the data, taking into account not only the location of the data (above or below the center), but also the relative distance of the data from that center.

For example, in a class of 11 students in a graduate seminar, the final exam grades are as follows:

100, 95, 94, 90, 85, 82, 79, 79, 76, 70, 53

The mode is the score that occurs most frequently (79), the median is the middle grade of the eleven (82), and the mean is the sum of these exam grades divided by the total number of such grades. In this case, the mean equals 82.1.

Whereas measures of central tendency establish centrality, it is also important to know how widely dispersed are the individual items in the distribution. The most common measure of dispersion is the standard deviation. Standard deviation is a measurement of the distance between the mean and the individual items in the distribution. Standard deviation is a particularly critical statistic in the interpretation of sample data and this same interpretation with respect to the mean in the context of the normal distribution is the key underpinning of sampling theory.

The Normal Distribution

Most features or characteristics (variables) of a population tend to be distributed in accordance with the commonly understood concept of the bell-shaped curve. For instance, most adult American men weigh between 150 and 200 pounds, with far fewer weighing less than 150 or more than 200 pounds. If the weights of all American men were recorded and their frequencies plotted, the distribution would most likely resemble the bell shape depicted in Figure 5.1, which is known statistically as the *normal distribution* or *normal curve*.

In the normal distribution, the mean is located at the exact center and peak of the curve, dividing the curve into two

Figure 5.1. The Normal Curve.

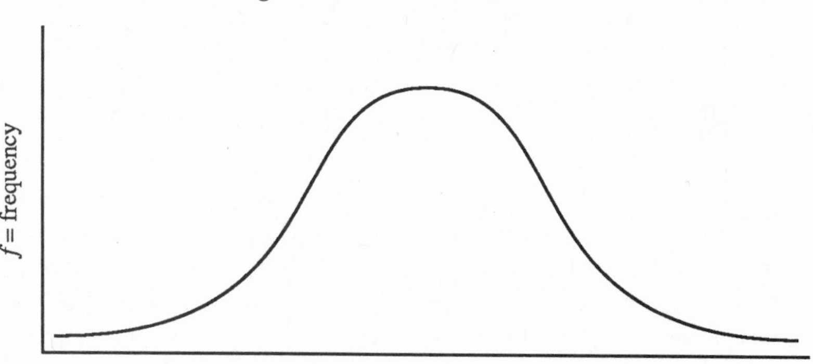

symmetrical halves, each the mirror image of the other. The normal curve is asymptotic to the *x*-axis. In other words, in both directions, the curve moves closer and closer to the *x*-axis but, in theory, never touches it.

Most cases in the normal distribution are clustered around the mean. In the example of the weights of adult American men, if the mean weight were 175 pounds, more men would weigh 170 pounds than would weigh 150 pounds. Similarly, more men would weigh 180 pounds than would weigh 190 pounds.

There are certain standard properties of the normal curve that convey how values of the variable are distributed around the mean. The measurement of distance from the mean is calculated in terms of the *standard deviation*. The standard deviation is, as the name implies, a measurement of dispersion around the mean in standardized units. Consequently, no matter what the variable is (for instance, weight, IQ scores, or income), a constant proportion of the total area under the normal curve will lie between the mean and any given distance from the mean as measured in units of standard deviation. The calculation of the true population standard deviation (σ) is as follows:

$$\sigma = \sqrt{\frac{\Sigma(x - \mu)^2}{N}} \tag{5.1}$$

where σ = true population standard deviation, μ = true population mean, and N = population size.

For any particular normal distribution, regardless of the mean or the calculated standard deviation, the number of cases between the mean (μ) and one standard deviation (1σ) always turns out to include 34.13 percent of the total cases (see Figure 5.2). Furthermore, since the normal distribution is symmetrical, the identical proportion of cases will lie below the mean (that is, between μ and -1σ). Hence 68.26 percent of all cases in the entire population will be found within one standard deviation of the mean in either direction. Similarly, 95.44 percent of all

Figure 5.2. Area Under the Normal Curve, in Percent, by Standard Deviation.

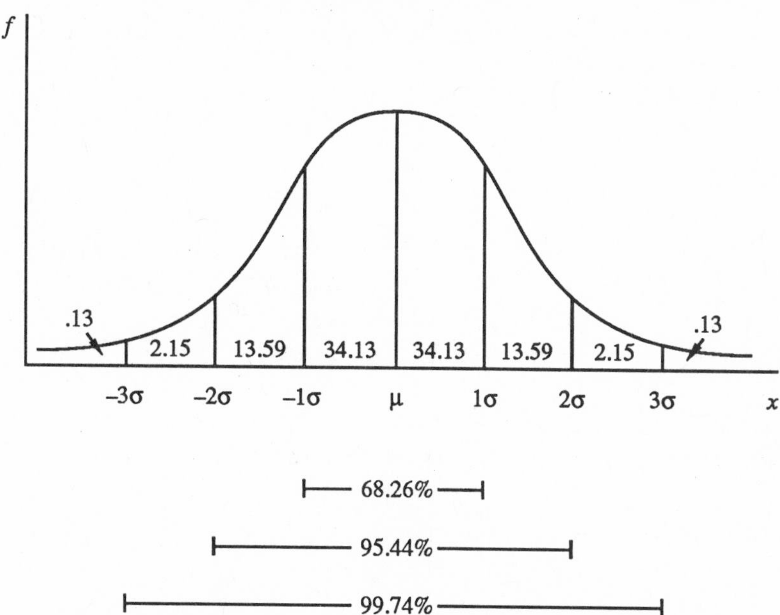

cases are to be found within two standard deviations and 99.74 percent within three standard deviations. It should be clear, therefore, that a very small number of cases exists farther than three standard deviations from the mean.

In the example of adult American male weights, given the mean weight of 175 pounds and an associated standard deviation of 30 pounds, it can be expected that 68.26 percent of the males would weigh between 145 and 205 pounds, 95.44 percent of the males would weigh between 115 and 235 pounds, and almost all men (99.74 percent) would weigh between 85 and 265 pounds.

The distribution of IQ scores is also an excellent example of normality. With an overall mean IQ of 100 and a standard deviation of 15, the percentage of scores contained within the ranges of standard deviations is as shown in Exhibit 5.1. From this exhibit, it should be apparent why a score of 140 has been

Exhibit 5.1. Range of Hypothetical IQ Scores ($\mu = 100$, $\sigma = 15$).

Range of Scores	*Percentage of Cases Within Range*
85–115	68.26
70–130	95.44
55–145	99.74

generally accepted as being a particularly high, sometimes meriting the label "genius." However, what if a researcher wanted to know approximately how many cases could be expected to be found above or below that "genius" score of 140? The ranges of standard deviations in Exhibit 5.1 do not seem to lend themselves to such a determination, but in fact they do. It is possible, in the normal distribution, to calculate the relative position of any score by converting it into fractional units of standard deviations, known as *Z* scores. This conversion can be accomplished through the following formula:

$$Z = \frac{x - \mu}{\sigma} \tag{5.2}$$

where x = individual score, μ = mean of the population distribution, σ = standard deviation of the population, and Z = standard deviation unit scores. When converting to *Z* scores, the population mean (in this case, $\mu = 100$) is represented by a *Z* score of 0 $[(100 - 100)/15 = 0]$. Applying 5.2 to the IQ score of 140 generates a *Z* score as follows: $Z = 140 - 100/15 = 2.67$.

In other words, a score of 140 is 2.67 standard deviation units to the right (positive) of the mean ($Z = 0$) on the normal curve. In order to comprehend this score in the context of relative position in the distribution, it is necessary to find the percentage of cases that are above or below 2.67 units. That is accomplished by consulting the Table of Areas of a Standard Normal Distribution given in Resource A. A *Z* score of 2.67 (column A) represents the point on the curve at which 99.62 percent of all scores are lower than the subject score of 140 and only 0.38 percent are higher. The determination of the percentage of all scores below $Z = 2.67$ is derived from column B in Resource A, which shows 49.62 percent of scores existing between the mean and the Z under consideration. Since the properties of the normal distribution stipulate that 50 percent of all cases are on each side of the mean, adding the 50 percent of cases below the mean to the 49.62 percent of cases above it (column B) yields 99.62 percent.

The Theoretical Basis of Sampling

Thus far, the discussion has focused on the normal distribution of *every* case in a population. It should be evident that such complete information is rarely available. Gathering data from every member of a population is, in most cases, either logistically impossible or economically infeasible. Therefore, it has become practical for samples of the population to be selected so that generalizations can be inferred from the sample to the total population. These generalizations find their statistical basis in the characteristics of the normal distribution.

As stated in Chapter One, the average layperson is quite skeptical about the prospect of making generalizations from a single sample. Therefore, let it be assumed that in order to determine the mean adult American male weight and to simultaneously appease this skeptic, the researcher suggests that 100 separate, mutually exclusive samples be conducted from the same population and that the mean of each of the 100 sample mean weights be calculated in order to estimate the total population's mean weight. The skeptic agrees, feeling somewhat more confident of the accuracy of these results compared to those of a single sample. The researcher would first select 100 samples according to principles that will be fully established in Chapters Six and Seven; he or she would then calculate the mean weight from each of the 100 samples. Table 5.1 presents such sample data, and Figure 5.3 plots these sample means and depicts them as normally distributed.

The distribution of sample means presented in Figure 5.3

Table 5.1. Distribution of 100 Hypothetical Sample Mean Weights.

Sample Means (pounds)	*f*
184	1
183	1
182	2
181	4
180	5
179	7
178	9
177	9
176	10
175	11
174	10
173	9
172	8
171	6
170	3
169	2
168	2
167	1
Total	100

Figure 5.3. Distribution of Sample Means.

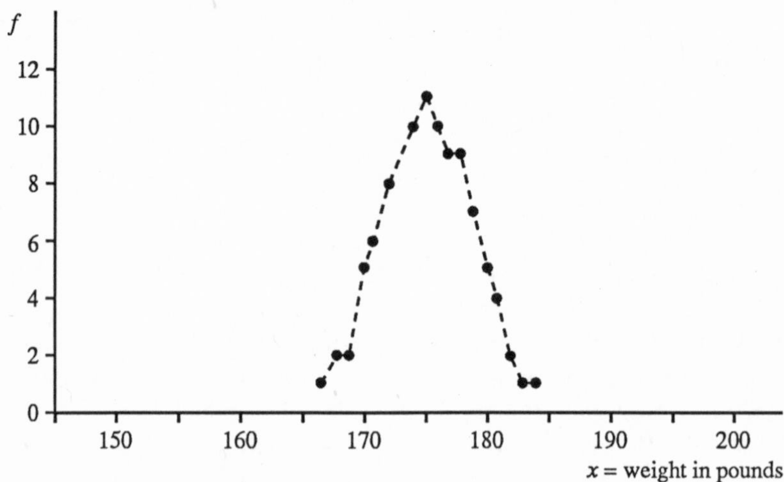

has certain properties that give it a critical role in the sampling process. These properties can be stated as follows:

Property 1: The distribution of sample means will approximate a normal curve as long as the sample size of each individual sample is reasonably large (generally over 30). This remains true whether or not the raw data are normally distributed (Krueckeberg and Silvers, 1974, p. 118).

Property 2: The value of the mean of sample means ("the mean of means") approaches the true population mean. The larger the number of samples, the closer the approximation to the population mean. This property is referred to as the central limit theorem.

Property 3: The standard deviation of the distribution of sample means (called the *standard error*) is smaller than the standard deviation of the total population. There can be a great deal of heterogeneity in the total population. Some males may weigh 100 pounds, others 300 pounds or more. However, when sample means are used, the variation among the mean weights will be significantly less than with the raw data because of the summarizing nature of the mean (Figure 5.4). The standard error is estimated to be

$$\sigma_{\bar{x}} = \frac{\sigma}{\sqrt{n}} \cdot \sqrt{\frac{N-n}{N-1}} \tag{5.3}$$

where $\sigma_{\bar{x}}$ = standard error, σ = population standard deviation, n = number of sample means (sample size of sampling distribution), and N = true population size.

It should be noted that Equation 5.3 takes into account the true population size (N) in the calculation of the standard

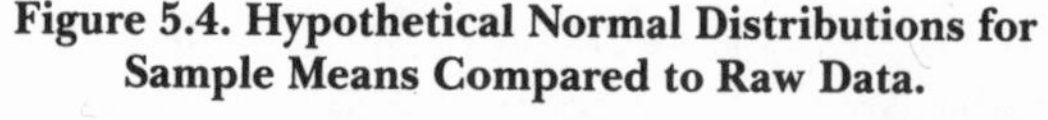
Figure 5.4. Hypothetical Normal Distributions for Sample Means Compared to Raw Data.

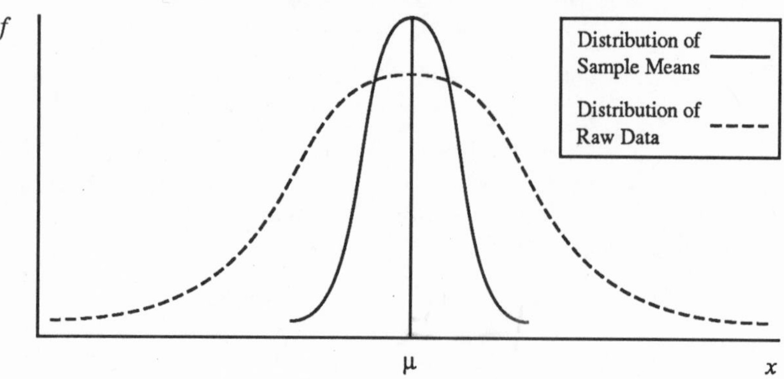

error. As the population size increases, it can be seen that $\sqrt{(N-n)/(N-1)}$ approaches 1. Hence with large populations, the standard error approaches

$$\sigma_{\bar{x}} = \sigma/\sqrt{n} \tag{5.4}$$

The expression $\sqrt{(N-n)/(N-1)}$ has come to be known as the *finite population correction* (Yamane, 1967, p. 161).

Generalizing from a Single Sample

Sampling theory invokes the three properties discussed above for purposes of justifying the use of one single sample to make inferences about a larger population rather than conducting many separate samples, as the skeptic would have the researcher do. The latter process is, of course, quite costly and time consuming—hence the desirability of being able to generalize from a single sample.

The assumption of normality (Property 1) allows probabilistic judgments to be made about a population based on one sample. It does so by making use of the standard area proportions under the normal curve as they apply to the distribution of sampling means (Property 2) and the standard error for this distribution (Property 3).

For example, with regard to the weights of American males (Table 5.1), the mean weight ($\overline{X}$) of the sample means is 175. The central limit theorem (Property 2) stipulates that this mean approaches and is a good estimate of the true population mean. The example postulated a population standard deviation of 30 pounds, the number of samples taken was 100; hence, the standard error of the distribution of the 100 sample means equals $\sigma_{\overline{x}} = \sigma/\sqrt{n} = 30/\sqrt{100} = 3$.

Property 1 permits us to adapt this information into the context of the normal curve (Figure 5.5). In this example, 68.26 percent of all sample means can be expected to fall between 172 and 178 pounds. In the case of the 100 sample means conducted at the skeptic's request, therefore, it is expected that 68 or 69 samples would indicate mean weights between 172 pounds and 178 pounds. Similarly, 95.44 percent of all sample means should lie between 169 pounds and 181 pounds and 99.72 percent of all sample means should be found between 166 and 184 pounds. Another way to look at these sample means is in probabilistic terms. In other words, given a true population mean of 175 pounds, if only one single sample were to be conducted, the chances of the sample's mean weight being within the 172- to 178-pound range is 68.26 percent (.6826 in probability terms) and there is a .9544 probability of the sample mean being within the 169- to 181-pound range. This idea of assessing one single sample in such probabilistic terms is the essence of sampling.

Confidence Intervals

The example above made use of population parameters such as μ and σ. However, the researcher rarely, if ever, is actually in possession of such information, and the procedure for estimating μ from many sample means is antithetical to the objective of using one single sample in order to make probabilistic judgments about the population. When the single sample is analyzed in probabilistic terms, it can serve as a reasonable surrogate for what may otherwise be a prohibitively costly and time-consuming series of separate samples.

Equation 5.3 can be adapted to accommodate the results

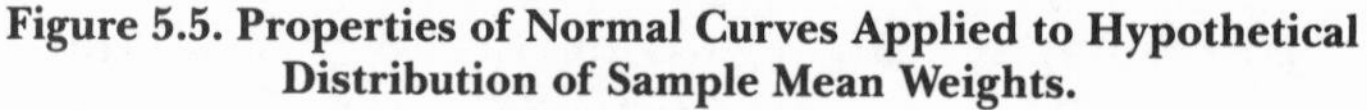

Figure 5.5. Properties of Normal Curves Applied to Hypothetical Distribution of Sample Mean Weights.

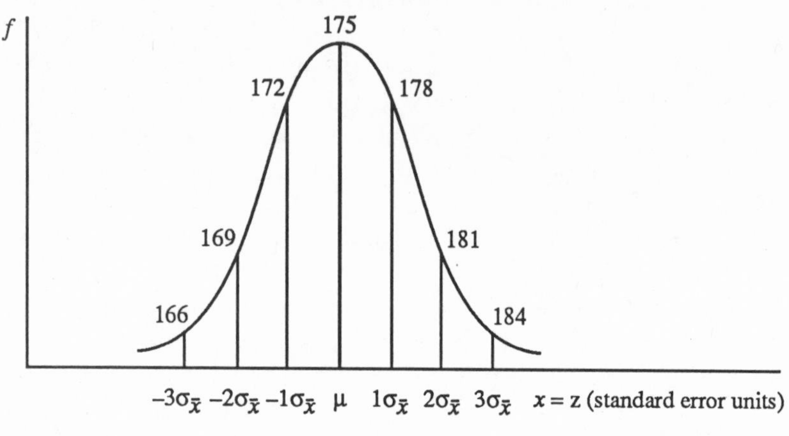

of a single sample through the process of substitution. The researcher can substitute the standard deviation of a single sample (s) for the population standard deviation (σ). In actuality the best estimate of s contains the finite population correction and can be expressed as $s = \sqrt{(n-1)/n}(\sigma)$, where n = sample size of the single sample. Again, as n grows large, the factor $(\sqrt{n - 1)/n})$ approaches 1. Hence, for large samples (generally $n \geq 30$), s approximates σ.

The researcher can further estimate the population mean (μ) by using the sample mean ($\overline{X}$) and the sample size of the single sample instead of the number of samples assumed to have been conducted. Equation 5.4 ($\sigma_{\overline{X}} = \sigma/\sqrt{n}$) can be expressed in its single-sample form as follows:

$$s_{\bar{x}} = \frac{s}{\sqrt{n}} \tag{5.5}$$

where n = sample size (number of cases in a single sample), $s_{\bar{x}}$ = the standard error of the mean for the single sample, and s = the sample standard deviation.

$$s = \sqrt{\frac{\Sigma(x - \bar{x})^2}{n}} \tag{5.6}$$

The researcher can make these substitutions because the probability of the conformity of the normally distributed sample to the true population is known. Hence, adjustments to account for any potential differences between the sample and the true population are possible. These adjustments to a single sample are manifested through the use of *confidence intervals*. By mere chance alone, some difference between a sample and the population from which it is drawn must always be expected to exist. The population mean (μ) will, in all likelihood, never be the same as the sample mean ($\bar{x}$), and the population standard deviation (σ) is highly unlikely to be the same as the sample standard deviation (s). These differences are known as *sampling error* and they can be expected to result regardless of how scientifically the sample has been selected and implemented.

Suppose that in a single sample of 400 adult American male respondents, it is found that the mean sample weight ($\bar{x}$) is 176 pounds with a standard deviation (s) of 25. Applying Equation 5.5, the standard error is obtained as follows:

$$s_{\bar{x}} = \frac{25}{\sqrt{400}}$$

$$= \frac{20}{25}$$

$$= 1.25$$

It is known that there is .6826 probability that the mean of any sample drawn from a population will be within one standard error of the true mean (Figure 5.5). Hence, the researcher is 68.26 percent confident that $\bar{x} = \mu \pm s_{\bar{x}}$ or that $\bar{x} \pm s_{\bar{x}} = \mu$.

In terms of the specific example:

$$176 = \mu \pm 1.25$$
$$176 \pm 1.25 = \mu$$
$$174.75 \leq \mu \leq 177.25$$

The researcher is 68.26 percent confident that, with a sample mean of 176 pounds and a sample standard error of 1.25 pounds, the true population mean lies between 174.75 and 177.25 pounds. As long as the true population mean lies within this interval, the individual sample mean will lie within one standard error of it. The probability of this occurrence is .6826. Hence, based upon the sample, there is 68.26 percent confidence that the researcher has identified the interval within which we will find the true population mean.

In most scientific investigations, a confidence level of 68.26 percent is not satisfactory. It is common for a researcher to seek either a 95 percent or 99 percent level of confidence. The choice of a confidence level is often a tradeoff among economy, precision, and risk of error. The factors associated with the choice of a confidence level will be discussed in Chapters Six and Seven. Referring to Figure 5.5 and Resource A, it can be shown that a standardized Z score of ± 1.96 encompasses approximately 95 percent of all cases and a Z score of ± 2.575 encompasses approximately 99 percent of all cases. Thus, the 95 percent and 99 percent confidence intervals take on the following configurations:

$$(95\%) \quad \mu \in \bar{X} \pm 1.96 s_{\bar{x}} \qquad (5.7)$$

$$(99\%) \quad \mu \in \bar{X} \pm 2.575 s_{\bar{x}} \qquad (5.8)$$

In other words, the researcher can be 95 percent confident that μ is located in the range expressed by the set $\bar{X} \pm 1.96 s_{\bar{x}}$ and 99 percent confident that μ is a member of the set $\bar{X} \pm 2.575 s_{\bar{x}}$.

In the example of American male weights, based on the single sample, we can be 95 percent confident that the true mean weight of adult American males is between 173.55 and 178.45 pounds. Similarly, we can be 99 percent confident that the true mean weight is between 172.78 and 179.22 pounds. Hence, through the use of confidence intervals, the researcher is able to determine that the true population mean can be estimated within a fixed interval range based on one sample mean. Notice should be taken that, for any given sample size, the more rigorous the level of confidence demanded, the more broadly delineated the confidence interval must be. By broadening the confidence interval, the researcher can mitigate the risk of making an error in generalizing from the sample to the population at large.

Proportions

The reader is more likely to be familiar with the concept of confidence intervals in the context of percentages (proportions). Almost everyone has been exposed to political public opinion polls, either by reading the results of such polls in the newspapers or by being a respondent in one. The typical results of a public opinion poll may, hypothetically, appear as follows: Twelve hundred (1,200) scientifically selected respondents were asked to state their preference between Senator Smith and Congressman Williams for the office of president of the United States. The survey contains a margin of error of ± 3 percent. The results of the survey are as follows:

Smith	47%
Williams	45%
Undecided	8%

Such reports rarely contain specific references to confidence intervals and confidence levels, but these results fit precisely into the interpretive context discussed above with regard to interval scale data. The true meaning of this survey finding is that the researcher is 95 percent confident that Smith has between 44 percent and 50 percent of the vote (47% ± 3%) and that Williams has between 42 percent and 48 percent. This is comparable to the interval scale example above, when the researcher was 95 percent confident that the mean weight of adult American males was between 173.55 and 178.45 pounds.

In general, the results, when given in terms of proportions, can be expressed as follows:

$$(95\%) \quad p = \bar{p} \pm 1.96\sigma_{\bar{p}} \tag{5.9}$$

$$(99\%) \quad p = \bar{p} \pm 2.575\sigma_{\bar{p}} \tag{5.10}$$

where p = true population proportion, $\bar{p}$ = sample proportion, and the standard error of the mean proportion is expressed as

$$\sigma_{\bar{p}} = \sqrt{\frac{\bar{p}(1-\bar{p})}{n}} \tag{5.11}$$

where n = sample size.

It is helpful to note the parallel between Equation 5.11 (standard error for proportions) and Equations 5.4 and 5.5. The equation for the standard deviation of a proportional distribution is $\sigma = \sqrt{p(1-p)}$. Just as with interval data, the equation for standard error requires the standard deviation to be divided by $\sqrt{n}$. Hence, the standard error of a proportional distribution is $\sigma_{\bar{p}} = \sqrt{(p(1-p)/(n)}$.

Let it be assumed that it is much later in the presidential campaign than when this poll was initially taken, and Senator Smith would like to know the current status of the campaign; he commissions a sample survey of 2,000 registered voters, which finds Smith's support to be 52 percent. Encouraged by this finding, but understanding the concept of sampling error, Senator Smith would like to know the margin of error associated with this poll. In other words, can the campaign staff really be confident that Smith possesses majority support? Senator Smith has asked his statistician to respond to that question at a confidence level of 99 percent. Equation 5.10 yields the following result:

$$
\begin{aligned}
p &= \bar{p} \pm 2.575\sigma_{\bar{p}} \\
&= .52 \pm 2.575\left(\sqrt{\frac{(.52)(.48)}{2{,}000}}\right) \\
&= .52 \pm 2.575(.011) \\
&= .52 \pm .028
\end{aligned}
$$

Thus, Senator Smith can be 99 percent certain that his campaign has between 49.2 percent and 54.8 percent of the vote. He may be somewhat disappointed that majority support cannot be claimed with 99 percent confidence, but it is better not to be misled by the poll that indicated 52 percent support than it would be to proceed as if majority support were certain.

The reader should now appreciate how the results of one single sample can be used to draw conclusions about the larger population of which it is a part. These conclusions are derived by recognizing the nature of sampling error and determining its extent through the use of confidence intervals derived from the properties of sampling theory.

Exercises

1. Calculate the standard errors for the following sample survey findings:
   a. $\bar{x} = 10$, $s = 2$, $n = 50$
   b. $\bar{p} = .75$, $n = 100$
   c. $\bar{p} = .33$, $n = 400$
   d. $\bar{x} = 3{,}000$, $s = 500$, $n = 700$
2. A researcher is interested in determining the mean income of attorneys in a particular major metropolitan area. A survey is conducted using a sample of 400 attorneys who are selected according to the accepted principles of survey research. It is found that the sample mean income is

$120,000 and the sample standard deviation is $25,000. The researcher wishes to be 95 percent certain that the mean income reported to the study's sponsor is accurate. Given that the sample mean is subject to sampling error, calculate the appropriate confidence interval.

3. A survey of 1,000 scientifically selected respondents indicates that 55 percent of them favor the mayor's proposed mass transit development program and 45 percent are opposed. The mayor and other members of the city council wish to be 95 percent certain that they have majority support before proceeding with the project. Does the 95 percent confidence interval assure them that they have more than 50 percent support?

Chapter 6

Determining the Sample Size

A crucial question at the outset of a survey research project is how many observations are needed in a sample so that the generalizations discussed in Chapter Five can be made about the entire population. The answer to this question is by no means clear-cut; it requires the careful consideration of several major factors. Generally speaking, the greater the level of accuracy desired and the more certain the researcher would like to be about the inferences to be made from the sample to the entire population, the larger the sample size must be.

Determinants of Sampling Accuracy

There are two interrelated factors that the researcher must address with specificity before proceeding with the selection of a sample size: *level of confidence* and *confidence interval*. The level of confidence is the risk of error the researcher is willing to accept in the study. Given time requirements, budget, and the magnitude of the consequences of drawing incorrect conclusions from the sample, the researcher will typically choose either a 95 percent level of confidence (5 percent chance of error) or a 99 percent level of confidence (1 percent chance of error). On the other hand, as discussed in Chapter Five, the confidence interval determines the level of sampling accuracy that the researcher obtains. In this chapter, it will be shown that selection of the sample size is a primary contributor to the researcher's success in achieving a certain degree of sampling accuracy. That is to say, sample size is directly related to the accuracy of the sample mean as an estimate of the true population mean.

The reader will recall that the equations for the standard error for samples containing interval scale variables (Equation 5.5) or proportions (Equation 5.11) included a factor (n) representing sample size. For any given sample standard deviation, the larger the sample size, the smaller the standard error. Conversely, the smaller the sample size, the larger the standard error. For instance, if a sample of 100 respondents indicates a mean income of \$20,000 per year with a sample standard deviation of \$3,000, the standard error and associated confidence intervals, with 95 percent or 99 percent levels of confidence would be calculated as

$$s_{\bar{x}} = \frac{s}{\sqrt{n}}$$

$$= \frac{3{,}000}{\sqrt{100}} = \frac{3{,}000}{10} = \$300$$

95 Percent Confidence Interval	*99 Percent Confidence Interval*
$\bar{x} \pm 1.96 s_{\bar{x}}$	$\bar{x} \pm 2.575 s_{\bar{x}}$
\$20,000 ± 1.96(\$300)	\$20,000 ± 2.575(\$300)
\$20,000 ± \$588	\$20,000 ± \$773

Hence, the researcher can be 95 percent certain that the true mean income for the population is between \$19,412 and

$20,588, or 99 percent certain that the true mean is between $19,227 and $20,773.

If, on the other hand, the available sample contains 400 responses, the standard error and associated confidence intervals would be calculated as

$$s_{\bar{x}} = \frac{\$3,000}{\sqrt{400}} = \$150$$

95 Percent Confidence Interval	*99 Percent Confidence Interval*
$20,000 ± 1.96($150)	$20,000 ± 2.575($150)
$20,000 ± $294	$20,000 ± $386

Therefore, with a sample size of 400 rather than 100, the researcher has been able to narrow the interval by 50 percent for each level of confidence, respectively, but this 50 percent narrowing has required that the sample size be quadrupled. If the sample size were to be increased to 1,000, the 250 percent increase in sample size from 400 would reduce the confidence interval by only an additional 37 percent. It is noteworthy that such reductions in confidence intervals can, in fact, be achieved, but at the potentially high cost of a substantially larger sample size.

The process of selecting a sample size requires that the researcher determine an acceptable range of uncertainty, given the time and cost constraints of the study. In the above example, for instance, if the researcher determines that the study can tolerate no more than a $300 margin of error (confidence interval) in either direction from the sample mean, she or he would not be satisfied by the 100-person sample at either level of confidence but would be better served by the 400-person survey. The researcher must also understand that this 400-person survey permits only 95 percent rather than 99 percent certainty of the stated confidence interval.

In this particular example, a level of confidence of 99 percent and a preestablished acceptable margin of error of $300 cannot be achieved. The researcher must decide which is preferable: an interval of ± $294 with 95 percent confidence or an interval of ± \$386 with 99 percent confidence. There is no fixed criterion by which to make this choice. The researcher must make this determination on a case-by-case basis and in accordance with the particular goals and objectives of the study. However, in the event that the researcher insists, satisfying each of the stricter criteria can still be accomplished, but only by increasing sample size. This interrelationship among level of confidence, confidence interval, and the effect of sample size upon them makes the determination of sample size an absolutely vital component of the sample survey process.

The researcher should consider the following guidelines in the selection of sample size:

- The greater the consequences of generating data that might lead to incorrect conclusions, the greater the level of confidence the researcher should establish. In practical terms, this involves a choice between the 95 percent and 99 percent levels of confidence.
- In most cases, the researcher can be satisfied by choosing the 95 percent confidence level, which implies a 5 percent risk that the confidence interval is incorrect.
- The margin of error or confidence interval must be established. The researcher will generally find 3–5 percent to be satisfactory for proportional data. Interval data margins of error must be established on a case-by-case basis depending on the unit of measurement, magnitude, and range of the particular variable.

Determination of Sample Size for Variables Expressed in Terms of Proportions

Determination of sample size for data given in terms of proportions is somewhat more straightforward than when the variable is on an interval scale. Hence, it is this methodology that will be introduced to the reader first. The relationship among the confidence interval, the level of confidence, and the standard error of the sample can be expressed by the following equation:

$$C_p = \pm Z_\alpha(\sigma_p) \tag{6.1}$$

where C_p = confidence interval in terms of proportions, $Z_\alpha = Z$ score for various levels of confidence (α), and σ_p = standard error for a distribution of sample proportions.

The formula for the standard error of the true population mean proportion is $\sigma_p = \sqrt{(p(1-p)/(n)}$; substituting it into Equation 6.1, we can rewrite the equation as follows:

$$C_p = \pm Z_\alpha \sqrt{\frac{p(1-p)}{n}} \tag{6.2}$$

Solving for n yields

$$n = \left(\frac{Z_\alpha \sqrt{p(1-p)}}{C_p}\right)^2 \tag{6.3}$$

In order to proceed with the calculation of specific sample sizes (n), the values of Z_α, C_p, and p must be established. As discussed, Z_α is most commonly set at 1.96 for the 95 percent level of confidence or 2.575 for 99 percent. The confidence interval C_p is typically set not to exceed 10 percent and is more frequently set in the 3–5 percent range depending on the specific degree of accuracy to which the findings must conform. As we have seen, the true proportion (p) is unknown. The most conservative way of handling this uncertainty is to set the value of p at the proportion that would result in the highest sample size. This occurs when $p = .5$; Equation 6.3 can be further refined, therefore, to read

$$n = \left(\frac{Z_\alpha(.5)}{C_p}\right)^2$$

because $\sqrt{.5(1-.5)} = .5$.

Now, let it be supposed that a government decision maker is in the process of determining an appropriate sample size for a study of public opinion concerning community service system adequacy. The question to be posed is whether or not the respondents find community services to be adequate. Percentages responding "yes" and "no" are to be tallied and presented for review. For purposes of this study, the decision maker feels that it is important for the sample proportion to be accurate within ±4 percent of the true proportion, and it is felt that 95 percent confidence in these findings would be satisfactory in order for the information to be effectively used. To obtain the appropriate sample size for this study, the researcher can substitute numbers into Equation 6.4 as follows:

$$n = \left(\frac{1.96(.5)}{.04}\right)^2$$

$$= 600.25$$

The calculated n must be rounded to the next highest whole number, so that, in this case, a sample size of 601 persons is required.

The reader should keep in mind that $Z_\alpha = 2.575$ can be substituted for $Z_\alpha = 1.96$ when 99 percent confidence is required and that the confidence interval (C_p) also can be varied according to the researcher's requirement for various levels of sampling accuracy.

For each level of confidence (95 percent or 99 percent), required sample sizes can be calculated for various confidence intervals in terms of proportions by operationalizing Equation 6.4. Table 6.1 portrays the calculated required sample sizes under these conditions.

It should be noted, once again, that there is an important inverse relationship between the sample size and the standard error, as manifested in the confidence interval. In order to narrow the confidence interval, a substantial increase in the sample size is required—an increase that can quickly become cost prohibitive.

Selecting a Sample Size When the Population Is Small

As discussed in Chapter Five, sampling theory and the equations derived from it assume a large population size. Therefore,

Table 6.1. Minimum Sample Sizes for Variables Expressed as Proportions.

Confidence Interval (Margin of Error, %)	*Sample Size*	
	95% Confidence	*99% Confidence*
± 1	9,604	16,590
± 2	2,401	4,148
± 3	1,068	1,844
± 4	601	1,037
± 5	385	664
± 6	267	461
± 7	196	339
± 8	151	260
± 9	119	205
± 10	97	166

the assumption underlying the calculation of sample sizes in Table 6.1 is that the general population from which the sample or samples are taken is large. If, however, the population is not large, the standard error must be recomputed with the finite population correction included. The formula for sample size in this case becomes

$$n = \left(\frac{Z_\alpha \sqrt{p(1-p)}}{C_p} \cdot \sqrt{\frac{N-n}{N-1}}\right)^2$$

Having introduced a factor for n on each side of the equation, we must solve for n again. Doing so yields the following:

$$n = \frac{Z_\alpha^2[p(1-p)]N}{Z_\alpha^2[p(1-p)] + (N-1)C_p^2} \qquad (6.6)$$

Replacing p with .5, as discussed previously, the general equation for sample size in all populations—both large and small—becomes

$$n = \frac{Z_\alpha^2(.25)N}{Z_\alpha^2(.25) + (N-1)C_p^2} \qquad (6.7)$$

In practice, since the finite population correction approaches 1 in large populations, this adjusted sample size determinant is used only when populations are not large, and we continue to use Equation 6.4 and Table 6.1 when the population is large.

The distinction between "large" and "not large" will be addressed shortly, but prior to doing so, an example of the required sample size from a small population is in order. If a researcher seeks to determine the political party preferences of the 2,500 professors at a large state university and does not have the time or financial resources to interview them all, a sample of professors can be taken. The researcher must decide how many professors to survey and establishes that a 95 percent level of confidence will be satisfactory along with a margin of error that does not exceed ± 3 percent. Applying Equation 6.7, the following is obtained:

$$n = \frac{(1.96)^2(.25)(2{,}500)}{(1.96)^2(.25) + 2{,}499(.03)^2}$$

$$= \frac{(3.84)(.25)(2{,}500)}{(3.84)(.25) + (2{,}499)(.0009)}$$

$$= \frac{2{,}408}{.9604 + 2.249}$$

$$= 749$$

If the researcher wished to be 99 percent confident of the ± 3 percent margin of error, the following sample size would be required:

$$n = \frac{(2.575)^2(.25)(2{,}500)}{(2.575)^2(.25) + 2{,}499(.03)^2}$$

$$= 1{,}061$$

Comparing these results to those in Table 6.1, it can be seen that, in the case of this relatively small population, the researcher can obtain 95 percent confidence interviewing 749 professors instead of 1,068, as indicated in Table 6.1, and 99 percent confidence can be achieved with 1,061 interviews in-

Table 6.2. Minimum Sample Sizes for Selected Small Populations.

	Sample Sizes					
	95% Level of Confidence			*99% Level of Confidence*		
Population Size (N)	*±3%*	*±5%*	*±10%*	*±3%*	*±5%*	*±10%*
500	250[a]	218	81	250[a]	250[a]	125
1,000	500[a]	278	88	500[a]	399	143
1,500	624	306	91	750[a]	460	150
2,000	696	323	92	959	498	154
3,000	788	341	94	1,142	544	158
5,000	880	357	95	1,347	586	161
10,000	965	370	96	1,556	622	164
20,000	1,014	377	96	1,687	642	165
50,000	1,045	382	96	1,777	655	166
100,000	1,058	383	96	1,809	659	166

Note: The choice of ±3%, ±5%, and ±10% for confidence intervals is based on the tendency of researchers to commonly use these intervals or a similar range of intervals in the design of their survey.

[a] Population sizes for which the assumption of normality does not apply; in such cases, the appropriate sample size is 50% of the population size.

stead of 1,844. These differences arise from the logical fact that fewer interviews are needed from a very small population in order for that population to be adequately represented by the sample.

Table 6.2 reflects the application of Equation 6.7 for various population sizes for the 95 percent and 99 percent levels of confidence and for confidence intervals of ±3 percent, ±5 percent, and ±10 percent. Notice that, as the population size (*N*) reaches 100,000, the required sample size approaches those listed in Table 6.1. Hence, a population size greater than 100,000 can be considered an appropriate definition of a large population and, conversely, populations of 100,000 and smaller are to be considered small. For particularly conservative confidence intervals and very small population sizes (designated in Table 6.2 by a superscript *a*), the assumption of normality does not apply. Very small populations are most accurately characterized in terms of a hypergeometric distribution, which is an advanced concept not addressed in this book (see Lieberman and Owen,

1961, pp. 3–22; Schlaifer, 1959, pp. 363–365). In certain cases, therefore, Equation 6.7, which is derived from properties of the normal distribution, does not yield appropriate sample sizes. In lieu of this equation, a sample size of 50 percent of the population size has been determined to provide the required accuracy (Yamane, 1967, p. 582). In sum, the survey administrator will never require a sample size in excess of 50 percent of the total population that the sample represents. This rule has particular significance when it is necessary to undertake internal surveys of organizations with a small population base. Examples of such surveys are employee satisfaction polls and job performance evaluations.

Determination of Sample Size for Interval Scale Variables

Large Populations

If some sample data are in the form of interval scale variables, Equation 6.1 must be adapted as follows:

$$C_i = \pm Z_\alpha(\sigma_{\bar{x}}) \tag{6.8}$$

where C_i = confidence interval in terms of interval scale, $Z_\alpha = Z$ score for various levels of confidence (α), and $\sigma_{\bar{x}}$ = standard error for a distribution of sample means.

Using Equation 5.4 ($\sigma_{\bar{x}} = \sigma/\sqrt{n}$) and substituting it into Equation 6.8 results in the following equation:

$$C_i = Z_\alpha\left(\frac{\sigma}{\sqrt{n}}\right) \tag{6.9}$$

Solving for n yields

$$n = \frac{Z_\alpha^2 \sigma^2}{C_i^2} \tag{6.10}$$

In order to proceed with the calculation of specific sample sizes (n), the values of Z_α, C_i, and σ must be established. As discussed, Z_α is most commonly set at 1.96 or 2.575; C_i is generally set in the context of the variable under study, as the research study dictates; and σ is estimated from the sample data themselves by s, the standard deviation of a single sample distribution, as discussed in Chapter Five. Hence,

$$n = \frac{Z_\alpha^2 s^2}{C_i^2} \tag{6.11}$$

Suppose that a researcher is interested in obtaining a sample from a large population of households in County X in order to determine the mean household income. The goals are to select a sample size that will yield a margin of error (confidence interval) of no more than ± \$1,000 and to be 95 percent certain of this result.

A problem exists, however, because a value for the sample standard deviation must be obtained. There is no simple parameter to use as there is with proportions (namely, $p = .5$). Since it is not at all likely that accurate information about the population parameters will be known before the completion of the survey, only a reasonable estimate of s can be made. There are two alternative methods of making this estimate:

1. The researcher may wish to use any previous information that is available (for example, another survey of this population that can provide the necessary mean and standard deviation for a key variable).
2. A pilot survey or pretest (see Chapter Two), conducted on the population, will yield a mean and standard deviation that can be used as estimates for the proposed sample.

Because a pretest should be conducted as a critical part of the survey process in any case, it is generally more feasible and efficient to use this method for the estimate of the sample standard deviation.

Based on a pretest of households in County X, a preliminary estimated mean of \$30,000 and standard deviation of

$6,000 are determined. The researcher may now use this information to operationalize Equation 6.11 to yield the following sample size:

$$n = \frac{(1.96)^2(\$6{,}000)^2}{(1{,}000)^2} = \frac{138{,}297{,}600}{1{,}000{,}000} = 139$$

This sample size of 139 respondents may strike the reader as being somewhat small in view of proportion sample sizes, where it would correspond to a margin of error of approximately ± 8 percent. The $1,000 margin of error here would be less than 8 percent, based on the $30,000 mean. The reader should be aware, however, that the relationship should not be drawn between margin of error and mean, but between margin of error and standard deviation. In terms of proportions, standard deviation always equals .5. The ratio of margin of error to standard deviation, in this example, is $.08/.5 = .16$. The interval data contained here can be assessed similarly, generating the same ratio of margin of error to standard deviation:

$$\frac{\text{Margin of error}}{\text{Standard deviation}} = \frac{1{,}000}{6{,}000} = .167$$

Small Populations

As is the case when calculating sample sizes for variables in the form of proportions, an adjustment must be made to Equation 6.11 when the general population is small (under 100,000). The finite population correction regarding proportions, $\sqrt{(N-n)/(N-1)}$, is also applicable to interval scale variables. Equation 6.11 becomes

$$n = \left(\frac{Z_\alpha^2 s^2}{C_i^2}\right) \cdot \left(\sqrt{\frac{N-n}{N-1}}\right) \qquad (6.12)$$

which can be written as

$$n = \frac{Z_\alpha^2 s^2}{C_i^2 + Z_\alpha^2 s^2 / N - 1} \tag{6.13}$$

In the example regarding household income in County X, suppose that the administrator wishes to research household income in only one small community within the county. This community has a population of 5,000 people. The researcher, as before, is interested in determining a sample size that will yield a margin of error (confidence interval) of no more than ± $1,000 and wishes to be 95 percent certain of the result. A pretest has estimated a mean of $30,000 and a sample standard deviation of $6,000. The researcher may now use this information to operationalize Equation 6.13 to yield the following sample size:

$$n = \frac{(1.96)^2(6{,}000)^2}{(1{,}000)^2 + \frac{(1.96)^2(6{,}000)^2}{4{,}999}}$$

$$= \frac{(3.8416)(36{,}000{,}000)}{1{,}000{,}000 + \frac{(3.8416)(36{,}000{,}000)}{4{,}999}}$$

$$= \frac{138{,}300{,}000}{1{,}000{,}000 + 27{,}665.05}$$

$$= 135$$

As with proportions from small populations, the reader should note that fewer respondents are required from the smaller community than from the entirety of County X to attain the same level of confidence and margin of error. Assuming the requisite characteristics of the normal distribution, this difference in sample size should be intuitively clear. Because interval scale variables will tend to provide an enormous and unbounded range of possible values, tables of minimum sample size, such as Tables 6.1 and 6.2 for proportions, are not feasible for the interval scale. Equations 6.11 and 6.13 must be applied in each case.

Determination of Sample Size When Both Proportional and Interval Scale Variables Are Present

In most surveys, both proportional scale variables and interval scale variables are present. For example, the researcher is usually interested in determining the proportion of respondents who are identified as male or female and may also be interested in knowing what proportion of respondents intend to vote for a particular candidate. At the same time, he or she often wishes to obtain knowledge regarding respondents' household income, age, or years of formal education. These latter variables are expressed in the form of the interval scale. It may be difficult to ascertain which equation or equations to use in order to determine the appropriate sample size for such a survey. The researcher must make certain that the largest sample size requirement is satisfied. Hence, for all interval scale variables and for those proportional variables with varying margins of error or levels of confidence, the researcher must calculate the required sample sizes by using the appropriate equations or tables and must establish a survey sample size equal to the largest required individual variable sample size.

For example, if the researcher calculates that the age variable requires 300 respondents in order to satisfy the research needs, that the income variable requires 350 respondents, and that the proportional variables all require a total sample size of 385 respondents, she or he would determine that at least 385 respondents must be secured and that this determination represents the overall survey sample size.

In most instances, in order to avoid this repetitive and laborious process, a survey administrator will use Table 6.1 to select a sample size associated with an overall margin of error and level of confidence. This sample size will generally satisfy the most stringent requirement of the interval scale variables. The reader, however, is cautioned that if a particular interval scale variable is highly critical to the focus of the survey, it would be prudent to make certain that the general sample size also meets the requirements for that particular variable.

Exercises

1. A statewide public opinion survey of 200 respondents is being conducted by Candidate Jones. Jones wishes to be 95 percent confident that the margin of error is ± 5 percent. Is the sample size sufficient to satisfy Jones's requirements. If not, what minimum sample size does Jones need.
2. Calculate the minimum required sample size for the following confidence levels and margins of error for a survey conducted in a city with a population of 40,000.

	Margin of Error (%)	*Confidence Level (%)*
a.	± 4	95
b.	± 6	99
c.	± 9	95
d.	± 2	99

3. Calculate the minimum required sample size for the following confidence levels and margins of error for data gathered from surveys conducted in the State of New York.

		Margin of Error	*Confidence Level (%)*
a.	Mean height of adult males ($s = 3$ inches)	± 0.5 inch	95
b.	Mean age of entire population ($s = 15$ years)	± 2 years	99
c.	Mean income of teachers ($s = \$11,000$)	± $1,000	95

Chapter 7

Selecting a Representative Sample

Although sample size is very important, it is by no means the only determinant of what constitutes adequacy of representativeness. It is critical that the sample be drawn according to well-established, specific principles. The purpose of this chapter is to discuss these principles and the various methods of sample selection that have been adapted and derived from them.

Identification of the Sampling Frame

The first consideration in deriving a sample is specification of the *unit of analysis*. The unit of analysis is the individual, object, institution, or group of individuals, objects, and/or institutions that bear relevance to the researcher's study. This relevance relates to the concept of a *general universe or population*. The general population is defined as "that abstract universe to which [the researcher] assumes, however tentatively, that his findings will apply" (Sjoberg and Nett, 1968, p. 130). In other words, it is the theoretical population to which the researcher wishes to generalize the study's findings. This population is composed of units, which become the units of analysis for purposes of the study. Specifically, a unit of analysis can be a person, a household, a social organization, a political jurisdiction, a corporation, an industry, a hospital, or a geographic entity, among others, depending on the nature of the conceptual general population.

The designation of a general population, although useful for conceptualizing the purpose and objectives of a study, is not necessarily conducive to the actual selection of a sample. Let us suppose that a study intends to generalize its findings to the residents of an entire metropolitan area. The general population can be considered to be those people who reside within the political boundaries of the area under study, and the unit of analysis is the individual resident. The process of selecting a representative sample requires, at its theoretical optimum, that the researcher know where and how to contact each person in the population. From a practical standpoint, it is highly unlikely that all members of the general population can be identified and contacted. People die and are born every minute; some people live in unrecorded accommodations (for example, the homeless); and others cannot be contacted for various personal reasons. Herein lies the essence of the statistical necessity for establishing an intermediate step between the general population and the actual sample—the development of a *working population.* The working population is an operational definition of the general population that is representative of the general population and from which the researcher is reasonably able to identify as complete a list as possible of members of the general population. This list is known as the *sampling frame*, and it is from this list that the actual sample is eventually drawn.

To illustrate the concepts of general population, working population, and sampling frame, suppose that a researcher is studying factors associated with economic disadvantage and poverty in New York City. The general population is to consist of all economically disadvantaged people in New York City. There are no lists of such a population. Therefore, the researcher must substitute a working population for this general population; he or she must find some other, identifiable population that can be claimed to correspond to the general population closely enough to be considered its surrogate. The designation of a working population requires the researcher to operationalize the concept of economic disadvantage. There are a variety of definitions of economic disadvantage. The federal government has established poverty-level criteria; poor families receive government aid from various federal, state, and local programs; and other agencies have their own measure of economic disadvantage. Based upon any one or any combination of these definitions, a list of persons that constitutes the sampling frame can conceivably be obtained.

It is not possible that any of these lists, either alone or in combination, will be complete and exhaustive in nature. Recognizing this, the researcher will want to select a list, or combination of lists, that maximizes representativeness and minimizes systematic omissions. In constructing the sampling frame, therefore, the researcher should attempt to determine the extent to which members of the working population have been excluded from this list and to decide whether these excluded members differ in any systematic manner from those who are included on the list.

In this example, the researcher may legitimately choose to define the economically disadvantaged as consisting of households with annual incomes below the federal poverty standard. This definition identifies the working population. The researcher might then identify a sampling frame consisting of individuals who receive funds through the program Aid to Families with Dependent Children (AFDC), which requires, for qualification, a household income below the federal poverty level. The researcher is likely to encounter a systematic omission in this list, however, which is sufficient to render it unrepresentative: the omission of individuals who may be economically disadvantaged but who do not have children and who are, therefore, not eligible for this program. If the individuals who are omitted are very similar to those who are included in all or most of the important categories (for example, ethnicity, age, and sex), the omission would not be considered to be systematic. However, in this case, since AFDC serves only families with children, the list does not include individuals or families without children whose income is sufficiently low to otherwise qualify. Such an omission is clearly systematic in the sense that there is a clear and important difference between those who are included and those who are excluded. A systematic omission of this nature renders the sampling frame unrepresentative of economically disadvantaged persons and, therefore, unacceptable. The researcher must search for an alternative sampling frame, which eventually will consist of another list (or combination of lists) of people with incomes below the poverty level and that does not contain such a systematic omission.

As another example of systematic omissions (frequently referred to as "biases"), social researchers wishing to study Hispanics often use telephone directories to compile their sampling frame from lists of persons with Spanish surnames. This approach has two easily recognizable biases.

First, telephone directories can exclude the poor, who cannot afford telephones, and the wealthy, who have more unlisted numbers than other groups; these directories also tend to exclude the more mobile members of the community, for whom this listing would be out of date. Second, this sampling frame would tend to omit Hispanics without Spanish surnames or those who have changed their names by marriage or for other purposes.

It is usually impossible to eliminate all bias. Other factors, such as the availability of data and the convenience and cost of deriving such lists, must be considered. In the ideal, the sampling frame would be a complete list of members of the working population. However, no list can be expected to be perfectly complete, and it is therefore important for the researcher to be reasonably satisfied that the working population and derivative sampling frame represent the general population as closely as possible.

By this point, the reader should have detected that, in an actual research study, the compilation of a sampling frame can be quite complicated. For example, the authors were involved in a research study that required the identification of all "Single Room Occupancy" (SRO) hotel units within the City of San Diego, California (general population). SRO hotels are those typically occupied by very-low-income transient residents on a month-to-month basis. Generally, these hotels are older structures with small, sparsely furnished rooms. In order to begin the process of identifying a sampling frame, an operational definition of SRO parameters (working population) was required. The philosophical approach established by the researchers in deriving this working population and consequent sampling frame was that, in the interest of completeness and accuracy, only the hotels or apartments that were obviously not SROs would be excluded. Hence, only residentially zoned property and properties with rents that were clearly too high, such as the major luxury hotels, were eliminated immediately. The remaining hotels and apartments constituted the working population. It was recognized that some recipients of the survey would not actually be SROs, but it was decided that this was acceptable in order to achieve as complete a sampling frame as possible. In recognition of this, the survey itself was designed to permit respondents to quickly and easily designate themselves as non-SROs.

The compilation of the sampling frame required the researchers to consult a variety of basic information sources. Four separate sublists were developed, eliminating duplications, and then were combined to form the final list of potential SROs, which comprised the sampling frame.

The first of the four sublists was a list of sixty-six downtown SROs enumerated in a June 1985 report by the San Diego Housing Commission. This list was limited to downtown San Diego and had been the accepted official list of SROs in use.

The second list was derived from the records of the City Treasurer's office. Transient occupancy tax (hotel room tax) lists from several different years were cross-checked against each other and against the list of sixty-six downtown SRO hotels to eliminate duplications.

The second list was then pared down by examining the rates of these hotels as elaborated on in various publications containing room rental rate information. All hotels with daily rates above $35 were eliminated based on research which demonstrated that the hotels offering long-term rentals generally charged monthly rates at least ten times their daily rate. A monthly rate in excess of $350 would take a property well outside of the rate limitation of $320 per month, as defined in the city's SRO ordinance.

The third list emerged from the City Planning Department's land use grouping analysis. All "hotels/motels" and "transient/residential hotels" are listed by the City Planning Department by parcel number and address whether or not they have paid transient occupancy taxes. All entries on the two prior sublists were deleted from this third list in order to eliminate duplication.

The fourth list was formed from a variety of data sources, including newspaper "room for rent" advertisements, the Yellow Pages, interviews with government staff, and physical inspection of targeted areas that tended to contain more of these housing types. All four lists were consolidated, and a sampling frame of 347 properties was compiled for the survey.

Sources of Population Lists

The SRO example mentioned a variety of lists and other data sources. Knowledge of where and how to obtain population lists is critical to the success of the sample survey process. The telephone directory is one of the most common sources of population lists. It has many advantages including its ready availability, its alphabetical listing of a very large percentage of households, and the inclusion of addresses and telephone numbers. Despite the minor disadvantages of the telephone directory that were mentioned previously, this list is one of the most comprehensive and widely used sources of information in survey research.

A similar source of working population lists is the reverse city directory. This volume, which is generally published annually for purchase by interested parties, lists the name, address, and telephone number of each listed telephone subscriber organized by street rather than subscriber's name. For ease of reference, the streets are listed alphabetically. The disadvantages associated with the telephone directory also apply to the reverse directory: dated information, unlisted telephone numbers, and the tendency to omit those who do not have telephones. Some such directories include a separate listing of telephone subscribers according to telephone exchanges. This becomes very useful in targeting specific communities or districts for a study.

Voter registration lists are generally available for purchase from the county's registrar of voters. These lists contain all residents aged eighteen or older who have registered to vote, listed in alphabetical order by precinct. The entries include political party affiliation, address, and, sometimes, telephone numbers. The main advantage of this list is in its politically active, adult population that has demonstrated an interest in current public affairs. Thus, political pollsters find the voter registration list to be a useful sampling frame for their studies.

Other sources of population lists, each with its own relative advantages and disadvantages deriving from the nature of the listed clientele, are

- *Water and electric meter lists:* Widespread use of water and electricity makes such lists relatively complete and thereby beneficial. The major difficulty in using these lists lies in the omission of multiple-dwelling units covered by the same meter.
- *Department of Motor Vehicle registrants:* Automobile ownership and use is quite widespread, making such lists good general sources and excellent specialized study sources.
- *Mailing services:* Computerized services exist that provide lists of postal patrons by zip code for a fee. This type of service is most useful in studies focusing on specific geographic areas.
- *Magazine/newspaper subscriber lists:* For special population segments (for example, middle-class women, sports enthusiasts, or teenagers), magazine subscriber lists offer an excellent targeted population listing of people with particular interests and, frequently similar demographic characteristics.

These lists are expensive and are sometimes difficult to obtain.

For more specialized studies, such as the SRO study discussed above, the researcher must be somewhat more creative in the development of a working population and sampling frame. There are no standard or fixed rules other than maintaining representativeness and avoiding systematic bias to the maximum extent possible. If serious systematic bias cannot be avoided and no alternative sampling frame is available, the researcher must detail the nature of this bias in the final report to avoid misleading its readers.

Probability Sampling

Sampling methods can be categorized into *probability sampling* and *nonprobability sampling*. In probability sampling, the probability of any member of the working population being selected to be a part of the eventual sample is known. This implies extensive and thorough knowledge of the composition and size of the working population. In nonprobability sampling, on the other hand, the selection process is not formal; knowledge of the working population is limited, and, hence, the probability of selecting any given unit of the population cannot be determined.

There are two characteristics of probability samples: (1) the probability of selection is equal for all members of the working population at all stages of the selection process, and (2) sampling is conducted with elements of the sample selected independently of one another (one at a time).

For example, consider a working population that consists of 100 persons whose names are written on equal-sized pieces of paper and placed in a hat for selection. The pieces of paper are thoroughly mixed and selected one by one, without being seen, until the sample size is obtained. This is a probability sample. Of course, when a piece of paper is selected from the hat to become part of the sample, the remaining papers no longer have the same probability of selection as the previous ones. For instance, originally each member of the working universe had a 1-in-100 chance of selection. After 25 are selected, those remaining would have a 1-in-75 chance of selection. This might seem to violate the first rule of probability sampling (equal probabilities), but, for practical reasons, it has come to be permitted as long as the chances for selection are equal at any given stage in the sampling process. This is called "sampling without replacement," and it is particularly acceptable when the working population is relatively large, because the probability differences from stage to stage are negligible.

There are several methods of drawing probability samples from the working population. The method chosen depends on a variety of factors, such as the manner in which the sampling frame is constructed and the focus of the study.

Simple Random Sampling

The best-known form of probability sample is the *simple random sample*. The usual procedure is to assign a number to each potential respondent, or sampling unit, in the sampling frame. Numbers are then chosen at random by a process that does not tend to favor certain numbers or patterns of numbers, and the sampling units selected become part of the sample itself. A common procedure for accomplishing this random process is to use a table of random numbers. Table 7.1 is an abridged table of random numbers. It is used in the following way.

Suppose that there are 500 people in a working population and a researcher wishes to select a random sample of 10 persons. Each person must be assigned a number ranging from 001 to 500. Using Table 7.1, the researcher arbitrarily selects a starting column or row of numbers and proceeds in any chosen direction (upward, downward, or across), looking for numbers between 001 and 500. In order to identify numbers from 001 to 500, the researcher must choose any three of the five digits given. In this case, let it be assumed that the process starts at line 9, column 2, and that it has been decided to proceed downward, looking at the first three digits in each random number for numbers between 001 and 500. The first number encountered is

Table 7.1. Abridged Table of Random Numbers.

	Column				
Line	*1*	*2*	*3*	*4*	*5*
1	11404	10478	24317	60312	25164
2	65621	95574	93724	49741	65251
3	93998	73709	00325	78627	36815
4	22667	52883	05673	74698	64385
5	33362	68724	52681	31148	83761
6	07236	66537	70834	33260	72583
7	31768	30247	90313	77538	05367
8	54121	21768	09324	79572	29734
9	68417	97521	56698	09525	76354
10	93561	63399	84743	39751	29448
11	31790	95267	75464	05783	98523
12	48585	66947	30541	64728	90400
13	93614	13143	58366	05070	37304
14	00071	86770	43287	07386	16458
15	48277	34132	73045	41818	07465

975; the second is 633. Neither of these numbers falls within the required range, so the search is continued with 952, 669, and 131. The first sample member has been found—sampling unit number 131. The next relevant number is 341 at the bottom of column 2. The researcher then continues on to the top of column 3; proceeding in this way, the third number of the sample is located—243. The reader should verify that the other seven sample numbers are as follows: 003, 056, 093, 305, 432, 497, and 311. If this process causes the researcher to arrive at a number that has already been selected for the sample, it is simply skipped, consistent with the premise of sampling without replacement.

Systematic Random Sampling

All probability sampling methods are actually variations of simple random sampling. *Systematic random sampling*, for instance, is an adaptation of the simple random process that is used when the working population list is quite large and the sampling units cannot be conveniently or feasibly numbered. If the working population consisted of 3,000,000 people and the drawing of a sample of 1,500 people was required, the process of numbering and selecting from a table of random numbers would be prohibitively burdensome. A systematic sample assumes that the sampling frame, or working population list, is randomly distributed; therefore, the researcher can systematically choose sample members by selecting them from the list at fixed intervals (every *n*th entry). For instance, the 1,500 sample members represent 1 out of every 2,000 people on the working population list (3,000,000/1,500 = 2,000), so if the selection process were to count to every 2,000th sampling unit from a starting point on the list selected at random, it would be expected that a random sample would exist. The starting point must be chosen between the first and two thousandth sampling unit on the list; otherwise the working population list will be exhausted before the sample selection is complete. Once again, the table of random numbers can be useful in the sample selection process—this time for choosing a starting point. Without looking at the table, the selector should arbitrarily pick a starting point (for example, column 4, line 30). Better yet, the selector can eliminate even this small potential for bias by asking someone else to choose a column and row or to point on the page while blindfolded.

It is rare for the systematic process to yield fixed intervals that are whole numbers without a fractional remainder. In the above case, if the working population were 3,100,000, the requisite fixed interval would be 2066.67, which would require truncating the decimal (Krueckeberg and Silvers, 1974, p. 38). As another example, suppose that a working population consists of a list of 250 students and the researcher requires that a sample of 9 students be selected. Dividing the working population of 250 by the desired sample size of 9 yields 27.8. This decimal is truncated (not rounded), leaving the whole number 27; hence, every 27th person on the list would be selected. The starting point would be any number between 1 and 27, selected randomly as discussed above. If the starting point happens to be 7, then the sample of 9 would consist of the following sampling units: 7, 34, 61, 88, 115, 142, 169, 196, and 223. If the decimal were rounded instead of truncated, the sample would include student number 252, who does not exist in the population of 250 students. On the other hand, truncation does tend to eliminate certain sampling units from the possibility of being selected. In this case, students 244 through 250 could never be selected. However, since the working population list is assumed to be random, this tendency to eliminate a small number of possible sample members is also random and therefore far more acceptable than choosing nonexistent sampling units.

Taking this process one step further, let it be supposed that the persons numbered 34, 61, and 115 refuse to respond or cannot be reached for an interview. The researcher is then faced with having to select three alternate respondents. Systematic sampling proceeds as follows: The remaining unselected working population sampling units are renumbered from 1 to 241 to account for the nine sampling units previously selected. This remaining number is divided by the required three respondents. Thus, 241 is divided by 3 to yield 80.3. Then, every eightieth person is selected starting with any number (selected at random) between 1 and 80. If the starting number is 60, the sample of three would include the sixtieth, one-hundred fortieth, and two hundred twentieth person on the list. This procedure is repeated, if necessary, until nine respondents have been successfully interviewed.

Stratified Random Sampling

Another adaptation of the simple random sampling process is known as *stratified random sampling*. Stratified sampling consists of separating the elements of the working population into mutually exclusive groups, called *strata*; random samples are then taken from each stratum. For example, a researcher may be interested in voter opinion concerning the issue of gun control. It is considered important to analyze the population by ethnic group affiliation. Accordingly, the sampling frame is separated into strata based on ethnicity. The primary purpose in this sample selection process is to make certain that each stratum is represented by an adequate sample size. This is much more

Table 7.2. Proportionate Sample Representation for a Hypothetical Ethnic Distribution.

Ethnic Group	*Population Size (in thousands)*	*%*	*Expected Proportionate Sample Representation*	*%*	*Expected Proportionate Sample Representation with Maximum ± 10% Margin of Error*	*%*
White	6,000	60.0	360	60.0	600	60.0
Black	1,500	15.0	90	15.0	150	15.0
Hispanic	1,500	15.0	90	15.0	150	15.0
Asian	1,000	10.0	60	10.0	100	10.0
Total	10,000	100.0	600	100.0	1,000	100.0

likely to occur when selection is performed by stratum than by an overall population random sampling procedure. Table 7.2 presents a hypothetical overall breakdown of the working population by ethnic group and the expected random sample representation of the various groups proportionate to their number in the overall population, based on a sample size of 600.

If the researcher were to proceed with random sampling procedures, it could be expected that the sample sizes of the ethnic strata would approximate the proportions they represent in the overall population. Hence, the researcher might consider, in advance of ultimate sample selection, that the sample is likely to have approximately 360 whites, 90 blacks, 90 Hispanics, and 60 Asians. However, since ethnicity has been established as an important criterion in the study, the researcher must now recognize that the number of blacks, Hispanics, and Asians to be sampled in the study is probably going to be too small to achieve certain requisite margins of error (for example, ± 10 percent). Table 6.1 indicates that these expected group sizes do not meet sample size requirements for a margin of error of ± 10 percent (95 percent level of confidence), thereby calling into question the researcher's ability to make reasonably accurate generalizations concerning these groups. A practical rule of thumb is that a 10 percent margin of error is the maximum that should be tolerated for any group or subgroup within the overall sample.

Hence, a sample size of approximately 100 is required for all strata and substrata. If the researcher, therefore, wants to attempt to achieve at least the ± 10 percent margin of error for each stratum, the overall sample size will have to be increased accordingly to reasonably ensure that each group will meet that threshold. For example, since Asians represent 10 percent of the population (Table 7.2), a total sample size of a minimum of 1,000 persons will be required in order to anticipate approximately 100 Asian respondents (10 percent) within that sample. Table 7.2 further demonstrates that a sample size increase above 600 would also be required for black and Hispanic populations. Increasing the sample size, however, can have serious cost considerations and may not be within the researcher's budget or time frame.

Stratified sampling offers to the researcher a method by which the margin-of-error requirement of a maximum of ± 10 percent for each stratum can be satisfied while still keeping the overall sample size at 600, as long as at least 100 persons are interviewed in each stratum. Table 7.3 shows the recommended disproportionate sample sizes by stratum for this particular example. The samples must now be selected randomly from four separate sampling frames within the total population. In essence, the researcher will have selected four distinct random samples. At this point, the reader should note that in the case of small populations, equation 6.7 and Table 6.2 should be utilized for purposes of determining the sample size of each stratum. This will reduce the requisite sample sizes.

The difficulty with disproportionate stratification is that the overall sample is now skewed toward the smaller strata. Blacks, Hispanics, and Asians are overrepresented, and whites are underrepresented. A weighting procedure must be employed to analyze the data with regard to the total population. In order to achieve this objective, the researcher must restore proportionality to the strata. One way to implement this weighting procedure is to duplicate the sample responses according to weight. The process involves dividing the expected proportionate sample representation (with its margin-of-error requirement) by the disproportionate sample size to obtain prelimi-

Table 7.3. Stratified Sample Representation for a Hypothetical Ethnic Distribution.

A	B[a]	C	D	E	F
Ethnicity	*Disproportionate Sample Size*	*Expected Porportionate Sample Representation with Maximum ± 10% Margin of Error*	*Preliminary Weight (C/B)*	*Final Weight*	*Weighted Sample Size (B × E)*
White	300	600	2.0	4	1,200
Black	100	150	1.5	3	300
Hispanic	100	150	1.5	3	300
Asian	100	100	1.0	2	200
Total	600	1,000			2,000

[a] The allocation of the total sample size among the strata is somewhat discretionary as long as the maximum margin-of-error requirement is met. It is recommended, however, that stratum sample sizes be as consistent as possible with their expected proportionate sample representation.

nary weights. In this example, these preliminary weights are indicated in Table 7.3 as white = 2.0, black = 1.5, Hispanic = 1.5, and Asian = 1. The overall sample, therefore, can be constructed by duplicating the responses of the white participants, randomly selecting one-half of the black and Hispanic participants' responses to add to the existing sample responses, and keeping the Asian responses as they are. There is, however, a problem with the random selection of one-half of the black and Hispanic responses; that is, the initial sampling error will have been compounded by a second sampling error. Therefore, weights should be derived in the form of whole numbers. If this is done, no secondary sampling procedure is necessary. This example would easily lend itself to final weights of white = 4, black = 3, Hispanic = 3, and Asian = 2, which result in the final weighted sample presented in Table 7.3. It must be made abundantly clear to the reader that such weighting procedures are for the purpose of combining the results of a disproportionate survey in order to analyze the overall population according to its true proportions. The margin of error for the overall study remains consistent with the true sample size (those who were actually interviewed, not the weighted totals). Each stratum is also analyzed in accordance with a margin of error dictated by its actual sample size. Thus, results related to blacks, Asians, and Hispanics will contain margins of error of ± 10 percent, whites ± 6 percent, and the overall sample ± 4 percent at the 95 percent level of confidence.

The example provided allows for a relatively neat and convenient weighted sampling process. It is more than likely, however, that preliminary weights might not be so easily manipulated algebraically to achieve the final weights. For example, assume that preliminary weights were as follows:

White	2.75
Black	1.95
Hispanic	1.33
Asian	1.00

It is readily apparent that whole number final weights are not easily discernible from these preliminary weights. In such a case, approximations of proportionality by using whole number final weights are acceptable, as long as these approximations are reasonably close to the expected proportions within each stratum. The researcher can justify such approximations by considering that, even if a larger proportionate sample of 1,000 were conducted, the likelihood is small that actual strata sample sizes would fall exactly in line with the expected proportions. This process would lend itself to final weights of white = 8, black = 6, Hispanic = 4, and Asian = 3, as determined in Table 7.4. The determination of the whole number factor is done on a case-by-case basis and is the lowest whole number that, multiplied by the preliminary weights, results in tentative final weights that are reasonably close to whole numbers.

The inclusion of the tabular display of disproportionate sample data in the final report requires special attention and is discussed more fully in Chapter Eight.

In telephone surveys, there is a special variation on the concept of stratified random sampling. This variation is called

Table 7.4. Weighted Values for a Hypothetical Ethnic Distribution.

	Preliminary Weights	×	*Whole Number Factor*	=	*Tentative Final Weight*	*Final Weight (Whole Number)*
White	2.75		3		8.25	8
Black	1.95		3		5.85	6
Hispanic	1.33		3		3.99	4
Asian	1.00		3		3.00	3

random digit dialing; it consists of stratifying the working population geographically by area code and/or telephone exchange and then, through the use of a random numbers table, selecting four- or seven-digit numbers, as appropriate, to complete the telephone number in order to contact potential respondents.

Let us suppose that a researcher needs to select a sample of 1,000 households in a small city with four telephone exchanges (578, 279, 594, and 265). Information provided by the telephone company indicates the number of residential telephones in each exchange as shown in Table 7.5.

It can be seen in this table that the 20,000 residential telephones in the city have been stratified by telephone exchange, and a sample size for each stratum has been determined in proportion to the total number of residential telephones in that stratum. Using a table of random numbers, the researcher can select 200 four-digit numbers for the 578 exchange, 250 for the 279 exchange, 350 for the 594 exchange, and 200 for the 265 exchange. As with systematic random sampling, nonworking numbers, or those that represent housholds with no response or

Table 7.5. Total Residential Telephones for Random Digit Dialing Process.

Exchange	*Residential Telephones*	*%*	*Proportionate Sample Size*
578	4,000	20.0	200
279	5,000	25.0	250
594	7,000	35.0	350
265	4,000	20.0	200
Total	20,000	100.0	1,000

a refusal to participate, should be replaced with other random numbers.

Cluster Sampling

The final frequently used probability sampling technique is known as *cluster* or *multistage sampling* (sometimes called *area sampling*). A cluster sample is a variation of a simple random sample in which there is a hierarchy of sampling units. The primary sampling unit is a grouping (or cluster) of the individual elements that are the focus of the study. This grouping must be a well-delineated subset of the general population that is considered to include characteristics found in that population. Such groupings typically consist of counties, cities, census tracts, census blocks, and so forth. The secondary sampling units are the individual elements within these clusters from which information is to be solicited. These units are selected for study at random during subsequent stages of the process. Cluster sampling arises predominantly from situations in which population lists are incomplete at the individual level but are complete at some more aggregated level.

To illustrate cluster sampling, suppose that the researcher for a private marketing firm wishes to identify all persons between the ages of eighteen and twenty-one in County X. It is clear that no complete or even nearly complete list of such persons would be available. A field project that would attempt to formulate such a list would most likely be totally infeasible and, if not, it would be prohibitively expensive. Furthermore, even if such a list could be constructed economically, the random sample of respondents drawn from it would likely be widespread, resulting in a good deal of traveling if, for instance, face-to-face interviews were required. Hence, the researcher can employ cluster sampling in the following manner:

Stage 1: List all census tracts in County X.
Stage 2: Select a random sample of tracts from the list according to Table 6.1 or 6.2, whichever is applicable.[1]

Stage 3: Select a random sample of census blocks from the random sample of census tracts according to Table 6.1 or 6.2.

Stage 4: Select a random sample of households on each block.

Stage 5: Interview selected households.

To concretize the application of these stages, assume that the researcher begins with 500 census tracts in County X. A random sample of these tracts (95 percent confidence level, ± 3 percent margin of error) would require 250 tracts to be included (Table 6.2). Assume further that these randomly selected 250 census tracts contain 50,000 census blocks. Of these blocks, a sample of 1,045 should be randomly selected (Table 6.2). From these 1,045 blocks, a random sample of 1,045 households will be selected in order to meet the overall criteria of ± 3 percent at a 95 percent level of confidence. These 1,045 households, therefore, have been selected without the potentially significant expense of having to list each and every household in the population. This can represent a substantial cost and time savings. Furthermore, the sample households will have been selected in 250 census tracts rather than the entire 500. This results in a potentially more concentrated interviewing effort. The disadvantage of this procedure is the possibility of sampling error (Chapter Five) occuring in each of the stages; hence, there is a compounded chance of error. However, under many circumstances (especially in face-to-face, in-person interviews), the practical time and cost advantages tend to outweigh this technical disadvantage.

In certain situations, clusters are known to be substantially different from one another in terms of size or homogeneity of the clusters' populations. Stratified cluster sampling must be used in such circumstances. For instance, in most states, the population tends to be concentrated in a handful of counties. If clustering is to be performed by county, it is possible to underrepresent or even completely overlook these large counties. In order to avoid this lack of representativeness, it is necessary to stratify counties based on population size (for example, 1,000,000 residents and above versus fewer than 1,000,000 residents). Clusters can then be selected from each of these strata in order to assure adequate representation. The principles of stratified sampling, including weight adjustments, must be applied to the stratified sample clusters as appropriate.

Nonprobability Sampling

The essential characteristic of nonprobability sampling is that the researcher does not know the probability that a particular respondent will be selected as part of the sample. Therefore, there is no certainty that the probability of selection is equal among the potential respondents. Without such equality, the researcher cannot analyze the sample in terms of the normal distribution. Therefore, the sample data cannot be used to generalize beyond the sample itself because the degree of sampling error associated with the sample cannot be estimated without an assumption of normality.

In spite of these obvious shortcomings, nonprobability sampling can be helpful to the researcher. It is considerably less complicated in terms of strict adherence to the tenets of random sample selection and is, therefore, much less costly and time consuming than probability sampling. The primary advantage of nonprobability sampling rests in its usefulness in the preliminary stages of a research project. In Stage 3 of the survey process (Chapter One), for instance, the researcher must ensure that there is adequate knowledge of the investigative area before constructing specific questions. The use of a nonprobability sample can quickly generate a preliminary understanding of some of the key issues underlying the research study. It is also the primary means by which researchers pretest and refine their survey instrument, as discussed in Chapter Two.

The most common example of a nonprobability sample is a "sidewalk survey," where interviewers, for instance, may interview passersby at a shopping center. The general population in this example is shoppers. Strict adherence to the principles of probability sampling would require the compilation of a list of all such shoppers as the working population. In the case of a sidewalk survey, this working population is typically not enumerated, and, consequently, the probability of selection from that working population of any particular passerby cannot be determined. Furthermore, under these circumstances, there can be a significant element of individual interviewer discretion in the selection of interviewees that might compound the existing uncertainty about whether the sample truly represents the general population.

There are several types of nonprobability samples. The sidewalk survey is an example of *convenience sampling*, in which interviewees are selected based on their presumed resemblance to the working population and their ready availability. Frequently, students are interviewed in their classrooms, enabling the researcher to contact large numbers of respondents in a relatively short period of time at minimal cost. It is important to reemphasize that the researcher cannot generalize the findings in such cases beyond the sample itself. These findings can only be used as an informal base of preliminary knowledge in preparation for a survey research project based on probability sampling.

Another type of nonprobability sample is known as the *purposive sample*. In the purposive sample the researcher uses professional judgment in the selection of respondents. For example, a researcher may be interested in gathering information about problems related to juveniles in a particular community. Key respondents, whom the researcher considers to be particularly knowledgeable about the subject, may be selected for interviews. These respondents may include such people as the directors of social service agencies, law enforcement personnel, judges, attorneys, and educators. Responses to a set of questions may then be summarized as part of a larger study concerning juvenile problems.

A similar nonprobability sampling technique is *snowball sampling*. Snowball sampling is particularly beneficial when it is difficult to identify potential respondents. Once a few respondents are identified and interviewed, they are asked to identify others who might qualify as respondents. Suppose that a researcher has initiated a study that necessitates the interviewing of drug abusers who have not sought medical or social assistance. Quite obviously, such respondents could not be easily identified. However, the researcher may be able to identify and interview a small number of drug abusers using personal reconnaissance. Snowball sampling could then be invoked by relying on these initial respondents to provide access to other drug users.

Quota sampling is a nonprobabilistic form of sampling in which the researcher ensures that the sample reflects the overall population with regard to one or more specific variables that have been identified as important to the objectives of the study. Assume that a researcher is particularly interested in ensuring that the sample represents the larger population in terms of sex. If the total population is 55 percent female and 45 percent male, the researcher should make certain that the sample reflects the same proportions. On the surface, this technique would seem to mirror that of proportionate stratified sampling. The difference, however, as with other nonprobabilistic techniques, exists in the fact that the selection of quota sample respondents for each subgroup is not done randomly. Rather, sample selection involves the discretion of the interviewer. The interviewer's responsibility is to obtain a sample allocated in accordance with a ratio of 55 percent female to 45 percent male. How this is actually attained is of secondary importance. However, as a note of caution for this and other nonprobabilistic techniques, researchers should still attempt to minimize readily mitigable biases in the selection process. Efforts should be made to achieve some balance of other population characteristics within the subgroups. For example, the selection of each gender group should include as broad a representation of characteristics such as age and ethnicity as possible; obvious over- or underrepresentation of such characteristics should be avoided.

Endnote

1. The most extensive treatment of a method of selecting the number of clusters to be sampled is contained in Scheaffer, Mendenhall, and Ott, 1986, pp. 197–222. They presented a complex and innovative formula for determining the

number of clusters to be included in a cluster sample, which can be shown at the 95 percent level of confidence as follows:

$$n = \frac{N\sigma_c^2}{N\left(\frac{B^2\overline{M}^2}{4}\right) + \sigma_c^2}$$

where n = number of clusters selected in a simple random sample, N = number of clusters in the whole population, σ_c^2 = population variance associated with the sizes of the clusters in the population, B = margin of error (confidence interval) in terms of either proportions or interval data, and $\overline{M}$ = mean cluster size for the whole population.

The formula will tend to yield a number of clusters to be sampled that is somewhat lower than the number generated by Tables 6.1 and 6.2. It does so because of two factors:

a. A preliminary sample is required in order to estimate $\overline{M}$ and σ_c^2.
b. There is an implicit assumption that there will be a full canvassing of all members of the clusters selected.

Hence, this formula has the advantage of a greater geographic concentration of clusters, but there are disadvantages in terms of the costs involved in conducting an adequate preliminary sample and in obtaining a 100 percent census within the clusters themselves. Also, because of the smaller number of clusters, there is a greater likelihood of needing to stratify the cluster sample. On balance, we believe it to be more consistent with the needs of the readers of this book, in terms of practical applications, cost factors, and other such considerations, to use the approaches presented in Chapters Six and Seven in the application of cluster sampling.

Exercises

1. You are interested in performing a survey that involves an attempt to identify the reasons associated with locational

preferences among suburban dwellers. Identify the general population and a working population for this study. Suggest possible sources of population lists for constructing the sampling frame.

2. Twenty persons out of a class of 50 students are to be randomly selected for participation in a certain experimental project. Assume that these students have been numbered from 1 to 50. Use Table 7.1 to select the twenty participants.
3. You wish to survey 370 doctors regarding their perception of medical ethics. The American Medical Association has provided an unnumbered list of the 41,000 doctors in your state. Apply the procedure of systematic random sampling to indicate where on this list you would start the sample and how you would proceed to obtain the complete sample.
4. The list provided by the American Medical Association (Exercise 3) also indicates the ethnic background of each doctor. The total ethnic breakdown is as follows:

	f	%
White	34,000	82.9
Asian	4,000	9.8
Black	2,000	4.9
Hispanic	1,000	2.4
	41,000	100.0

The study seeks to make generalizations according to ethnicity with a margin of error of 10 percent.

a. What would you expect to be the ethnic distribution of your 370-person sample in Exercise 3?
b. You determine that a disproportionate stratified sample is needed in order to satisfy these requirements. What is the disproportionate ethnic breakdown of your sample? (*Note: The population size is small.*)
c. Calculate the weights to be applied to each disproportionate subgroup in order to convert each to proportionality.

5. A study of undocumented aliens is about to be undertaken. The researchers find that they do not possess sufficient

information about the important issues facing these individuals to construct a thorough survey questionnaire. Therefore, they need to gather preliminary information from this group. How can the researchers use the much less expensive nonprobabilistic sampling techniques to obtain this preliminary information?

a. Convenience sampling:____________________________

____

b. Purposive sampling:______________________________

____

c. Snowball sampling:_______________________________

____

PART THREE

Analyzing and Reporting Survey Results

cluded from the analysis. For example, suppose that it is found through a survey research study that football fans earn a statistically significant higher annual income than nonfootball fans. Prior to making a policy decision based on such a finding, the researcher should analyze other variables that might be suspected of influencing the independent variable (football fans) and the dependent variable (annual income). One such variable would be the sex of the respondent, because football fans tend to be predominantly male and income levels are higher among males. It may be, therefore, that the preliminary finding is erroneous and that the actual independent variable is gender. If this should actually be the case, then the relationship between football fans and income is said to be *spurious*—or not genuine.

There are a variety of advanced statistical techniques that are designed to measure the influence of more than one independent variable on a dependent variable, and, thereby, identify spurious relationships. Foremost among these techniques are multiple regression analysis, two-way analysis of variance, and partial correlation, all of which are beyond the scope of this text.

Exercises

1. The following matrix of cross-tabulated response frequencies has been provided in a computer printout. The categories are ethnicity and political party preference.

	White	*Black*	*Hispanic*	*Asian*	*Total*
Democrat	200	120	100	50	470
Republican	350	10	40	30	430
Independent	50	20	10	20	100
Total	600	150	150	100	1,000

   a. Use the data from this matrix to construct a contingency table. Make certain that the independent and dependent variables are appropriately placed on the columns and rows.
   b. Calculate the chi-square and interpret its meaning.

Table 9.7. Level of Tolerance Toward Stress by Coffee-Drinking Status of Respondent.

	Coffee Drinker		*Non-Coffee Drinker*	
Level of Tolerance	*f*	%	*f*	%
Very tolerant	40	16.0	20	13.3
Somewhat tolerant	25	10.0	20	13.3
Neither tolerant nor intolerant	75	30.0	45	30.0
Somewhat intolerant	60	24.0	50	33.4
Very intolerant	50	20.0	15	10.0
Total	250	100.0	150	100.0

c. Calculate an appropriate measure of association and interpret its meaning.

2. Consider the survey results in Table 9.7 concerning coffee drinkers and their psychologically determined levels of tolerance in times of stress.
   a. What preliminary conclusions might you draw from these survey results?
   b. Calculate the chi-square. Can it be established that statistical significance exists with 95 percent confidence?
   c. Would the Median Test be appropriate? If so, perform the Median Test. How does this change your answers to parts a and b?
   d. Are there other variables involved that you suspect might be contributing to a potential spurious relationship between the variables in question?
3. The City of Willowbend conducted a sample survey of 400 voter registrants to determine whether or not voters have a favorable attitude toward the city's newly proposed growth management plan. The city was not only interested in voter preference but also in how this preference relates to voter income level. Accordingly, the sample respondents were asked to indicate their annual household income in the context of certain fixed categories. The results of the income question and the growth management preference question were cross-tabulated. The results of that cross-tabulation are presented in Table 9.8.

Table 9.8. Voter Preference Regarding Growth Management Plan by Annual Household Income for the City of Willowbend.

Attitude Toward Growth Management Plan	*Annual Household Income*											
	Under $10,000		*$10,000–$19,999*		*$20,000–$29,999*		*$30,000–$39,999*		*$40,000 and Above*		*Total*	
	f	%	*f*	%	*f*	%	*f*	%	*f*	%	*f*	%
Favor	8	66.7	81	88.0	48	25.3	13	18.3	9	28.0	159	39.8
Do not favor	1	8.3	9	9.8	130	68.4	50	70.4	18	48.0	208	52.0
No opinion	3	25.0	2	2.2	12	6.3	8	11.3	8	24.0	33	8.2
Total	12	100.0	92	100.0	190	100.0	71	100.0	35	100.0	400	100.0

a. Use the chi-square test to determine whether or not there is a statistically significant relationship (95 percent level of confidence) between voter attitude concerning the growth management plan and annual household income. (*Hint:* Consider sparse cells and regroup categories accordingly before calculating the chi-square.)
b. Calculate an appropriate measure of association.

Chapter 10

Preparing an Effective Final Report

The final report is the vehicle for communicating to the audience the conclusions and recommendations derived from the study. It should be viewed by the researcher as integral to the survey research process as a whole and, therefore, the research process should not be considered to be complete until the final report has been prepared and disseminated. Within the report, the analysis of the data, including tables, graphs, and other statistical presentations, should be well organized and clearly explained so that the intended audience can comprehend the essential findings of the study. This chapter suggests an appropriate format and useful guidelines for preparing a formal report of survey research findings.

Report Format

There are several fundamental considerations that must be taken into account as the final report is prepared. These considerations are explained in the following sections.

The Title

The report should contain a title that identifies the focus of the research. The title should be clear and succinct. Frequently a subtitle can help to further clarify the subject matter of the research. For example, a research report concerning growth control limitations in New York State was titled "Issues Concerning Economic Growth: A Critique of Oswego County's Proposed Countywide Impact Fee Program." The title should be included on the cover of the report along with the names and affiliations of the authors. The date of report dissemination should also be included, as should the client or sponsor for whom the study was conducted. Exhibit 10.1 is an example of a well-constructed cover page. The title should also appear within the report either on a separate title page or at the top of the first page of the report.

Executive Summary

The reader of the report frequently finds it helpful for a short summary of findings to be included at the beginning of the report. This summary can serve as a source of reference after the report has been read and can also serve as the basic source of information about the report itself for audiences that are only peripherally interested in the subject matter.

Introduction to the Study

The report should start by providing the audience with some background about the subject matter of the study and by placing the study into an appropriate perspective with regard to the history and current significance of the research topic. Major social and political events of the time that the researcher feels have some bearing on the responses should be presented in the introduction. The introduction must also contain a clear statement of the specific purpose of the study, which describes the issues and explains why the researchers decided to pursue the subject in this fashion and at this time.

Exhibit 10.1. Example of Cover Page.

Issues Concerning Economic Growth: A

Critique of Oswego County's Proposed

Countywide Impact Fee Program

prepared by

XYZ Research Corporation

for

The Oswego County Taxpayer's Association

July, 1991

Review of Preliminary Research

The initial processes undertaken by the researcher in identifying the research focus and helping to develop the actual research instrument should be summarized. This includes a review of existing literature consulted and a discussion of the key groups and individuals who participated in the development of the information base from which the pretest and draft questionnaire evolved. The specific questions at issue or research hypotheses to be tested should be stated and shown as having been directly derived from this preliminary research. The hypotheses should be presented in the context of the information required from the study. That is, the researcher should indicate what the research is designed to discover that was heretofore unknown.

Method of Research

Sample Selection. The report should detail the procedures employed in selection of the sample. This discussion must include an explanation of how an appropriate working population was identified to represent the general population. The determination of the sampling frame should be discussed, including any potential systematic biases. Also to be included in this discussion are the determination of sample size (specifying the level of confidence and confidence interval) and the specific sampling method employed in the selection of the final sample.

Survey Procedure. The survey method should be discussed, including the recruitment and selection of interviewers for telephone and in-person surveys, procedures employed in the initial mailing for mail-out surveys, follow-up procedures, response rates, and the time frame of the study. Patterned biases that may have been identified in the interviewing process must be identified and explained. Their potential effect upon survey results should be indicated.

Data Analysis. The researcher should briefly describe the statistical methods used in data analysis, including all applicable tests of significance and measures of association. Included in this section are explanations of the meaning and importance of these tests and measures.

Research Findings

The major part of the report consists of the research findings. This portion is composed largely of tables and graphs, with appropriate descriptive and analytical statistics, accompanied by written explanations of the tabular and graphic results. The tables and graphs should be integrated within the text and not aggregated separately from it in an appendix, for instance. A table or graph should appear in the text as close to its initial mention as possible, while ensuring that it is fully contained on one page; it must not span more than one page. It has been found that this placement of tables and graphs within the text lends itself to increased convenience for the reader, who can study the researcher's interpretation of the data while maintaining ready visual access to the data themselves.

A frequency distribution table should be prepared for each survey question, and contingency tables should be presented at the researcher's discretion within the framework of the research issues under consideration. This discretion should be guided, in part, by the statistical significance of any apparent relationships among the variables involved. Each contingency table must be accompanied by the most appropriate test of statistical significance and, if signifcant, by a measure of association with some comment regarding the relative strength of the variables' assocation.

Conclusions

The report should conclude with a strong section that draws implications from the findings, indicates relationships and trends among the various tables and graphs, and relates the findings from the study to any relevant previous studies or literature. When appropriate, policy recommendations should be put forth, and, finally, opportunities for further research should be discussed.

Bibliography

Important publications and documents consulted during the research process should be listed in a bibliography at the end of the report.

Appendixes

Certain information should be attached to the report in the form of an appendix. Such material always includes a copy of the survey instrument itself with the raw frequency data indicated for each question (frequently referred to as a "data sheet"). Other potential appendixes may be the verbatim open-ended response worksheet and detailed explanations of certain statistical techniques and/or sampling procedures, including all applicable mathematical equations, which are much better placed in the appendix than in the body of the report itself.

There is a considerable amount of discretion involved in choosing the material that is to be included in an appendix. The overriding principle is to include material that the researcher feels would be beneficial to the reader, but that would tend to interrupt the readability of the report. This allows the researcher to maintain a pleasant communicative flow in the report itself, while still providing all the important information to readers of the report.

Additional Considerations for Formally Reporting Survey Results

Within the report framework, there are further issues, particularly with regard to format and style of writing, that the researcher should address in the preparation of the final report. These issues can be organized into three general categories: (1) vocabulary, jargon, and statistical notation; (2) reporting of numerical detail; and (3) reporting of statistical significance and sampling error.

Vocabulary, Jargon, and Statistical Notation

The audience and/or client must be considered in deciding on the writing style and the extent of professional vocabulary to be used. If a report is prepared for a technically oriented audience (for instance, engineers, doctors, scientists, or accountants), the researcher may feel more comfortable using terms that are regarded as specific to their particular discipline. The more general or diversified the audience, however, the less technical the language should be, as long as meaning and substance are not sacrificed. An example of such a general audience would be the people who would read a research report summarizing the results of a community public opinion survey.

The report should not overly rely on the use of statistics and statistical notation as substitutes for descriptions of the relationships involved. For example, it is more informative to an audience to say that there is a moderate correlation between the ethnicity and income of the citizens in a community than to write only that the ethnicity/income Cramer's $V = .35$ for the survey under study. The use of the word "correlation" is preferable to the use of "Cramer's V" to communicate the applicable relationship. In general, it is better to use descriptive words (for instance, mean, test of significance, and measure of association or correlation) than to rely entirely on statistical notations such as $\overline{X}$, χ^2, and V. Statistical notations should be used only once in the written portion of the report—after the technique's initial mention. For instance, when chi-square is first mentioned, it should be followed by the parenthetical reference (χ^2), as indicated in the following example: "The chi-square test of significance (χ^2) for the relationship between political party affiliation and sex of the respondent did not establish the existence of a statistically significant relationship between the two variables." After this initial reference, the use of any statistical symbol should be confined to the tables and mathematical displays only.

The choice of particular words is very important. Be

careful not to give the impression that survey findings are universal. Instead of writing, "The people feel that. . . ," write, "Most people feel that. . . ," because it is highly unlikely that all people will have the same opinion. Be careful when using words such as "strong" or "significant," for instance; these words and certain others connote statistical relationships that may mislead the readers as to the true meaning of what is being communicated. It is more meaningful to indicate that a particular issue has "substantial support" rather than "significant support" when reporting results without the use of significance tests. This is especially true in reporting frequency distributions. The researcher must also be careful to avoid the use of emotive or judgmental words—words that denote surprise, discomfort, or displeasure. For example, a report should not contain the phrase, "It was particularly upsetting to find that. . . ."

For ease of reading, footnotes should be used sparingly. Important material should be incorporated into the body of the text as much as possible. Reference citations should always be embodied within the text in accordance with the format (author, year, page). Each citation should correspond to a full bibliographic reference at the end of the report. Content notes (explanatory digressions that, in the judgment of the researcher, would tend to obstruct the flow of the text) should also be used as infrequently as possible, but when they are used, they should be placed at the bottom of the page for ready reference.

Reporting of Numerical Detail

The written portion of the report should indicate percentages, fractions, or ratios rather than absolute frequencies. That is, rather than reporting that 475 Democrats oppose gun control, it is more informative to say that 65.8 percent of the Democrats oppose gun control, or that nearly two-thirds of the Democrats oppose gun control. When the overall sample is quite small or when a particular subgroup within the sample is small, the researcher should report both the percentages and the corresponding frequencies. For example, rather than reporting that "40.0 percent of black office workers favor a change in their union contract," it is more appropriate to report that "in a survey of sixty office workers, twenty of whom are black, eight black workers (40.0 percent) favor a change in their union contract." In this way, the reader will not be misled into believing that this particular finding is more substantial than it actually is.

Use whole numbers and common fractions whenever possible. Instead of reporting that "men favor an issue more than women by a ratio of 1.85 to 1," it is better to say that "nearly twice as many men favor this issue than do women." This approach lends itself to significantly more pleasant reading, while providing the audience with the specific numerical detail in the accompanying tables. Similarly, it is better to report that approximately one-fourth of a population expressed a certain attitude than that seven thirty-seconds did (which actually may be more accurate but is much more difficult to translate into a commonly understood quantity).

The tables will provide all the necessary details a reader may wish to garner from the results of the study. Accordingly, the researcher should avoid reporting an excessive amount of detail and should, instead, selectively report the few salient details that bear most directly on the focus of the study. Rather than reporting detail as follows: "Concerning mode of transportation to work, 68.2 percent use automobiles, 23.7 percent use public transit, 4.8 percent walk, 2.9 percent ride bicycles, and 0.4 percent use taxis and other dial-a-ride services," the researcher should report the information by stating that "over two-thirds of the population (68.2 percent) use automobiles and nearly one-fourth (23.7 percent) use public transit." If the research has a particular focus regarding one of the other modes of transportation, it should be commented on, but otherwise, the written portion of the report should highlight only the critical findings.

It is not necessary to write about all tables. However, their presence should be mentioned by table number, and the reason for their presentation should be stated. References to the tables can be separate or in grouped form. For example, the researcher may indicate that "Tables 3.3–3.8 summarize the general characteristics of the population." However, the information in some of these tables may be perfectly obvious from looking at the table and may not be sufficiently noteworthy to require further elaboration.

Decimals should be rounded to the nearest tenth. For example, 32.58 percent should be reported as 32.6 percent.

Reporting of Statistical Significance and Sampling Error

When a finding that the researcher considers to merit discussion within the report is also statistically significant, the researcher should report the level of significance. If the finding has met the requirements for being significant at both the 95 percent and 99 percent levels of confidence, the report should indicate that "statistical significance has been established at the 99 percent level of confidence." If, however, the finding is significant at the 95 percent level but not the 99 percent level, the report should indicate significance at the 95 percent level. When a finding is important to the study in terms of its relationship to certain research hypotheses, but the tests fail to establish statistical significance at 95 percent or 99 percent, the researcher should still report the finding but should also indicate that statistical significance has not been established.

Periodically, during the course of the report, it is a good idea to remind the reader that the results that are being reported are subject to a certain margin of error. These reminders should be incorporated subtly into the written report without obstructing its flow or appearing to apologize or serve as disclaimers. For example, a report might contain the following statement: "Out of the total population, 55.0 percent of the men and 52.0 percent of the women favor abortion, subject to a margin of error of ±5 percent." These reminders should be relatively infrequent but sufficient in number to prevent the reader from forgetting this important limitation of the data.

When a result cannot be fully explained in terms of the relationships underlying the findings, as in the case of suspected spuriousness, the researcher should not attempt to conceal this lack of definiteness, but should, instead, clearly state the nature of the uncertainty and suggest further research on the issue. Also, if the sample is nonprobability (for example, quota, convenience, purposive, or snowball), the researcher must be careful to avoid generalizations beyond the sample itself. She or he must be constantly cognizant of the fact that a nonprobability sample is not scientifically representative of a larger population. Therefore, references to the sample in the report should be in terms of "respondents" or "the sample" rather than in general population terms such as "Americans," "men," or "blacks."

Exercises

1. Table 10.1 lists certain issues identified by residents of Hamilton as needing government action. Using the data contained in this table, write a paragraph for inclusion in a final report that summarizes and highlights residents' opinions regarding the identified issues. Be sure to follow the guidelines outlined in the chapter.

Table 10.1. Issues Identified by Residents of Hamilton as Needing Government Attention.

Issue	*f*	%
Traffic problems	2,252	25.3
Too much growth	1,847	20.8
Undocumented alien problems	1,404	15.8
Maintaining rural environment/open space	383	4.3
Crime and drug abuse	680	7.6
School crowding/quality	783	8.8
Too few recreational activities	286	3.2
Government inefficiency and lack of response	154	1.8
Need for more commercial development	311	3.5
Need for beautification program	119	1.3
Need for government services[a]	678	7.6
Total	8,897[b]	100.0

[a] Government services include libraries, sewers, water, rent control, pedestrian safety, property taxes, and street maintenance and repair.

[b] Since each respondent had the opportunity to designate as many issues as he or she wished, the total number of responses exceeds the number of cases in the file.

2. Tables 10.2 and 10.3 examine shopping patterns among various ethnic groups residing in the community of City

Table 10.2. Area Where Convenience Goods[a] Are Purchased Most Frequently.

	Mean Number of Shoppers									
	White		*Black*		*Asian*		*Hispanic*		*Total*	
Commercial Area	$\overline{X}$	%	$\overline{X}$	%	$\overline{X}$	%	$\overline{X}$	%	$\overline{X}$	%
City Heights	195	44.1	65	51.6	18	47.3	56	50.0	334	46.5
Midcity (other than City Heights)	119	26.9	30	23.8	10	26.3	27	24.1	186	25.9
Nearby regional shopping center areas[b]	60	13.6	17	13.5	5	13.2	16	14.3	98	13.7
Other[c]	68	15.4	14	11.1	5	13.2	13	11.6	100	13.9
Total	442	100.0	126	100.0	38	100.0	112	100.0	718	100.0

Note: $\chi^2 = 3.80$, not significant at 95% (critical $\chi^2 = 16.92$, $df = 9$).

[a] Convenience goods include groceries, medical supplies, do-it-yourself products, and dining out.

[b] Nearby shopping centers include Mission Valley (Mission Valley), Fashion Valley (Mission Valley), College Grove (East San Diego), and Grossmont (La Mesa).

[c] "Other" responses include various locations throughout San Diego that are generally closely tied to the location of the respondent's workplace.

Table 10.3. Area Where Shopping Goods[a] Are Purchased Most Frequently, by Ethnic Group.

	Mean Number of Shoppers									
	White		*Black*		*Asian*		*Hispanic*		*Total*	
Commercial Area	$\overline{X}$	%	$\overline{X}$	%	$\overline{X}$	%	$\overline{X}$	%	$\overline{X}$	%
City Heights	28	6.6	20	16.0	8	20.5	11	9.9	67	9.6
Midcity (other than City Heights)	115	27.1	37	29.6	9	23.1	27	24.3	188	26.9
Nearby regional shopping center areas[b]	175	41.3	44	35.2	11	28.2	51	46.0	281	40.2
Other[c]	106	25.0	24	19.2	11	28.2	22	19.8	163	23.3
Total	424	100.0	125	100.0	39	100.0	111	100.0	699	100.0

Note: $\chi^2 = 19.86$, significant at 95% (critical $\chi^2 = 16.92$, $df = 9$).

[a] Shopping goods include appliances, specialty goods, clothing, furniture, toys, and sporting goods.

[b] Nearby shopping centers include Mission Valley (Mission Valley), Fashion Valley (Mission Valley), College Grove (East San Diego), and Grossmont (La Mesa).

[c] "Other" responses include various locations throughout San Diego that are generally closely tied to the location of the respondent's workplace.

Heights. The residents were asked where they shopped most often for convenience goods, such as groceries, medical supplies, and dining out (Table 10.2), and for shopping goods, such as appliances, furniture, and clothing (Table 10.3). Write an account, for inclusion in a final report, that addresses the most salient relationships in these tables.

Resource A

Table of Areas of a Standard Normal Distribution

(A) Z	(B) Proportion of Area Between Mean and Z	(A) Z	(B) Proportion of Area Between Mean and Z
0.00	0.0000	0.10	0.0398
0.01	0.0040	0.11	0.0438
0.02	0.0080	0.12	0.0478
0.03	0.0120	0.13	0.0517
0.04	0.0160	0.14	0.0557
0.05	0.0199	0.15	0.0596
0.06	0.0239	0.16	0.0636
0.07	0.0279	0.17	0.0675
0.08	0.0319	0.18	0.0714
0.09	0.0359	0.19	0.0753

(A) Z	(B) Proportion of Area Between Mean and Z	(A) Z	(B) Proportion of Area Between Mean and Z
0.20	0.0793	0.55	0.2088
0.21	0.0832	0.56	0.2123
0.22	0.0871	0.57	0.2157
0.23	0.0910	0.58	0.2190
0.24	0.0948	0.59	0.2224
0.25	0.0987	0.60	0.2257
0.26	0.1026	0.61	0.2291
0.27	0.1064	0.62	0.2324
0.28	0.1103	0.63	0.2357
0.29	0.1141	0.64	0.2389
0.30	0.1179	0.65	0.2422
0.31	0.1217	0.66	0.2454
0.32	0.1255	0.67	0.2486
0.33	0.1293	0.68	0.2517
0.34	0.1331	0.69	0.2549
0.35	0.1368	0.70	0.2580
0.36	0.1406	0.71	0.2611
0.37	0.1443	0.72	0.2642
0.38	0.1480	0.73	0.2673
0.39	0.1517	0.74	0.2704
0.40	0.1554	0.75	0.2734
0.41	0.1591	0.76	0.2764
0.42	0.1628	0.77	0.2794
0.43	0.1664	0.78	0.2823
0.44	0.1700	0.79	0.2852
0.45	0.1736	0.80	0.2881
0.46	0.1772	0.81	0.2910
0.47	0.1808	0.82	0.2939
0.48	0.1844	0.83	0.2967
0.49	0.1879	0.84	0.2995
0.50	0.1915	0.85	0.3023
0.51	0.1950	0.86	0.3051
0.52	0.1985	0.87	0.3078
0.53	0.2019	0.88	0.3106
0.54	0.2054	0.89	0.3133

(A) Z	(B) Proportion of Area Between Mean and Z	(A) Z	(B) Proportion of Area Between Mean and Z
0.90	0.3159	1.25	0.3944
0.91	0.3186	1.26	0.3962
0.92	0.3212	1.27	0.3980
0.93	0.3238	1.28	0.3997
0.94	0.3264	1.29	0.4015
0.95	0.3289	1.30	0.4032
0.96	0.3315	1.31	0.4049
0.97	0.3340	1.32	0.4066
0.98	0.3365	1.33	0.4082
0.99	0.3389	1.34	0.4099
1.00	0.3413	1.35	0.4115
1.01	0.3438	1.36	0.4131
1.02	0.3461	1.37	0.4147
1.03	0.3485	1.38	0.4162
1.04	0.3508	1.39	0.4177
1.05	0.3531	1.40	0.4192
1.06	0.3554	1.41	0.4207
1.07	0.3577	1.42	0.4222
1.08	0.3599	1.43	0.4236
1.09	0.3621	1.44	0.4251
1.10	0.3643	1.45	0.4265
1.11	0.3665	1.46	0.4279
1.12	0.3686	1.47	0.4292
1.13	0.3708	1.48	0.4306
1.14	0.3729	1.49	0.4319
1.15	0.3749	1.50	0.4332
1.16	0.3770	1.51	0.4345
1.17	0.3790	1.52	0.4357
1.18	0.3810	1.53	0.4370
1.19	0.3830	1.54	0.4382
1.20	0.3849	1.55	0.4394
1.21	0.3869	1.56	0.4406
1.22	0.3888	1.57	0.4418
1.23	0.3907	1.58	0.4429
1.24	0.3925	1.59	0.4441

(A) Z	(B) Proportion of Area Between Mean and Z	(A) Z	(B) Proportion of Area Between Mean and Z
1.60	0.4452	1.95	0.4744
1.61	0.4463	1.96	0.4750
1.62	0.4474	1.97	0.4756
1.63	0.4484	1.98	0.4761
1.64	0.4495	1.99	0.4767
1.65	0.4505	2.00	0.4772
1.66	0.4515	2.01	0.4778
1.67	0.4525	2.02	0.4783
1.68	0.4535	2.03	0.4788
1.69	0.4545	2.04	0.4793
1.70	0.4554	2.05	0.4798
1.71	0.4564	2.06	0.4803
1.72	0.4573	2.07	0.4808
1.73	0.4582	2.08	0.4812
1.74	0.4591	2.09	0.4817
1.75	0.4599	2.10	0.4821
1.76	0.4608	2.11	0.4826
1.77	0.4616	2.12	0.4830
1.78	0.4625	2.13	0.4834
1.79	0.4633	2.14	0.4838
1.80	0.4641	2.15	0.4842
1.81	0.4649	2.16	0.4846
1.82	0.4656	2.17	0.4850
1.83	0.4664	2.18	0.4854
1.84	0.4671	2.19	0.4857
1.85	0.4678	2.20	0.4861
1.86	0.4686	2.21	0.4864
1.87	0.4693	2.22	0.4868
1.88	0.4699	2.23	0.4871
1.89	0.4706	2.24	0.4875
1.90	0.4713	2.25	0.4878
1.91	0.4719	2.26	0.4881
1.92	0.4726	2.27	0.4884
1.93	0.4732	2.28	0.4887
1.94	0.4738	2.29	0.4890

(A) Z	(B) Proportion of Area Between Mean and Z	(A) Z	(B) Proportion of Area Between Mean and Z
2.30	0.4893	2.65	0.4960
2.31	0.4896	2.66	0.4961
2.32	0.4898	2.67	0.4962
2.33	0.4901	2.68	0.4963
2.34	0.4904	2.69	0.4964
2.35	0.4906	2.70	0.4965
2.36	0.4909	2.71	0.4966
2.37	0.4911	2.72	0.4967
2.38	0.4913	2.73	0.4968
2.39	0.4916	2.74	0.4969
2.40	0.4918	2.75	0.4970
2.41	0.4920	2.76	0.4971
2.42	0.4922	2.77	0.4972
2.43	0.4925	2.78	0.4973
2.44	0.4927	2.79	0.4974
2.45	0.4929	2.80	0.4974
2.46	0.4931	2.81	0.4975
2.47	0.4932	2.82	0.4976
2.48	0.4934	2.83	0.4977
2.49	0.4936	2.84	0.4977
2.50	0.4938	2.85	0.4978
2.51	0.4940	2.86	0.4979
2.52	0.4941	2.87	0.4979
2.53	0.4943	2.88	0.4980
2.54	0.4945	2.89	0.4981
2.55	0.4946	2.90	0.4981
2.56	0.4948	2.91	0.4982
2.57	0.4949	2.92	0.4982
2.58	0.4951	2.93	0.4983
2.59	0.4952	2.94	0.4984
2.60	0.4953	2.95	0.4984
2.61	0.4955	2.96	0.4985
2.62	0.4956	2.97	0.4985
2.63	0.4957	2.98	0.4986
2.64	0.4959	2.99	0.4986

(A) Z	(B) Proportion of Area Between Mean and Z	(A) Z	(B) Proportion of Area Between Mean and Z
3.00	0.4987	3.20	0.4993
3.01	0.4987	3.21	0.4993
3.02	0.4987	3.22	0.4994
3.03	0.4988	3.23	0.4994
3.04	0.4988	3.24	0.4994
3.05	0.4989	3.25	0.4994
3.06	0.4989	3.30	0.4995
3.07	0.4989	3.35	0.4996
3.08	0.4990	3.40	0.4997
3.09	0.4990	3.45	0.4997
3.10	0.4990	3.50	0.4998
3.11	0.4991	3.60	0.4998
3.12	0.4991	3.70	0.4999
3.13	0.4991	3.80	0.4999
3.14	0.4992	4.00	0.49997
3.15	0.4992	∞	0.50000
3.16	0.4992		
3.17	0.4992		
3.18	0.4993		
3.19	0.4993		

Resource B

Glossary

Ambiguous questions: Confusing questions that a respondent can reasonably interpret in more than one way.

Bar graph: Graphic display of data that plots the categories of the variable along the horizontal axis and the frequency of response along the vertical axis, with a solid bar representing volume of response.

Biasing words and phrases: Words and phrases that elicit emotional responses rather than reasoned and objective answers to the question that contains such wording.

Chi-square test: A statistical significance test used for variables that have been organized into categories and presented in a contingency table.

Closed-ended questions: Questions that provide a fixed list of alternative responses and ask the respondent to select one or more of the alternatives as indicative of the best possible answer.

Cluster (multistage) sampling: The process of randomly selecting a sample in a hierarchical series of stages represented by increasingly narrow groups from the working population.

Computer software packages: Prepackaged statistical programs, for use on microcomputers, that facilitate analysis of survey data.

Confidence interval: A probabilistic estimate of the true population mean based on sample data. It represents the margin of error, which indicates the level of sampling accuracy obtained.

Contingency table: A tabular display presenting the relationship between two variables.

Control variable: The variable that is held constant in a three-way cross-tabulation in order to display the data by using contingency tables.

Convenience sampling: Type of nonprobability sample in which interviewees are selected according to their presumed resemblance to the working population and their ready availability.

Cramer's V: A measure of association used for categorical data that is calculated directly from the chi-square statistic.

Data entry: The process of entering the raw data from completed questionnaires onto the computer.

Degrees of freedom: Number of cells that are free to vary. Once the values of these cells are known and once all row and column totals are known, the values of all other cells are fixed.

Dependent variable: The variable that is being explained or is dependent on another variable.

Direct measurement: Information-gathering technique that involves the direct counting, measuring, or testing of data.

Draft questionnaire: A draft of the survey instrument that is prepared at the conclusion of the preliminary information-gathering process and prior to implementation of the pretest.

Filter or screening questions: Questions that require some respondents to be screened out of certain subsequent questions and/or disqualified from participating in the survey at all.

Finite population correction: Adjustment of the standard error in order to account for small population sizes.

Fixed-alternative response categories: A list of response choices associated with closed-ended questions.

Focus group: A technique used prior to questionnaire development in order to gather preliminary information about the subject under study. Individuals who are deemed to have some knowledge of the issues associated with the research study are brought together in a structured setting and led in a roundtable discussion by a group leader.

Frequency distribution: A summary presentation of frequency of response for each category of the variable.

Frequency polygon (line graph): Graphic technique for interval data only. A line connects points representing the midpoint of the class interval (horizontal axis) and the frequency of response (vertical axis).

General population: The theoretical population to which the researcher wishes to generalize the study findings.

Histogram: A variation of the bar graph that plots interval data categories along the horizontal axis in proportionate, rather than equal, widths.

Inappropriate emphasis: The use of boldface, italicized, capitalized, or underlined words or phrases within the context of the question that may serve to bias the respondent.

Independent variable: A variable that explains changes in another variable.

In-person interviews: Interviews in which information is solicited directly from respondents in a face-to-face situation.

Interval scale data: Data involving a level of measurement that establishes an exact value for each category of the variable in terms of specific units of measurement.

Interviewer instructions: Explicit instructions to the survey administrator concerning how to properly administer and complete the questionnaire.

Level of confidence: Degree of confidence associated with the accuracy of the measurements derived from sample data.

Level of wording: A guideline for the development of questions that instructs the researcher to be cognizant of the population to be surveyed when choosing the words, colloquialisms, and jargon to be used in the questions.

Likert scale: A scaled response continuum measured from extreme positive to extreme negative (or vice versa) in five, seven, or nine categories.

Mail-out survey: Printed questionnaires disseminated through the mail to a predesignated sample of respondents. The respondents are asked to complete the questionnaire on their own and return it by mail to the researcher.

Manipulative information: Explanatory information in a questionnaire that is intended to provide necessary background and perspective, but serves instead to unduly bias the respondent.

Mean (arithmetic mean): The mathematical center of the data, taking into account not only the location of the data (above or below the center), but also the relative distance of the data from that center.

Measure of association: A measure of the strength and direction of the relationship between two variables.

Measure of central tendency: Statistics that provide a summarizing number to characterize what is "typical" or "average" for particular data. Mean, mode, and median are the three measures of central tendency.

Median: The value of the variable that represents the midpoint of the data. One-half of the data will have values below the median and one-half will have values above it.

Median Test: A variation of the chi-square test of significance for use with ordinal and interval data under certain circumstances.

Mode: The category or value of the data that is characterized by possessing the greatest frequency of response.

Multipurpose questions: Questions that inappropriately elicit responses for two or more issues at the same time.

Nominal scale data: Data that involve a level of measurement that simply identifies or labels the observations into categories.

Nonprobability sampling: A method of sample selection in which the probability of any particular respondent being selected is not known.

Normal distribution: Data distributed in the form of the symmetrical bell-shaped curve, where the mode, median, and arithmetic mean have the same value.

Observation: An information-gathering technique that involves the direct study of behavior, as it occurs, by watching the subjects of the study without intruding upon them.

Open-ended questions: Questions that have no preexisting response categories and that thereby permit the respondent to answer in his or her own words.

Ordinal scale data: Data involving a level of measurement that seeks to rank categories in terms of the extent to which these categories represent the variable.

Phi: A measure of association that is a variation on Cramer's *V* and used only for 2 × 2 contingency tables.

Pie chart: Circular graphic technique that displays information as proportions of the whole.

Postcoding: The process of coding responses to open-ended questions or other questions that are not involved in the precoding process.

Precoding: The placement of numeric codes for each category of response at the time that the questionnaire is prepared in final form for administration.

Pretest: A small-scale implementation of the draft questionnaire used to assess such critical factors as questionnaire clarity, comprehensiveness, and acceptabiity.

Probability sample: Sample with the following two characteristics: (1) probabilities of selection are equal for all members of the working population at all stages of the selection process and (2) sampling is conducted with elements of the sample selected independently of one another. Probability samples are often referred to as *random samples*.

Purposive sampling: Type of nonprobability sample in which the researcher uses judgment in selecting respondents who are considered to be knowledgeable in subject areas related to the research.

Questionnaire editing: The examination of finished, returned questionnaires for accuracy, legibility, and completeness (often referred to as the "cleanup" process).

Quota sampling: Type of nonprobability sample in which the researcher deliberately selects a sample to reflect the overall population with regard to one or more specific variables that are considered to be important to the study.

Random-digit dialing: Use of the random numbers table to generate telephone numbers for the purpose of contacting potential respondents.

Respondent: The person who replies to the questions in the survey instrument.

Response rate: Percentage of the potential respondents who were initially contacted who actually complete the questionnaire.

Sample survey research: Survey research conducted by interviewing a small portion of a large population through the application of a set of systematic, scientific, and orderly procedures for the purpose of making accurate generalizations about the large population.

Sampling error: The likelihood that any scientifically drawn sample will contain certain unavoidable differences from the true population of which it is a part.

Sampling frame: The list of members of the working population from which the actual sample is eventually drawn.

Scaled responses: Alternative responses that are presented to the respondent on a continuum.

Secondary research: A means of data collection that consists of compiling and analyzing data that already have been collected and that exist in usable form.

Simple random sampling: The random selection of numbers of the working population for inclusion in the eventual sample.

Skewed distribution: A non-normal frequency distribution with some extreme values, either high or low, that cause the three measures of central tendency to deviate from one another.

Snowball sampling: A type of nonprobability sample in which the researcher identifies a few respondents and asks them to identify others who might qualify as respondents.

Spuriousness: An apparent relationship between two variables that is found, upon further analysis, to be the result of the interaction of a third variable.

Standard deviation: A measure of data dispersion that depicts how close the data are to the mean of the distribution.

Standard error: The standard deviation of a distribution of sample means as opposed to the distribution of raw data of a single sample.

Standard Z score: See Z *score.*

Stratified random sampling: Separation of the working population into mutually exclusive groups (strata); simple random samples are then taken from each stratum.

Survey administration: The implementation of the precoded final questionnaire in the survey research process.

Survey research: The solicitation of verbal information from respondents through the use of various interviewing techniques.

Systematic random sampling: Adaptation of the random sampling process that consists of selecting sample members from a list at fixed intervals from a randomly chosen starting point on that list.

Telephone survey: Information collection through the use of telephone interviews that involve a trained interviewer and selected respondents.

Tests of statistical significance: A series of statistical tests that permit the researcher to identify whether or not genuine differences exist among variables.

Three-way cross-tabulation: The method by which the relationship among three variables is presented in a series of contingency tables.

Unit of analysis: The element (person, household, or organization) of the population that represents the focus of the research study.

Variable fields: Computer spaces allocated and corresponding to a variable in the questionnaire.

Venting questions: Questions in which the respondent is asked to add any information, comments, or opinions that pertain to the subject matter of the questionnaire but that have not necessarily been addressed throughout the main body of the questionnaire.

Working population: An operational definition of the general population that is representative of the general population and from which the researcher is reasonably able to identify as complete a list as possible of members of the general population.

Z *score:* The conversion of calculated standard deviations into standard units of the normal distribution.

Resource C

Answers to Selected Exercises

Chapter 4

1. The survey question may be precoded as follows:
   01 ______Automotive/automotive-related
   02 ______Professional
   03 ______Services
   04 ______Restaurant
   05 ______Retail
   06 ______Entertainment
   99 ______Other, please specify
2. Postcodes are as follows:
   a. Dry cleaning (03)
   b. Hotel (07) Hotel/motel
   c. Pediatrican (02)
   d. Gas station (01)

e. Jewelry store (05)
f. Bar (06)

Chapter 5

1. a. .28
   b. .04
   c. .02
   d. 18.9
2. \$120,000 ± \$2,450
   \$117,550 – \$122,450
3. Yes; confidence interval is 55% ± 3% or 52%–58%

Chapter 6

1. No; a minimum sample size of 385 is required.
2. a. 592
   b. 456
   c. 119
   d. 3,755
3. a. 139
   b. 373
   c. 465

Chapter 7

1. General population—suburban residents
   Working population—households located in suburban census tracts
   Population lists—reverse telephone directory; utility customer lists; mailing services
2. Using the last two digits in each random number and selecting, at random, a starting place of line 4, column 2, by reading the table from left to right, the following twenty numbers will be selected: 24, 48, 36, 37, 34, 47, 13, 38, 21, 17, 25, 43, 23, 41, 28, 14, 4, 32, 18, and 12. (*Note:* The final selection of random number 12 requires returning to the top of the table.)

3. Begin the sample by randomly selecting a number between 1 and 110. Starting with the name corresponding to that randomly selected number, select every 110th name on the list.

4. a. 307 White
36 Asian
18 Black
9 Hispanic
370 Total

b. 96 White
94 Asian
92 Black
88 Hispanic
370 Total
(based on Equation 6.7)

c. 31 White
4 Asian
2 Black
1 Hispanic

Chapter 8

1.

a. **Table 8A. SAT Scores Among High School Seniors.**

Score	*f*	%
1,400–1,600	20	3.3
1,200–1,399	80	13.3
1,000–1,199	161	26.8
800– 999	209	34.9
600– 799	100	16.7
400– 599	30	5.0
Total	600	100.0

Note: Missing cases = 50.

The reader would be correct in selecting any one of the first four categories for rounding up to 100 percent. The authors recommend selecting the category with the largest frequency.

b. The distribution in Table 8A is basically characteristic of a normal distribution.

c. Mean

2. a. Median

c. 4

3.

a. **Table 8B. Citizen Rating of Police Effectiveness.**

Rating	*Value*	*f*	*%*
Highly satisfactory	1	140	28.0
Satisfactory	2	190	38.0
Neutral	3	75	15.0
Unsatisfactory	4	75	15.0
Highly unsatisfactory	5	20	4.0
Total		500	100.0

b. Mean: 2.29 using the Likert scale as indicated in Table 8B.

c. Bar graph, pie chart, frequency polygon

Chapter 9

1.

a. **Table 9A. Political Preference by Ethnic Background.**

	Ethnic Background									
	White		*Black*		*Hispanic*		*Asian*		*Total*	
Political Preference	*f*	*%*	*f*	*%*	*f*	*%*	*f*	*%*	*f*	*%*
Democrat	200	33.3	120	80.0	100	66.7	50	50.0	470	47.0
Republican	350	58.4	10	6.7	40	26.7	30	30.0	430	43.0
Independent	50	8.3	20	13.3	10	6.6	20	20.0	100	10.0
Total	600	100.0	150	100.0	150	100.0	100	100.0	1,000	100.0

b. $\chi^2 = 178.24$ (significant at 99% level).

c. Cramer's $V = .30$ (moderate association).

2.

b. $\chi^2 = 10.12$ (significant at 95% level).

c. Yes; Median Test $\chi^2 = .02$ (not significant).

3.

a. $\chi^2 = 167.16$ (significant at 99% level).
b. Cramer's $V = .46$ (relatively strong association).

Bibliography

Abrahamson, M. *Social Research Methods.* Englewood Cliffs, N.J.: Prentice Hall, 1983.

Babbie, E. R. *Survey Research Methods.* Belmont, Calif.: Wadsworth, 1973.

Backstrom, C. H., and Hursh-Cesar, G. *Survey Research.* (2nd ed.) New York: Wiley, 1981.

Bailey, K. D. *Methods of Social Research.* (2nd ed.) New York: Free Press, 1982.

Blalock, H. M., Jr. *Social Statistics.* New York: McGraw-Hill, 1972.

Converse, J. M. *Survey Research in the United States.* Berkeley: University of California Press, 1987.

Dans, J. A. *Elementary Survey Analysis.* Englewood Cliffs, N.J.: Prentice Hall, 1971.

de Vaus, D. A. *Surveys in Social Research.* London: Allen & Unwin, 1986.

Devine, R. P., and Falk, L. L. *Social Surveys: A Research Strategy for Social Scientists and Students.* Morristown, N.J.: General Learning Press, 1972.

Dillman, D. A. *Mail and Telephone Surveys.* New York: Wiley, 1978.

Draper, N. R., and Smith, H. *Applied Regression Analysis.* New York: Wiley, 1966.

Glock, C. Y. *Survey Research in the Social Sciences.* New York: Russell Sage Foundation, 1967.

Hoinville, G., and Jowell, R. *Survey Research Practice.* Portsmouth, N.H.: Heinemann Educational Books, 1978.

Kish, L. *Survey Sampling.* New York: Wiley, 1965.

Korin, B. P. *Statistical Concepts for the Social Sciences.* Cambridge, Mass.: Winthrop Publishers, 1975.

Krueckeberg, D. A., and Silvers, A. L. *Urban Planning Analysis: Methods and Models.* New York: Wiley, 1974.

Levin, J., and Fox, J. A. *Elementary Statistics in Social Research.* New York: HarperCollins, 1988.

Lieberman, G. J., and Owen, D. B. *Tables of the Hypergeometric Probability Distribution.* Stanford, Calif.: Stanford University Press, 1961.

Marsh, C. *The Survey Method.* London: Allen & Unwin, 1982.

Meier, K. J., and Brudney, J. L. *Applied Statistics for Public Administration.* (rev. ed.) Pacific Grove, Calif.: Brooks/Cole, 1987.

Miller, W. L. *The Survey Method in the Social and Political Sciences.* London: Frances Pinter, 1983.

Moser, C. A., and Kelton, G. *Survey Methods in Social Investigation.* New York: Basic Books, 1972.

Nachmias, D., and Nachmias, C. *Research Methods in the Social Sciences.* (2nd ed.) New York: St. Martin's Press, 1981.

O'Sullivan, E., and Rassel, G. R. *Research Methods for Public Administrators.* New York: Longman, 1989.

Ott, L., Mendenhall, W., and Larson, R. F. *Statistics: A Tool for the Social Sciences.* (2nd ed.) Boston: Duxbury Press, 1978.

Parten, M. *Surveys, Polls, and Samples: Practical Procedures.* New York: HarperCollins, 1950.

Poister, T. H. *Public Program Analysis.* Baltimore, Md.: University Park Press, 1978.

Rosenberg, M. *The Logic of Survey Analysis.* New York: Basic Books, 1968.

Rossi, P. H., Wright, J. D., and Anderson, A. B. *Handbook of Survey Research.* Orlando, Fla.: Academic Press, 1983.

Schaeffer, R. L., Mendenhall, W., and Ott, L. *Elementary Survey Sampling.* (3rd ed.) Boston: Duxbury Press, 1986.

Schlaifer, R. *Probability and Statistics for Business Decisions.* New York: McGraw-Hill, 1959.

Sjoberg, G., and Nett, R. *A Methodology for Social Research.* New York: HarperCollins, 1968.

Smith, H. W. *Strategies of Social Research.* (2nd ed.) Englewood Cliffs, N.J.: Prentice Hall, 1975.

Sudman, S. *Reducing the Cost of Surveys.* Hawthorne, N.Y.: Aldine, 1967.

Sudman, S. *Applied Sampling.* Orlando, Fla.: Academic Press, 1976.

Suits, D. B. *Statistics: An Introduction to Quantitative Economic Research.* Skokie, Ill.: Rand McNally, 1963.

Warwick, D. P., and Lininger, C. A. *The Sample Survey: Theory and Practice.* New York: McGraw-Hill, 1975.

Weisberg, H. F., and Bowen, B. D. *An Introduction to Survey Research and Data Analysis.* New York: W. H. Freeman, 1977.

Welch, S., and Comer, J. *Quantitative Methods for Public Administration.* Homewood, Ill.: Dorsey Press, 1988.

Witzling, L. P., and Greenstreet, R. C. *Presenting Statistics.* New York: Wiley, 1989.

Wolf, F. L. *Elements of Probability and Statistics.* New York: McGraw-Hill, 1962.

Yamane, T. *Statistics: An Introductory Analysis.* (2nd ed.) New York: HarperCollins, 1967.

Young, P. V. *Scientific Social Surveys and Research.* Englewood Cliffs, N.J.: Prentice Hall, 1966.

References

Bailey, K. D. *Methods of Social Research.* (2nd ed.) New York: Free Press, 1982.

Blalock, H. M., Jr. *Social Statistics.* New York: McGraw-Hill, 1972.

Krueckeberg, D. A., and Silvers, A. L. *Urban Planning Analysis: Methods and Models.* New York: Wiley, 1974.

Poister, T. H. *Public Program Analysis.* Baltimore, Md.: University Park Press, 1978.

Schaeffer, R. L., Mendenhall, W., and Ott, L. *Elementary Survey Sampling.* (3rd ed.) Boston: Duxbury Press, 1986.

Schlaifer, R. *Probability and Statistics for Business Decisions.* New York: McGraw-Hill, 1959.

Sjoberg, G., and Nett, R. *A Methodology for Social Research.* New York: HarperCollins, 1968.

"What Does Your Family's Future Hold in Alpine?" Alpine *Sun,* Oct. 11, 1989, p. 12.

Yamane, T. *Statistics: An Introductory Analysis.* (2nd ed.) New York: HarperCollins, 1967.

References

Bailey, K. D. *Methods of Social Research.* (2nd ed.) New York: Free Press, 1982.

Blalock, H. M., Jr. *Social Statistics.* New York: McGraw-Hill, 1972.

Krueckeberg, D. A., and Silvers, A. L. *Urban Planning Analysis: Methods and Models.* New York: Wiley, 1974.

Poister, T. H. *Public Program Analysis.* Baltimore, Md.: University Park Press, 1978.

Schaeffer, R. L., Mendenhall, W., and Ott, L. *Elementary Survey Sampling.* (3rd ed.) Boston: Duxbury Press, 1986.

Schlaifer, R. *Probability and Statistics for Business Decisions.* New York: McGraw-Hill, 1959.

Sjoberg, G., and Nett, R. *A Methodology for Social Research.* New York: HarperCollins, 1968.

"What Does Your Family's Future Hold in Alpine?" Alpine *Sun,* Oct. 11, 1989, p. 12.

Yamane, T. *Statistics: An Introductory Analysis.* (2nd ed.) New York: HarperCollins, 1967.

Index